25
LIBRARY
TERRACE

Also By Natalie Fergie

The Sewing Machine

25 LIBRARY TERRACE

NATALIE FERGIE

embla
books

First published in the UK in 2025 by

embla
books

An imprint of Bonnier Books UK
5th Floor, HYLO, 105 Bunhill Row,
London, EC1Y 8LZ

A CIP catalogue record for this book is available from the British Library.

ISBN: 9781471419423

Also available as an ebook and an audiobook

1

Typeset by IDSUK (Data Connection) Ltd
Printed and bound in Great Britain by Clays Ltd, Elcograf S.p.A.

The authorised representative in the EEA is Bonnier Books
UK (Ireland) Limited.
Registered office address: Floor 3, Block 3, Miesian Plaza,
Dublin 2, D02 Y754, Ireland
compliance@bonnierbooks.ie
www.bonnierbooks.co.uk

For librarians, everywhere

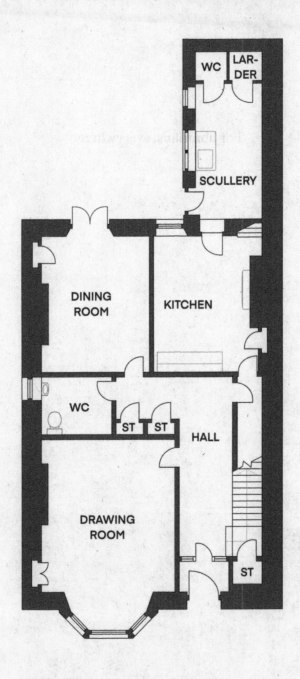

GROUND FLOOR

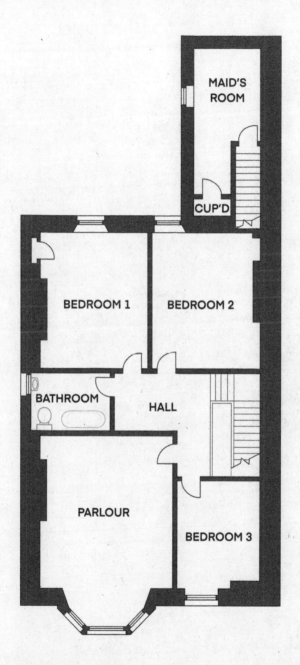

MAID'S ROOM

CUP'D

BEDROOM 1

BEDROOM 2

BATHROOM

HALL

PARLOUR

BEDROOM 3

FIRST FLOOR

2011

2011

Chapter 1

February 2011

Tess squeezes the trigger.

The drill screams into life. She lets it slow to a stop and dumps it onto the huge coffee table beside her recent purchases. 'DIAMOND TIPPED' proclaims the packaging, with a shooting star which reminds her of a toothpaste advert. She unwraps the drill bit with some difficulty and holds it up to the light. It must be a very small diamond, she thinks, glancing down at her left hand.

In the kitchen, she turns on the tap at the sink and squirts a healthy dollop of green washing-up liquid into her palm. She holds her hands under the icy stream and watches as a white froth of extravagant soapy bubbles appears. The ring spins on her finger, but it doesn't come off. Too many doughnuts, she thinks. A cold ache, not dissimilar to the frozen feeling in her chest, begins to spread downwards to her fingers and upwards to her elbow. She twists the ring around and around until she is able to pull it over her knuckle and drop it into the sink.

Back at the coffee table she arranges the other items from her shopping trip. A fifty-metre roll of yellow masking tape, a tube of superglue and a pack of Brillo pads. Yellow reminds her of happy times. It's the colour of custard and daffodils and good cheese. Blood red, for anger and pain,

3

would have been more appropriate but the store hadn't offered that option.

Patrick has ever so helpfully left the chuck key attached to the drill cable. She opens the jaws wide enough to insert the bit. As she tightens the chuck she gives the key a vengeful extra-tight twist and squeezes the trigger a second time. There is a bark from upstairs. Baxter, locked safely in the bathroom, is protesting.

A long time ago, when she was about six, her father had fitted a shelf in the family's bathroom. He wasn't what anyone would call a handyman, and he had therefore consulted the *Biggest Ever Book of DIY*, a hopeful, but underused, Christmas gift from her mother. She remembers that masking tape had been an essential piece of kit for the task.

Tess scrubs a corner of the immaculate, craftsman-made table with a Brillo pad until the oiled surface is back to naked wood. She leans down to table height and blows the pink powder away. Scissors make short work of the lid on the tube of superglue. She spreads it liberally across the back of Patrick's phone, taking care to avoid the switches on the side. While she waits for the £400 device to bond permanently to the bare timber, she goes back to the kitchen, fills the kettle and waits for it to boil. From the window she looks out at the neatly mown front lawn which is his pride and joy.

Coffee made, she retrieves her engagement ring from the sink, and carries the mug back to the living room. Her hand shakes, but for once she leaves the splashes on the table where they land and doesn't race for a cloth. The coffee is too hot to drink, and she puts the mug down without bothering to use a coaster. She turns the phone on, rips a couple of pieces of masking tape from the reel and arranges them in a cross, right over the messaging app Patrick uses. And then she puts the ring on top of the tape.

Her hand is surprisingly steady as she positions the point of the drill bit through the ring and exactly in the centre of the papery kiss. She squeezes the trigger again, and leans forward to add her body weight to the grind of the drill.

The *Biggest Ever Book of DIY* was right, she thinks, as the metal spike begins to split the yellow cross. This is not difficult at all. She pushes down, feeling the drill hesitate a little as it goes through the glass screen. It jumps slightly at the level of the components before it rushes downwards into the beautiful spalted ash. When the chuck is almost at the level of the screen, she stops.

The phone is skewered to the table by the drill, with the ring sandwiched between them, like a piece of modern art.

*

There is nothing else to be done. The carpets have been vacuumed, the bathroom scrubbed and taps polished, and the houseplants have been watered. She has tidied the garden, bagged up the last of the fallen leaves for mulch and dealt with the lawn. The last thing she does is to take her own phone back to factory settings. She can't bear to look at it any longer.

It would be so easy to be vindictive, she thinks, as she stands on the doorstep and locks the door for the final time.

Baxter sits patiently on the path and she bends over to pick up his lead. 'Come on, Bax. It was me who signed the adoption papers at the Dog and Cat Home, so there's absolutely no doubt that you are all mine.'

She eyes the keyhole, the tube of superglue in her hand.

Chapter 2

February 2011

'Good afternoon, M and P Legal.'

The solicitor's receptionist is calm and competent, thinks Tess. The same attributes she tries to offer her clients. Correction. The attributes she *tried* to offer her clients. Past tense. She waits while another four calls are answered and put through before approaching the desk.

'May I speak with Fiona Reid, please? I don't have an appointment but I'm a friend. Sort of, anyway.'

'I'll check her diary for you.' The receptionist wiggles the mouse on her desk and her eyes flick across the computer screen. 'She's due in court this afternoon. Let me just see if she's in her office. Your name is?'

'Tess Dutton.'

'One moment, please.'

There is a discreetly muffled conversation.

'She'll be down in a few minutes.' The receptionist looks at Baxter and smiles. 'We don't often have dogs visiting us.'

A few minutes later a slim woman arrives. Her formal suit and precise haircut are at odds with her words, which tumble out into the reception area in a chaotic rush.

'Tess! I've been trying to get in touch with you for *days*. Is your phone not working? What on earth has happened?'

'Hi, Fiona.' Tess chooses just one of the questions to answer. 'I'm OK, but I had to take a couple of weeks off.' She gets the good news part out. 'Don't worry, I won't leave you in the lurch, I just needed a bit of space to think.'

Fiona glances at her watch. 'I don't have much time. Can we do this at my place later?'

'As long as the kids aren't within earshot.'

'How urgent is it?'

'Fairly urgent. Today. This evening. Tomorrow. It can't really wait any longer than that.'

'Tonight then, about eight? They go to their dad's at seven, so we'll have the place to ourselves.' She studies Tess. 'You can't give me some idea?'

Tess can feel her throat tightening. 'I'll explain tonight, but the short version is that I need somewhere to live, and that means Baxter as well.'

Fiona knows exactly what is required. 'I'll order pizza.'

*

Back in her office, Fiona picks up her phone and scrolls to the very bottom of her contacts list. She taps the screen.

The call is answered on the fourth ring.

'Twenty-five.'

'Hello, Georgia. It's Fiona. I'm sorry to call you out of the blue, but I think I may have someone for you.'

'I'm seventy-one, Fiona. I spend my days reading. I help my friend with his allotment and I write angry letters to politicians. I'm not sure I have either the time or the energy for anyone new. Not after the last time.'

'I do understand, but our agreement is that I let you know as soon as possible, and make sure you've got all the information you need. I'll see what else I can find out, and if you decide to go ahead, it'll be Alasdair who deals with the arrangements, as usual.'

'I'll think about it over the weekend.'

'Thank you. I wouldn't ask if it wasn't important.'

'I know.'

The call ends.

Fiona sits at her desk for a few minutes, remembering.

1908

Chapter 3

March 1908

The yell could be heard from the street outside the house.

John Black stopped stroking his moustache and screwed up his eyes, trying to see past the piles of masonry and lead pipes lying in what would eventually be his front garden. The yell had become a scream of pain and it was heading in his direction.

A man covered in pale plaster dust appeared at the rectangular opening where the front door would soon hang, dragging a lad behind him. 'Hurry!' he shouted, and headed towards a standpipe in the street where he turned the tap on and let water flow out across the not-yet cobbled ground. Despite the noisy protests, he pushed the lad's head under the gush.

'Keep still! The water has to get into your eye.' The screaming stopped as the scrawny lad spluttered and coughed. Every so often there was a gasp and a shout, but the man was determined to keep the lad's head under the flow of water. A second boy of about the same age appeared.

'Get a pail!' the man demanded. 'And make sure it's empty.'

The boy vanished back inside the house and returned quickly with a heavy galvanised bucket, bashed about the rim.

The injured lad was silent now. He had been set back onto his feet and stood shivering, his head soaking wet, water dribbling down onto his shirt. The man rinsed the grey bucket out three times and then filled it with fresh water.

'Sit there,' he instructed. The lad did as he was told and sat down on a stack of planks. Beside him was a heap of long larch poles and coiled ropes; last week these had been the scaffolding for the house. 'You need to take handfuls of water from the pail, like this,' the man demonstrated, 'and then hold your hand against your eye and tip your head back. I want you to use the whole pail of water. And when you've done that there will be another pail. Over and over again. Have you got that? Do you understand?' The lad nodded.

All this activity unfurled in front of John Black, who was standing on a rutted path that would soon be the pavement. He unbuttoned his overcoat. 'Here,' he said, stepping forward, 'he's freezing cold. Put this around him.'

The plasterer looked up, taking in the smart hat and formal suit. 'That's kind of you, sir, but your coat will be ruined.'

'This is going to be my house, and I think a few marks on a coat is a small price to pay for looking after one of the young men who is building it for me.' He held the heavy wool coat out, its satin lining catching the low afternoon sunlight. 'Please, take it.'

The plasterer took the coat. 'Thank you. He's chilled, that's for sure.'

'And his face? What happened?'

'A dod of lime plaster in his eye. It's caustic. It will have burned.'

'In his eye? My God.'

'I'm sure he'll be fine after a few days. We got it rinsed out very quickly. You really can't delay with this kind of thing.'

'What age is he? He looks so young.' John frowned. 'Is it safe for him to be here?'

'He's fourteen,' the man lied. 'He's not missing any school. I pay him, and he takes the wage home to his mother. She's a widow. It all helps a little.'

John listened, but was unconvinced. 'Very well. I'll leave you to get on. I need to get home now.' He crossed his red woollen scarf over his chest, tucked the ends under his arms and fastened the buttons on his suit jacket. 'It's been rather a day.'

The plasterer hesitated, clearly unsure how to respond.

'I had thought that this house would be where my wife and I would bring up our family, but according to the doctor we saw this morning, she is quite unwell, and now I am uncertain about almost everything.' It was somehow easier to tell a complete stranger about his circumstances than it would have been to disclose them to a friend on the golf course.

'I hope the news isn't as bad as you fear, sir.' The man held out his hand, and John grasped it, feeling the man's callused skin against his own office-smooth fingers.

'Thank you. Please keep the coat, it may be useful to the lad.' He judged the plasterer to be a similar build to himself. 'Or to someone else.'

He looked back at the house, noticing for the first time that someone had chalked a 2 and a 5 in large numbers on the stone lintel above the door. He turned and picked his way back along the uneven road surface of Library Terrace, rubbing his hands together in the brisk air because his leather gloves were in the pockets of the coat that was no longer his, and it would have been churlish to go back and ask for them.

Finlay and Ann would be waiting for him at home. He had no idea how he was going to tell them the news about their mother.

1910

Chapter 4

November 1910

Ursula sat in the silent office. As usual, she was the last person to leave. She liked the edges of the day best; the first moment when the noisy printing presses came to life in the morning, and then the satisfying sight of stacks of leaflets and programmes and catalogues all piled up ready to be shipped out to customers at the close of business. She knew she was going to miss it all.

The company's keys lay beside her gloves on the desk, next to the bottles of black and red ink. She took a sheet of headed paper from the drawer and threaded it around the typewriter roller, rested her fingers on the keys, looked ahead and began.

Friday, 18th November 1910

Dear All,

I have come to know and respect each one of you since I arrived at Black's from London three years ago, and I want to thank you from the bottom of my heart for the well-wishes you have expressed today. Your generosity of spirit has warmed me greatly.

*As I am sure you all realise, I could not have antici-
pated leaving the company under such circumstances
and your kindness is very much appreciated. From
Monday, my place will be taken by Miss Wilma Jackson, who is joining the office staff from the Education
Department at Edinburgh Corporation. I think she
will be a little better prepared than I was when I started
to work here. Specifically, I have ensured that there is no
point in sending her to the warehouse for 'a long stand',
and while you may have caught me with 'tartan ink',
I'm sorry to say that won't work either.*

Ursula smiled at the memory of her embarrassment. She
had learned that these pranks were only played on people
who were liked; the more officious members of the team
were left well alone.

*It's a little early, but since this is my last day, and I won't
be here in the office to speak to each of you in person
when you collect your wages, I want to wish you and
your families a peaceful Christmas season and good
health for 1911.*
With very best wishes,
Ursula Smith

*

Ursula climbed the stairs to her top-floor tenement flat in
Comiston. As she walked past the door of the flat below, she
heard a key turn in the lock. There wasn't time to escape.
She pasted a smile onto her face and turned to greet her
downstairs neighbour.

'I hear you are leaving us, Miss Smith?' The woman's tone was somehow accusatory. 'There have been quite a few people marching up and down these stairs, for a viewing.'

'I am indeed. I hope they haven't caused too much noise.'

Miss Gibb sniffed, determined to get as much information out of Ursula as possible. 'Where is it that you are off to, then? I saw the intimation in *The Scotsman* last week. Quite a step upwards, I think.'

Why is it, Ursula wondered, that some people simply cannot be happy about the good fortune of others? Not a word of congratulation or good wishes was being offered, even though a little warmth would cost Miss Gibb nothing. 'Thank you. As I'm sure you will remember from the newspaper, our wedding is next month, so I will only be here for a few more weeks.' She deftly avoided giving any information about her new address. 'The landlord has asked me to find someone suitable to take over the tenancy for my flat and I have met their request.'

'Who will we be getting above us, then?' Miss Gibb was clearly unhappy. 'I hope they will be quiet and respectable. As you know, we cannot abide disturbance.'

Ursula smiled. 'A respectable married couple will be moving in. I believe they have a young daughter and there is a new baby expected early next year.'

'A baby?' Horror was written all over Miss Gibb's face.

'They are delighted to be so near to the primary school. I think they intend to stay until the children are quite grown up. It will be good to have some stability, don't you agree? There is nothing worse than new tenants moving in and out all the time.' She paused. 'I'll be leaving behind most of my furniture, so at least you won't have the disruption of a removal company carrying wardrobes and tables up and down the stairs.'

A man's voice came from within the flat, impatient and demanding. 'Margaret!'

'Yes, Father, I will be with you in a moment.' Miss Gibb seemed suddenly weary.

'Come here! Come here right now. I need my dinner cut up and it's going cold.'

Miss Gibb melted back into the flat without so much as a goodbye.

As Ursula climbed the last flight of stairs, she chided herself for being uncharitable. The new family would inevitably make noise, and Mr Gibb would moan endlessly to his daughter because he was housebound and there was no one else to complain to. And Miss Gibb, who had never said 'please just call me Margaret', and who rarely left the flat because of her responsibilities, would have to cope with it all.

Ursula thought about how different her own life was going to be, and how fortunate she was to be loved by a good man. She knew it would not make Miss Gibb any happier to be told about Library Terrace, nor the people who lived there. It might even have the opposite effect.

Chapter 5

Early December 1910

It was Sunday morning when the mystery began. As usual Isobel had made breakfast and set it out in the dining room before returning to the kitchen to get on with the rest of her chores. Bacon, square sliced sausage and scrambled eggs were on offer in warmed dishes, and the silver toast rack was full of neatly cut triangles.

Ann daydreamed her way through most of the meal, not paying much attention to a rather boring discussion between Father and Finlay about some engineering difficulty at the printing works. The two of them moved on to talking about something that Finlay found entertaining, and without warning, the atmosphere suddenly changed.

'It's time you realised that these are serious matters,' Father almost exploded with frustration.

Ann didn't properly understand what the problem was and scrabbled backwards through the half-heard conversation, trying to work out what had caused such annoyance. She didn't dare ask, and took tiny nibbles off the crust of a piece of toast as she tried to make it last as long as possible without it looking as though she was messing with her food.

'It really wasn't like that, Father,' Finlay protested. 'They were barely holding hands. That's what was so amusing.'

Father clattered a spoonful of marmalade onto his plate so hard it spilled over onto the tablecloth. 'You will come to the parlour at eleven o'clock sharp, and we will discuss this *privately*.' He used his napkin to wipe the crumbs from his luxuriant moustache, got up from the table and left the room. He was followed a minute later by Finlay, who appeared to have lost his appetite. The marmalade spoon was left where it had landed, the tablecloth spattered with sugary preserve.

After she had left enough time to be sure that no one was coming back, Ann seized another piece of toast and spread it thickly with butter because there was now no one to comment or prevent her from doing so. She was just swallowing the last mouthful when there was a knock at the door.

'Oh!' The maid stopped in her tracks, unsure whether to stay or to leave. 'I beg your pardon, Miss Ann, I thought everyone had gone upstairs. I'll clear the table, if you're finished?'

Ann nodded and reached for the last slice of toast. It didn't enter her head that like every maid in the street, Isobel would have been up since before six, and might have welcomed some cold leftovers to help her get through the rest of the morning.

Isobel looked at Ann, who still had crumbs around her mouth, and at the sticky tablecloth which would now need to be laundered, and said nothing about any of it.

*

Listening at keyholes often meant you only heard part of a conversation, but practice had taught Ann to be patient. She had developed the fine art of fading into the wallpaper and knew about a lot of things that went on in the house by simply remaining silent when conversations happened around her. Father was not beating around the bush. She recognised the tone.

'Finlay, you are seventeen, and it's time for me to give you the same simple advice that your grandfather gave me.'

There was an indistinct interruption from her older brother who, judging by the lower volume, was standing at the far end of the first-floor parlour, beside the window which overlooked the street. He would be able to see the top branches of her little cherry tree in the front garden. In spring there would be tiny new buds on it, and pink blossom would follow. Ann had planted it with Father in the autumn of 1908 when she was ten; they had just moved into 25 Library Terrace, and she thought of the small tree as her own personal property. Cherry was a sweet name which would make people smile, she thought. Her own name felt very plain and boring in comparison.

Her back hurt from leaning forward at an awkward angle, but she ignored the ache and pressed her ear even closer to the keyhole. She could feel the cold brass on her skin and smell the Bluebell polish Isobel used every week.

'I haven't finished speaking!' Father was on the war path.

'I apologise,' came her brother's voice, conciliatory, and deeper than his father's, with no trace of the mid-teen creaks of earlier years.

'I repeat, you are seventeen now, and it's important that you understand how the world works.'

'Yes, Father. You were saying about the two things?'

Ann held her breath as she strained to hear the words.

'Two things will get you into trouble in life.' Father's voice strengthened. 'Your stick and your signature.' There

23

was a pause. 'And if you remember that, son, you will avoid a lot of life's difficulties.'

Ann frowned. A stick and a signature? It didn't make any sense. But before she could puzzle it out, she realised that heavy footsteps were heading towards the door, and only a few seconds remained before she would be discovered. She slid the book she was carrying onto the carpet runner, pushing it in the direction of her bedroom with her foot as though she was playing a giant game of shove ha'penny, and then moused her way towards it with soft steps, avoiding the creaky floorboard in the middle in a way that Isobel might have recognised. She was four feet from safety when the parlour door opened, and she quickly pulled her hair out from behind her ear to hide the indentation of the keyhole. 'Sorry, Father. It slipped out of my hands.'

'You must be more careful. Books cost money.'

She could tell that he wasn't truly cross with her.

'Is Miss Smith here yet?' he continued. 'I need to speak with her about our wedding. It's only two weeks away now.'

'I know. I am so excited about it.'

'She will make changes here, I expect, and we will all have to get used to those, but if everyone tries their best, I hope it won't be too difficult.'

Ann bent down to pick up the book. 'She arrived a little while ago. I think she's in the kitchen with Isobel. They were going to discuss the order for the butcher, I heard them speaking about it when she was here yesterday afternoon.'

Finlay appeared in the parlour doorway, 'I wouldn't say no to a cup of tea, Annie Bee.' He winked at her, knowing full well that her habit of listening at keyholes had almost been her undoing.

*

Ann waited until after lunch, when she knew Father and Miss Smith had gone out for their usual walk to Blackford Pond, before she went into the kitchen.

Isobel was scrubbing a saucepan at the scullery sink, almost up to her elbows in hot water. She turned at the sound of the door opening. 'Are you looking for something, Miss Ann?'

Ann sat down at the table. The smell of biscuits seeped out from the oven in the black range behind her, and the heat warmed her back. 'This must be a nice room to work in,' she said, 'it's always so warm and cosy.' She began to doodle with her finger in the scattering of flour that had been left behind on the table. The swirls and loops she created made channels which she dusted over, before starting again with a fresh pattern.

Isobel pointed upwards to the small room above the scullery. 'You should be here in the morning when you've just come down from up there and it's still dark. It's not so cosy when the fire's almost out and Jack Frost has tried to poke his long fingers under the back door.' It was said without any malice, but it was the truth, nonetheless. 'Better watch out or you'll be getting flour in those long plaits of yours and they'll go hard and crusty. You'll not be happy when it has to be brushed out. You'd better come over here and put your hands in the sink for a moment; we don't want you getting into trouble.'

Ann swished her fingers in the soapy water and looked around for something to dry her hands with. She didn't see the blue kitchen towel which hung on a nail right beside the scullery sink. Instead, she walked back into the warm kitchen and picked up a tea towel from the neat pile of freshly ironed laundry on the big table. Isobel watched as her just-completed work was undone, but said nothing.

Natalie Fergie

Ann dried her hands carefully. 'Father has been talking to Finlay.'

'I expect he had something important to say, Miss Ann.' Isobel lifted the heavy pan out of the washing-up water and put it on the wooden drainer.

'He said that there were two things that would get Finlay into trouble.'

'And what would those be, miss?'

'Your stick and your signature,' Ann checked her fingernails for bits of flour she might have missed, 'which I don't really understand. I thought that perhaps you might be able to tell me?'

Isobel's face seemed to be stuck. She coughed and guddled about in her pocket for a handkerchief while she worked out how to answer. 'I'm not sure I know, Miss Ann,' she said at last.

'Never mind. I'll ask Miss Smith, if I remember.' Ann felt her cheeks start to flush. It had happened a few times over the last month, and she assumed it was just one of the things that meant you were almost finished with being twelve. 'Maybe it would be better to talk to Miss Smith about my birthday instead of silly sticks. Do you know that from today, it's exactly four months until I will be thirteen?' She walked to the door, leaving the crushed tea towel on the table and a snowfall of flour on the floor. 'And have you heard that The Great Lafayette is coming to Edinburgh? That is very exciting indeed.'

Chapter 6

January 1911

Ursula had insisted on walking Ann to school on the first day of the new term. She wasn't sure she would do it every day, but it had seemed important to make an effort at least once. On her way back she glanced surreptitiously through the iron railings of the other houses in Library Terrace and tried to get a sense of who her new neighbours were from their taste in curtains and furniture. As she reached number 25, she paused, still not quite believing that this was now her home.

The stained glass in the inner door to the hall gleamed and sprinkled blue and green across the floor as she entered. Her umbrella, neatly furled and ready to use, was propped up against the coat stand. The recent spell of dry weather had stopped her taking it with her on every trip, but as she hung up her coat and removed her hat, she reflected that she was bound to be caught out eventually.

The hall smelled of beeswax polish with a hint of roses. It wasn't an unpleasant scent, but it was the choice of another woman, and one of the many things that she planned to change, a little at a time. The pace would need to be slow and imperceptible, unlike the breakneck speed of events since their wedding just before Christmas. It was scarcely believable to her that she had been married to John for only a matter of weeks, and in the space of a few words in front of a minister, she had become the wife of her former employer and taken on two almost grown children. Life with a live-in maid was already proving to be rather different from living on her own in a compact tenement flat, with just a little help from the laundry service.

She looked at the hall clock; at this hour John would be delegating the organisation of the second print runs to his supervisors, and doubtless he would be being awkward with the new secretary Ursula had selected to replace her. In time, Wilma Jackson would manage him well enough, she thought.

With Finlay and Ann at school, and John at work, she realised she was alone in the house for the first time since the wedding. There was Isobel, of course, but she didn't count. Not really.

At the end of the hall, past the big staircase on the right, was the first of a pair of doors that led to the kitchen and scullery, one door set at right angles to the next. She opened each one in turn; a curious arrangement, she thought, but clearly designed to avoid noise and cooking smells from making their way into the house, while at the same time preventing any glimpse of the place where the work really happened.

She could see Isobel standing at the draining board in the scullery, peeling carrots, swaying from side to side and singing, slightly out of tune. Labelled canisters of flour and sugar and oatmeal had been set out on the wooden kitchen table, along with a green tin of treacle, in preparation for the morning's baking session. Ursula watched the young woman working. In the short time since the wedding, she had waited to see how things were done in the house. Her experience as John's secretary had taught her that there was no point in rushing to change what might not be broken.

Isobel had served basic meals which might be described as satisfactory rather than exciting. Even Christmas dinner had been quite a simple affair. Ursula hadn't felt able to start any new traditions, but it had turned out there were no old ones worth keeping anyway. It was time to be a little more assertive.

She needed to understand everything there was to know about the running of the house: ordering the groceries, doing the accounts, arranging the laundry collections, and supervising the cooking and cleaning. Other married women managed their households efficiently so there was no reason she shouldn't be able to accomplish it, even though she had come to the job rather later than most. It was the start of a new year, and a new life, and it was time to take charge. She tried to ignore the butterflies in her stomach.

Isobel finished the carrots and swept the orange slivers into a bucket with the side of her hand. She turned to walk back into the kitchen and stopped suddenly when she saw Ursula.

'I beg your pardon, Miss Smith. I mean Mrs Black. I didn't hear you come in.'

Ursula smiled briefly. Even smiling was a worry. How to be polite and command respect, but at the same time never be over-friendly, which, she had been told by her mother many years earlier, was the worst thing to do when you were dealing with staff.

'I suppose I will get used to walking into this house without knocking, now that I live here.'

Isobel blushed. 'I am sorry, Miss, Mrs Black. I didn't mean . . .' She lowered her head and rubbed her hands dry on her apron.

'We are both going to have to get used to this new situation.' Heavens, but this is complicated, thought Ursula.

'You worked for the late Mrs Black for some time. She selected and employed you and she will have had her own ways of doing things. I'm a stranger and this is different for both of us.'

'I promise I'll do my best. I'm a good maid and a hard worker. You'll not be disappointed.'

'Isobel, I have been visiting this house every week for more than six months. I have no concern whatsoever about your work. Anyone who can manage Mr Black as well as two children without it all going to pieces deserves a medal in my opinion.' She smiled. 'Not that Finlay is really a child any more. He is taller than any of us.'

Ursula picked up a parcel which was lying on the long table next to the flour and sugar, a brown paper-wrapped box about nine inches by six, tied securely with string. 'Did this come today?'

'Yes, miss. First post. The postman didn't want to let it fall through the letterbox onto the floor in case it was something fragile, so he brought it round to the back.'

Ursula frowned. 'He came to the scullery door? Did you not hear him knock at the front?'

'I was taking in the kitchen cloths from the washing line. I thought I might as well take advantage of nature's bleach.' Isobel put her hands behind her back and crossed her fingers to protect herself against the lie. She and the postman had an arrangement, and he sometimes called in on his route and used the scullery lavatory in return for the occasional quarter-pound of cinnamon balls from the confectioners on the High Street. Or it might sometimes be Edinburgh Rock. Either way, it suited both of them.

Ursula put the parcel down again. 'I suppose he's a tradesman, of sorts, and it's certainly better than taking packages back to the sorting office and causing delay.'

She looked around the room. It was not an inspiring place; the putty-coloured walls were serviceable but drab and seemed to suck the life out of the weak winter light outside. On a cloud-heavy day it was positively gloomy, and in the evening the gas lighting did a less than adequate job.

'I should probably do an inventory,' said Ursula, with no enthusiasm. Opposite the window was a large built-in dresser; she opened a drawer and saw neatly organised rows of knives and forks – the everyday sort, not the best silverware, which was kept in the sideboard in the dining room. The drawer beside it held kitchen tools: a potato masher, a grater and a rolling pin, among other things.

'There's no need,' Isobel replied. 'The ledgers are in the last drawer, the one with the key. Everything is written down, and the order book and the invoices are kept there too. Mrs Black,' she paused before correcting herself, 'the late Mrs Black was very particular.' She straightened her back. 'She was always checking up on things.'

Ursula didn't reply, wondering briefly if her predecessor had good reason for scrutinising the work of the young woman in front of her.

Isobel tried again. 'I can take the ledgers out for you so you can go through them, if you like? I could put them in the dining room. It's warmer than the parlour upstairs.'

'What did the late Mrs Black do?'

'She did it all on a Monday, sitting in the drawing room at Mr Black's desk – before she got too unwell, of course.'

'And is the fire lit in the drawing room?'

Isobel shook her head and hastened to explain. 'I thought everyone was going to be out all day today and if that's the case I don't light it again until three o'clock in the winter, and only then if Mr Black is entertaining. Everyone usually just goes straight upstairs to the parlour after dinner.' She began to undo her kitchen apron. 'I'll go and light it now.'

'That won't be necessary.'

'But I thought—'

'The dining room is warm because the fire is still alight from breakfast, yes?'

Isobel nodded. 'I need to add more coal, though, and open up the damper if you're going to be in there.'

'Perhaps for today, I will just sit here at this table in the kitchen and work my way through all the papers and books.'

'You want to sit in the kitchen?'

Ursula looked at Isobel's scandalised face. 'It's warm. It's clean. You have scrubbed the floor this morning; the mop is drying out there,' she pointed towards the scullery, 'I can see it from where I'm standing.'

'Yes, Mrs Black. I wash it down twice a day.'

'I will undoubtedly have many questions and I don't want to walk back and forth from the dining room every time there is something I need to clarify. There is no point in me asking John,' she corrected herself, 'Mr Black, because judging by the fullness of the drawer, all he has done is pay the bills without filing anything.'

'He has been very busy.' Isobel was defensive. 'And it's been nearly eighteen months since Mrs Black . . .'

'Eighteen months of muddle, by the look of these papers.' Ursula turned back to the table and moved the tin of treacle and the flour canister to one side. 'You don't need to make excuses for how things are; I have eyes and I do understand how it's been. But it's time for me to sort out the housekeeping so things will run more smoothly in the future. I've waited until the year has turned, just to let everything settle down, but the sooner I start, the better.'

She lifted the ledgers and papers out of the drawer and set them out in piles on the table. 'I'm well used to organising offices, after working as Mr Black's secretary for the last three years here in Edinburgh, and at another company in London before that. Organising a household is not going to be so very different. I will try not to disturb your cake making. It is cake, I take it?'

'Yorkshire parkin, miss.'

'Very good.' Ursula glanced at the parcel. 'And I'll open that later.'

Chapter 7

January 1911

The winter light had faded and the gas mantles had been lit by the time Ursula, with Isobel's help, had managed to disentangle the threads of numbers in the main ledger. The leather-bound volumes from nineteen previous years were stored high up in one of the cupboards, and after studying three of the most recent books Ursula didn't feel strong enough to spend hours poring through the rest of them. Her predecessor's handwriting was unfamiliar and difficult to decipher, especially as the hand which had held the pen had obviously become shaky near the end. It seemed there had been little in the way of domestic financial management for some time, with sheaves of invoices to be cross-checked, and worryingly, some recent bills that were stamped UNPAID in red. When at last every set of figures had been entered into a new page in the ledger, and the columns added up, Ursula could see that there was a discrepancy of more than fifty pounds. She checked her addition and subtraction several times, but there was no doubt.

She knew she would need to talk to John about this to make sure there were no other bills unaccounted for or invoices outstanding. While it seemed a terrible thing to do, her instinct was to abandon the half-used book and begin again with a fresh set of accounts, and she decided to ask John to bring a new ledger home from the storeroom at the office. He had said he would leave her to organise the household, in fact he had seemed relieved about it, and she could now see why.

'I need to check what there is in the pantry,' Ursula said.

'Of course,' replied Isobel, her voice tight. She had watched the checking and rechecking of the columns of figures with increasing alarm.

They went through the shelves of jars and cans together. It was tempting to make a proper list of what was there, but now she was standing looking at the packets and bags and tins, Ursula could see that the kitchen was operating with a very limited palette of ingredients. It hadn't escaped her notice that the food served was plain to say the least, but until now she had left the meals and routines as they were, unwilling to be too much of a new broom.

She turned to Isobel. 'Is this it?'

The young woman nodded.

'So how does it work, with Mr Black's preferences?'

'I always do the best I can with what is ordered.' Isobel frowned before continuing. 'On Monday I make pie from the leftovers of the joint we have on Sunday; quite often that's mutton, or sometimes it's beef.'

Ursula smiled encouragement. 'I have noticed that you have a light touch with pastry.'

Isobel barely noticed the compliment. 'Or sometimes I use a layer of sliced tatties instead of the pastry.' She paused. 'I mean potatoes, sorry. And vegetables. Cabbage or carrots. On Tuesday and Wednesday there are faggots. I make those with minced beef and pork from the butcher, and there's mashed potatoes and turnip and gravy. In the winter months I make enough for two days and put the dish on the cold stone shelf in the larder at the back of the scullery. But in the summer they won't keep for a second day, so I make them fresh each morning.'

'Go on.'

'Thursday is braised liver. Friday is fish. And on Saturdays Mr Black used to take the children out for lunch when he got home from the office, and they had a big plate of sandwiches and cakes and biscuits for tea instead of a proper meal. That was before you . . .'

'Right.'

'And in the mornings, there's porridge and toast and marmalade, except for Sunday when there is the big breakfast: tattie scones, sliced sausage, bacon, eggs, and more toast and marmalade, and sometimes honey as well. But of course you know that.'

'Anything else?'

'Every day Mr Black takes a sandwich to work, two slices of bread with cheddar cheese and chopped dates. He always has the same thing.'

Ursula forgot her mother's advice and smiled to herself. She had seen John sit at his desk every day and unwrap his sandwiches, and watched as he folded the greaseproof paper into a precise rectangle afterwards before throwing it in the wastepaper basket. Sometimes he missed.

'Since,' Isobel hesitated, 'since the late Mrs Black has been gone, I've had to make plans for what is eaten, and I've offered to put other things in the sandwiches but Mr Black always says no.'

'I don't think either one of us will win that battle. I asked him about it once when there was no one else in the office and he told me it meant he didn't have to make a decision about something as straightforward as lunch, and he could think about more important things instead.'

Isobel glanced up at the clock, calculating the time needed for the work she hadn't yet done and mentally reshuffling her tasks for the rest of the day.

'Puddings?'

'I sometimes make crumble if there's fruit. Master Finlay's little plum tree at the end of the garden gave us a small harvest last September, even though it's only been planted since they moved here. He asked for a plum tree and Miss Ann asked for the cherry tree in the front garden.' She pointed to the lower shelf in the open larder where crimson-filled glass jars were arranged in a line, labelled neatly. 'Those are spiced plums. I added some from the greengrocer so there were enough. My aunt gave me the recipe for them. Sometimes I make Eve's pudding, and there's custard. Or I make rice pudding, or blancmange, or junket. And there were raspberries and blackcurrants in the garden last year so I made summer pudding a few times when the berries were ripe.'

'And you have been with the family how long, Isobel?'

'Since they moved here, after the house was built. Before that they were in a big tenement flat in Bruntsfield and there was another maid who didn't come with them. She said it was too much for her.'

'So that's just over two years?'

'More or less, miss. The late Mrs Black felt that a routine for the meals was important. But this house hasn't really been run in the same way as the others in the street.'

'Oh?'

Isobel looked down at her shoes. 'Some of the other maids, we talk, you know. They tell me that the ladies in their houses are interested in the food and how it's prepared, so they do it together. They try new things.'

'And you've never done that?'

'Mrs Black, sorry, the late—'

Ursula shook her head. 'There is no need to correct yourself all the time, I understand what you mean.'

'Well, the late Mrs Black wasn't interested. Maybe it was because she was poorly. But even before she was really ill, she just gave lots of instructions. I did my best, though it wasn't always good enough, I'm afraid. I'm a plain cook, not a fancy one. Towards the end it was easier for her to just let me do everything, and she stopped commenting on what I made. And afterwards I had even less time for all the cooking because I was doing so many other things as well.' Isobel waved her arm as though to envelop the house in a bedsheet. 'There is a lot to get done. I had to come up with a plan I could repeat because it was the only way I could manage it all. I'm very sorry. I've done my best and I don't want to speak out of turn, but it was the only way. And Mr Black was sad for a long time, and the children couldn't decide what they wanted, so I did it all for them. If you want to have a new maid, I can look for another position.' Isobel was now talking to the floor, her head bowed.

Ursula looked at the tired young woman, who was wiping her hands on her apron over and over again, and shook her head. 'It hasn't been an easy time for anyone.'

'Before I started here, I spoke to the maid from the Bruntsfield flat and she told me that Mrs Black had her ways.'

'Ways?' Ursula was flummoxed. Louise Black was an enigma. It was like having a sainted body in the house who could not be criticised or have her methods challenged. But from the little John had told her, Louise had not been the easiest of people to live with. There were a lot of rules, for a start. 'Sit down with me, please.'

Isobel pulled one of the wooden chairs out from the table and waited.

Ursula sat down and tapped the dark green binding on the ledger with her fingers. 'There are going to be some changes.'

Isobel looked at her miserably. She remained standing. 'Yes, miss.'

'First, I am now Mrs Black so there will be no more miss, if you don't mind.' She paused. 'And secondly, there will be no more liver in this house. Or faggots. And while there might be a plan, we won't be having the same thing every Tuesday as though we are in a regiment of the Cameron Highlanders. Tell me, do you *like* to cook?'

'I don't mind it. But I'm not sure I'm any good at it. My friends,' Isobel waved her hands again to encompass the houses on either side, 'well, they make all sorts and I've just never had the opportunity because—'

'I understand,' Ursula interrupted. She opened the ledger and looked again at the column of figures, now in her own handwriting. 'Right, Isobel. In the house in which I grew up, the food was very different from this. My father's mother was German, and when she was a child in Berlin there were often visitors from all over Europe.' She counted the countries off on her fingers. 'France, Italy, Austria and Switzerland for a start. There was a lot of cooking and baking. Especially the baking part. I think a small amount of variety, introduced a little bit at a time, will definitely be the order of the day now I am in charge.' She smiled. 'And there is no time like the present, so I think we should make a plan for next week, together. These unpaid bills may mean we need some new suppliers, although heaven knows I am sure they all talk to one another.'

'Yes, Mrs Black.'

'I will need your advice before I place the orders. I'm sure you have an opinion on the best greengrocer and butcher to use, for a start. If you can tell me which shops we have accounts with, and which ones you think send good-quality produce, that would be very helpful.'

Isobel felt the tension in her shoulders begin to ease. She thought about the columns of figures and the unpaid bills and the checking. All of the checking. She crossed her fingers; if she was careful, perhaps this would be alright after all.

Chapter 8

January 1911

'I completely forgot, John,' said Ursula at breakfast, 'a parcel arrived yesterday. I left it in the kitchen.'

'A parcel for me?' he replied.

'Maybe it's for me!' Ann couldn't keep the excitement out of her voice. 'After all, it's my birthday soon, and I hope there will be presents.'

Ursula shook her head. 'I'm afraid it's for me.'

Ann slumped in her seat, disappointed.

Ursula squashed the urge to walk through to the kitchen and collect the package. 'I'll ring the bell and Isobel can bring it through.'

Finlay, engrossed with spreading butter right to the edges of his toast so there was no part of the surface left uncovered, didn't look up. 'She won't hear it. She's up the garden doing something with clothes pegs and the washing line. I saw her walk up there with a basket a couple of minutes ago.'

'I'll get it, it might be for me after all.' Ann didn't wait to be told she couldn't go, and was off her chair and out of the room before anyone could stop her.

'She's going to be impossible.' Finlay lifted the slice of perfectly buttered toast to his mouth. 'Anyone would think no one in the history of the world had ever had a birthday before, and it's still months away.'

Before John had the opportunity to admonish his son, Ann was back.

'It does *say* your name on the outside,' she put the package down beside Ursula, 'but that might be a mistake?'

'Let me see.' John held his hand out for the parcel and looked closely at the stamps before passing it back. 'A couple here for your collection, Finlay.'

'Is it a present for me, then?' Ann's impatience got the better of her.

'I don't think so, my dear.' John looked at his pocket watch and checked it against the clock on the sideboard. 'I need to get moving; if the printing presses aren't running properly on a Monday we never catch up for the rest of the week.' He smiled at Ursula. 'But of course, you'll remember that.'

'Indeed.'

'Last night's dinner was excellent.' He rubbed his stomach. 'I am very much looking forward to tonight's meal.'

*

Ursula carried the parcel back into the empty kitchen. 'Hello?' She heard a scraping noise coming from the maid's room above the scullery, followed by footsteps clattering down the uncarpeted staircase. Isobel appeared, twisting her long hair into a bun and pinning it awkwardly.

'Sorry, Mrs Black. I was just tidying myself up, it's been a bit of a rush this morning.'

'I need to speak to you about tonight's dinner.'

'The pie?'

'No, not the pie, which I am sure will be perfectly adequate. I mean the vegetables.'

'The vegetables?' Isobel echoed.

'I was wondering what you have in the larder, and hoping there is something more interesting than cabbage.' Ursula started to walk towards the scullery and the larder with its cold marble shelf.

Isobel got there before her. 'There are onions and potatoes and at least a pound of carrots.'

'I was hoping we might have some parsnips. I have an idea for them.'

'Sorry. Perhaps if they are added to the order for next week?'

'Maybe the carrots would do.' Ursula moved back into the kitchen and unlocked the tall cupboard beside the range. 'Do we have any honey?'

'Of course, Mrs Black. It's on the breakfast table every Sunday. Are you wanting me to make a cake?'

Ursula shook her head. 'My mother used to make roast parsnips with honey and sage, and I was just thinking it would be more interesting than plain boiled carrots.'

'There is sage. It grows up at the end of the garden. Miss Ann and I planted it last summer; we grew it from some seeds the postman gave me.'

Ursula turned around at the second mention of the postman in as many days. 'Really?'

'I cut it down at the end of the summer and dried it above the stove. There's a full jar of it behind the cornflour.' She pointed into the cupboard. 'And rosemary, and some thyme as well.'

'And this is all from the postman?'

Isobel blushed. 'The seeds were. The rosemary was a cutting from his allotment. He's always telling me we could grow more in the garden here.'

'Is he indeed?'

Isobel felt some sort of explanation was needed. 'We just share a few words when he brings the parcels. It's been the same postman now for all the time I've been here.' She tried to change the subject. 'How do you cook the parsnips with honey?'

'I can't really remember. I just thought we could try it. Like roast potatoes, I suppose; part cook them and then toss them in the honey and sprinkle sage on top, or thyme, perhaps.'

'Or both?'

'Quite possibly.'

'And then you just roast them in the oven?' Isobel was willing to try anything if it stopped Ursula asking about the postman. She didn't want her supply of Edinburgh Rock and boilings to stop.

'Why don't you try it with a bit of golden syrup the first time you do it? That will be less wasteful if it doesn't work.' Ursula picked up the parcel. 'Now what I actually came in here for is a pair of scissors, to cut this string. Are they in the middle drawer?'

Isobel held her hand out for the package. 'I can undo those knots for you if you like. It won't take a minute, and string is always useful for tying a cloth around the top of the bowl when I'm making a steamed pudding.'

Ursula shrugged. 'You can try if you want; they look very tight to me.'

But in no more than a minute or two, the string was untied and zigzagged in a twisted loop around Isobel's fingers, making a sort of bow. She handed the loosely wrapped parcel back.

'Thank you.' Ursula turned to leave. 'I'll take it upstairs. The breakfast things are still to be cleared in the dining room and you'll be able to get on with doing that if I'm not in the way.'

Isobel picked up the empty tray and hid her disappointment well. She, like Ann, was very keen to know what was inside the mysterious package.

Chapter 9

January 1911

The knock at the scullery door was hesitant, and Isobel didn't hear it at first. She was concentrating on lifting a tray of jam tarts out of the oven and it was only when the knock came a second time that she glanced across at the kitchen window and saw the familiar face of the postman. She put the hot baking tin down on the table and hurried to answer the door.

'Morning, Duncan. Come away in and get a heat in front of the range.'

'You're on your own, then?'

'It's just me for the next hour or so.'

He stepped into the scullery and closed the door behind him. 'I'll be glad to get indoors for a wee while, and no mistake. This city always lives up to its reputation. Even when it's sunny, there's a wind.'

'I'll leave you to . . .' She glanced towards the far end of the scullery where the door to the lavatory was kept firmly closed.

'Thank you kindly.' He heaved the canvas mail bag off his shoulder and put it down next to the sink with a groan. 'I thought things would ease off after the turn of the year, but no, the whole world is sending letters and cards as though there is a second Christmas on the way.'

'I can give you a scone if you like? I made them yesterday.'

'If you're sure you can spare one, that would be most welcome.'

Isobel opened the cake tin and selected the most mis-shapen scone: golden brown, with crunchy demerara sugar on the top and studded with sultanas. It took only a minute to split it and spread it with butter and raspberry jam. She popped it into a brown paper bag saved from the greengrocer's delivery and set it down on the table.

Duncan washed his hands at the scullery sink when he was finished. She had always insisted on this, and he went along with her rules.

'How are things with you then, Isobel?' He pointed to the door that led to the hall. 'Is she settling in?'

'I think so.'

'No problems?' He paused. 'You're not thinking of moving on?'

'I'm not. Not yet, anyway.' She counted the tarts in her head as she transferred them onto a wire rack to cool. 'She seems alright so far. But a lot of people are nice to begin with, and then they change later.'

'I'll keep my fingers crossed for you.'

'I'm not sure she really knows how to treat me. One minute she seems quite happy with my work, and then an hour later I feel as though she's checking up on every-thing I do.'

'She's not like the last one, though?'

Isobel shook her head. 'No. But I'm not counting my chickens.'

'And she is kind to the young girl? That's what matters the most.' He picked up the paper bag and looked inside. 'A scone and raspberry jam. You have a good heart, Isobel. My wife will be very jealous. She often talks about last year, when you made that cake for her birthday. My grandchildren were happy too, they talked about it for weeks.' He took hold of the top corners of the bag and twirled it around in the air, twisting it closed.

'I'm not sure I can promise you a cake this year. It was easier when it was just me, but most days I've got Mrs Black for company now.'

'But she is kind?' he repeated. 'To the girl?'

'As far as I know.' She studied her hands, wrinkled and red from washing the dishes. 'I do hope so. Miss Ann had enough trouble with her mother, she can't be dealing with any more.'

He hoisted the mail bag back onto his shoulder. 'I'd better be off. Your neighbours might be taking notes.' He reached forward and touched her arm. 'You did your best, Isobel. That's all any of us can do.'

'I suppose. If only I had realised sooner.'

He shook his head. 'And what could you have done?'

'I don't know.'

'Nothing. You could have done nothing.'

'But—'

'You have to stop blaming yourself, Isobel. It was not your fault.' He opened the scullery door. 'I'm sorry, I really must go.'

'Wait a minute!' Isobel rubbed her forehead, leaving a floury mark. 'I've been thinking that we need a sign. Something so you know whether I'm on my own in the house or not.'

'I suppose we don't want anyone finding me in here when I should be out delivering.'

'I'll put the blue jar of soft soap on the scullery window-sill when she goes out, and I'll take it away when she's here. It's not as though you call in every day, and it's easy to see from the back gate.'

'Right you are.'

'If you see the jar then the coast is clear. And as long as you are ready to say you made a mistake if you do see her, that'll make it alright.'

'We can try that. I just don't want you to get into trouble.'

'I'll be fine. We can do this. Give my regards to your wife.'

After he left, she put the blue jar on the windowsill. It looked pretty there, with the winter sunlight catching the sheen of the pottery. And half an hour later, when she heard Ursula return and the front door banging, she moved the jar further along the workbench. No one would notice, she was sure of it. People were not aware of things that did not affect them. That was how all the trouble had started before, with folk, and good ones at that, simply not noticing what was happening right under their noses.

Chapter 10

January 1911

Ursula sat on the padded stool in front of her dressing table. She pulled the hairpins out of her bun and shook her head to loosen her hair before running her fingers through it. She was not a proud woman, but she was quietly pleased that despite being well into her forties, her hair was still the same colour as it had always been, with only a few sprinkles of white creeping in at the nape of her neck. And since she couldn't see the back of her head unless she was sitting with the dressing-table mirrors angled just so, it didn't trouble her.

'I know it's still a way off, but we need to discuss Ann's birthday present,' she said to John, who was already sitting up in bed with his nose in a book.

'Mmmm?'

'Ann's birthday?' She began to brush her hair from root to tip. It was so long she could sit on it.

He lowered the book, resting it on his chest. 'I thought maybe a set of encyclopaedias.'

'I'm not sure. I think we need to be treating her like the young woman she is about to become. Someone who will marry one day.' Ursula's brushing halted for a few seconds. 'And anyway, doesn't Finlay have encyclopaedias she can look at?'

'He'll move away soon. He'll go to university and I'm sure the books will go with him.'

She tried again. 'There's plenty of time for learning at school. Ann needs to have a gift that is pretty. I'm sure all her friends have nice things; in fact I've noticed a few of them starting to put their hair up.'

'She's a child. Her brain needs to be fed.'

Ursula unscrewed the lid from the jar of vanishing cream and applied small dots of it to her face. Three on the forehead, two on each cheek, one on her chin. She began to stroke the cream in. 'I don't think you realise, but she's not a little girl any more. Her shape is changing. I'm not sure she has even noticed it herself yet.'

He didn't reply.

'I was thinking that Finlay could give her something for the garden. From what I remember of last summer, she seems to like being outside.' She leaned forward to examine her face in the mirror. 'I ordered a few packets of seeds for the flower border; that's what was in the parcel she was so interested in. Maybe he could give her those. There are snapdragons and cosmos and sweet peas. All of them could be cut for the table.'

John nodded, approving of this part of the plan, at least. 'She's been very interested in the garden ever since we planted the cherry tree together. I will discuss your idea with Finlay.' He put his bookmark in between the pages. 'I do have one suggestion, though. I saw in the newspaper a few days ago that The Great Lafayette is coming to perform in Edinburgh. They say he's a personal friend of Mr Houdini.'

Ursula finished smoothing in the cream and studied her reflection again to make sure she hadn't missed anywhere.

John continued. 'I've heard her talking about it with Finlay. She is quite obsessed with the idea of lions and horses on the stage and is fascinated by all the illusions.'

Ursula turned to face him. 'This is an excellent idea. If you want her to learn things, what better way than to be actually in the theatre where it is happening, and watch it all unfold? Are the tickets on sale yet?'

'I'm not sure. I wonder if you two ladies might like to go? Finlay puts up with all her chatter about it but I can see that he thinks it is rather beneath him.'

'I could go with her, and it certainly would be fun. But maybe she would prefer to go with you?'

'With me? Why?'

Ursula spoke as one might to a small child. 'Because *you* will be able to explain it all and reveal the mysteries.'

John laughed. 'I don't know if I'm up to that particular challenge. I'm quite sure his secrets are extremely well hidden.'

'Nonetheless, I think it would be rather splendid for the two of you to go. You are away so much with the business, and I see her every day. It would be a special experience she can share with you, and you alone. We all need that sort of thing with our parents.'

'I don't think her mother would have agreed with you; she couldn't wait to pack Ann off to be a weekly boarder when she was seven years old.'

Ursula shuddered. 'I'm very glad she's at home with us now. I cannot imagine doing such a thing.'

'What Louise wanted, Louise got. She was a force of nature, until she became unwell.'

Ursula, who disliked Louise more with every passing day, added this to the pile of grudges upon which she would never be able to act. 'I will go, but only if you really don't want to. I do think the two of you should have the excitement.'

'Very well, though it will depend on the dates, of course. The performance will be at the Empire Palace Theatre. Perhaps you could see if the tickets are on sale next time you are in town. In fact, since it's a special occasion, you might try for a box?'

'I'll certainly find out what's available. It may be more fun to sit with the rest of the audience though.' Ursula stood up from the stool and began to braid her hair. 'I think this birthday is important. My mother gave me a handbag for my thirteenth birthday. It was blue to match my eyes, and I've been thinking I would like to do the same for Ann. A bag to match those green eyes of hers.'

'What does a girl of thirteen want with a handbag?'

Ursula sighed. 'Where shall I start? To begin with, dresses don't have proper pockets. We put our handkerchiefs up our sleeves. Without a bag, we have nowhere to put our coin purses, and nowhere to put a comb or . . .' she paused ' . . . other necessaries.'

John stared at Ursula. 'She hasn't . . .?'

She twisted an elastic band around the end of her braid and walked across to the bed.

'No, but it may not be long. Another year, perhaps.'

'A handbag is an excellent suggestion.' He closed his book and put it on his bedside table. 'Would you like me to come with you to choose it?' The tone of his voice clearly indicated that he could think of few chores that would be worse.

Ursula smiled. 'Your presence will not be required. I think I can manage on my own. It's the first birthday since I became part of the family and I would like to make it special for her.' She folded the eiderdown back and slipped between the sheets, snuggling down until her head was on his shoulder. 'I know it isn't until April, but I should like to know that I've managed to find just the right thing.'

'It seems like only yesterday that she was born in the Bruntsfield flat. We didn't make it to the nursing home across the Meadows. It was about twenty minutes from start to finish. No time for a midwife or a doctor. Louise wanted another boy, and was determined to call him Anthony, but we got Ann instead.' John pulled Ursula close. 'Such a lot has happened since then. It hasn't always been easy, but I am a very lucky man to have you as my wife.'

Chapter 11

January 1911

Ursula had a Plan with a capital P. She would go to Robert Maule's department store at the foot of Lothian Road. If they didn't have what she wanted, she would walk along Princes Street to Jenners, and if that failed, she would go to R.W. Forsyth. Surely there would be something suitable in one of the three biggest stores in the city.

She left the house promptly at half past ten, well wrapped against the cold. The tram was crowded and she was relieved to get off it and into the fresh air, but despite spending twenty minutes in Maule's she wasn't excited by any of their offerings, so she continued along the north side of the street on foot. Behind the large display in the Singer shop she could see a couple, the man holding forth about something and his wife standing rather unhappily beside him as he pointed at a grand cabinet and gesticulated.

She pulled her scarf around her face against the chill wind that had blown up from the Forth and pushed on to the other end of the street.

There were several bags in Jenners that were vaguely possible, but none that really seemed to be right for Ann. Ursula was disappointed, but bought a packet of six white handkerchiefs for John. He didn't need them, but she enjoyed seeing the overhead pneumatic tubes that took cash and sent it to the cash room in a vacuum system, whooshing back to the servers a few minutes later with the change and a receipt. She repeated her search in R.W. Forsyth, but there was nothing suitable there either. It doesn't matter, she told herself, it's more than three months until the big day. Plenty of time.

She continued her walk to the North British Station Hotel at the eastern end of the street, and promised herself she would come back for afternoon tea another day, before turning right and heading across the North Bridge.

Waverley station sat in the deep cutting below the bridge. Soot and smoke hung in the air. Whistles blew, and the carriages bumping over the joins in the rails created the metallic smoky smell of adventures in Ursula's imagination. On some days she walked down the long ramps from Waverley Bridge into the station itself and sat on a bench in the ticket hall with no intention of travelling anywhere, just to enjoy the anticipation of a potential journey. But today was not the day for such musing and she continued to walk, the wind cutting through her coat as she headed towards James Thin the bookseller. She would look for a gift for John, she decided. Maybe Sir Arthur Conan Doyle had written a new novel.

*

An hour later, after browsing many of the shelves in the bookshop, she was both hungry and ready to leave. She tucked her scarf snugly around her neck and headed up towards the theatre, clutching her purchase. On the opposite side of the road was a café she hadn't noticed before and despite the fact that she wanted to be home in plenty of time for Ann to get back from school, she crossed over to investigate, dodging an oncoming tram as she did so.

A man encased in a long white apron, with his sleeves held away from his wrists by elasticated metal bracelets around his upper arms, opened the door before she reached it. A bell rang above her head as she entered, and again as the door closed.

'Welcome to Café Vegetaria,' he said, and showed her to an empty table.

'Thank you. I am in rather a hurry, so could you just bring me tea, please? And maybe a sandwich. Ham and mustard, if you have it?'

'I can offer you the tea, madam, but not the ham sandwich. This is a vegetarian establishment.'

'Oh?' Ursula, normally unflustered, found herself suddenly without a response.

'We have cheese sandwiches, with or without pickle, or perhaps you would prefer a nice warming bowl of leek and potato soup?'

Ursula had no desire to find somewhere else to have a meal, and she was already seated, so to stand and leave now would be embarrassing. This would have to suffice. 'Do you have no meats at all?'

'None.' The man glanced up at the clock on the wall. 'But we are still serving our sixpenny lunch. Soup and bread, and then a hot savoury course, which today is a rather splendid beetroot and carrot crumble with vegetable gravy.' He paused. 'All followed by pudding with cream.'

'That sounds like quite a lot,' she replied, distracted by the large posters on the walls. 'If I could just see the menu, that would be helpful.'

'Of course.' He left, returning with a folded card which bore the words 'Café Vegetaria' on the front.

She scanned it quickly. 'I'll have a pot of tea, and some of the beetroot crumble, please.' She glanced at the loaded plates of the nearby customers. 'Just a half portion will be sufficient, I think.'

He brought the food a few minutes later, along with a leaflet headed 'Vegetarian? Why not?' and left her to read it in peace.

Ursula was suddenly famished. She broke up the crumble with her knife and fork, and while she waited for it to cool, she picked up the leaflet and studied it. A half-memory of something she had read in the past danced around the edge of her thoughts. Something about suffragettes being vegetarians. She set the leaflet aside and picked up the menu to look at it properly. At the bottom, below the details of sixpenny teas and shilling dinners, she read: 'The promoters of this venture give not less than 50 per cent higher remuneration to their helpers than is paid elsewhere.' Below this were two more words. 'No tipping.'

She enjoyed the crumble, and the crusty brown bread and butter that had arrived with it, unrequested, and examined her surroundings. A poster on the wall beside her declared: 'Staff wanted. Lowest wages paid 15s a week of 54 hours. All meals and uniform provided.' A second poster announced: 'Census Meeting. Bring Your Friends.' She poured herself a cup of tea and opened her bag to retrieve her diary and a pencil. The black covers were new-year stiff, and the weekly format was just big enough for her appointments. She turned to the address section at the back and started to write.

15 shillings x 52 weeks = 780 shillings
780 divided by 20 shillings to the pound = £39 a year
9 hours a day for 6 days = 54 hours

She frowned and checked her calculations. The truth began to slowly dawn on her that Isobel, who was up before six in the morning, and not in bed before ten at night, seven days a week, was working almost twice as many hours as the young women in the café, even after she took account of her half-day off.

Ursula shook her head and checked the figures for a third time. This surely couldn't be right. But her arithmetic seemed to be correct. How much were they paying Isobel? She couldn't remember exactly, but she was sure it wasn't anything close to thirty-nine pounds a year. Of course, Isobel lived above the scullery so she didn't pay rent, but even when Ursula factored this in, she was left with an uncomfortable feeling in the pit of her stomach, one she knew would not go away until she had checked the ledgers at 25 Library Terrace and asked John about Isobel's wages.

When she eventually left the café, the leaflet folded and stowed safely in her bag, she was so preoccupied with everything she had learned that she completely forgot to go to the theatre to enquire about tickets for The Great Lafayette.

Chapter 12

Early February 1911

'Are you unwell?' John asked Ursula when they were out for their usual Sunday morning walk. 'You barely touched your meal yesterday evening. I don't think you've eaten a proper dinner all week.' Nothing got past him and it could be both a blessing and a curse.

'I'm experiencing a prolonged episode of indigestion,' she lied. 'Some foods seem to make it worse. I'm going to speak to Isobel and see if we can change the meals a little.'

He frowned. 'This is how Louise's illness began. She lost her appetite. Are you sure you don't need to see a doctor?'

'Definitely not. I expect it will pass in a few days.' Ursula linked arms with John, not caring what anyone might think. 'Could you remind me how much you pay Isobel? I couldn't find the details in the household ledgers.'

'Eight shillings and sixpence a week. It used to be seven shillings and ninepence, which is just over twenty pounds a year. But after Louise died I decided to increase it because Isobel was taking on more responsibility than before, and I didn't want her to leave us.'

'So that's how much a year?'

'A shade over twenty-two pounds.' He smiled. 'I think she was rather surprised, but I was glad to do it. We really would not have managed without her. Why do you ask?'

Ursula stepped to one side to avoid a puddle. 'I read something earlier in the week about wages, that's all. Nothing with which you need to concern yourself.'

*

Rather than ringing the call bell from the drawing room to summon Isobel and interrupting her work, Ursula walked the few steps across the hall into the warm kitchen.

'I think I need your help, Isobel. I am in somewhat of a quandary.'

'Of course, if there is anything I can do, I will, Mrs Black.'

Ursula sat down at the table and pointed to the other chair. 'Come and sit with me for a minute.' She put a piece of folded paper on the table beside the teapot. 'There is a café on Nicolson Street which I've visited a few times now, and I like the food they serve there.'

Isobel nodded. 'And you would like to try some of their ideas?'

'I would. There is one problem, though.' She looked out of the window at the wintry sky for a moment. 'The food is vegetarian. There is no meat or fish in the meals.'

'None at all?'

'None at all,' Ursula echoed. 'But I like it, and the more time I spend there, the more I have struggled to eat our meals. I push the meat around the plate and . . .'

'I've noticed,' Isobel said quietly. She didn't want to appear cheeky.

'I know I'm not explaining properly what the problem is.' Ursula sighed. 'The truth is, I don't really understand it myself.'

Isobel twisted the long ties on her apron around her fingers. 'I thought my cooking was displeasing you for some reason.'

'Not at all.' Ursula thought of the posters on the walls of Café Vegetaria. 'Over the last few weeks, since I have been going to the café, I have begun to think of us as more of a team, Isobel.'

'A team?'

'Yes. We work together to run the house.' Ursula found herself deliberately ignoring the views of her mother, who had always insisted on a certain distance between staff and family. 'I know that I'm your employer, but it seems to me that things are changing in the world.'

Isobel risked a smile. 'I think I might like to be part of a team,' she said carefully.

Ursula pushed on without really listening. 'But now there is the meat question, and I can't bring myself to bring the fork to my mouth. I don't know what to do about it.'

Isobel trod her way cautiously through this new way of thinking. 'I wonder what Mr Black thinks?'

'He has noticed. He notices everything. It's his way. I told him that meat gives me indigestion and he has accepted that, for now. But we,' she slipped into using the new signifier without noticing, 'well, we need to do a bit of thinking, Isobel. I know we do some of the cooking together now, but I'm going to need your assistance with this. I don't want to change what the rest of the family eats.' She stopped for a moment. 'At least not yet.'

'Are you wanting your food to look like their food, but without the meat?'

'That's exactly it. I've copied down some of the dishes from the menu. The place is called Café Vegetaria, which is a rather pretty name, I think.' She unfolded the piece of paper and pushed it across the table.

Isobel leaned forward to study the words. 'Leek and barley soup,' she read out loud. 'Broth. Vegetable pie. Carrot and beet crumble with herbs. Nut roast with gravy. Cheese soufflé. Macaroni with Italian sauce.' She looked up. 'None of that looks very complicated, except maybe the nut roast. And I've never made an Italian sauce.'

'I've been thinking it may be a bit tedious if all we have is soups and pies.'

'That's true.' Isobel tried out the new role which had been thrust upon her. 'I don't think it will be too difficult, not if we make a plan.'

Ursula could feel the strain easing. Being in charge of the meals was a chore; it was necessary, but definitely not her favourite occupation. She would much rather be reading a book, or sitting in Café Vegetaria listening to the conversations and fresh opinions which swirled around her there.

Isobel opened the small drawer below the tabletop and took out a sheet of paper with a notice printed on one side. She turned the paper over. 'We can keep it simple for the next wee while and see how it goes.' She licked the tip of the pencil and started to write, thinking aloud as she added things to the list. 'Everyone likes a proper pie with a good pastry crust. If I do that twice there won't be any complaints. I'm sure I can find something different from beef or mutton for yours and with any luck no one will notice.' She tapped her forehead with the blunt end of the pencil. 'Macaroni once. Cottage pie with mash on top. I would need to think about what could be a substitute for the escalopes. Perhaps I could make a risotto? One of my friends is in a house where the grandmother is Italian. She's always talking about making a big flat round bread with tomatoes and cheese and anchovies on it. We could leave the anchovies off for you, of course. I don't suppose this place has a recipe book? It wouldn't help their trade.'

'I don't know, but James Thin is just over the road. I'm going back to the café tomorrow. I'll ask the server if he has any suggestions.'

'I'll keep this list in my pocket for now. I know Mr Black doesn't often come into the kitchen, but Miss Ann does, and she's very inquisitive.'

'She is indeed.' Ursula pointed at the paper. 'Is that an advertisement for the theatre?'

Isobel nodded. 'The Great Lafayette is coming to town. I don't fancy it myself, far too noisy for me, but Miss Ann gave me the notice anyway. She hasn't stopped talking about it for weeks.' She pushed her chair back from the table. 'I'll make a pie for this evening. In fact, if I make individual pies for everyone it won't be much extra work and it'll be less obvious.' She turned and lifted the coal scuttle to slide another rush of fuel onto the grate. 'I just need to fire the oven a bit so it's hot enough for a nice pastry crust.'

They looked at one another across the kitchen, each aware that their relationship had shifted slightly, and neither of them was sure that she wanted it to go back to how it had been before.

Chapter 13

Late February 1911

Ursula wasn't sure why Café Vegetaria exerted such a pull on her. Since the start of the month she had found herself there several times a week. There were rarely any male customers and the ladies who were gathered at the tables in pairs and threes and fours seemed to be regulars who nodded and smiled at her when she went in. Occasionally someone would play a tune on the piano in the corner. On this particular Wednesday, there were no free tables and she stood a little hesitantly near the door.

'If you wouldn't mind sharing?' said the server.

She shrugged. 'That would be fine.'

'If I can find you a seat, what would you like today?'

'A pot of tea, please, and perhaps some of the date and walnut loaf I enjoyed so much last time, if you have any?'

He walked across the café to a table where a woman sat alone. Ursula saw them exchange a few words and the woman laughed. He pulled out the rush-seated chair opposite her, waved Ursula over and then left, without providing any introductions.

Once Ursula was seated, the stranger offered her hand. 'Mary Young.'

The woman's grip was unexpectedly firm. She looked a little older than Ursula, with smooth skin and absolutely white hair.

'Ursula Black. Thank you for agreeing to share your table. I hope I won't disturb you.'

'Not at all. It is always pleasant to have some company.' She looked directly at Ursula, in a slightly disconcerting manner. 'I think I've seen you before?'

'I've eaten here a few times.'

The woman nodded encouragingly and Ursula found herself adding to the conversation without realising she was being drawn in. 'It's an interesting place.'

'It is indeed,' replied her new companion, stirring what appeared to be a large cup of cocoa. 'Are you a vegetarian?'

Ursula wished she had ordered cocoa too and was momentarily flustered by such a direct inquisition. 'No. Well, not really. Not yet. I am making a few changes, but I have the views of my family to consider.'

'It's so much less costly than buying meat. And it's a lot quicker to prepare meals compared with the time some tougher joints and cuts require.'

Ursula nodded. 'I've discussed it with our maid. We plan to try some new ideas, but it's not easy. Do you know something about it? Could you suggest a book, perhaps? Or a pamphlet?'

Mary Young stuck her hand up in the air where it could be spotted by the server. He hurried over. 'This lady is interested in your recipes.'

Ursula shook her head. 'Oh no, I wouldn't presume to ask for any professional secrets.'

'They aren't secrets.' The man smiled at her. 'Mrs Young knows we usually have a few copies of Dr Allinson's book in the office. I believe it provides the most comprehensive information on the subject, and of course, it has been written by an eminent doctor and a proponent of Hygienic Medicine.'

Ursula frowned. 'Hygienic Medicine?'

Her dining companion answered the question for her. 'Good health through a vegetarian diet, plenty of exercise, fresh air and regular bathing.'

'I see.' Ursula looked up at the server. 'Well, if you do have a copy of the book, perhaps you could add it to my bill?'

He nodded. 'I'll check with the manager and leave it at the desk for you.' The café bell jangled as the door opened and he hurried away to greet another small group of customers.

'Tell me about yourself, Ursula.' It was a demand. 'I do love to meet new women. Fresh company is so stimulating.'

'I'm not sure what you might find of interest.' Ursula felt it would be rude not to comply. 'I live in between Morningside and Newington, with my husband and his two children,' she began, unsure of what was required. 'It's not far from the Observatory, actually. My husband's first wife died eighteen months ago.' She stopped, unaccustomed to providing a curriculum vitae to a complete stranger, and looked around the café for inspiration. On the wall opposite was a poster emblazoned with the word 'CENSUS' in capital letters. 'This will be our first census as a family.'

Mary Young leaned forward and spoke ever so slightly more softly. 'And are you going to complete the form?'

'My husband will do that, as head of the household. Those are the rules, surely?'

'Not everyone will be obeying the rules, though, will they?'

'They won't?' Ursula felt like a child who has unexpectedly stumbled into an adult world and doesn't understand the vocabulary.

'Do you read the newspapers, Ursula?'

'I look briefly, over breakfast. My husband takes *The Scotsman* to work and it doesn't usually come home with him in the evening.' Ursula took the initiative at last. 'Will you be completing it?'

There was a firm head-shake. 'Definitely not, and my husband will not be doing it on my behalf either. I will not be counted if I do not count.'

'I beg your pardon?'

'If the government will not give me the vote, and allow my opinions to be heard, then they shall not count me in the population. The census questions are not legitimate anyway. No one should be filling it in, man or woman.'

'Not legitimate?' Ursula felt as though she was behaving like a parrot.

'The questions are biased. It's well known in my circles. They are asking about women's fertility. It's horrible.' Mary Young was clearly furious about the issue. 'And what's more, we have no idea why they are collecting such personal information and what use they may find for it.'

'How do you know this?' Ursula was unable to hide her disbelief, but at that moment a waitress arrived with her order, and there was a break in the conversation while her tea was poured and things arranged.

'I have my sources.'

'And do you think that this protest, this not completing the forms, will get you the vote?'

'I don't know if it will get *us* the vote, Ursula, but we have to try. All women should have their voices heard at the ballot box, everyone from maids to countesses. Or do you not think that your opinion has the same worth as that of your husband?'

'I suppose it does.'

68

'You mentioned children. Boys or girls?' The bluntness was astonishing.

'Finlay is seventeen and Ann is twelve. She will be thirteen in April.' Ursula was glad of the change of subject. 'That's why I was out today. It's my third attempt to buy her a handbag, or maybe something that can be worn across her shoulder.'

'Thirteen is an important age. I happen to know of a woman who may be able to help, if you would like to give your daughter something unique?'

Ursula took a small bite of cake.

'She makes beautiful bags,' Mary Young continued. 'Her father wouldn't let her work in the family leather business, so she set up on her own instead. I do like a bit of gumption. I'll give you her address.' She took a used envelope and a pencil from her bag and wrote on it in copperplate handwriting. 'The place is not far from here. She works from her home, in Marchmont.' She handed it over. 'We should be supporting other women in their businesses, wherever we can.' She looked around her and lowered her voice again. 'This place is the exception, because the manager is one of us.' She finished her cocoa.

Ursula was losing track of the many threads in the conversation. She was unsure how to respond.

'I would happily have spent another hour talking to you, Ursula. We could have had more cake or even stayed here for lunch, but unfortunately, I have an appointment and I need to be on my way.' She stood up. 'I do hope we will meet again. Dr Allinson's book is very interesting.' Mary Young pulled her gloves from her pockets. 'Oh, just one last thing. You may find it useful to buy some sago on the way home. He is rather keen on the stuff.'

Ursula couldn't determine from Mrs Young's tone whether this was a good or a bad thing.

Natalie Fergie

When she paid her bill at the desk a few minutes later, the server handed her a brown paper bag with a yellow book visible inside. 'The manager found you a copy'.

'This looks rather clandestine,' she said.

'There is much that is hidden in this world,' he replied enigmatically. 'I do hope you find it useful. And although you think I would be giving away our secrets, please ask me anything at all if the information within is unclear.'

Ursula put the book into her bag and stepped outside onto the street. It was a bright February afternoon, but with no discernible warmth. Her head was full of the conversation she had just had. Should she be reading the newspaper more thoroughly? And where was the nearest dry goods store that would be able to supply her with a pound of sago?

She paused as she left the café, and prepared to turn to the left, back down towards Princes Street and the tram home. But on the spur of the moment, she changed her mind, turned right and set off towards the Empire Palace Theatre to investigate the price of tickets to see The Great Lafayette.

Chapter 14

Early March 1911

Ursula was unsure about simply turning up at someone's private residence without an appointment, but short of writing a letter in advance there seemed to be no other way of visiting the young woman who made the bags. She was surprised to find that the street was one she had walked down many times before and yet she had never been aware that there was a business behind the shiny black front door. It was a main door, she noted, not a flat inside a tenement stair, and as she walked up the path she saw a small card in the window. 'Elizabeth Forrester, seamstress and leatherwork.'

She knocked on the door. It had a less than supremely polished brass handle and she noted that the letterbox could have done with a bit of elbow grease as well. The maid was clearly slacking. From outside, she could hear the sound of the inner door being opened, followed by a clatter. Presumably the keys have been dropped, she thought. She could have sworn there was a curse hanging in the air.

A slight young woman opened the storm door. 'Yes?'

Ursula introduced herself. 'I am Mrs Ursula Black. Your name was provided to me by Mrs Mary Young.' She didn't get any further.

'You've met Mary! A wonderful supporter of the cause. Do come in.'

Ursula managed to conceal her surprise at the casual greeting, but did as she was asked and waited in the tiled vestibule as the main door was relocked behind her.

'Just follow me.' The young woman walked briskly along the corridor that led to the back of the flat. The smell of a cake being baked, or perhaps it was biscuits, escaped from the kitchen.

'Please take a seat in my workroom. I need to take an apple pie out of the oven, I won't be a minute.'

Clearly the maid is indisposed, thought Ursula, looking around the room. A black Singer sewing machine, unlike any she had seen before, dominated the space in front of the window where there was most daylight. There were no chairs, just an adjustable stool in front of the machine. Beside it lay an instruction book with 'Model 29' printed on the front. A large waist-high bench, about the size of the kitchen table at 25 Library Terrace, stood in the middle of the room, and on the opposite wall was a tall grid of shelves, at least a yard deep. A tantalising hint of colour poked out from each square section where the end of a roll of leather or fabric protruded, and the whole edifice was arranged like a vertical rainbow with a column of scarlet and claret, followed by another of rust and autumn leaves, and then ragwort and mustard, before shading into several sections containing any green she could possibly have thought of.

Elizabeth Forrester returned from the kitchen still wearing her apron and dispensed with formalities without being given permission. 'So, Ursula, how can I help you today?'

'I mentioned to Mrs Young, to Mary,' Ursula didn't know what name to use, 'that it will be my husband's daughter's thirteenth birthday in a few weeks. I thought that perhaps it was time she had a bag of her own instead of relying on me or her sleeves to carry a handkerchief and other items.

She seemed very sure that you would be able to advise me, or even sell me such an item.'

Elizabeth seemed delighted. She smiled broadly, reached for a large book with the word 'ORDERS' stamped on the cover, and opened a cupboard in the dresser behind her.

'Oh yes. I am sure I can help with that. How exciting, a new bag.'

She pulled out a stack of boxes from inside the cupboard. 'Let me show you a few of these; they are waiting to be collected. Please have a look and see if there is anything you like.'

Ursula began to remove the lids from the boxes, one at a time. The bags were not the usual smooth leather, as she had expected, but pliable suede, and although this would make them less hardwearing, she realised immediately that the softer material was much more suitable for Ann. There were practical everyday bags in natural taupe and brown and black, which were useful enough but rather sombre. The colours of the evening bags were brighter. Strawberry pink and peacock blue and even a particularly bright yellow. She examined them inside and out. It was important to inspect the workmanship, to make sure this was a proper business and not just some young woman playing while she waited for a husband. Ursula stopped herself. It was an uncharitable attitude to have. She blushed and bent her head.

Elizabeth moved a fearsome pair of cutting shears aside and leaned forward on the table, resting on her elbows. 'Should I assume this is an item that will be used a lot, rather than just being brought out for special occasions?'

Ursula nodded. 'Sometimes things which are beautiful are saved for best, and I'm guilty of that myself, but I want this to be a bag which is robust enough that it can be used without any worry, while at the same time it needs to be pretty.'

'What about something like this?' Elizabeth went up on her toes and reached to the back of the cupboard for another box. She took off the lid and pushed it across the table to Ursula. 'It's a new design. Some of my customers request these colours in particular.'

The bag was a vibrant violet, with two tassels, one on each side, and a braided silk strap. It was secured with a gold-coloured clip fastening. The soft suede pouch was lined with pale green silk, and there was a further pocket inside, in cream.

'This is perfect. Just the right size, and not too heavy.'

'I'm afraid it's the only one I have. The customer is coming to collect it tomorrow, but I could make you another one just like it. It would take me about two weeks. Would that give us enough time before this momentous birthday?'

'It would.' Ursula stroked the suede and turned around to look at the multicoloured grid behind her. 'I wonder if you might make it in a different colour?'

'As long as I have it in stock.'

'Ann has the most beautiful green eyes. Could you suggest something which would complement them?'

Elizabeth walked over to the grid and selected three rolls of supple suede. She set them out on the bench, unrolling each one in turn. 'Like this? I'm expecting a new delivery of the braided silk for the straps next week.'

'In that case I'll trust your judgement. Any one of these would be delightful.'

'And for the lining?'

'I'm happy to have whatever you think is most appropriate.'

Elizabeth smiled. 'Of course. Now, I am running a very small enterprise here, so I ask for a deposit of twenty-five per cent to cover the cost of the materials. It amounts to half a crown and the total will be ten shillings.'

A young woman who knows her mind, thought Ursula, I rather like that. She took her purse from her bag and opened it. 'Two weeks?'

'Two weeks. You may collect it from here. I do have some of my designs for sale in a shop in Stockbridge but I prefer to keep these particular bags here in my workshop. No point in inviting comment unnecessarily.'

Ursula handed over the half-crown, realising as she did so that when the full cost of the bag was paid, it would amount to more than a week's wage for Isobel.

'Thank you.' Elizabeth Forrester slipped the coin into a deep pocket in her skirt. 'As a rule, I don't send letters out to advise that an item is ready. It can cause unwanted questions for some of my customers. Shall we just say two weeks from today? Noon?'

'Yes, that would be ideal. My step-daughter has become very inquisitive about the letters which arrive. She thinks that every envelope contains a secret birthday gift.' As she walked back to the front door, Ursula wished, not for the first time, that her own dresses had pockets. 'I don't suppose . . .'

'Mmmm?'

'It's not important. I will ask you about another matter when I collect the bag. Good afternoon to you.' She stepped out onto the path and behind her Elizabeth Forrester started to close the door.

'My apologies for shutting you out so quickly but it's a cold day and the heat escapes so fast.'

And with that Ursula found herself outside the flat and heard the key turned in the lock with almost unseemly haste. She pulled on her gloves and set off for home. Things are changing, she thought. They are changing all around me and I'm not sure I can keep up with it all.

Chapter 15

March 1911

'Show me then,' John said to Ursula on the Sunday afternoon two weeks before Ann's birthday. 'I want to see what sort of gift could possibly be an improvement on a nice set of encyclopaedias.' He winked at her. 'This had better be good.'

She smiled and patted the two white boxes on her lap. 'It *is* good. In fact, I was so impressed I went back the day after I placed the order and chose a second for myself. It will go with my best dress, the deep purple one with the lace at the neck. I won't use it until after Ann's birthday, of course.'

She passed him the smaller box first. The lilac bag with silver tassels nestled in a crinkle of white tissue paper.

He felt the texture of the suede, not wanting to leave any marks on its softness. 'Very nice. I'm sure you will look extremely elegant carrying that.'

'And this is Ann's.' She passed the second box over to him. 'Green, as we agreed, to match her eyes. Each bag has an additional pocket inside in cream which makes it easier to see your things in poor light.'

He examined the bag, opened the clasp with care and ran his fingers over the purple silk lining. 'I'm sure she'll be delighted.'

'Thank you.'

'For approving of your choice of gifts?'

'Yes, for that . . .'

'Is there something else?'

Ursula sighed. 'I suppose I'm finding things a little more difficult than I expected.' She was unsure how to continue. 'I want to thank you for your reassurances about my position in the family.' She rewrapped the bags in their tissue paper slowly and slipped them back into the presentation boxes. 'I am a bit worried about Ann.' She searched for the right words. 'Finlay is brusque with her sometimes. Do you remember how he teased her about the encyclopaedias last week? I don't think he means it badly but I can see that she has noticed. Young girls can be easily hurt.'

'That young man is trying my patience at the moment. He gets these new ideas from his friends at school and I'm sure he copies their behaviour. They did not allow such free thinking when I was a pupil.'

Ursula was beginning to regret having raised the matter and found herself unexpectedly defending Finlay. 'I expect it will pass. He is probably testing out what it is to be a man. And he's itching to be independent.' She stood up and put the boxes back in their hiding place in the oak chest beneath the window.

'Well, he is certainly testing *me* on occasion and I don't mind admitting it. And too much independence won't help him in life. I had to have a talk with him before Christmas about taking care. I'm not sure he took much notice of me, though.' He waited until she was seated beside him again and took her hand. 'You were right about the bag. Now that I've seen it, I understand. I was wrong to suggest the encyclopaedias.'

'You weren't wrong at all, and I'm sure if she wants encyclopaedias in the future then they can be provided. I do

Natalie Fergie

find it so interesting to observe how different they are. Ann is less impetuous and far more cautious for a start. So far, anyway.'

'Long may it last.' John picked up his book and found the postcard that was marking his place. 'And I am sure Ann will be delighted to have something a grown-up lady would have. It will add to the gift considerably. I'm very pleased you chose one for yourself too. Where did you buy them in the end?'

'In Marchmont. From a young woman who has a workshop at her home in one of the tenements there. She works from her flat, in the back room next to the kitchen.'

'And how did you find out about her?'

'Mrs Young gave me her details . . .' Her voice trailed away.

'Ah yes, I'm sure you've mentioned her before. She has been quite an influence over these last few weeks.'

She waited to see what he would say next.

'So are you going to boycott the census, Ursula? Are we going to break the law? That's what this is leading up to, I think?' He studied the postcard as though he had never seen it before. 'It might escape Ann's notice that her bag is in suffragette colours, but I have certainly noticed, and so will Finlay.'

'Break the law?'

'It's against the law not to complete the census, and if you're in the house, I must put your name on the form.'

'What do you mean, "if I am in the house"?'

'Those are the rules.'

'Where else would I be?'

'You tell me.' He studied her face.

A sudden realisation came over her. 'You have been to Café Vegetaria!'

78

He nodded.

'You have been spying on me!'

He held up his hand to stop her, but it had no effect.

The words gushed out of her. 'I have seen over the last few weeks that I can make decisions for myself, without needing to always consult others. And I have even changed what I eat and I feel much better for it.'

'And did I object?' He squeezed the question in but she ignored him.

'I've made new acquaintances beyond the wives of your business associates, who all talk about the world as though it is something they merely observe rather than something they might improve.'

He gave up trying to say anything meaningful and waited until she was finished.

'I do not want to go to rallies and throw bricks through windows. I do not want to hand out leaflets or get arrested. But I have opinions, and they may be rudimentary in some spheres, but I have the right to express them, and I have the right to . . .' She paused. 'I have the right to try to elect a government which represents me. *Me*. Not you, nor the Bridge Club nor even Mrs Young. My opinions are my own. And while I'm saying all this I would like you to bring the newspaper home after work so that I may read it too.' She ran out of steam.

'I see,' he said calmly. 'And if you don't want to go on marches and you don't want to protest, how are you going to achieve these goals you are so passionate about?'

Her energy evaporated, as quickly as it had arrived. 'I don't know.'

'But—'

'I'm not sure. Do I have to be completely certain about everything immediately?'

'No, of course not. I don't know why you are so upset.'

She found a second wind. 'Is the journey to finding out not equally important? If discovering things is not exciting, why does Finlay have encyclopaedias, for goodness' sake?'

'Stop.'

'Why? Am I not allowed an opinion?'

He shook his head.

'I am not?'

'No. I mean yes, of course you are. Please look at me.'

She shook her head.

'I went to the café to see where you have been spending so many hours.' He sat up straight. 'I am rather ashamed to say that I went to see if it was a suitable place. I have in fact been more than once. And I have drunk cocoa and that Brunak stuff, which I have to say is quite ghastly, and I have listened to the conversations that happen there. Anyone observing me would have thought I was reading my newspaper, the one which I will of course now leave here in the morning for you, rather than taking it into the office. I've been there four times in total. They might almost know me as a regular customer now.'

Ursula's thoughts were taken over by a rush of questions. Four times? He had been to the café not once, but *four times*? Why had he not mentioned it? Was he about to forbid her to go back?

John stroked his moustache, completely unaware of her turmoil. 'And what I initially thought was somewhere where there were some very odd opinions and ways, now seems to me to be an important meeting place for new ideas, and for actions which may change the world for the better.' He looked at her closely. 'So tell me, do you not want to march and protest?'

'I do not.'

'So, what is it that you *do* want?'

She was silent for a full minute.

'I want to avoid being listed on the census. The statement is quite right. If we aren't represented then our details shouldn't be recorded.'

'I am to break the law?'

'No.' She stood up at last and turned to face him. 'The census counts those who are in a property at midnight. If I'm not here then you are not lying.'

'And you will be where, exactly? I overheard talk of all-night walks on Bruntsfield Links and the Meadows.'

'There is another plan, but it's a secret.'

'And are you quite sure you'll be safe?'

'Yes, quite sure.'

'And how were you going to enact this plan without me knowing?'

She dared a smile. 'I hadn't quite worked that out, to be entirely honest with you.'

'I see. And is there anything else you want to do that I should or should not know about?'

She decided to strike while the iron was hot. 'There are two things.'

'Go on.'

'First, I think that Ann should read the newspaper, some parts of it anyway. I can find things during the day that are suitable and she can read it when she comes home.'

John nodded his agreement. 'And we can discuss them over dinner, which will be far more interesting to me than the colour of her new hair ribbons. And the second thing?'

'I need your permission to do this.'

He raised his eyebrows. 'My permission?'

'Well, not exactly, but you always deal with the money in the house. You give me a housekeeping allowance but I don't know how much else there is.'

'You want me to show you the bank account?'

'No. But I need you to increase the allowance.'

'Why?'

'Because I want to pay Isobel more than we do now. She isn't just a maid. She is doing more of the cooking and making a good job of it. And to allow her to do that, we also need to buy some equipment so that her other chores don't take as long.'

'Equipment?'

Ursula saw that it was an all-or-nothing moment. 'There has been nothing new since Louise died. There are new kitchen appliances for sale now. But they use electricity.'

'You think we should have electricity installed in the house?'

'I do.' Ursula pointed at the gas-lit glass globes on the walls. 'We would have better lighting and everything would be more efficient, and it would be cleaner and less work. This is a new and exciting world and we must be part of it.'

He smiled.

'You agree with all these things?'

'I will need to make enquiries about the electricity, but yes, I agree.' He lifted his book back up and slid the postcard into the back page, ready to use again. 'Just promise me that you will be safe on census night. Your well-being is the most important consideration.'

Chapter 16

Monday 3 April 1911

The sun was barely up when Ursula returned to 25 Library Terrace on the Monday morning after the census. The lock on the door to the scullery at the back of the house was stiff and she had deliberately taken the key with her the previous evening in case she had needed to get back in the middle of the night without waking everyone. Or at least, that had been her plan, but it wasn't working out that way.

The hinges squeaked as she pushed the door open and when she stepped into the scullery, she was met by a startled Isobel, rolling pin aloft.

'My God, Mrs Black!' Isobel had clearly been ready and willing to use the weapon, in both terror and self-defence. 'I'm sorry for cursing, but you did give me a fright.'

'I apologise,' replied Ursula. 'I had hoped to get in without any fuss. What time is it?'

'It's just before six.'

'I'm so tired, it's no wonder I'm feeling the cold.' Ursula moved into the kitchen and loosened her headscarf. She draped her heavy woollen coat across one of the chairs before sitting down. 'I think I'll just stay here for five minutes and get warm before I go upstairs. Maybe I should take my shoes off here; I don't want to leave dirty footprints on the stair carpet as I go up.' She took a breath to allow for the tightness of her corset, and bent forward to undo her shoelaces.

'The kettle's almost boiled, will I make you a pot of tea?'

'Or cocoa? It feels like bedtime to me; I've been awake for most of the night.'

'Mmmm?' Isobel didn't want to ask the obvious question, and busied herself with a pan and a bottle of yesterday's milk from the cold store.

'That was quite the most rule-breaking thing I have done since I was about nine years old, but it was worth it.' Ursula yawned and stretched. 'I've been at a protest to try to get us the vote.'

'The vote? You mean Votes for Women?'

'That's right. Do you think you would vote, Isobel, if you had the chance?'

'I think so. Not sure it's ever going to happen, mind.'

'Well, in this life, if you don't ask, you don't get. That's what my father used to say.'

Isobel went to the scullery briefly to rinse out the milk bottle. 'Where was your protest? If you've been out walking the streets since you left last night then it's small wonder you're exhausted.'

'It was in the same place I got the yellow cookery book, in Café Vegetaria on Nicolson Street. We stayed there all night, about two hundred of us. The curtains were closed and the lighting was kept low. We talked and ate cherry cake and cheese sandwiches, and we drank tea and there was a sort of play put on by some of the women, which was rather good fun. I don't have a dramatic bone in my body, though, so I didn't participate in it. And then at about five, before it was properly light, people began to leave. Someone had peeked through the curtains and there were two policemen standing in one of the doorways opposite. They had been there all night so I expect they were rather cold, and this morning they were writing things down. Counting us, I suppose. One of them was talking and the other was writing. But it was still pretty dark and I'm not sure they would have been able to recognise any of us. We all had our hats and scarves on, so I don't know what the point of the activity was. I expect some superior had told them to do it and they didn't have any choice.' She paused. 'Choice is such a powerful word. I am accustomed to choosing what to do, and not having other people direct me. I used to run the office at Mr Black's company; I started as just a typist, but quite quickly I was promoted. I hired staff, ordered stationery, made appointments. I was good at my job, and that meant I was trusted with choices. Everything seems so different now.'

Isobel lifted the pan off the heat just in time. Burnt milk would have made the kitchen stink for days. 'Weren't you frightened you might be arrested?' She poured the frothing liquid carefully onto a mixture of cold water and sugar and cocoa which she had mixed to a smooth paste, put the cup on a matching saucer and set it down in front of Ursula.

'For what? For staying in a café all night? No crime was committed.'

'But what about the census? Mr Black was completing the form last night and he asked my age so he could write it down. I didn't realise that your name wasn't there with the rest of us.'

Ursula sat up straighter in the chair. 'There's a five-pound fine for not completing the form correctly, but I wasn't here so it wasn't necessary for me to be listed. Although in point of fact if I don't want to appear on the records I should not be back in the house before noon today.' She looked at Isobel. 'But if you don't tell anyone, and I go straight to bed before Finlay and Ann catch sight of me, they will never know. I can't see Mr Black giving the game away, and if I am discovered, despite my efforts, and have to pay a fine then I will take the money from my savings. I don't expect anyone else to do that for me.'

'I think you are very brave. I'm not sure I would have the nerve.'

'Truth be told, I'm not sure I'll do anything like it ever again. And I'm very pleased to hear that you would vote if you had the opportunity.' Ursula laced her fingers around the warm cup and sipped her cocoa. 'I've been thinking about it a lot, and there are other ways I can make a difference. For a start, I can make sure that Ann is educated about things, not just about how to choose a husband and entertain at an afternoon tea party. She should have a career in something she loves.'

Weariness made Ursula forget the social boundaries her mother had instilled in her. 'I was never encouraged to have ambitions in that way. My father didn't object to me working, but my mother didn't approve at all. She said it was unnecessary and unladylike and it would stop me finding a husband. She was furious when I went to help in an office for a friend of the family, but I discovered the work suited me so I moved to another company where I had a salary, and then another one, and that made her even more cross. She was a good person. I loved her dearly, and she just wanted me safely married and settled. But she was from a different time and she didn't like change. If I hadn't gone out to work, I would never have met Mr Black.' She took another sip of cocoa. 'But I think she would be happy if she could see me now, and that's something, I suppose.'

Isobel didn't want to interrupt; she had wondered for a long time how it was that Ursula had ended up moving the four hundred miles north.

'The owner of the last company I worked at was often the worse for a bottle of wine at lunchtime. He was late for every meeting. One afternoon I needed to hold the fort for an hour, as usual, and Mr Black arrived for his appointment. I had to make excuses and be polite, and by the time the owner came back from his lunch I had inadvertently convinced Mr Black to buy his supplies from another business entirely. A few weeks later he wrote to me and offered me a job. It was around the time when the late Mrs Black started to become unwell and he was quite distracted. He said he wanted a safe pair of hands to run his office during a difficult time, and he offered to pay my train fare. I arrived at Waverley with two suitcases and I stayed in a boarding house for a month while I looked for somewhere to live. I started my life again, from nothing, really. My parents were both gone by then, and there was a small inheritance and nothing to keep me in London. Moving to Edinburgh was the biggest decision I've ever made in my life. Even bigger than getting married.'

Isobel didn't know what to say, so she completely ignored the unexpected disclosure and simply nodded.

'You must be tired after being out all night.'

'I am, rather. I need to decide what to do next. I can write letters and deliver leaflets, but I don't want to go to rallies or put myself out there in public. It's not really me, I'm not . . .' she hunted for the right word, ' . . . an exhibitionist.' She drank more cocoa. 'This is very good, thank you.'

'You're welcome.'

'The other thing I can do is to look after you better. My conversations with the other women over the last few weeks have made me realise that.'

'*Me?*'

'You are my employee, and you live in my house and therefore I feel a sense of responsibility towards you. I have been discussing it with Mr Black and we have agreed that you will have an increase in your wage. And you will have a few hours off during the week as well as your Saturday afternoon. The fires will need to be done, of course, and the dinner made, but I see no reason why you shouldn't have a little time to go to the library; there's one on the end of the road after all. Or you may want to go and feed the ducks at Blackford Pond, or just walk along the street without a shopping bag in your hand and a list in your pocket.'

Isobel looked at Ursula in astonishment.

'I may not be taking part in protest marches, but I can make a difference in my own home and that is at least as important.' Ursula drained the cup and put it on the table. 'And now I'm going to go upstairs before inquisitive young people see me and start asking questions.' She scooped up her coat and scarf and left the kitchen, leaving her shoes where she had discarded them, and the cup on the table for Isobel to clear, even though the scullery sink was less than a dozen paces away.

Isobel sat down and stared at the fire in the belly of the range for a few minutes, feeling its warmth before getting to her feet again. 'Just wait till the girls around here get to know I'm getting a pay rise *and* some more time off. That's going to set the cat among the pigeons and no mistake. I wonder if Mrs Black has any idea what she might have started.'

And then she picked up Ursula's abandoned shoes and set them down neatly beside the back door, ready for polishing.

Chapter 17

April 1911

'I have decided,' announced Ursula at breakfast on Saturday, the day before Ann's birthday, 'that I am not going to eat meat any more. It disagrees with me.'

'No more bacon for Sunday breakfast?' said Finlay immediately. 'Or sausages?'

Ursula shook her head. 'Not for me, but you can still have these things.'

'Or haggis,' he persisted, 'or duck at Christmas?' He was just warming up. 'Or roast pork and apple—'

'Finlay, *stop*,' demanded John. 'There is no need for you to be concerned if your own food is unaffected.'

Ursula was surprised. John had initially thought that changing what she was eating would be a short-term matter, and he hadn't made a fuss about it, but recently he had said he wanted her to see a doctor. Clearly her refusal to seek medical advice had now been accepted.

He continued. 'Ursula has researched this, and has, indeed, acquired a new book on the subject. We have discussed it thoroughly and I agree that it is the best way forward.'

Ursula frowned. 'You've seen the book?'

'Naturally. I am aware of everything that goes on in this house.'

This was absolutely not the case, and they both knew it.

Finlay sighed. 'Vegetables and more vegetables.'

'Enough!' John was displeased.

'What about birthday food?' said Ann, in a small voice. 'What about tomorrow?'

Ursula smiled. 'There will of course be your favourite afternoon tea. Are you looking forward to being thirteen?'

'I am. A bit, anyway.'

'That doesn't sound very excited to me.'

'My friends have all been given special gifts on their birthdays, but Finlay has been telling me for months that I will be getting a set of encyclopaedias.'

'Has he really?' Ursula stared hard at Finlay and then looked back at Ann. 'Well, let me tell you, my dear, your brother doesn't know very much about your birthday so I wouldn't trust anything he says.' She took a piece of toast from the rack and put it on her plate. 'Now, pass the marmalade please, I am hungry this morning.'

*

After the breakfast things were cleared, when Finlay was out with his friend Daniel, and Ann was curled up on her bed reading, Ursula and Isobel met in the kitchen to plan the meals for the week with the assistance of Dr Allinson's yellow book.

Separately, they had studied it, and come to quite different conclusions.

Ursula turned the pages and peered at the small text. 'He says sago should be added to every meal.'

'I saw that. But I'm not sure how you add sago to a cake,' said Isobel carefully. 'Maybe we could start with the easy changes like vegetable pie fillings, and I could try making these lentil sausages as well. We can worry about the sago later.'

'I confess I was dismayed to read that it should be in every *single* meal,' admitted Ursula. 'It's not my favourite food at all.'

Isobel picked up the book. 'If you look at the menu for a week written by *Mrs* Allinson, I think you'll find Dr Allinson and his wife don't think the same thing.' She turned the pages. 'See?' She stopped her finger on the paper. 'It's here on page ninety-one.'

'Really? I don't think I read that far,' confessed Ursula.

'I read that chapter before anything else. It appears to have been written by,' she peered at the page, 'Anna P. Allinson. And it gives her address too, look. 4 Spanish Place, Manchester Square, London.'

'I suppose I could write to her, since she has kindly provided us with her details.'

'I don't know that you'll have to do that. She gives a week of meals but it's really a week of three-course dinners.' Isobel looked up at Ursula triumphantly. 'I've read every one of the twenty-one suggestions, and there's only one that has any sago in it.'

'*One?*'

'Just one.' Isobel smiled. 'It makes me wonder if the person who was giving the instructions was not the person carrying them out, if you see my meaning.'

'Perhaps I can put the pound of sago I bought last month to the back of the pantry,' said Ursula. 'I've never liked the stuff.'

Isobel sat down at the table without asking permission. 'What would you like to eat next week, I mean after tomorrow's birthday food?'

'I'm not sure. I think you've read this book more thoroughly than I have. What would you suggest?'

Isobel was ready for the question. 'What we've been doing for the last few weeks was taken from the menu from the Café, but I think I can do better than that now.' She pulled a piece of paper from her pocket and read from it. 'Lentil Rissoles, page twenty-four. You can have those instead of meatballs.'

Ursula turned the pages of the little book. 'Right. What else?'

'Onion Tart, page twenty-six. I can make two, and just put bacon in one of them.'

Ursula turned the page and nodded agreement.

'Macaroni Cheese, page thirty-one.' Isobel was just warming up. 'Everyone will eat that. I might even be able to make a macaroni cheese pie; I've seen them in the bakers, although they don't appear in this particular book. But there are other pies, and I can make almost anything into a pie if I think hard enough about it.'

Ursula smiled. 'Mr Black does like his pies.'

'I'll make a different pie for another day, and I'll make two, like the tarts, so one has meat in it and the other doesn't. Oh yes, and on the bottom of the page before the macaroni, there is a nut roast, just like the one you told me about. I've never made such a thing, but I could do a small one for you to try, and if you like it then you could have that instead of whatever roast meat everyone else is having on a Sunday. At least you won't only be having potatoes and veg and Yorkshire pudding.'

'True. Trying to hide the fact that I haven't eaten the meat on my plate, just to stop Finlay asking questions, has been rather tiresome.'

Ursula counted up on her fingers. 'That's five things, if we include the nut roast.'

'I found a curry too, it's back on page twenty-four beside the rissoles.'

'A curry.' Ursula leaned back a little in the kitchen chair. 'Have the family ever had curry before?'

'Not in my time. But it would be easy enough to make one for the family from the leftover roast, and you could have whatever vegetables you liked in yours. Carrots are nice and sweet, and perhaps some sultanas. And what about ham in a tomato sauce with rice, for them, just seasoned a little bit, and you could have a risotto instead?'

Ursula nodded and held out her hands with fingers outstretched. 'Seven.'

'Page twenty-one. Butter Beans with Parsley Sauce. That would work just as well with a couple of pieces of haddock for everyone else. And Miss Ann isn't that keen on fish anyway so she might join you.'

'That's eight meals now.' Ursula closed the book. 'Goodness but this is difficult.'

'I don't think it is, not really. And especially when you think how over-and-over again the meals have been for the last two years, and before that as well.'

'You think something new might be welcomed?'

'It might be, as long as people aren't set against it from the start.'

'You mean Finlay.'

Isobel smiled. 'As long as Master Finlay has a nice pudding, he'll be happy. That's the way to his heart.'

'I do hope so, because he's not making life very easy for me at the moment.' Ursula realised that her private thoughts on the matter had slipped out into the room. She hastened to change the subject. 'Now, we need to make some preparations for the birthday girl's big day tomorrow. Ann has asked for drop scones in the morning, with syrup, which seems simple enough. I've ordered a cake from the baker on Morningside Road and it will be delivered this afternoon to the scullery door so Miss Curious doesn't see it arriving. I know you'll be out, so I'll sit here in the kitchen and wait for it. I assume there is enough space for me to hide it in the larder?'

'I could have made a cake.'

'I know you could, but you would have spent your afternoon off doing it and that would not be fair.' Ursula was determined that Isobel's Saturday afternoon off should remain sacrosanct. 'What about the food for tomorrow afternoon?'

'I'll do that in the morning. I think you said there are three girls coming? There will be the cake, of course, and I'll make a big plate of cheddar cheese sandwiches with plenty of Marmite. That's her favourite. She would lick the knife I use for the spreading if she got half a chance.'

Chapter 18

Sunday 9 April 1911

Ursula didn't believe in making people wait all day for their birthday presents. She had called Finlay into the parlour the night before and explained that he must be up, dressed, and in the dining room at eight o'clock, and not a minute later, even though it was Sunday, and he would normally have been a little slower to rise. He wasn't impressed but the sight of his father on the other side of the room had quelled any objections he might have otherwise voiced.

By a little after seven, Ursula was downstairs. She helped Isobel make the batter for the drop scones and went through to the dining room one last time just before eight o'clock to make sure everything looked pretty. As requested, John and Finlay were sitting at the dining table, on time, waiting slightly impatiently for Ann to wake up and get out of bed. Isobel had been tasked with going outside to knock on the front door very energetically at five past eight, and if that failed, she was going to ring the bell a few times. It was only a couple of minutes after the loud banging when they heard the first squeak of the floorboards on the landing upstairs.

'Hello?'

Ursula put her finger to her lips to stop the others replying.

'Where is everybody?'

They heard Ann's footsteps as she came down the stairs, and then the dining-room door opened slowly.

'Happy Birthday!' Ursula allowed John to go first, and then Finlay, before she joined in.

'Oh! This isn't what usually happens.' Ann stared, wide-eyed, at the large box which took up at least a third of the table, and the smaller packages which were beside it. 'Is this all for me?'

'It is indeed.' John got to his feet and wrapped his arms around her. 'Happy Birthday, little one.'

'But shouldn't we wait until later? I mean, presents are for the afternoon when visitors come, aren't they? That's what Mother always said.'

'We thought you might like them a bit earlier this year,' said Finlay. He tapped the top of the large box. 'After all, you'll be wanting to start using your encyclopaedias.'

Ann's face fell. 'I suppose so.'

Ursula took charge. 'Isobel has made drop scones, and there is warm syrup to pour over them. We thought you might like to open your presents first, because syrup is sticky.'

'You definitely don't want the pages to get stuck together,' Finlay added.

Ann realised that the only empty seat was the one Father used, at the head of the table. He pointed at it. 'Today, you are the most important person in the house, so you take my chair.'

Two parcels were arranged in the space where the place setting should have been. Ann took her seat and lifted the first one off the top. It was covered in what looked like newspaper and was tied up with garden twine. Ursula hadn't seen the wrapping until Finlay had added it to the collection last night. She approved of his creativity.

Ann read the label: 'From Finlay'. She undid the knotted string and pulled the paper aside. 'Seeds!' She spread the packets out on the table. 'This is *so* exciting! Snapdragons, and cosmos, and calendula and poppies and nasturtiums and marigolds, and ooooooh, sweet peas.' She shook the wrapping paper. 'And basil and chives and parsley as well.'

Ursula glanced at Finlay. She had provided the nasturtiums and the cosmos, but the rest were nothing to do with her. He was smiling to himself, unaware of exactly how much he had just shot up in her estimation.

Ann wanted to study all the seed packets in detail, one at a time, but she realised everyone was waiting for her to move on to the next gift. 'I'll need to learn all the Latin names. Maybe the encyclopaedias will help me with that.' She arranged the envelopes carefully in alphabetical order, and then stopped for a moment to study the words on the wrapping. 'This is from a seed catalogue.' She looked at Finlay. 'Where did you get it?'

John cleared his throat. 'We were printing them for a garden supplier last week. It's one of the first big sheets off the press, before we do a proper print run. Your brother thought you might like it.'

'A whole catalogue.' The excitement in Ann's voice was unmistakeable. 'That's like giving me two presents at the same time. Thank you very much.' She smiled at Finlay. 'If you want to help me plant some of them, that would be alright.'

'They are all for you,' he replied quickly. 'I'm not the gardener in the family.'

Ann put the seeds and the catalogue aside and studied the next parcel. The cream-coloured box was tied around and around with enough green hair ribbons to last for several weeks even when Ursula had allowed for the current rate of loss. Ann undid the bows and paused to enjoy the moment. She knew that this was her real present, with the encyclopaedias still ahead of her. The lid of the box was stiff, and it took a moment to loosen it, but when she managed to get it off and she saw what was inside, she didn't know what to say. Sitting in crinkly tissue paper was something she hadn't even known she wanted, until it was suddenly there in front of her. Her very own grown-up bag, in her favourite colour in the whole world. 'Is this really for me?' She lifted it out of the box and got off Father's chair so she could put it across her shoulder, and twirled around to see what it felt like.

'It's from both of us,' John said, with an unexpected catch in his voice. 'Ursula thought it was time you had something that befits a young lady of thirteen, and I agree with her.'

Ann snapped the catch open and looked inside. 'It's purple!' She found the second clip and undid it. 'And there's another pocket as well. Look, Finlay. Isn't it splendid?'

From the other end of the table, Ursula saw that John had been right, and Finlay had indeed seen the significance of the green, purple and cream. He looked at his sister, enjoying her delight for a second time, and then glanced across at Ursula and nodded, very slightly. Not approval, exactly, but an acknowledgement.

Ann took the bag off and stowed it carefully in the box. 'I think I know what this is,' she said, nudging the huge cardboard box on the table, which had no birthday wrapping at all. To her surprise, the box moved. She pushed it a little harder and it moved again.

'Perhaps if we put this on the floor for you?' said John. He lifted it down onto the carpet without any effort. 'How peculiar, it's not heavy at all.'

Ann came over to have a closer look. 'I think it must be empty.'

'Are you sure?' John was enjoying himself. 'It's very securely packaged. Do you not want to see what's inside?' He took one of the best knives off the table and cut the string. 'There, now you can have a proper look.'

Finlay and Ann looked at one another. He shrugged. 'Don't ask me. I have no idea.'

Ann moved the cardboard flaps out of the way and peered inside. 'There's an envelope at the bottom.' She reached down to pick it up.

The suspense was broken by the arrival of Isobel, who came in carrying a tray. The smell of warm drop scones was instantly recognisable. 'Oh, I'm sorry, I thought you might be ready for these. I can come back later.'

'Not at all.' Ursula had an idea that Isobel's curiosity had got the better of her. 'Just put it on the sideboard and we'll be ready in a few moments. The birthday girl has found a mysterious envelope and we all want to know what's inside it.'

Ann went back to her appointed seat at the head of the table and sat down. 'Not encyclopaedias, then,' she whispered to herself as she sliced open the flap of the envelope with a butter knife. She pulled out two pieces of card and gasped. 'Tickets!' She could hardly speak. 'Tickets to see The Great Lafayette at the Empire Palace Theatre on Tuesday the ninth of May.'

'I will take you to the theatre,' said John. 'It's the late performance and Ursula thought that you and I might like to have an adventure together, just the two of us. What do you think?'

'I would like that very, very much.' Ann looked at each one of them in turn. 'Thank you. I think being thirteen is going to be my best year ever.'

Chapter 19

May 1911

On Monday evening, the day before the much talked-about theatre excursion, John was unwell. A sore throat had reduced his words to a rasp, and Ursula had called the doctor, concerned that he might have diphtheria.

'Laryngitis,' said the doctor, addressing John. 'You need to speak as little as possible, and under no circumstances must you go to work.'

'But what about taking my daughter to the theatre? It's her birthday treat.' John squeezed the words out. 'We are going to see The Great Lafayette tomorrow evening.'

The doctor shook his head. 'I would not recommend it. If you cannot remain silent, or near silent, for a few days, you may cause permanent damage to your vocal cords.' He turned to Ursula, who was standing at the end of the bed. 'I feel that going into a crowded place is not to be recommended at all.'

John was not pleased. His face betrayed him, but it seemed there was no argument.

'I'll show you out, Doctor,' said Ursula.

John heard snatches of instructions as they walked down the stairs, and then the sound of the big front door closing.

'But what about the theatre?' he croaked when she reappeared.

'I've been thinking about that.' Ursula sat down on the edge of the bed. 'Finlay can take her, and I will stay here to look after you.'

He shook his head.

She took his hand. 'Finlay is seventeen, and he can be quite responsible when he wants to be.'

'It was supposed to be a special night out. Just the two of us, that's what you and I planned for her.'

'There will be other visits to the theatre.' She put her finger to her lips. 'No more talking. Ann will understand, and Finlay is going to university later this year. He will be completely occupied with his studies and all his new friends. There may not be many more occasions where he will escort her, and behave like the older brother he actually is.' She patted the counterpane. 'Now, please, you really must rest your poor voice. I'm going to ring for Isobel to bring you a drink. It's not too late and I am sure she won't mind.' She stood up. 'You work very hard for all of us and you're always thinking about other people, and now it's our turn to look after you.'

John shook his head.

'Very well, I won't ring for her. But in that case, I insist on making you a hot toddy. Some honey and lemon to soothe that throat of yours? I am sure I can manage that on my own.' She kissed his forehead. 'Tomorrow, the doctor said you should start having salt water gargles, four times a day, so I'll let Isobel know in the morning and she can bring them to you at the proper times.'

He pulled a face.

'No arguments! I'll bring the children in to see you before they go to school.'

*

In the morning Ursula ushered Ann and Finlay into the bedroom as promised. John was sitting up in bed wearing his blue and cream striped pyjamas and looking rather flushed. His voice was husky but he had improved a little.

'As you can see, your father is quite poorly. The doctor came last evening and has given strict instructions that he must rest and not talk.'

John made the sign of buttonholing his lips and pulled the eiderdown up to his chin.

Ursula looked at the two school-uniformed children. 'This has left us with rather a difficulty.'

'The Great Lafayette,' said Ann, crestfallen. 'We won't be able to go.'

'You *will* be going. I have a solution.' Ursula turned to Finlay, who was staring out of the window, not giving anyone his full attention and obviously embarrassed at seeing his normally robust father in bed. 'Finlay, you will take Ann to the theatre this evening.'

Finlay's head snapped around to look at his father. He ignored Ursula completely. 'I have choir after school, I won't be back in time.'

'You don't yet know what time you will be needed,' Ursula pointed out. 'And I will write to the choirmaster and explain the circumstances. And if a letter from me is insufficient, your father will write one as well.'

'He won't let me off attending if I am going to the theatre instead,' protested Finlay. 'We are rehearsing for the end-of-term concert.'

'Then I won't tell him. I will simply say that due to illness, you are needed at home.'

'You're going to lie?'

'No. It's the truth. You are needed to look after your sister.'

'Look after me?' It was Ann's turn to protest. 'I'm thirteen years old, I don't need anyone to look after me.'

John looked from one face to the other. He took a sip of water and spoke, very quietly, so they had to come closer to the bed to hear what he was saying. 'Very well, we shall return the tickets to the box office and the whole outing will be cancelled.'

'That's not fair!' Ann exclaimed. She glowered at Finlay. 'This is your fault. I'm going to school now. I suppose I am still allowed to do *that* by myself?' She stomped out of the room.

'I was joking,' said Finlay, raising his shoulders in an exaggerated shrug.

John beckoned him closer, so Finlay would be able to hear him. 'It didn't sound like it. But the ball, as they say, is now in your court, son.'

'Oh *alright*,' replied Finlay, dragging out the syllables. He looked at the clock on the mantelpiece. 'If you can dash me off a note I will take it in tomorrow. I can't wait for it now, I'm already late.' He left the room, clearly feeling as though he had been hoodwinked into something he didn't want to be any part of.

'That went well!' Ursula could not remain quiet, and her voice shook.

John smiled at her and responded, his voice creaking and almost vanishing in places. 'Sssssshhhh. It went exactly as I thought it would. Finlay hates choir so he will be glad of the excuse, and Ann will be grateful to be able to go on the outing. I think it's a good result.'

There was a tap at the bedroom door and Isobel entered carrying a tray with a teapot on it, and a slice of toast on a side plate.

'Toast water,' she announced. 'It cures everything. And it's better when freshly made.' She put the tray down on the dressing table.

'Toast water?' mouthed John to Ursula, but Isobel was too quick and she saw him.

'Yes, Mr Black. You break up the toast and put it in the pot with the hot water and wait for ten minutes, and then you pour the water into the cup. I brought a strainer for you as well.' She straightened up, looking rather pleased with herself. 'It's a well-known remedy.'

On the other side of the room, Ursula tried not to laugh.

Chapter 20

Tuesday 9 May 1911

'Are you ready yet?' Finlay waited in the hall with his coat on. He leaned against the narrow table and drummed his fingers on the polished mahogany.

Ann appeared at the top of the stairs. Her hair had been put up for the occasion, and she wore her best dress and coat, and her new green bag hung diagonally across her body. She walked down slowly, not wanting to disturb her new hairstyle.

He looked up at her, realising for the first time that his little sister was not so little any more. 'Very nice,' he said grudgingly.

Ursula frowned at him from the drawing-room doorway.

'Not that you need me to say that,' he added.

'I've put some money in this envelope with the tickets,' said Ursula, handing it to Finlay, 'so you can catch a cab there and back. You'll be able to catch one at the rank near Morningside station, and it will take you to the end of Chambers Street. You can walk up from there, it's not more than a couple of hundred yards.' She gave Ann a hug. 'The performance won't finish until after eleven o'clock and your father told me that he wants you to do that rather than getting the tram. And when you come home there will be cocoa and cake and you can tell me all about it. I want to hear every detail.'

*

The crowd outside the theatre was huge. Everywhere there were people in their best dresses and suits, pushing their way towards the entrance. Finlay was determined to do things his way. 'You need to hold my hand.'

'Really?'

'Yes. Definitely.'

'I'm almost grown up now and that's what little children do.'

'I don't want to lose you.'

'But I'm right here beside you, you can see me.'

'Do you know how many tickets have been sold for tonight?'

'No, but I expect you're going to tell me.'

'Three thousand. There are two thousand, nine hundred and ninety-eight other people here, wandering about, and they will *all* be trying to find their seats. They'll be standing up at the ends of the rows, talking with their friends and we will have to get past them.'

'Three thousand? I don't believe you.'

'Father told me before we left.'

'Oh.' If her father had said it, Ann decided it must be true. 'Alright then.'

'Trust me, I don't want to be holding my little sister's hand in public either, but Father would never forgive me if I lost you.'

The throng of people in the street outside had been compressed into the stalls and balcony seats inside, with some lucky ticket holders having one of the boxes on either side of the wide stage. As they went into the auditorium, they could hear the orchestra, the string section following the lead of the First Violin as they tuned their instruments from his notes.

Finlay found their seats, near the middle of a row in the stalls, and they settled down. Ann looked at the programme Finlay had bought for her. 'Do you know how he does the illusions?'

'No one knows,' he replied. 'It's all a secret. If we knew, we wouldn't be here.'

'I suppose we all hope we can work it out by watching very carefully. My friends at school will be so envious. None of them have seen The Great Lafayette.'

'I don't understand why you are so obsessed with him.'

She didn't answer right away because a large man was requesting that she stand up to let him pass. Seated again, she tried to explain. 'It's just the magic, the not-knowing. It's like a big puzzle with lots of pieces and you can't tell which is the important one that is going to make it all work. And of course, there are the animals. The horse and the lion. I've only seen lions at the zoo. I wonder if it's a tame lion?'

Finlay laughed. 'I don't think any lion is ever truly tame.'

'That makes it even more exciting, don't you think?' replied Ann, ignoring the put-down. She settled herself into the seat and opened the programme.

Chapter 21

Tuesday 9 May 1911

Afterwards, they stood outside in the street and watched the flames shooting upwards into the sky. Smoke poured from the theatre roof and the sound of crackling timber came from inside the building.

Ann would not let go of Finlay's hand. They stood, transfixed by the spectacle, until they were shepherded away by the police. A group of soldiers appeared, seemingly from nowhere, and set about clearing a path right up the centre of Nicolson Street for the fire brigade. Policemen moved the many hundreds of stunned theatregoers away from the inferno so the fire tenders could get as close as possible to the blaze.

On the other side of the street, scantily dressed residents from the flats opposite the theatre stood on the pavement, unable to believe what they were seeing. They held on tightly to their bare-footed children as the water from the fire tenders ran in little rivers down the gutters towards Chambers Street. As the heat intensified, the glazing in the tenements cracked and splintered.

There were no cabs.

As they walked along Melville Drive, beside the Meadows, they could see the orange glow in the sky reflected in the tenement windows.

Finlay held Ann's hand tightly all the way home and she didn't complain at all.

When they reached Library Terrace, he turned and hugged her. 'I would never, ever have left you behind, Annie Bee.'

Ann was still too shocked to speak.

Ursula answered the door. 'Did the performance go on late? It's past midnight.' She sensed something was wrong. 'What's that smell?'

'Smoke,' said Finlay. 'There was a fire. A big fire. I am not sure how we got out of the theatre at all, to be truthful.'

'Are you sure you're alright?' She ushered them into the hall where the light was better and examined their faces. She needed to know they weren't hurt.

'We are both safe. Nothing to worry about,' replied Finlay. 'But I need to speak to Father and tell him that myself. I'm sure you understand.'

'Of course. He will want to hear what has happened, as I do. He managed to get out of bed after you left and was determined to stay up until you got home.' She sniffed. 'But first I want you to take your coats off so the smoke doesn't affect his throat. I'll come up with you so he doesn't get a shock, and then I'll ask Isobel to make you some hot milk.'

*

They sat around the fire, a smaller one this time, contained behind a fireguard and with coal instead of the burning curtains and theatre seats.

Isobel brought hot milk as requested, and Ursula poured a little brandy into Finlay's cup without being asked. 'Stay, Isobel. I'm sure you want to know about this as much as we do,' she said.

John made a space on the couch and beckoned Ann to sit beside him. 'Now we are all here, please tell us what has happened. Start at the beginning,' he croaked. Ann sat down, but didn't cuddle in.

'We arrived a little early,' Finlay began, 'and we managed to get to our places without any great difficulty. Every seat was sold, I heard the ushers talking to one another. It was a full house. The performance started on time and it was really very good. I honestly did not expect to enjoy it as much as I did.' He stopped. 'It feels so wrong to say that now.' He coughed into his handkerchief and looked at the speckles of grey on the cotton lawn fabric, surprised to see evidence of the night's events in front of him.

'Go on,' said Ursula.

'The finale was called The Lion's Bride. Everyone had been talking about it in the audience, saying how it was the most exciting thing you would ever see. I was rather sceptical, but it started off very well.' He rubbed his hands through his hair and lifted them to his face. 'I can still smell the smoke.'

'Isobel will draw you a hot bath before you go to bed. Please continue, if you can.' Ursula's voice was soft and encouraging.

'It's hard to know what actually happened. Everyone thought the flames were part of the illusion, so we just sat there. No one moved at all. There was even some cheering at the spectacle. And then all of a sudden, the orchestra began to play "God Save the King", and even then, to start with, no one moved. But of course, once we realised what they were playing we all stood up, because, well, because it was the national anthem and that's the correct thing to do. By then we could see the flames had spread to the stage, and everyone knew that something was wrong. The safety curtain was brought down, but it didn't go low enough to reach the stage. There was a gap at the bottom, about three feet, I think, and then there was a loud whoosh, just like when you put a piece of newspaper over the fire here to get it going and you take it away suddenly and all the air rushes in and the flames leap up.' He took a sip of the hot milk and tasted the brandy. 'It sounds silly now, but as it was happening, I was thinking about it as though it was a physics question in a school exam. I was working out the theory of it all as it unfolded in front of me.'

No one interrupted him as he tried to relive the course of events as accurately as he possibly could.

'And then everyone tried to get out at the same time. There was some panic, but mostly people were just determined, and there was shouting, of course, but it wasn't chaos. It was like a drill. Everyone did what they were supposed to do. And I took Ann's hand and I didn't let go. I think she fell on the stairs going towards the exit, and I'm afraid I just yanked her up.' He was crying now, and looked over at his sister who was still sitting like a lump of wood beside her father. 'I couldn't bear to have lost you, Annie Bee.'

Ann nodded, but didn't say anything.

Ursula passed him her own clean handkerchief, and he wiped his eyes, leaving grey streaks on the cotton fabric.

'When we got outside the street was packed. No one seemed to want to leave. People were trying to find friends in the crowd, and mothers and fathers were looking for their children. That's when things got much more frantic. There was a lot of desperate shouting. And then the police came, and there were lines of soldiers who seemed to appear from nowhere and then the horses and the fire tenders arrived, but by that time the theatre was quite ablaze.

The firemen had brass on their helmets which reflected the flames so it looked as though their heads were on fire. They were so brave. Going into a burning building. Into danger, without a thought.' He stopped for a moment. 'I've never thought of it like that before. What it would be like to just follow an order when you know that you might come to harm?'

'Take your time,' whispered John. 'There is no rush.'

Finlay took another sip of his drink before continuing. He was so intent on getting the details right, he barely noticed that his father had spoken. 'All of a sudden, I was exhausted. It was as though everything had been sucked out of me and I wasn't sure my legs were going to hold me up any more. But Ann was standing there beside me and I wanted to get us away. The theatre was still on fire and the whole street might have gone up in flames and I knew we needed to get home. We walked back. I didn't want to get a tram, and I know you gave me the money for a cab, but I couldn't see one, and anyway, I needed to walk and breathe cool air. I'm afraid I made Ann walk too. I hope that wasn't unutterably cruel, but I couldn't have gone inside a cab, I just couldn't. I didn't want to be shut in a box.' He looked across at his sister. 'I don't think we said a word all the way back, did we?'

Ann shook her head.

'I have a few questions,' said John, his voice still hoarse. 'But at the moment I am so happy that you are both safe. Ann, I want you to go with Isobel and she will help you wash, and you can get into your night clothes and come back here so I can say goodnight.'

John waited until they had gone before he spoke.

'I'm not sure I would have had the presence of mind that you did, Finlay. And I cannot tell you what a debt I owe you. Is there any news of what happened? Do you know if everyone got out alive?'

Finlay shook his head. 'I'm afraid I only know as much as I've told you. It was bedlam outside with so much noise. The inferno was still raging when we left. I think the whole building will be gone by the morning in spite of the firemen and their equipment. The blaze seemed to get established in just a few minutes. I think there must have been flammable materials on the stage for the illusions, because it got out of control very quickly. I'm worried about Ann. She hasn't said a word since we got out of the place. At one point she slipped from my grip as we tried to get out of the stalls and I made a lunge for her bag. I'm afraid I may have torn the strap and she'll be very unhappy about that. After that I just held her hand and didn't let go. She may even have some cuts and bruises. I'm so sorry. I did my best.'

John stood up and walked over to where Finlay was sitting. 'I think you may have saved her life as well as your own.' His voice cracked as he spoke and held out his hand.

Ursula watched from her chair. She wondered why men were so formal all the time, and silently promised herself that Finlay would not be like that. It was not too late to show an example.

Chapter 22

Thursday 11 May 1911

'I'm beginning to regret encouraging Ann to read the newspaper so thoroughly,' said Ursula to John as she handed him his hat and umbrella in the hall.

'I agree, she does seem to be overly interested in all the details of the fire.' His voice was almost recovered now, only faltering if he talked too much or too loudly. 'But it's too late to put the genie back in that particular bottle, I fear. When is the funeral?'

'On Sunday.'

'So soon?'

'It seems so.'

'Perhaps all this will be less important to her after it's over.'

'I was wondering,' Ursula paused, 'if I should take her to see it.'

He stopped walking towards the door.

'Are you serious? Taking a child to something like that?'

'Not to the actual funeral. But the newspaper says that tens of thousands of people are expected to come out onto the streets to pay their respects, and I thought we might be able to get a glimpse of the procession, if we were to get up early.'

'Is that a good idea?'

'I'm not sure what else will help. She is obsessed with it. And because he was an illusionist she is half-convinced that he isn't really dead and that he will reappear in a swirl of brocade and silk and shout something suitably theatrical. Perhaps if she sees the procession, she will understand that it is real.'

'I can see your reasoning.' He turned again for the front door, and with one hand on the handle, he continued. 'But allow me to think about it, please. You do have some rather unusual ideas sometimes.'

*

Rugby had given way to cricket at school and on Saturday morning Finlay had left early to prepare for a match, taking his breakfast with him.

John cleared his throat. 'Ann, I was wondering,' he said and then corrected himself, '*we* were wondering if you would like to see the funeral procession for The Great Lafayette tomorrow. I understand that it will be very well attended.'

Ursula looked up from her bowl of Dr Allinson's Power cereal. She was unsure whether or not it was to her taste, but it was recommended, so she was doing her best with it.

John reached across the table and took Ursula's hand and squeezed it. 'It was a good suggestion, and now that I've had time to consider it, there seems to be no reason not to attend.'

Ann raised her head from counting the embroidered flower petals on the tablecloth. 'I think,' she said carefully, 'I would like that very much.'

'I expect your brother will accompany you.' He looked at Ursula and saw the tiny barely-there shake of the head. 'Or perhaps we could all go, if it's important to you.'

'Yes please.'

'Very well. I've finished reading the newspaper for now so I want you to look at it and find out the route of the procession and the time.' And with that he pushed his chair back and stood up. 'I will be in the drawing room if anyone needs me.'

*

They arrived at the roadside early. Ann let go of Ursula's hand and pushed her way to the front. The procession was slow. A single black horse pulled a large floral display mounted on the back of a carriage. 'THE LAST ACT' was picked out in flowers on the front of it. A brass band followed the carriage, and trumpets, trombones, clarinets and other instruments were played all along the route. Two more black horses, with plumes of black feathers sprouting from their harnesses, pulled a second carriage, upon which lay a coffin. This was followed by a car. A Mercedes, Finlay noted.

But it was Ann who noticed that instead of the Mercedes symbol on the car radiator, there was a polished metal model of Beauty, The Great Lafayette's dog, who had died just a few days before the fire. Inside the car, she had read in the newspaper, was Mabel, his Dalmatian. No people were in the car, just Mabel. Ann didn't know whether to cheer or to be quiet.

They made their way back home afterwards as two pairs. Finlay walked beside his father, discussing the cricket scores from the day before. Ursula could hear him talking about ducks, and there always seemed to be so many numbers. She and Ann followed on behind.

'Tell me what you are thinking,' said Ursula.

'There were a lot more people than I thought there would be.'

'In the procession?'

'No, on the pavements. I expect that's because he is so famous. When you die, or Father dies, I don't expect there will be many people. Finlay has a *lot* of friends but I don't suppose even he will have a big funeral.' Ann kicked a small stone into the road. 'And when it's my turn I'll be dead so it won't matter anyway. I won't see it.'

Ursula was so shocked she didn't know what to say.

'I'm not going to go and see Mother any more.'

'I beg your pardon?'

'When we go and put flowers on the grave. I'm not going.'

'I think your father may be disappointed.'

'I'll say I have a headache. Or I'll think of another reason, like laryngitis. Once I've not been going for a while, he won't ask about it.'

'May I ask why you don't want to go?'

Ann didn't say anything for half a road of houses.

'Ann?'

'Because she wasn't a nice person.'

'What a thing to say!'

'She wasn't. *She* would not have held my hand so tightly and rescued me from the fire. *She* would have rushed out and left me behind to burn.'

'I'm sure that's not true.'

'And I am sure that it is. And she would never have let me read the newspaper; she said those were things for boys, even when I could read quite well. But mostly it's because she was horrid to Isobel. She used to make her cry. I heard her sometimes, shouting and shouting when Father was out. And Isobel was sad. I heard her telling the postman that she was going to leave us and find another position.'

'I see.'

'And even when she was ill, at the end, she still shouted, just not as loudly. Nothing was ever right. Ask Finlay.'

'I most certainly will *not* ask him.'

'If you did, he would tell you. She had a shout for everything, but only when Father was not in the house to hear her. I don't know why she had children if she hated us so much.'

'Is there anything else?'

'I don't want to call you "Mother".'

'I've never asked you to do that.'

'I know, but I think Father would like it. He sometimes says "ask Mother" to me, and I'm not sure if it's because he forgets or because it's something he wants. So I try not to call you anything.'

Ursula realised that this was true, and she had never noticed. 'I see.'

'I had a mother and she was not nice. She used to say bad things about me. She whispered them in my ears so no one else would hear. And you don't do things like that if you love someone, so she definitely didn't love me. She once told me she named me Ann because it was the least interesting name she could think of. She didn't even put an e on the end of it.'

'Finlay calls you Annie Bee sometimes. Is that because your initials are A.B.?'

'He only does it when he's being nice.' Ann looked across at Ursula. 'It's because I had lots of black hair when I was born, and then my skin turned yellow for a few days. He was four and a half, and he thought I looked like a bumble bee.'

Ursula listened. She listened more intently than she had ever done in her life.

'You are nice to me and nice to Finlay and especially nice to Isobel.'

'But you don't want to call me Mother?'

'No, I don't.' Ann was suddenly so definite and so confident it was breathtaking. 'I had someone called Mother and she is gone now and I'm glad.' The silence continued for a few more houses. 'I would like to call you Ursula.'

'I see.'

'And I want to be like you. I don't want any more meat on my plate.'

They had fallen further behind John and Finlay, Ursula deliberately slowing down so that the conversation would be private. She could already anticipate how John was going to take all this. It was not going to go down well.

Chapter 23

June 1911

Isobel enjoyed making scones more than almost any other kind of baking. It was quick, and she felt it required some deftness with the temperature of the butter and the oven. It wasn't as easy as it looked, and if pushed she would have said that it made her feel rather clever. She held the sieve high over the earthenware mixing bowl and shook it gently so the white powder fell in a cascade, gathering air as it fell, mixing flour and baking powder together. She chopped the butter with a blunt knife against her thumb and began to rub the mixture into fine breadcrumbs. This was what she enjoyed most, the transformation from one form to another; she had heard Finlay talking to his friend Daniel in the garden about changing states. He had said it was chemistry, and she supposed that baking was a sort of chemistry, but a lot more genteel than the bangs and smells the two young men had been describing. He was clever, she thought, the sort of person who would change the world, given a chance.

Ursula appeared in the doorway, interrupting Isobel's thoughts.

'Isobel, I need to talk to you.'

'Yes, Mrs Black.'

'I have been thinking about something for several weeks, and I need you to be honest with me.'

Isobel stopped mixing the scone dough and rested her hands on the edge of the bowl. 'Of course.'

'I want you to tell me your impression of the late Mrs Black.'

Isobel hesitated before replying. 'Why is that, if you don't mind me asking?'

Ursula sat down on one of the kitchen chairs and pointed at the other chair.

'Just tell me what you think.'

'I'm not sure I want to do that,' said Isobel eventually. She stayed on her feet.

'Why not?' Ursula had discovered that it was better to be direct with Isobel.

'I don't want to speak ill of the dead.'

'There is something ill to be said, then?'

Isobel was trapped by her own words. 'I'm not sure how it would be helpful.'

'It would be helpful to *me*,' Ursula said, emphasising the last word. 'I've been told some things and I want to know if they are true,' she paused, 'before I speak to my husband.'

'I might lose my job.'

'You won't.'

'I might, if Mr Black doesn't like what I would tell you.'

'Please let me be the judge of that.'

Isobel sighed.

'Just tell me whatever you want to, or not. And if you really don't want to say anything, then we will leave it at that.'

Ursula waited. It would have been easy to pepper the space with more questions, but she allowed the silence to rest until Isobel might be ready to speak.

'Well, as you know, I came to the house when it was new, almost three years ago,' Isobel began. 'Ann was ten and Finlay was fourteen. A little while after everyone moved in, things seemed to be alright. Mrs Black was . . . I'm not sure how to describe it. Shall we say there wasn't much patience inside her. And then one afternoon there was a knock on the scullery door, and there was a woman outside, a bit older than me. She had a message for me. She told me to be careful. And I asked her what she meant and she said she hadn't been able to get another place after she had worked for Mrs Black.'

Ursula frowned. 'Did she tell you why that was?'

'She said that word had been put about that she was unreliable. That she wasn't clean in her habits and she was loose with her morals.'

'And these rumours had come from . . .'

'From Mrs Black. The woman could not prove it, of course, but she said that she'd been offered plenty of positions but as soon as her references were taken up, the offers were withdrawn.'

'And had she done anything to deserve these statements?'

'I didn't ask. But I assumed the fact that she was warning me meant that there was no truth in them at all. She said that the problem had started when she decided not to move to Library Terrace. She was a small woman and she had a rasp to her breathing. She said the house would have been too much for her. She had looked all over the place. Situations in *The Scotsman*, and some agencies as well. In the end she stopped trying and went back to her family. They have a smallholding near Haddington. She was up in Edinburgh that day to go to the Infirmary for her lungs and she took it upon herself to come and speak to me, and she left me her address, in case I should need it.'

'And then what happened?'

Isobel rubbed her forehead, leaving a floury mark. 'Nothing.'

'Nothing at all?'

'Nothing until a few weeks later. Then one day Mrs Black accused me of eating more food than I was entitled to. She said she had been monitoring it and that I was having more than my share and that the food was hers to give out and not mine to take. And she accused me of improper relations with the postman. She said that it was disgusting how I was carrying on with him.'

'The same postman we have now? But he must be about fifty years old and you are barely twenty!'

'I'm twenty-two, it was on the census form.'

Ursula skimmed past the reminder. 'This is scarcely believable.'

'I promise you, it's all true. She would give me my portions of food. I wasn't allowed to serve myself. If there was nothing left after dinner, I didn't get anything.'

'Did that happen often?'

'Often enough. I learned very quickly to put a slice of bread in my pocket during the day, just in case, and to eat when she was out, make extra soup, that sort of thing. In the end I just made the meals a bit bigger so there was always something left over. Not so much more that she would notice, but enough to be sure I could have something.'

'Why didn't you leave? I mean, I'm very glad you didn't, but why not?'

'Because of the children.'

Ursula put her head in her hands.

Isobel was now quite unable to stop.

'It was alright when Mr Black was in the house. Everything was quiet and respectful. But when he was at work, she shouted at me. Now, I understand that maids get shouted at sometimes, but when the children came in from school, she shouted at them too.'

'Often?'

'Most days. If their rooms were untidy, or a book was left out of place or there was a mark on a coat, or even if they weren't feeling well. It was like a tap being turned on and off. You didn't know who you were getting or what would make her shout. It wasn't something you could guess in advance. Master Finlay was at high school by then. He made sure he was in every sports team, in the debating society, in the chess club and in the choir. Anything that meant he was out of the house until after Mr Black came in from work at six. I saw him in the evenings when he came back from all these activities and I could have sworn he had been standing on a street corner to avoid coming into the house; he was so wet and cold sometimes he could hardly undo the buttons on his coat.'

'And Ann?'

'Miss Ann just hid. She hardly came out of her room unless it was necessary. She said she had headaches. She had so many of these mystery headaches that Mr Black took her to see a doctor at the Sick Children's Hospital. Of course, there was no headache when she was not with Mrs Black. It all feels like a long time ago now. Ann was so quiet. She barely spoke. I think she thought that if she didn't say anything then she couldn't be wrong. It probably went on for about a year, with loud shouting almost every day. And then Mrs Black got more ill. She didn't have the breath to shout because of the disease in her lungs. The sickness sort of stole her voice. After that there wasn't real out-loud shouting, but shouting in whispers. Sneaky shouting that no one can hear unless they are up close. I still call that shouting. Miss Ann couldn't hide in her room any more because her mother needed her to fetch things and be her errand girl. And that was when Ann used to come to me in the kitchen. And she would tell me things.'

'Things?'

'About how she was an idiot, and how she would never marry because she was an ugly girl. And I realised there was no point in telling her she was wrong, because I was just the maid and she was being told these things by her mother who was much more important.'

'So what did you do?'

'I just listened to her. I would ask her about school and just let her blether away. And I taught her about things, things that make you clever because other people don't know them.'

'I don't understand.'

Isobel walked over to the window. 'How many kinds of birds do you think we have in the garden?'

'I don't know. I've never thought about it.'

'Try.'

'Starling, blackbird, blue tit, sparrow, maybe a pigeon or two.'

'Next time you see Miss Ann, ask her. There are eighteen. Probably more. And ask her about the mosses and the lichens on the walls. We know all the names.'

'How do you know these things? Were you brought up in the country?'

Isobel laughed. 'In the country? No. I'm from Gorgie. I went to the library when I was out doing the shopping and borrowed a few books for her. We learned them together, here at the table in the kitchen. Mrs Black didn't know because she was in her bed by then and too poorly to be down here. Noticing things is a skill, my teachers at school told me that. Miss Ann knows about a lot of things, much more than people imagine.'

'But why doesn't she talk about all this?'

'Because talking about things that matter gets you into trouble. Or at least it used to, when Mrs Black was here.'

'You taught her to be curious.'

'I suppose. She discovered it was a good feeling to find things out.'

'And then Mrs Black died.'

Isobel nodded. 'And Mr Black was very sad for a long time.'

'From your voice it sounds as though there is more to say about that.'

'No one else was sad. No one.' Isobel folded her arms. 'Why are you asking me all this?'

'Because I needed to know. Mr Black wants the children to call me Mother, but Ann is refusing to do it. He is cross with her and thinks she is being stubborn for no reason. Ann wants to call me Ursula.'

'If you don't mind me saying, Mrs Black, I think that's a great compliment. It's possible that, in her mind, Mother is not a good word.'

Ursula nodded. 'That's what she said and I didn't fully understand why.'

'What are you going to do now?'

'I want to speak to Finlay. And after that, I need to talk to my husband.' She paused. 'Are you making fruit scones?'

'Cheese.'

'Good. I'm hungry.' She took a plate down from the dresser. 'Eighteen different birds? Perhaps I need to go to the library too.'

Chapter 24

July 1911

Ann lifted the heavy watering can and struggled down the garden with it. The prolonged dry weather meant her little patch of ground was thirsty. Last year's rosemary bush, grown from a cutting from the postman, had survived, and her carefully sown birthday seeds had already germinated and grown into a carpet of tiny plantlets. There were two sections: a flower bed and a herb patch, and she was most concerned about the herbs because she knew Isobel liked to use them to cook with. She didn't hear Finlay coming up behind her.

'Hello, Annie Bee.'

'You shouldn't creep up on people like that!'

'Sorry.' He pointed at the watering can. 'Would you like me to fill that back up for you?'

'Please.' She handed over the grey galvanised can and bent down to rub the fragranced rosemary spears and the little furry sage leaves between her fingers.

'Shall I water them for you?' he said, when he came back.

She shook her head. 'I know you gave me all these seeds, but you don't know what you're doing. It needs to be done properly.' She took the watering can from him. 'What do you want?'

'I was wondering if you're looking forward to seeing the new King and Queen next week. It's going to be quite a spectacle, I think. There's a big procession planned, all along Princes Street.'

'I'm not going.' Ann leaned over to inspect the smaller seedlings.

'But they might never come back to Edinburgh!' Finlay couldn't keep the astonishment out of his voice. 'Not ever.'

'I don't like being in a crush of people.' She dribbled some water onto the dry earth and turned to look up at him. 'Being squashed up with all the crowds at The Great Lafayette's funeral procession was very difficult for me. I thought you would understand that.'

He nodded. 'I suppose.'

'Is there something else?'

He pushed a mess of misbehaving curls out of his eyes. 'Well, I wanted to ask you something, actually. It's the *Daily Mail* Circuit of Britain on Saturday.'

'What's that?'

'A contest between thirty aeroplanes, like a race in the air. It's about a thousand miles around the country in a circle. It starts and finishes at the famous Brooklands racing circuit, near London.'

'I've never heard of it, so it can't be that famous.' Ann drizzled water into the centre of the bed, giving the mint and the lavender a good drink.

'There's a prize of ten thousand pounds.'

She stopped what she was doing and looked up at him. '*How* much? That sounds like an awful lot. Are you sure?'

'I'm certain. They set off in a few days' time. And I want to go and watch the aeroplanes land up at Redford Barracks. Father doesn't approve of the race at all, he thinks it is terribly dangerous, so I've told him that Daniel and I are going out for a walk.' He watched her progress with the watering. 'But the thing is, I might be back a bit later if the pilots are delayed.'

'Why?'

'I don't know, all sorts of reasons. Anything could happen. There are forest fires in Perthshire at the moment, and with all this heat there might be thunderstorms. Apparently, this month is the hottest July ever recorded.'

'Why are you telling me this?'

'I'm relying on you to make up an excuse for me if anyone notices I'm back late.'

'Can I come with you?'

'No, silly. That would mean there won't be anyone to cover, will there?'

'I'm not silly. And I want to come.'

'I can't take you, Annie Bee.'

'I would be very quiet.'

'I'm sorry, but if you come too then I will get caught. They aren't due to land until three o'clock so I think I'll be fine.' He bent down and pulled at some leaves, trying to be helpful.

She slapped his hand. 'Stop it! You don't know what you're doing. That's my thyme plant you're pulling at. She won't like being messed with.'

'I'm going to see them, whether you help me or not. But I'm hoping that if I'm late you'll be able to distract everyone. I promise I'll do something nice for you to make up for it.'

Ann aimed a stream of water at the curled parsley.

'I suppose so.' She held the empty watering can out for a second refill. 'But I won't forget you said that.'

*

129

Ann grumped her way through breakfast the next morning.

'What on earth has got into you?' Ursula asked.

'I don't feel well. Maybe I should go back to bed.'

Ursula put her hand on Ann's forehead. 'I don't think you have a fever and you aren't vomiting or shivery.'

Ann slumped her shoulders.

'I think you are well enough to go out. Now off you go and put your shoes on. I need to collect a few things at the dry goods store up at Church Hill and you can come with me. Your father says we should get them delivered but it's a lovely day and I would like the fresh air.'

Ann pushed her chair back. 'Finlay,' she began, and then she saw his face, not pleading exactly, but wary. 'Finlay is going to take me to Portobello for an ice cream before I go back to school.'

He frowned.

'That's what you said, Finlay, isn't it?'

He gave in and nodded. 'I think it will be a nice afternoon trip.'

Satisfied, Ann walked up the stairs to her bedroom, and no one except Isobel, who was rubbing the brass door handles and finger plates with Bluebell metal polish, noticed that Ann's lips moved with every step.

*

When they eventually got back from the grocery shopping, which had taken far longer than expected, Ursula said she was going to a meeting. Everyone else was out. Finlay was seeing Daniel, Father was at work and Isobel was nowhere to be seen. Ann really didn't feel well. Her belly was uncomfortable and she had little stabby pains deep inside. She went back into the garden and watered her herbs, but it was too hot to be outside for long. She headed back upstairs, her lips moving as she climbed.

'Oh!' she said, as she walked into her bedroom.

Isobel was sitting on the bed with Ann's jewellery box beside her.

'Isobel! What are you doing?'

The necklaces Ann had been given after her mother died, which she had expressed no interest in wearing, were set out across the counterpane. They had been carefully arranged by colour: pearls, then coloured beads, then jet. And beneath them on the next row there were the rings, all of them still too big for her.

Isobel looked up and glanced at the alarm clock. 'Oh, Miss Ann! I didn't know you were back.' She got off the bed, scooped the jewellery into the box and closed the lid. 'I'll get back to my cleaning.'

'I don't feel well and I am going to lie down for a little while. Why were you looking at my . . ?'

But Isobel was gone, leaving the door to swing closed behind her.

Ann sat down on her bed, undid her shoelaces and kicked her shoes off. She lay down and tried to think what Ursula would do, or Finlay, or Father, but she couldn't decide. Should she go and ask Isobel again? She had rushed off so quickly.

She eased herself back up and looked inside the jewellery box. Most of the items were from Louise. She didn't even know for sure what was in the box. Father had thought she might like them all nearby so she could feel closer to her mother after she had died and hadn't realised that this was the last thing she wanted, so the box had stayed mostly shut. The only necklace she really liked hadn't been Louise's at all. It was made from steel, each bead faceted like a diamond. And it wasn't kept in the box, it was in a little brass-coloured tin which said 'Ucal Bronchial Lozenges' on the outside, filled with bran. The bran, Isobel had told her, was to keep the steel beads dry and to stop them from rusting. It had been a gift from her grandmother when she was born and she kept it in the little bedside cabinet, underneath her handkerchiefs.

She opened the drawer. The metal tin wasn't there.

Ann knew then that she needed to wait for everyone to come home; this was not something she could sort out by herself. She lay back down on the bed, her stomach churning and stabbing and butterflies dancing inside her with the worry of it all.

*

Ann heard them come in, first Father, then Finlay, and finally Ursula, whose meeting had lasted much longer than she had planned. By the time everyone had come home, Ann had been to the toilet and seen the blood on her underwear. She had wiped herself and changed into clean things, and waited for Ursula to come and find her.

The air race and the jewellery box all seemed much less important now.

Chapter 25

July 1911

Two Saturdays after the jewellery-box incident, Finlay took Ann for ice cream in Portobello, as he had promised. They went on the tram and Ann counted the steps as they climbed up to the top deck because she couldn't help herself.

'Italian ice cream is the absolute best,' said Finlay after finding them a seat in the café and ordering from the waiter. 'One day I want to go to Italy and try it in the place it really comes from.'

'*This* Italian ice cream comes from here,' she replied.

It was eventually brought to their table in tall glasses. Finlay took a scoop of it with the long spoon and savoured the white deliciousness.

'And pizza,' Ann said. 'I want to taste real pizza, not just the kind Isobel has started to make.'

'And pizza,' he agreed.

'Are you going to tell me about the Air Race?' She was not in the mood for conversation and getting Finlay to talk about one of his enthusiasms was the easiest way to avoid having to make an effort.

'It was magnificent.' He drew the word out into individual syllables. 'The aircraft were going to land at Redford Barracks so everyone went there to watch them arrive. You had to pay a shilling to get close, and I wasn't expecting there would be a charge, but I had money with me.'

'Where did you get the money from?'

He blushed. 'I had the cab money from when we went to The Great Lafayette. No one asked for it back, so I kept it, like an emergency fund in case we're ever caught out again and need to get home quickly.'

Ann was not convinced. 'I don't think you should have kept it.'

'I've never spent a penny of it, until the Air Race. And the rest is there if we need it. Like today, if you felt unwell again like you did a couple of weeks ago—'

'Right,' said Ann, quickly changing the subject and going back to her ice cream. 'So, you paid the shilling and then what?'

'Nothing happened for quite a while and I was worried that I'd need to leave to get back home before they appeared. But then some men came out with big white sheets and they made a cross on the grass, and they got some Boy Scouts to help with putting bricks on the sheets so they didn't blow away.'

'Perhaps if you hadn't left the Scouts you wouldn't have had to pay the shilling.'

'Maybe.' He licked his spoon. 'We saw the planes approaching in the sky and we heard the engines. It was such a thrill. I've never seen anything so marvellous. When they landed, everyone cheered. Only four pilots finished the course. And that was it. I couldn't stay any longer because I had to come home.'

'It does *sound* exciting.'

'I'm sorry I haven't told you about it before but I couldn't risk anyone overhearing.' Finlay looked at her. 'You've been very quiet lately.'

'I know.'

'Is there anything the matter?'

Ann thought about the fact that she would have a visitor every month for the rest of her life, which was how Ursula had described it. 'No, nothing's wrong,' she lied.

'Ann Black, I don't believe you. You are keeping a secret.' He put the final spoonful of ice cream into his mouth and licked his lips.

'Me?'

'There is no one else called Ann Black in the vicinity, so yes, you.'

She scraped the last drop of melted ice cream from the tall glass and managed not to let it dribble on her dress. 'Well, yes. But you can't tell.'

'I can't promise you that. If you are in danger, I have to say something.'

'It's nothing like that.'

'Go on then, spill the beans.' He leaned back in his chair and looked around the café, waiting for her to divulge her important secret. 'What is it?'

Ann whispered, 'I think Isobel might be stealing things.'

He leaned forward. 'What?'

'Something is missing.' She looked down into the empty glass, unwilling to meet his eyes. 'It was when I was feeling poorly a couple of weeks ago. There was no one in the house and I thought she must be up in her room. I wasn't feeling well so I went straight upstairs to my bedroom, and there she was.'

'Doing what?'

'She had my jewellery box open on the bed and she was going through all the necklaces and rings.'

'Mother's things?'

'Yes. I'm never going to wear them, though, because she was a horrible person. I only keep the box to make Father happy. I don't even really know what's in it.'

'You've never done an inventory?'

She frowned. 'A what?'

'It's a fancy name for a list.'

'No, I've never done one of those.'

'So you don't know for sure if there *is* anything missing?'

'Not from that box.' She hesitated. 'But my little steel necklace, the one Grandma gave me when I was born? Well, that's gone.'

'You are quite, *quite* sure? This is a serious thing, Ann, saying someone is a thief.'

'The tin is not in the drawer where I keep it.'

'We need to go home,' he said. 'We must tell Father immediately.'

'It's Isobel's afternoon off. She told me she was going to sit in Princes Street Gardens and listen to the band that plays there. She was looking forward to it.' Her voice had an air of desperation. 'Do we have to say? I don't want to get her into trouble.'

'Neither do I, but we have to speak to them before she comes back. It's not the sort of thing you keep a secret. It really isn't.'

Ann could feel a mood descending on her. 'If you are absolutely sure,' she said eventually.

'I am. And there's no time to waste. It's after two o'clock and she will be back at six.' He pulled his new wallet out of his pocket. 'This is why you should always have an emergency fund. Remember that, Annie Bee, it's very important.'

Chapter 26

July 1911

'Ann thinks that Isobel is a thief.'

Seven words. In the time it took to say them Ann watched the faces in the drawing room change, from smiling to cautious, grave, concerned, even angry. She looked at the floor. Now that the words had been said by someone else it was impossible to take them back and hide them inside her. She hated these words, hated that she was the person who had raised the issue. 'I didn't say that.'

'You did,' said Finlay.

'I said that I thought she *might* be stealing things.'

John took charge. 'I want you both to sit down, and I want Ann to tell us precisely why she thinks this is the case.'

'I said might,' Ann protested. 'I didn't say she *is*, I said she *might* be. It's not the same.'

'Regardless, we need to know why you would think such a thing.'

Ann looked at Finlay, because he already knew and that made it easier. 'It was the day when I wasn't feeling well. I came home early and none of you were in. I found Isobel upstairs in my bedroom. She had taken all the necklaces and things out of my jewellery box and laid them out on the bed, and she was looking at everything very carefully.'

'Your mother's jewellery box?'

Ann nodded. Her bottom lip quivered.

'And is anything missing from it?'

Ann shrugged. 'I don't know.'

'How is it possible for you not to know?' His frustration at the whole situation spilled out. 'Isn't it obvious?'

She shook her head. 'I never look inside that box. I don't try the necklaces on or play with them, I don't care about them at all. You could give them all away and I wouldn't care.'

'Ann!' Finlay stared at her.

'You've forgotten what she was like. How mean she was. I don't want anything of hers anywhere near me.'

John frowned. 'I don't understand.'

Ursula's certainty cut through the room. 'I do. Isobel told me.'

'And you believe her? If she's stealing from us, how can we trust anything she says?'

Ursula stood up. 'Nothing is known to be missing.'

Ann shook her head. 'There is *one* thing. The necklace that Grandma gave me is gone.'

'If you will excuse me for a moment.' Ursula left them all sitting in silence and they heard her footsteps going up the stairs and then coming back down. She held out the brass-coloured lozenge tin. 'You mean this?'

Ann reached for it. 'Yes! This one. It was in with my handkerchiefs and when I looked for it after I saw Isobel in my room, it wasn't there.'

'I took it,' said Ursula. 'I noticed that the clasp was damaged, and some of the steel beads were rusting. I've had it polished for you. It was meant to be a surprise.'

Ann cupped the little tin in her hands. 'Thank you so much.'

John put his hands on the table. 'That's all fine and well but it doesn't explain why Isobel was going through

Ann's things.' He paused. 'Has anyone else noticed anything odd?'

'She has been more meticulous with the cleaning recently,' said Ursula carefully. 'Going into every corner, clearing out drawers, spring cleaning wardrobes and cupboards even though it isn't spring any more. It's as though she is searching for something. But I'm very uncomfortable talking about her like this when she isn't here.'

As though she had been summoned, Isobel walked up the front path, and they watched as she crossed in front of the bay window on her way to the side gate and the back garden.

It was John who fetched her from the kitchen and brought her through to the drawing room.

Chapter 27

July 1911

'Please sit down,' said John.

'I would prefer to stand, sir.' Isobel could not imagine what was happening.

John cleared his throat. 'I understand that you have been examining the contents of Ann's jewellery box.'

Ann wanted the floor to open up and swallow her. Anything to not be in the room.

To everyone's astonishment, Isobel looked each of them in the face, one after another.

'That's true.'

'This is a very serious matter. Would you care to provide an explanation?'

'I was looking for my property.'

John's eyebrows couldn't have risen any higher if he had forced them to. '*Your* property?'

Isobel reached into the neck of her dress and pulled out a length of black cotton cord. A coin was attached to it with a knot. 'This is mine. It's an 1889 penny from the year I was born. My late father drilled a hole in it and put it on a string for me. It's worthless, or at least it's only worth a penny to anyone but me. My father died when I was five and it's the only thing from him that I own.'

No one spoke.

'When I took up my position here, I kept it in my room. I didn't want to wear it in case the string broke and it got lost, so I kept it on a little earthenware dish on my shelf. And then one day, the dish and the coin were gone. The string was left behind and I could see it had been snipped with scissors. It wasn't an accident. And a few days later I found some pieces of broken pottery in the garden, up near the plum tree, where Miss Ann used to play at tea parties with her friends.' She looked at Ann. 'You were younger then. We hadn't been here long.'

'You thought Ann had taken it?' Ursula took over.

'I am sorry, but yes, I did.'

'Why didn't you say anything?'

Isobel looked straight back at Ursula. 'Because the late Mrs Black was not very kind towards her and I didn't want her to get into trouble.'

'Not very kind? I don't believe what I am hearing.' John turned furiously to Ann. 'Why did you take it?'

'I didn't!' Ann protested. 'I've never even been up the stairs to Isobel's room. I wouldn't dare.'

'Well, this is a full-scale mystery and no mistake,' said Finlay, stating the obvious.

Isobel sighed. 'It was the late Mrs Black.'

'I beg your pardon!' John was on his feet now. 'You are accusing my wife, my late wife, of theft?'

'I saw the coin in her jewellery box one day when she was getting ready to go out. It had the same hole, just above the Queen's head. She knew that I had seen it and she just closed the box. And you may as well know, she used to come into my room when I was out.'

'You must surely be mistaken.'

'No, sir, I am not.' Isobel looked back at him steadily. 'I would find things had been moved.'

John shook his head. 'I do not believe it.'

'What was moved?' Finlay's voice cut through his father's anger.

'All sorts of things. My pillows were turned over. My sheets untucked. My shoes pulled away from the wall and put the wrong way around. One time a clean apron was taken from my drawer and then it reappeared a few weeks later beside the wash stand, all crumpled. It wasn't anything I could complain about. But I knew she had been there.'

'Why would she do this?' said John.

'Power,' said Finlay.

His father looked at him in astonishment. 'Explain yourself!'

'It was to show she was in charge. No one could complain because there would be a huge fuss and we would be the ones in the wrong. She did it with my books.' He demonstrated with his hands. 'I would find my encyclopaedias with one book in the wrong place, so they were out of alphabetical order, or sometimes one volume would be replaced upside down. The pencils I had just sharpened would all be just a little bit blunt the next day. Once, she read my letters; I could tell because the paper was folded back in the opposite direction. The creases were in new places. She did it like that on purpose so it would be obvious to me but not to anyone else. It was her way of showing us that she could do what she wanted and go through our private things and we couldn't stop her. With everything else going on, especially when she was unwell, I didn't want to make a fuss. I tried to forget.' He looked at his father. 'She never did this to you?'

John shook his head. 'I don't think so. But I am not the most observant of people, and we shared a room, of course, so she had the right to be there.' His voice lost its edge. 'You should have told me.'

'Should is a terrible word,' said Ursula. 'Should is all about blame. Blaming oneself, blaming others.'

John turned back to Isobel. 'You found your necklace in Ann's box?'

'Yes, sir. Or at least, I found the coin. It was hidden under the tray at the bottom. I had to remove everything before I discovered it.'

'What I don't understand is how she managed to get into your room, Isobel.'

'It's very simple, sir; the door doesn't have a lock.'

'No lock?' It was John's turn to be surprised. 'But I remember buying locks and keys for every room in the house when it was built. It was one of the last things I paid for.'

'Oh, there was a lock at the beginning. But I came home from my afternoon off one week, and I found the keyhole jammed up with paper. The key was useless. And after that Mrs Black used to walk in whenever she felt like it. It wasn't until she was really quite ill and she couldn't manage to get up the stairs from the kitchen that the room was my own again.'

'Why have you never mentioned the lock not working?' John knew the answer to this question already. Isobel wouldn't have dreamed of complaining about anything like this. He made an effort anyway. 'I could have had it repaired for you.'

'It doesn't matter now. None of you would dream of coming in uninvited.' Isobel stood up straight, as though she had made a decision. 'But I understand if you would like me to leave. I was wrong to go through the jewellery box. I have broken the trust you had in me.' She turned around and left the room without waiting for permission.

'I am a charitable man,' said John, 'and I like to think the best of people, but this takes the biscuit. And for it to be happening under my own roof and me to be ignorant of it is shocking.'

Ursula pointed at Ann and Finlay. 'I hope that you two have learned not to be so quick with your assumptions.' She looked across the room at her husband. 'And you and I are going to speak with Isobel and see if we can persuade her to stay. I think that is the very least we can offer.'

Chapter 28

August 1911

Isobel was hurrying, Ursula could feel it.

'Is everything alright?'

'Yes, yes. I'm just making sure that all my jobs are done properly before I go off this afternoon.'

Ursula looked out of the window. 'It looks like another beautiful day.'

'Enough blue in the sky to make a sailor a pair of trousers, my auntie used to say. Everything is ready for dinner; there's a pie under a tea towel on the cold shelf in the larder so that's ready to go in the oven at five, and the potatoes are peeled and covered in water in the pan, but I haven't added the salt yet. And there's a jug of that sweet onion gravy that Master Finlay likes.'

'Thank you.' Ursula really wanted to know what Isobel's plans were but there wasn't a question-sized gap in the conversation.

'There's a fruit flan for pudding. I mean dessert. That's in the larder too. You just need to put cream with it. There might be a few more raspberries ripe in the patch down the garden that you can add if you like.'

'Won't you be back by six?' It wasn't like Isobel to be late. She had been so appreciative of the extra hours she now had to herself and always strived to make sure that her routine didn't disrupt the household.

'I expect so. I'm meeting a friend for an hour and she doesn't have as much time off as I do, so her afternoon is precious. I don't want to be late.'

Ursula nodded and poured herself another cup of tea.

The locksmith on Bread Street had been most helpful when Ursula had visited, and had supplied not just the lock and the new doorknobs, but also a rather pretty door knocker, and she had booked a lock fitter to install them all. He was coming this afternoon, while Isobel was out. It was to be a surprise.

*

It was well past seven o'clock when Isobel returned. She rushed in through the scullery door, gasping for breath, and found Ursula washing the last of the plates.

Isobel was horrified. 'What are you *doing*?'

'You weren't back, so I decided to wash up. It's not difficult, and I didn't want you to come back to a pile of dirty dishes. It's a lovely evening and everyone else has gone out for a walk.' Ursula wiped her hands on the towel that hung behind the door. 'I didn't want to go with them because I have a blister from my new shoes.'

'Right, I'll get my apron and if you would like to leave the rest of it now, I'll finish up.'

'There isn't anything to leave, it's all done. Really, it was just a few plates. You did all the dishes from the baking this morning. Don't forget that I lived alone before I came to Library Terrace so I'm not a stranger to hot water and soft soap. We kept some pie and some dessert for you.'

'Thank you.' Isobel took her coat off. 'I'll just put this in my room and I'll be back down right away to set up the breakfast things.'

Ursula nodded, and as Isobel put her foot on the first step, she smiled to herself.

A few seconds later there was a gasp. Ursula waited.

'What has happened to my door?' Isobel ran back down the stairs. 'It's locked and I can't get in.' Her voice began to break. 'Is this because of the jewellery box? I explained about that and I am so, so sorry.'

'Oh my goodness, absolutely not!' Ursula reached into her pocket and pulled out a shiny new brass key. 'This is for you. We all thought that as you are part of the household here, part of the family, really, you should have your privacy when you want it. I would never dream of coming into your room without permission, but after everything that happened before, we thought you might like to be sure of that.' She offered the key to Isobel. 'Although you probably won't want to lock the door when you are actually in the room, in case there is an emergency or something.'

'A fire.'

'Yes, a fire. But when you're up there, I thought that rather than shouting up as though you are a naughty child, I could use this instead?' Ursula pointed to a small brass door knocker which had been mounted on a piece of wood and fixed above the hand rail at the foot of the staircase.

Isobel took the key. 'Did the person who fitted the lock take the old one away?'

'It's outside. Finlay is fascinated by things like that and I thought he might want to take it apart and see how it works. It's on the scullery windowsill.'

Isobel fetched the old lock. 'Let me show you something.'

'What am I looking at?'

'She had the lock changed. It's not the one that was on the door to start with; that one was taken away when Mr Black was on a trip somewhere, and this one was fitted instead.'

'Why would she do that, if she intended to stuff it with paper?'

'That happened later. Look at the lock. You can only lock it and unlock it from one side, see? The keyhole the other side has been blanked off.'

Ursula frowned. 'I don't understand.'

'She could lock me in. And even if I had a key, I couldn't get out. She did that to make sure I was too frightened to go up to my room during the day. To make sure I was working all the time. She would lock it in the morning when I came down and not unlock it again until after eight o'clock at night. And then when she got bored of that, she stuffed all the paper in so anyone could come up at any time. Not that they did, but it was another way to make me worry.'

Ursula shook her head. 'I cannot imagine why you stayed.'

'I told you. It was because of the children. I knew that if she was doing this to me then she was almost certainly practising so she could do it to them.' Isobel looked down at her new key. 'Especially Miss Ann. It wasn't a secret that she had never wanted a daughter, and she blamed her for the troubles.'

'Troubles?'

'Women's troubles. She never said what they were but it was seemingly Miss Ann's fault. She was born so quickly that I think there was, well, I think there was an injury, you know. And she wasn't the same afterwards.' Isobel surveyed the clean scullery. 'But that's enough of the past, don't you think? If there's nothing else, I'll eat my supper, and then I can get on with laying the table for breakfast.'

*

After she had eaten the pie and the slice of flan, and had done the last of her chores, Isobel went in search of Ursula and found her sitting in the dining room. Evening sunshine stretched long shadows across the table.

'I need to speak with you, Mrs Black. I haven't properly thanked you for the lock and the door knocker.'

Ursula put down her pencil and closed her diary. 'You are very welcome. It's the least we could do for you.'

'It's just . . .' Isobel was distinctly uncomfortable about something.

'Go on.'

'Well, it's just that after I saw my friend this afternoon, I went to see about a new position. With everything that's happened I wasn't sure if you *really* wanted me to stay. I needed to see if there was another house that would offer me a place so I went for an interview. Someone told me there is a big household in the Grange who are looking for a maid and that the family are good, you know?' Isobel looked past Ursula and fixed her eyes on the clock on the mantelpiece. From ten feet away she could see that the dark wooden case needed dusting.

'And were you offered the job?'

'I was. Subject to references, of course.'

Ursula felt her stomach tighten. 'When are you leaving us?'

'I haven't decided about it.'

'We will be very sorry to see you go, I hope you know that.'

Isobel sat down on one of the best dining chairs, without asking permission. 'It's a good situation, and there is a kitchen-maid who would be beneath me, so it would be a promotion, sort of.'

'I see.'

'But I would be going back to having just a half-day off each week, and it would be on a Sunday, when the shops and things are closed.' Isobel paused. 'And the lady asked me all sorts of questions but she didn't give me a chance to ask any of my own.'

Ursula waited for Isobel to untangle her thoughts.

'She walked me around the house so I could see what needed to be done, and then she showed me the kitchen. The house has electricity and I think she was rather proud of it. But in the cold cupboard there was a chicken with its head still on, and there were sausages and some black pudding ready for the Sunday breakfast. It struck me that I've hardly cooked anything like that since the start of the summer. Mr Black has stopped expecting his Sunday roast, and even Master Finlay has given up complaining about not having meat on his plate.'

Ursula couldn't resist a smile. 'I'm sure Finlay still eats it when he's out with his friends. And I know for certain that Mr Black enjoys a good meaty lunch when he is at the golf club, so he isn't missing out. But yes, that little yellow book has changed all of us.'

'You may be right about Master Finlay. It's just that, to be honest with you, I'm not sure I could go back to dealing with it all now.' Isobel stopped, as though she had made a decision. 'And I would miss everyone. I know I'm only the maid here, and even though I work hard, this is not an easy house to look after. The electricity in that house did look as though it would be a help.' She smoothed her skirt with her hands, trying to flatten the day's creases. 'But I've been going over everything in my head ever since I left. I even walked back to the Meadows and sat on a bench so I could have a proper think about it.' Isobel looked at Ursula. 'I feel as though I really belong here. You listen to me. That lady was very nice, but she didn't listen at all.' She pushed the chair back and stood up again. 'So I've decided that if you want me to stay, I will.'

The ticking of the clock seemed to fill the room.

From the moment Isobel had first mentioned her visit to the grand house in the Grange, which was undoubtedly a more prosperous residence than 25 Library Terrace, Ursula had felt a twist of anxiety in her stomach. Although Isobel was saying she would like to stay, Ursula wondered if it was time she laid her own cards on the table. This was not about kitchen-maids or electricity. She had to decide whether or not it was time to include Isobel in her plans.

'It's very important to me that you realise how much I appreciate your work in this house, Isobel,' she began. 'You could have just left us when I became vegetarian and you didn't do that. Between us we cooked two different dinners every night for several months and somehow we muddled through everything and learned the new recipes together. And after the circumstances with your necklace last month, it would have been completely understandable if you had decided to leave immediately, but you stayed.'

This was not at all what Isobel expected. She reached up to her neck and rubbed the old penny which was now threaded safely onto a silver chain which Ursula had given her. She didn't know where to put herself.

'And apart from those things, before I married Mr Black, you were the person who looked after Ann. I don't know how she would have survived without you.' Ursula paused. 'Although I worked in Mr Black's office, before that I had quite a privileged upbringing, and when I first came to this house I was not educated in the way things are for many women in this country. I thought it wasn't necessary to make changes, but I've learned a lot from the people I see at Café Vegetaria, and I have learned from you as well. I'm a different person now. You are partly responsible for that.' She leaned forward, her elbows on the table. 'You are not *just* a maid. You never were. And if you want to stay here and try to change more things with me, it would make me very happy.'

Isobel listened carefully to every word. And then she smiled.

'I think I would like that very much, Mrs Black.'

Chapter 29

August 1911

'School starts next week,' said Ursula. 'We will need to buy you some new pencils.'

John had already left for work, and Finlay had vanished upstairs.

'I know it does.' Ann was slumped in her chair at the dining table. 'And I'm the only one in the house going back. It's so unfair.'

'Finlay will be studying too, though.'

'I know, but he's nearly eighteen now and he'll be at university and that's quite different. No more school uniform, no more homework jotters, no more rules.'

Ursula reached for the last lonely piece of toast on the rack. 'That's mostly true, as far as it goes, but Finlay's life is not going to be a carefree sprint from lecture to tearoom with no work required in between. If he wants to succeed, he will have to work very hard.' She spread the toast with salted butter. 'Aren't you looking forward to seeing your friends again?'

'I suppose. Some of them have been away from Edinburgh for weeks and weeks. I'm not sure I would want to do that. I like being here with you and Isobel and I have my herb garden. I mean who would take care of all the watering it if I wasn't here? We haven't had any rain since the start of the summer. I have been counting the days off in my diary.' Ann frowned. 'Imagine if there isn't any rain until September. We might have no water in the taps, and my plants will die.'

'I don't think it will come to that.' Ursula sincerely hoped the weather would break soon. Her corsets were extremely uncomfortable and getting very stained with perspiration. 'If there is only one week of your holidays left, we must make the most of it. What would you like to do apart from going to buy new pencils? Perhaps a new book? Or I could take you for lunch at Café Vegetaria?'

'I'm not sure.'

'Would you like to help me put some pictures into my album, now that your father has collected them from the photographer?'

Ann brightened a little. 'Could I have some photographs of everyone? You know, in frames, so I could put them on my dressing table.'

'I don't see why not.'

'You and Finlay and Father. I would like to be able to see the pictures when I get up in the morning and before I go to bed at night.'

'But you see us all every day anyway.'

'Nonetheless,' Ann tried the word out, 'I would like to have photographs of my own.' All signs of lethargy gone, she slid off the chair. 'I will get ready straight away and we can make a start. Do you know what we are having for dinner tonight?'

'Haricot bean and tomato casserole with sage and walnut dumplings.' Despite the heat, Ursula knew this news would be well received.

'That sounds lovely, dumplings are my favourite.' Ann's shoes clattered along the tiled floor in the hall, and as she put her foot on the first of the carpeted stairs, she began to count under her breath.

*

'Who is this?' Ann looked closely at a photograph of a couple in their best clothes. A man with a large grey beard and heavy moustache seemed to look back at her, and in front of him sat a small woman who wore a dress with a lace collar, her shoes peeking out at the hem. She didn't have a hair out of place; it was as though she had been to have it styled especially for the occasion.

'My parents.'

'Tell me about them.'

'My father was an engineer, just as Finlay wants to be. He invented things and taught at a college for apprentices. I think he would have liked your curiosity; he never minded answering my questions, even when they were probably a bit foolish.'

'What was he called?'

'Bernhardt. He was from Germany, and he came to London when he was a very young child, just two or three years old. And then when he grew up, he changed his name.'

'You can do that?'

'You can. There are legal papers that need to be dealt with but I don't think it's very complicated. He was Bernhardt Schmidt, and he became Bernard Smith.'

'Why did he want to change it?'

'I'm not sure. He never spoke about it. Perhaps it was easier for him. He didn't have an accent; he sounded like you and me. Maybe he just wanted not to have to answer questions about where he came from all the time.'

'I didn't know you could change your name,' said Ann quietly. 'I thought you were stuck with whatever you were given.'

Ursula pressed on. 'And this is my mother, she was called Veronica.'

'Speedwell.'

'Pardon?'

'I read it in my flower book. Those little purple flowers that we get in the lawn if the gardener doesn't mow it often enough. They are called speedwell, and the proper official name for them is Veronica.'

'You've taught me something today.' Ursula touched the photograph with her forefinger. 'She was a kind woman, but she didn't always understand me. I think she would have liked to know she was named after a pretty flower.'

'Why are you called Ursula?'

'I was named after my grandmother, my father's mother.' She spread the loose pictures out on the table. 'Have you decided which of these new photographs you would like for your frames?'

Chapter 30

September 1911

Ann sat at the kitchen table, and watched Isobel knead the bread dough.

'You always look as though you are enjoying that.'

'There are a lot of things I *don't* like doing in this kitchen, like black-leading the range and mopping the floors, but yes, I do like making the bread.' Isobel pushed the edge of the dough away from her and then grabbed it and folded it over towards her before pushing it away again.

'It's another one of Finlay's chemistry things,' said Ann. 'Taking powder and water and salt and putting them all together to make something tasty.'

Isobel paused in the kneading. 'You are sounding very grown up, Miss Ann, if I may say so.'

Ann smiled to herself and patted her braids which, with Ursula's assistance, were now looped around her head like a halo. 'I have been thinking about how different things are now Ursula is here.'

Isobel continued to knead the dough.

'And I've been making plans for my herb garden for next year.'

'That sounds rather grand.' Isobel shaped the rounded dough into a ball and dropped it back into the earthenware bowl to rise. 'It's only September. Next year is a good way off.'

'I know, but I've been reading a book about choosing plants, and it says you should always plan things a long time before you need to do them. Have you got time to look at the garden with me now?'

Isobel looked up at the clock. 'I expect so.' She rolled up her long apron and tucked it into the waist strings. 'Just five minutes, mind.'

They went outside and walked up the bone-dry path to the carefully tended herb patch at the far end. It was the only part of the garden which was still green and healthy.

'What is it you want to do?'

'I want this to be useful, so I need to know which herbs you would like more of. I've only ever planted the cuttings from the postman, and the seeds Finlay gave me for my birthday. But we might want different kinds next year. I'm teaching myself the proper Latin names.' Ann pointed to each herb in turn. 'Rosmarinus, Thymus, Salvia, Mentha, Melissa, Allium, Ocimum, Petrocelium.'

Isobel was impressed. 'Very good. I think we might need more parsley, we use quite a lot of that. And sage, because of your favourite dumplings, and perhaps you could grow some lemon balm for salads?'

'My book says there is more than one kind of thyme and sage. I'll ask Ursula if I can buy some extra seeds. Do you think she'll say yes?'

Isobel leaned backwards to stretch her back a little. 'She might. You've worked hard at the digging and the weeding, and I'm impressed with how you've kept up with the watering. It's very handy for me to be able to walk up the garden and pick a bit of this or that to help the dinner along.' She bent down to nip off a few mint leaves and popped them into her mouth. 'They have such pretty names, that's for sure. Well, apart from the basil.'

Ann laughed. 'I know, Ocimum isn't very nice, not for something with such a good flavour. There are at least two sorts of sage, though.' She rubbed a velvety leaf between her fingers. 'There is this green Salvia and there's another one with purple leaves.'

'I'll use whatever you choose to grow. If you pinch out some of those chives and bring them inside for me now, I'll chop them up and put them in the dough instead of onion, and you can have chive rolls with your dinner this evening. Now, Miss Ann, I really must get on, so I'll leave you to your planning.' Isobel turned and headed back along the path to the scullery door, her skirts brushing against the herbs as she walked.

Left alone, Ann sat down cross-legged like a small child, and removed the folded paper from the cunning pocket which Elizabeth Forrester had sewn into the side seam of her dress. She opened it up and studied it. The diagram was clear enough, and she would certainly be needing more space next year, if Father agreed.

On the paper she had drawn out a series of concentric rings, with the herbs arranged inside the circles and the rosemary bush in the centre. The Latin names were listed neatly along one side of the paper, with arrows showing where everything would go.

She took a pencil from her pocket and spread the paper out on the dry, sun-warm flagstone path, and wrote in her best handwriting:

My New Herb Garden
She paused for a moment, and added:
By Annie Black

1921

Chapter 31

Monday 20 June 1921

The census collector adjusted his tie and pushed his shoulders back to make himself feel more official. It was midmorning and he was about a third of the way through his collecting round. Most of the houses in this part of Edinburgh had their outer storm doors open, allowing the sunshine to warm the tiled entrance between the main door and the partially glazed inner one. Each one, he noticed, had a slightly different pattern on the floor. Some featured a complicated central star, with smaller stars arranged around the edge in ochre and cream and pale blue. Others just had a simple rectangle surrounded by a number of borders. Most, but not all, of the entrance halls were gleaming. He could smell the fragrance rising from the wax-polished surfaces.

Almost every property had produced their census form. Some had been handed over by the lady of the house; he often heard the sound of young children filtering through to the front door. Other forms were brought forward by the maids, wiping their hands on their aprons and looking nervous, as though it would be their fault if there was an error on the paperwork.

He worked his way along Library Terrace, opening and closing the black iron gates with care, and assessing the capabilities of these same maids by the level of shine they had achieved on the brass door knockers. The main door of number 23 was painted a deep navy blue and the front garden was festooned with early sweet peas and scented nigella. The brasswork gleamed and the stained glass in the inner door was polished to a sheen. He lifted his hand to knock and paused as he thought he caught sight of a figure walking in haste across the hall. His cousin had been a maid before the war, and he remembered her telling him that every fingerprint on the polished brass had to be rubbed away. He was glad the census had been delayed. Collecting completed forms in June was easier than it would have been during the civil unrest in April. He was all for the quiet life.

No one came to the door. He knocked, knuckles on wood, unwilling to add to the maid's workload, and waited.

There was no reply. He knocked a second time and was rewarded by a flurry of activity in the hall. The door was opened by a woman of about forty, wearing a pink dress and carrying a coat draped over one arm. He couldn't for the life of him think why she would want a coat when the sun was splitting the sky, but women were a mystery to him; they had so many rules for everything.

'Yes?' She looked at the bag slung across his shoulder. 'If you're looking for Jane she's hanging out the laundry in the back garden, but I've asked her not to have callers unless it's her day off.'

'I'm not looking for Jane,' he replied. 'I've come to collect the census form your husband would have completed last night?' He made his voice go up at the end, so the statement sounded like a question. If the form hadn't yet been completed, it was less contentious.

'Ah yes, of course. It's in the dining room. One moment.'

He waited for what seemed like five minutes or more with the sun beating down, warming his back, and reminding him that he hadn't had a glass of water since breakfast. This delay invariably meant that the form hadn't been completed and there was some hasty scribing going on inside the house. Eventually, the woman reappeared, accompanied by a stocky, grey-bearded man.

'My father was just looking for his pen to sign in the correct place.' She handed him the form and he looked through all the entries, noting the smudged ink in a couple of places.

'That all seems to be in order. Thank you. I'll be on my way.'

He walked back towards the gate and then heard her voice calling him. 'There won't be anyone next door,' she said, pointing at number 25.

'At the moment? You mean they've gone out for the day?' He had a lengthening list of not-at-homes who would need another visit later in the week.

'No, I mean they aren't there. They've gone away to France, I think, or maybe Belgium?' She looked over her shoulder.

'France,' said her father. 'Not that there's much left of the place, by all accounts.'

The collector nodded. There wasn't a need for further explanation. 'Do you happen to know if their maid went with them?'

'I don't think so. The place is locked up. I can check with Jane if you need to know exactly where she is?'

'That won't be necessary. The enumerator for her district will deal with it.' He nodded a goodbye and closed the gate carefully behind him before continuing his route.

The garden of number 25 looked tired; no flowers here, he thought. The shutters were closed and the house seemed forlorn, as though the life had gone from it. There would be many missing names on the census forms this year. Men who had been listed in 1911 as schoolboys or stonemasons, bankers or butchers, who no longer commanded a line on the government document. Or at least, not on *this* document. They would be listed in other places, he hoped.

He lifted the latch on the gate of number 27. It squeaked into life as he pushed it open, and he could hear the laughter and squeals of excited children as he walked up the path.

A cornflower-blue door this time, the colour of fresh flowers and summer skies.

1931

Chapter 32

February 1931

Ann was so preoccupied with mental arithmetic as she walked home from the shops that at first she didn't see the man standing outside 25 Library Terrace. She only became aware of him when he reached for the latch on the gate. He looked up the path to the front door, and she saw him hesitate.

Her heart quickened. This was only to be expected after so many years, she thought.

He paused, and then stood up straight as though on parade, opened the gate and started to walk along the path. She held her breath, and watched, transfixed, as he stopped halfway and looked across to the cherry tree she had planted with Father in 1908. The flower bed beneath the tree was in an abandoned state, a tangle of dried-up geranium stalks that she should have tidied up last autumn.

The man touched the bark on the trunk of the tree and looked up at the network of twigs and buds above. He reached up for the end of one branch and bent it down close to his face to examine it before letting it go back to its original position. And then he stepped back onto the path, taking care not to crush the geraniums, despite their neglect.

He was three yards from the front door when she began to run. The library books in her basket clattered against the wickerwork, battering the corners off-square as they jolted up and down with every step.

He stood at the green front door, looking at it, with his hand raised, but for some reason not lifting the unpolished brass knocker. As she got to the open gate she saw that his overcoat was not new and his boots were worn down at the heel. All this she took in quickly, and she knew then, from his stance, that this was not Finlay, and that what her heart wanted was not what the evidence was showing her.

He heard her footsteps, turned to look at her, and lifted his cap.

The cap should have told her. Finlay would never have worn a cap like that, not unless he was playing golf with Father and the sun was going to get in his eyes. It was difficult to guess this man's age; in his forties, perhaps? Hair greying at the sides. Maybe five foot nine, definitely not six feet tall. Weary, accepting his situation, not challenging it.

'Can I help you?' she said.

He smiled, but the smile didn't get as far as his eyes. 'I was admiring your cherry tree.'

'I saw.'

'Wrong time of year to be pruning it, but it could do with some attention.'

'You are a gardener?'

'No. Not officially anyway, I just like trees. I'm a painter and decorator, been in business for almost twelve years, with good references.'

'And you're looking for work?' She saw his shoulders lose some of their squareness and watched him prepare for rejection.

'I know this is an unexpected call, and you may have someone in mind for your jobs already . . .'

'I'm sorry,' she realised as she spoke that she really *was* sorry, 'but I'm afraid I'm not in a position to have any decorating done at the moment.'

He nodded and stepped away from the door.

'I apologise for disturbing you.'

'You aren't, actually. It's just that I don't want anything done right now, this month or next. But if you leave me your details, I'll be in touch when I'm ready.'

'Thank you, that's very kind.'

'There isn't much work about at the moment, I suppose?'

He shook his head.

'I'm sorry,' she said again, unsure why she was apologising. 'Do you have a card I could take?' The first small drops of rain spotted the path and she turned her face to the sky to feel the tiny speckles kiss her cheeks.

'I've run out, I'm afraid, but I can write my details down for you.'

'Let me get the door open and I'll find a pencil.' She found her keys in her coat pocket and unlocked the door, pushing it hard at the point where she knew it always stuck in the frame. It didn't budge. She tried again. 'Bother. I usually use the back door because of this.' She relocked it. 'Follow me.'

They threaded their way up the path at the side of the house in single file and through the tall gate that led to the back garden. She turned the knob on the scullery door and went in. The man stayed on the back doorstep.

'Come in! You need to get out of the rain, and I don't want all the heat to escape.' She saw him hesitate. 'Please. It will get cold in here if the door is open, and there's nothing here worth stealing.' It was a phrase she had used many times before. She watched his face stiffen, but it was too late to apologise; the damage was done. She rushed on as though the words hadn't been said. 'You look cold. And we'll both get soaked if we stay outside.'

He stepped into the scullery as instructed, and closed the door behind him.

Ann had unlocked the door to the kitchen, and was already at the dresser, opening a drawer. 'Oh dear, this pencil is blunt.' She tried another. 'Blunt again.' She guddled about in the drawer. 'I don't suppose you have a pocket knife? Mine seems to have gone the way of so many things in this house.'

She looked back at him. He was already reaching into his coat pocket. She wondered fleetingly if this was wise, inviting a stranger into the house, and asking him to use a knife, not ten feet away from her. She held out two pencils as evidence.

He looked around the kitchen for a bucket. 'Will I sharpen them into the grate, to keep things tidy?'

'Please.' She reached into the drawer again. 'I might have a few more here for you, if you don't mind?'

'This is an impressive range,' he said as he moved the heavy fireguard out of the way. 'More and more people are having these removed and installing new gas cookers instead, but I do like a proper fire in the kitchen.' He rubbed his hands over the embers.

As he leaned forward she saw that his thick woollen overcoat had created the illusion of a well-built man but there was much less of him than she had realised. Money must be tight, she thought. Decorating won't be on many householders' list of essential spending plans during these difficult times. She took her own coat off and hung it on the hook on the back of the door between the kitchen and the hall.

He opened the knife and examined the blade. She had added other pencils to the pile; there were now more than a dozen in various lengths lying on the table.

'You draw?' He examined the lettering on the sides. 'Some of these are softer than the ordinary kind.'

'When I was younger. I'm just using them up before I buy more.'

He took the first one, laying it in the curve of the fingers of his left hand and putting his thumb on the shaft to grip it. She watched as he stroked the penknife firmly from painted wood to graphite tip, slicing off curls of cedar, one for each of the six sides of the pencil. He rotated it and repeated the process. There was, she noticed, a rhythm to the job.

He held the first pencil up vertically to check the grey lead was smooth and then sharpened it to a point with tiny, quick movements, before giving it a final check. He didn't say a word, just worked away in silence.

She took her diary out of her bag and opened it to the correct date. 'Now, tell me your name and how I should contact you when I'm ready for the decorating.'

'Anderson,' he replied. 'Keith Anderson. I don't have a telephone, but you could write? My workshop's just off Dalry Road. I'm not sure how much longer I'll be paying the rent on it, though.'

Ann nodded. 'If the information changes, please let me know.' She reached across the table for the cake tin. 'May I interest you in some parkin?'

Chapter 33

February 1931

The post was lying behind the front door when Ann got back from the greengrocer, basket in hand. She wrestled with the key, gave the heavy front door a mighty heave and stumbled forward with the momentum of her efforts as it opened. She made a mental note to write GET DOOR FIXED on her list of things that needed to be repaired. If it wasn't written down, it wouldn't get done.

Two items. A leaflet about the census, and an upside-down envelope. She nudged them aside with her shoe so they didn't get crumpled by the draught-excluding brush which was fixed to the bottom of the door. Her basket was heavy; as well as vegetables, she had bought flour and butter, and a quarter-pound of acid drops from the confectioners. Her treat for later.

She bent down to pick up the post and smiled as she saw the familiar cursive script in black ink. A letter from Isobel. It had been a while.

Ann was good at deferred rewards. She took the letter to the kitchen and put it on the table next to her knitting. The kitchen, and indeed the whole house, was cold. She had gone out early before relighting the range, but the fire was set, a criss-cross of twigs and newspaper, ready for her return. She tried not to light the big black-leaded monster in the morning unless she was sure she would be in for the day. Occasionally, if she had an afternoon errand, she would let the coals die down to just embers, and put the heavy fireguard over the firebox, and then stoke it back up on her return. It was risky to leave it burning when she went out, even with the guard firmly fastened to the hooks she had screwed into the wall, but since the range also heated the water in the tank above, it was a fine balancing act between safety and practicality.

She lit the single gas ring in the scullery, purchased after speaking to the decorator two weeks earlier, and put the kettle on to boil.

The house was silent apart from the ticking of the kitchen clock, and her own voice. She barely went into the rooms upstairs any more. They were clean enough, but living alone had meant making changes. The bedroom doors were left closed and the parlour unused, and she lived downstairs where there was everything she needed. The drawing room could substitute for a parlour if she ever had need of such a thing, and the old dining room with its glazed double doors opening onto the garden was now her bedroom. She had positioned a bird table outside and she could see the house sparrows and starlings clustering around it when she opened the curtains in the morning. Often, she got back into bed and watched them, just for the joy of it.

The big table in the kitchen was her office and her knitting station and her bakery. It suited her well enough to live this way. She could manage, financially. Her inheritance, and the recent sale of her father's business, had seen to that. She wasn't wealthy, but she was careful. Even with the depression, the interest on the capital sum meant that the bills were paid comfortably with funds left over to be invested, and she could always moderate the coal and the gas if required.

The small pebble in the base of the kettle rattled against the sides to let her know that the water was boiling. She filled the teapot, and turned it three times to the right, three times to the left and then three times again to the right, before pouring the tea into her cup. Finally, before sitting down at the table, she put a couple of lumps of coal on top of the kindling with the tongs and struck a match. At last, she picked up the envelope.

Part of the fun of getting a letter was the investigation before it was opened. The stamp, the postmark, the bent corners and, on high-quality paper, the water marks. Sometimes the ink on the address had run from where the envelope had fallen on a wet pavement, making new colours where the pigments had separated and then dried. 'Finlay could explain that to me,' she said out loud into the space in the air that had been largely empty for the two years since Ursula had died. Seven years since Father had passed away. Fifteen since she had heard Finlay's voice.

She lifted the breadknife and sliced open the flap.

Dear Miss Ann,
I hope this letter finds you well.

She lifted her cup and took a sip of tea before continuing.

I am afraid I have bad news.

Ann felt her heart begin to race.

The family I am employed by have decided they can manage without me. It is completely outwith my control, unfortunately.

This happened at the start of January, just after the turn of the year. I am sorry for not writing before now, but there has been so much to do, and I was unsure about my situation here. They have been kind, and have given me time, but I need to look for another place and there is not much in this area.

Ann knew what was coming and was already nodding her head before the question on the page was posed.

I know it is a terrible imposition, but I wondered if you might have need of a maid for a while, just until I manage to find a new position. I would not be any trouble and I have a little money saved. Perhaps there are jobs in the house you need help with? I will manage, because we have to, don't we?

I am sorry to ask, but I cannot think of another way. It is not a good time to be searching for work. It seems a lot of families have stopped having live-in domestic help, and that only leaves shops and factories.

There are so many men who are looking for employment now, and each and every one of them will be taken on before me.

I do understand if it is not possible, so please don't say yes out of pity.

I am sending my very best wishes for your health and well-being,

Yours,

Isobel

Ann went back to the beginning and read the letter again.

She calmed down and started to talk to the empty room, a habit formed in the two years of living alone.

'Where will she sleep? She can't go back up to the maid's room, that's totally inappropriate for a woman of her age.' Ann opened her diary to a page at the back and lifted one of the freshly sharpened pencils from the jam jar which lived within easy reach on the big table.

'I wonder if she has furniture. How might that be transported?'

She wrote:

ISOBEL
Furniture?
Move?
Which room?
When?

'There are enough beds and wardrobes here in the house. Maybe we could both move upstairs. Isobel could have Finlay's room.' She shook her head immediately, rejecting that particular option. 'Or maybe my old room? And we might be needing a dining room again eventually. I suppose I could have the main bedroom, although not right away.'

She retrieved a sheet of paper from the desk in her room and came back to the kitchen table to write.

My dear Isobel,

What dreadful news.
You may, of course, come back here. This is a generous house for one person. I didn't tell you before, but I came

close to selling it last year. So much has happened since I last wrote properly in November, and there wasn't space to squeeze it all onto your Christmas card.

As you know, Ursula and I kept Black's running with a manager in place until she died, but it was very difficult. Even with legal help, finding a buyer for the company and dealing with the sale was exhausting, despite being very necessary. I simply couldn't continue with it any longer. Father had always hoped that Finlay would come back after university and take over the reins. Ursula and I did our best as his substitutes, but the wholesalers didn't want to deal with women, no matter how competent, and by October last year I had come to the decision that it was time to close the doors. The sale finally went through last month. It was a sad day and I'm not sure quite what I will do with my time but I confess that I am relieved. It has been hard to manage everything alone, these last two years.

My solicitor told me that in the current economy, it is not a good moment to try to dispose of a large house either, so after reading your letter today, it seems fortuitous that I listened to his advice and stayed here at number 25.

You must come back as soon as possible. If Ursula were still here, I'm sure she would agree with me.

Please use the enclosed to buy your train ticket. And if you need to arrange for furniture and other things to be moved then let me know.

Yours,

Ann

She opened the drawer in the dresser where the ledgers were kept and lifted out the household cashbox. Inside, the coins were stored in little cloth bags, separate ones for sixpences and farthings and threepenny bits, and all the other denominations. A selection of bank notes from different Scottish banks in various colours and values were kept in the compartment below. She could remember Father meticulously examining each design with a professional jeweller's loupe whenever there was a new issue.

'Will ten shillings be enough?' There was no answer from the absent voices. 'A pound,' she decided. 'I don't want to embarrass Isobel by sending more.'

Ann kept £100 in the box, more or less; she disliked going to the bank and preferred to be more self-contained. She rifled through the notes and chose a Royal Bank of Scotland one-pound note with the bank's headquarters in St Andrew's Square on the reverse. 'A little bit of home,' she pronounced, as she closed the box and put it away.

Although she didn't like leaving the house with a fire burning, she put on her coat for the second outing of the day. 'If I run to the post office instead of walking, it won't take me long to get there and back. This needs to be sent without delay,' she said, as she fixed the fireguard back into place.

Chapter 34

Early March 1931

Ann raced down the foot ramps into Waverley station with her scarf trailing behind her as though she was still a child in the playground at primary school. She scanned the concourse for Isobel and eventually spotted the familiar figure, thinner than she remembered, standing beside a tall pillar near the booking hall.

'I am so sorry, Isobel,' she panted, 'the tram was full and I had to wait for the next one.'

'Don't fuss, it doesn't matter.'

Ann put her arms around Isobel and hugged her close. 'I am so glad you are here.' She looked down at two small brown suitcases and the battered handbag that was sitting beside them. 'Is this all you've got?'

Isobel shrugged. 'There really wasn't much worth bringing. It's just my clothes and a few keepsakes. I won't take up much room.'

'I can see that. It's a big house for just the two of us. I think we'll rattle about in it a bit.' Ann picked up the nearest case. 'Let me take one of these and we'll go up onto Princes Street and get the tram back, hopefully it won't be as full this time.'

*

Ann led the way around the side of the house to the scullery door. 'It's not that you shouldn't use the front door,' she explained, 'I don't want you to think that matters at all. It's just that the storm door is a bit stuck at the moment. I need to take some sandpaper or something to the side of it. The wood seems to swell whenever there is heavy rain and then the door jams.' She turned the doorknob and went inside, digging in her pocket for her key before unlocking the kitchen door.

'Still leaving it open, then?' Isobel nodded at the scullery door.

'You know how it is,' Ann replied.

'It's the same all over. Doors left unsecured, just in case.'

'I know it's probably unnecessary after all this time, but I can't help it. There was a man a few weeks ago who came to the front door. He was looking for work.' She sighed. 'And I could have sworn, I could really have *sworn* that it was Finlay. But of course it wasn't him, and I felt rather foolish.' She pushed the kitchen door open with her foot and the warmth from the cast-iron range rushed into the cold scullery, diluting the heat as it spread between the two rooms.

Isobel followed Ann into the kitchen. 'You left the fire lit?'

'In your honour. I didn't bank it up this morning so it's really only what's left from last night. I'm trying to train myself to be less obsessive about it, but it isn't easy. I even bought a new fireguard, see? I'll put some more coal on now, and then you can get settled.' Ann moved the heavy metal mesh, lifted the coal scuttle and shook some lumps onto the pale orange embers. 'I thought you could have my old room upstairs for now, and you can work out which one you want in a day or two.'

Isobel pointed to the narrow, carpetless staircase that led out of the kitchen and up to the room above the scullery. 'I was planning to go back to my old room.'

'I won't hear of it. Absolutely not.'

'Where are you sleeping, if you aren't upstairs? I'll not be moving you out of your own space.'

Ann smiled. 'Things have changed a little here. It took me some time to get used to being in the place by myself, and I swithered about it for quite a while. Couldn't make my mind up at all. In the end I commandeered the dining room as my bedroom because the doors open out to the garden. I got some help to move the furniture.' She opened the biscuit tin that was sitting on the big table. 'I made these for you.'

Isobel looked inside. 'Jumbles!' She picked one up. 'It's been a long time since I had one of these.'

Ann pushed the tin a little further across the table. 'Help yourself.'

'If you're sleeping in the dining room, where do you eat?'

'I do almost everything in here, because it's warm.' Ann opened her arms to include the whole kitchen. 'It means I only have two fires to light in the winter. And if I'm honest, most of the time I often only bother with this one.'

'You don't heat upstairs at all?'

'There isn't any point. It would be a waste of good coal. It's saved me a fortune, although I can feel the chill coming down the stairs to meet me in the mornings. But of course, all that will change as soon as you've decided which room you want.'

Isobel nibbled at the almond biscuit. 'I honestly would prefer to go back into my old room, for now at least. It's familiar so I think I'll sleep well up there.'

'I suppose that's alright, if you're completely sure,' Ann conceded reluctantly. 'But not if you're thinking of being the maid of the house again. I won't hear of it.'

'You'll be needing some help, though.' Isobel was already casting a surreptitious glance along the mantelpiece and checking for dust on the backs of the chairs.

'Times have changed, Isobel. I'm not saying it's been easy, but I've managed fairly well since Ursula died. The hardest thing has been the silence, and that won't be an issue now you're here.'

'I know what that's like. When there's no one to have a meal with, and you find yourself imagining the conversations you might have had.'

'Exactly. I walk around this place talking to myself so I don't forget how to use my voice, some days.'

'You can talk to me now.'

'I know.' Ann smiled and then frowned immediately afterwards. 'I don't like the idea of you being in that tiny room, though, especially when there isn't a fireplace up there. But if you really won't change your mind then I've got a little electric fire, and I insist you use it.' She put her hand into the biscuit tin and pulled out an irregularly shaped jumble. 'And you'll not be getting up before six in the morning either. You are my guest, so I don't want to find you down here stirring the porridge before I get up.'

'For now.'

'Pardon?'

'I'm your guest for now. But I'll be needing to find a way to earn a living soon. My savings are almost used up. And I have to return the money you sent. I mean, I'm very grateful to you, but I must repay it.'

Ann ignored the offer. 'I will cancel the champagne, then. And here was I thinking we would be having cocktails every evening and canapés at the weekend for guests.'

'I don't remember ever making a canapé in this house!'

'I was only joking.' Ann could feel her voice tightening. 'I don't miss my old life at all, Isobel. Just the people who were in it.'

Chapter 35

Early April 1931

The knock on the scullery door, left open in the spring sunshine to air the rooms, was hesitant. Ann would have missed it altogether had she not been in the kitchen, arranging damp sheets and towels onto the rails of the lowered pulley, ready for it to be hoisted back up above the stove for a final airing.

'One minute,' she called, dropping a damp tea towel back into the laundry basket before taking the two steps down into the scullery. 'Oh.' She smiled without being aware she was doing it. 'Mr Anderson, if I remember correctly?'

He smiled back. 'That's right. Keith Anderson. I remembered about your front door being stuck so I hope you don't mind me coming around the back.' He held out a large envelope. 'I'm trying to hand these out personally.'

'Hand out what?'

'Your census form. I'm one of the collectors, so if you could fill it in on the twenty-sixth of April, I'll be back some time after that to collect it and I'll take it to the enumerator's office.'

She took the envelope. 'Let's hope it's better than the last two they did.'

'I'm sorry?'

'The last two censuses.'

'I don't think I understand.'

'Never mind. Thank you for remembering about the door. We really must do something about it. It's very inconvenient.'

She put her hand on the doorknob, ready to close the door, but he spoke before she managed it.

'I was wondering, I hope this isn't rude, but would you mind if I washed my hands?'

Ann understood what he wanted right away. 'Of course you may.' She opened the door wider, so he could come in. 'You can see where the soap is beside the sink, and there's a towel on the roller on the back of the door here.' She pointed to the two doors at the far end of the scullery. 'It's the door on the left.'

'Thank you.'

She pulled the kitchen door half closed and went back to hanging up the last of the laundry. After a couple of minutes she heard the water flowing into the scullery sink. He tapped on the door when he was finished.

She beckoned him in and pointed to the empty kitchen chair. 'Perhaps you could go over the details with me, just so I ensure I fill it in correctly?'

'Of course.'

'It must be a long day for you, out delivering forms.'

'I'm glad of the work.'

She nodded. 'I read about the government giving the census jobs to people without other employment.'

'It's something, I suppose. But it comes with strings attached. The work is for several weeks, but we had to sign a paper saying that if we get an offer of other work in that time, we will refuse it.'

'That doesn't seem so bad; it's work, even if it's only for a month or two. Surely that's what matters?'

'It *is* bad, though. If a man has been out of work for six months and is taken on as a collector, what if he's offered a real job in those few weeks? A job that might last for months or even years? How could he turn that down?'

Ann frowned. 'So this *is* another tainted census.'

'I don't remember the '21 census being a problem. Apart from it being late because of the miners' strike, I mean.'

'If a strike isn't a problem, I don't know what is.'

'I suppose, if you put it like that . . .'

'I do. And that's before one considers the difficulties in 1911.' She glanced up at the clock, went over to the range and lifted the lid on a pot. 'It's my lunchtime. Would you like some soup? It's just carrot and lentil, nothing fancy, I'm afraid.'

He hesitated, and then gave in. 'That would be very kind.'

'Bowls and spoons are on the drainer in the scullery.'

He got to his feet and went to collect them.

'It's just me here today. Isobel is out looking for work, a bit like you.'

'Isobel?'

'My friend. She used to live here and has moved back for a bit.'

'There's not much work about. That's why I took this. Any wage is better than nothing at all, even with the strings.'

Ann scooped two great ladles of the soup into each bowl and put the bread and butter within reach. 'Help yourself. The bread is two days old, I'm afraid, but if we don't eat it up it will either be turned into bread and butter pudding this evening or fed to the sparrows. Have as much as you like.'

'Thank you. It's been a long time since breakfast.' He breathed in the aroma rising from the bowls. 'This smells wonderful. My mother used to say that good soup is a meal in itself.' He dipped the spoon into the soup at the side furthest away from him and lifted it to his mouth, sipping from the near side.

Ann noted his good table manners without realising she was doing it.

He paused before taking the next spoonful. 'What did you do about completing the last census?'

'My father would have filled it in if we'd been here but we were away in France at the time so we weren't recorded as existing at all. That is unacceptable in my opinion. We are citizens and we should have been counted.' She took a slice of bread and broke it into four. 'And this time it's just me and Isobel here in the house, so I'd better make sure I do it properly or you might get into trouble.'

'Why was the 1911 census a problem?'

'You don't remember?'

'Not really. I think I'd have been nine years old, maybe ten, depending on the date. My father would have filled it in for us.'

The result of her speedy mental arithmetic surprised Ann; despite her first impressions and his sprinkling of grey hair, he was three years younger than she was herself. 'It was the year when women all over the country refused to fill the form in,' she said.

He couldn't respond because his mouth was full of bread.

'No documentation without representation. That's what we wrote on the forms.'

'We?'

'Well, not me, I was too young, obviously, but Ursula wasn't recorded and my father didn't make a fuss. She went to a party instead so she wasn't even in the house at midnight.'

He swallowed the bread and took another spoonful of soup. 'Ursula is your sister? And she was a suffragette?'

'Ursula was my stepmother. And she wasn't a suffragette, but I think she might have wanted to be. She decided she had responsibilities here, so she did other things instead. I think sometimes you only realise how remarkable some people are when it's too late to tell them.' She buttered the torn bread, taking a thin skim of yellow right to the corners. 'But anyway, the whole census was wrong.'

'More wrong than the suffragettes not filling it in?'

'Far worse than a few empty lines on a census form, in my opinion. The government wanted to learn about the fertility of women, which is a private matter.'

'You seem to know a lot about it.'

'It was terrible. It's so important that we make sure things are done fairly, don't you think?'

He shrugged. 'Yes. But when you are at the bottom of the pile, it's hard to put that above getting food onto the table.'

Ann blushed. 'I apologise. I didn't mean to go on so much. Isobel is always telling me I get too involved in things, but it's hard sometimes, especially when it feels important.'

He supped the last dregs of the soup. 'At least the rain stayed away for me this morning; not sure I'll be so lucky this afternoon, mind.' He pushed his seat back. 'I'd better get moving.'

Ann took her courage in both hands. 'There's usually a pot of soup on the stove.' Her words came out in a rush before she had time to think twice. 'So, if you happen to be passing again and you'd like to have some lunch with an opinionated woman, just knock on the door.'

He seemed uncertain. 'That's very kind, but if you don't mind me saying, will other people not object to a man you don't know sitting in your kitchen and eating your food?'

'You mean Isobel?' She didn't wait for a reply. 'She'll be fine with it. That's not something I'm worried about. And anyway, it's my house so I make the rules.'

*

'You did *what*?' said Isobel when she came back from looking for work. It had been a fruitless search and to make matters worse it had poured all afternoon, and she was soaked from head to foot.

'I asked him in for a bowl of soup.'

'A stranger, in the kitchen? Are you mad?'

'He isn't a stranger.'

'And why would that be, pray?' Isobel took off her sodden shoes and set them down beside the range, but not too close.

'I've met him before. I'm sure I told you about me mistaking him for Finlay.'

'You did. But you didn't say he had come in on that occasion either.' She put her hands on her hips and winked at Ann. 'Is there something you aren't telling me, young lady?'

'Less of the young, I'm a mature woman. It'll be my birthday on Thursday and I'm expecting a cake with thirty-three candles on top.'

Isobel couldn't help but laugh. 'Mature is not really the word I would have chosen.'

'It's only happened twice.'

'And will there be a third time?'

'I don't know.'

Isobel sighed. 'I'm serious, do you know anything at all about him?'

Ann thought for a moment. 'His name is Keith Anderson. He's three years younger than me, but I think he looks older. He's a skilled tradesman, a painter and decorator. One moment . . .' She reached her diary down from the shelf on the dresser and flipped back to February. 'He has an address on Dalry Road, but it doesn't say whether it's a private address or a business address.'

'Anything else?'

'What do you mean?'

'Describe this man who has been sitting in our kitchen, just in case I meet him. I shouldn't want to be embarrassed. And if I ever need to give the police an idea of what he looks like, it would be helpful to know what to say.'

Ann sighed dramatically. 'He's not as tall as Finlay. He has brown hair, and it's going a little grey at the sides.' She looked out of the window at the drizzle. 'I suppose Finlay's hair would be like that now, if he were here.'

'Go on.'

'Mr Anderson is quite thin. His clothes seem to be too big for him. He has a soft voice. Doesn't say a lot. Has this knack of getting me to talk but doesn't really ask questions.' She paused. 'I'm not sure how he does that.'

'And he knows that you don't live here alone?'

Ann folded her arms defiantly. 'I mentioned you *several* times.'

'Good. There are plenty of odd folk around at the moment. People who are desperate. You think I'm joking, but we need to be careful.' She looked through to the scullery.

'No,' said Ann.

'I really think—'

'No. The scullery door stays unlocked.'

'Will you at least be more mindful about locking the kitchen door then? For *me*?' She pointed at the staircase. 'I sleep up there, remember. I could be murdered in my bed.'

'You could lock your door, if you wish? But I suppose you're right. I'll put some oil into the kitchen door lock this afternoon. It's rather stiff.'

'The census is quite soon, isn't it?'

'It's on the twenty-sixth, so I suppose we should have a look and see what the Government wants to know about us this time.'

Chapter 36

End of April 1931

'I saw Keith today.' Isobel was standing at the scullery sink and washing the dishes. She always claimed to be better at it than Ann.

'Oh really? You didn't say you'd gone out.'

'I wasn't out.' Isobel finished washing a sherry glass and set it down carefully on the drainer. 'He came here.'

Ann lifted the glass by the stem, and rolled it between thumb and forefinger, holding it up to the evening sunlight to check for smears. 'Oh?'

'I saw him outside in the street, looking up at the windows when I was scrubbing the front step. He was just as you described.'

'And you asked him in?'

'I did.' She glanced at Ann. 'He was collecting the census form, so I handed it over. And I asked him if he wanted a sandwich.'

'I'm surprised.'

'But you invited him in yourself, more than once, you told me so. And I thought that a man with so little money in his pocket would appreciate a kindness.'

'I suppose I did.' This was one of those moments, Ann thought, where there was a changing of the guard, where the old rules didn't apply any longer and must be abandoned.

'But of course, this is your home too, Isobel, so why shouldn't you have a guest for lunch?'

'Wait a minute . . . Ann Black, you are not jealous?'

'Jealous? Me? Why on earth would I be jealous of you having a visitor?'

'And now, miss, you are blushing.'

'I am not.'

'You are.' Isobel scrubbed at the dried-up egg on the plate. 'He's certainly easy on the eye, I'll give you that much.'

'Oh, stop that. Stop it right now.'

'I speak as I find, that's all.'

Ann shrugged. 'And what was *your* visitor saying?'

'He still has no work, apart from the census, and that's nearly finished now because the stragglers are almost mopped up. No one is having any painting or wallpapering done and the really big houses, up in the Braids and in the Grange, all have their preferred tradesmen who have worked for them for years so there's no room for anyone new. And those people aren't really affected by what's going on anyway, not in the same way as ordinary folk.'

Ann took the wet soapy plate from Isobel. 'I'm sorry to hear that.'

'He's having trouble paying his rent. I don't think he would have told you that, but he felt able to tell me.'

'Why do you say that?'

'Same reason everyone is. No work, and landlords who demand their shilling whether a tenant has got it or not. They've got the power to charge what they want.'

'No, not that! I mean why wouldn't he tell me?'

'Because he wants to impress you, of course.'

'So I will give him some work?'

195

'Ann, you can be so *dense* sometimes. He wouldn't tell you because he wants you to see him as a person you might want as a friend, not because he wants you to *employ* him.'

'I don't see why he would want to impress me. And anyway, he really does want me to employ him, that's why he came to the door in the first place, isn't it?'

Isobel could barely keep her face straight. 'I have said it before, and I'll say it again, sometimes you are not the brightest girl in the class, especially when it comes to matters of the heart.'

Ann shook her head. 'There are no matters of the heart or any other place going on.'

Isobel gave the water in the bowl a last swirl to check for rogue teaspoons, and then tipped it up to sluice the dirty liquid down the plug hole. 'You may think that now, but we'll see what comes out in the wash.'

Ann shook the damp tea towel and inspected it before deciding it would do for another day. 'I'm sorry he's having such trouble.' She folded the cloth, ready to put it on the pulley.

Isobel winked at Ann. 'He said he would come back next week, to say hello. And I'm not going to tell you which day so you can't go out to avoid him.'

'Honestly, Isobel. You should be called Mrs Matchmaker. He's a painter and decorator so he is hardly likely to fit in here.'

Isobel turned to face Ann. 'I *beg* your pardon?'

'I just meant that he probably doesn't like the things I like. It isn't as though he's a professional person.'

Isobel shook her head. 'I honestly never thought I would hear you say such a horrible thing.'

'It's true.'

'Is it now? And what about you and me, then? I'm not a professional person. I left school at twelve and I don't have a qualification to my name.'

Ann shook her head. 'It's different. You are clever, and you read, and you listen to the wireless and you are ... well, you are interested in all sorts of things. I could never consider being friends with someone who isn't curious. Man or woman. It would be so boring. The same conversations all the time.'

'I really am surprised at you.'

'Well, it's just the way it is.' Ann was angry now. 'And I'm going to be out all next week anyway, every single day. I have things I need to do. Things that are *not here*.'

Chapter 37

Early May 1931

The library was busy. It wasn't that people were returning books or borrowing new ones, nor even standing browsing the shelves, but almost every seat at the long tables was taken. The newspaper section was filled with men turning the pages slowly, working their way from the front covers to the back, reading every word and every advertisement. Ann initially thought they were looking for the job vacancies, but as she watched from her position at the reference table, with the *Guide to British Lichens* in front of her, she saw that they were prolonging their visits, delaying going back outside into the street and staying in where they could be distracted from life by the books and the newspapers. The hidden functions of a library are manifold, she realised.

She knew for sure that Keith Anderson would be visiting number 25 today. Isobel had started making bread as soon as breakfast was over, and she was making enough dough for three loaves instead of the usual two. And extra soup, and oaty biscuits as well.

'I'll be out all day,' Ann had said as she left the house.

Isobel had just smiled. 'I'll see you this evening, then.'

*

He arrived at the library just before lunchtime, about the same time she realised her bottom had gone numb from sitting on a hard wooden chair for more than an hour. She moved carefully to a recently vacated seat in the corner so she wouldn't be seen.

He selected a newspaper and took a seat a few rows ahead with his back to her. She could see that he read differently from the other men. He turned to the news first, and he had a little book beside him in which he wrote notes. After fifteen minutes or so he went back to the long rods which held the newspapers and exchanged *The Scotsman* for another broadsheet, then sat down again and worked his way through the news, taking his time and pausing to look off into the distance every so often before returning to the page and writing in his book. Ann wriggled. She needed to go to the lavatory, but the facilities were near the entrance and she would have to walk past him to get to them. Just as she thought that she couldn't wait any longer, he got to his feet and put the final newspaper back in the rack and started looking at the shelves. Non-fiction, she observed.

She seized her chance and headed for the WC. When she looked back before closing the door, he was at the table again, and engrossed in his reading. She didn't like the feeling this gave her.

*

The storm door at the front of the house hadn't yet been closed for the day when Ann walked into the hall. 'Hello!' she called.

There was no response. She hung her coat up and lifted the latest Lord Peter Wimsey novel from her basket. Between the hours she had spent at the library in the morning and the time in the café in the afternoon, she was halfway through it. She wore her stubbornness as though it were a lead dress.

'Did he come, then?' she said as she walked into the kitchen.

Isobel and Keith were sitting opposite each other at the table. A jigsaw was spread out in the space between them; the edges were complete, and some of the foreground. They both looked up at the same time.

'I didn't hear you come in,' said Isobel.

He stood up. More evidence of his good manners, thought Ann.

'Good evening. I'm afraid I'm taking advantage of your friend's hospitality. We started this and it's rather addictive. Just one more piece, you know?'

'A bit like knitting a sock,' said Isobel. 'One more row. And then another one.'

Ann felt like an intruder in her own house as the two of them laughed, sharing the moment. 'Did he come, then?' she repeated. 'The plumber about the problem with the hot water?' She threw the conversational curve ball to Isobel, who caught it, considered dropping it, and then decided to throw it back.

'No, not today. Are you sure it was this morning he was supposed to come?'

'That was what he promised. Perhaps the spare parts haven't arrived or something.' She paused. 'I do agree about jigsaws, Mr Anderson, they are very addictive.'

Isobel stood up. 'You have a go. I can't see any more pieces that will fit; I think I'm too close to it.' She went to the scullery to wash her hands. 'You know, this water seems alright now,' she called, with a hint of mischief in her voice as she ran the tap. 'Perhaps the system has fixed itself.'

'Let's hope so, I could do without another bill.' Ann sat down and studied their progress. She picked up a piece of sky and slotted it into place.

He was still on his feet. 'I think it's time I went. I'll not disturb your meal.' He picked up his cap from the back of the chair. 'Thank you for the bread, Isobel, and the soup.' He looked at Ann. 'And please, call me Keith, Miss Black.'

Ann saw that there was a paper bag with a fresh loaf poking out of the open end on the dresser, and beside it sat a large glass jar of what appeared to be Scotch broth.

She gave in. 'What's for dinner, Isobel?'

'Macaroni cheese, with crispy breadcrumbs on top and roasted red cabbage with walnuts,' replied Isobel. 'It's almost done.'

'Enough for three?'

'I would think so.'

Ann pointed at the chair he had just vacated. 'You may as well sit back down then, Keith.' She tried out the sound of his name. 'Dinner is almost ready.'

'Thank you.' He was clearly uncomfortable. 'But only if you are both sure; I don't want to impose.'

'We are sure, aren't we, Isobel? We quite often make extra, just in case. You never know who might call by at dinnertime.' She looked down at the jigsaw. 'We might need to move this along a bit to make room for us to eat, though.'

They managed to shuffle the puzzle along by taking a side each and moving it an inch at a time along the well-worn wooden table.

'There are plates in the cupboard behind you,' said Ann, 'and cutlery in the drawer below that. And if you don't mind, there's a thick mat on your left, to put the hot food on.'

Natalie Fergie

Isobel opened the oven, and the smell of melted cheese oozed across the kitchen. She lifted the round enamel dish out carefully. It was a bigger one than they normally used for the two of them; Isobel had obviously been scheming this all day. Ann had wondered about it before, and now she was sure of it.

When they were all seated, Ann put the serving spoon into the hot pasta and pushed it round so it was pointing at Keith. 'After you. Guests first.' She watched him eye up a quarter of what was in the dish and serve himself, taking care not to appear greedy. She was sure he would finish the final quarter at the end. He had a look of hunger about him, that was for sure.

Chapter 38

May 1931

'I think you should offer Keith a room here.' Isobel poured flour onto the scales from the mouse-proof tin in which it was kept.

'In this house?' Ann leaned back in the kitchen chair and studied her friend.

'Yes.'

'And turn it into a lodging house instead of a family home?'

Isobel sighed. 'There may be a possibility of it being a family home again one day. But at the moment it's just you and me and we only use the downstairs and often not even all of that. This kitchen is the warmest place so that's where we sit, and let's face it, the drawing room needs attention.'

'My father would turn in his grave.'

'That may be true.'

'And I don't know what Ursula would think.'

Isobel concentrated on weighing the flour for the pastry. Half Allinson's wholemeal, half white. She sifted them together, high above the bowl to aerate the flour, and then tossed the bran which was left in the wire sieve back into the bowl. 'Well, that's the thing.'

'What thing?'

'Pass me the butter, please.'

Ann lifted the lid off the butter dish and pushed it across the table.

Isobel eyeballed two ounces of butter and chopped it against her fingers with the back of a knife and started to rub the fat into the flour so it looked like breadcrumbs. When she was happy with the fineness of the mixture, she added cold water, a dribble at a time. 'What would she think, really and truly?' She gathered it into a dough with her hands and looked up at the clock. 'There isn't time to let this rest, I'm running late. I think I'll just roll it out now.' She paused. 'This is important, Miss Ann.' She only used this title when she was being serious about something and wanted to be listened to. 'What would Ursula Black do if she were here now?'

'I don't know. But why is it my place to bail him out? Why can't his family help?'

Isobel was ready for her. 'There isn't anyone. His father is dead, his mother is unwell and she lives with his aunt in Dundee. There's no room for him there, and it's too far away. And anyway, he isn't a child.'

'How do you know all this?'

'I asked. You know, like you do when you have a conversation with someone?' She finished shaping the pastry into a ball. 'There's no need to look so scandalised. I'm surprised you haven't discovered all this yourself, but I suppose the two of you are always too busy putting the world to rights to worry about the really important things in life.'

Ann was defensive. 'That's not fair. And what about brothers or sisters?'

'Some men don't want to bring up the past, even when they are asked. It hurts too much.' Isobel lowered her voice a little. 'He did have brothers. Two of them.'

Ann knew what was coming. She couldn't believe how insensitive she had been, or how foolish. What must he think of her? 'Tell me.'

'They were both killed on the first day at the Somme. They were never found. He's always wanted to go to Picardy and pay his respects, but never had the money to make the trip.'

'Their poor mother.'

Neither of them spoke for more than a minute.

Ann leaned her elbows on the table. 'Something else we have in common. There's no proper grave to visit, so you always wonder.' She rubbed her face. 'And you always hope, even when it makes no sense.'

'I know.'

'Finlay hasn't gone, you know?' Ann pointed at the scullery. 'I still want to believe that he's going to walk right through that door one day. He'll say, "Long time, no see, any stories, Annie Bee?" in that sing-song way, just like he used to when he came home on leave.' She stared at the door between the scullery and the kitchen, *willing* it to open. 'It's been fifteen years and I still miss him so much.'

The kitchen was quiet, apart from the tick of the clock on the mantelpiece, and the occasional coal spark.

It was Isobel who broke the silence. 'Are you going to do it, then? You could start with Keith and see how it goes.'

'I don't know. I'm not sure I could have a man in the house.'

'We would get used to it. And he's here almost every day now anyway.' Isobel chanced a wink. 'I can't imagine why that would be.'

'Yes, but men are so *big*, even when they aren't. Their voices are huge and they take up so much *space*. They leave the lavatory seat up, and there will be arms and legs and muscles everywhere.'

Isobel didn't respond. She scattered flour onto the table and rolled the pastry out with the rolling pin. A quarter-turn and a few rolls backwards and forwards and then the same again. She opened the door to the pantry and brought out a jar of crimson fruit. 'This is the last of the plums. Until September anyway.'

'The trouble with spiced plums,' replied Ann, attempting to change the subject, 'is that they are altogether too good. Every year I think I have bottled enough from Finlay's tree and every year I am wrong.'

The smell of cinnamon and cloves escaped from the jar as it was opened and they both breathed it in. Isobel spooned the fruit into a white enamel pie dish. 'If I save the juice and add a little more sugar, it would make a syrup, and we could have it poured over something else later in the week. Keith likes a pudding.'

'Oh, do stop it. I get the message.'

Isobel lifted the pastry onto the rolling pin carefully, and flopped the sheet neatly onto the dish before trimming off the extra pieces with a knife and crimping the edges deftly between finger and thumb. Two slashes in the top and it was ready for the oven.

'Right.' Ann folded her arms. 'You've obviously made your mind up about this already.'

Isobel rolled the cut-off strips of pastry into a ball and held it out on the palm of her hand. 'Jam tarts? Or do you want to eat it raw, like you did before you were all grown up?'

Ann took the lump of dough. 'You are avoiding giving me an answer.' She pulled a small piece off and popped it into her mouth.

'In most things, I do share what I think, and I'm grateful that you listen to my opinion. But in this situation we aren't equal. It's your house. And that means it's your decision.' She rubbed her hands together to dislodge the scraps of dough from between her fingers. 'And a little bit of you thinks he isn't good enough.'

Ann didn't speak until she had eaten the rest of the pastry, one small torn piece after another. 'Alright. I give up. I was wrong and I know that now, but you really aren't helping.'

Instead of starting to clear up, Isobel sat down at the table, her hands clasped in front of her. 'Very well, Miss Ann, you really want to know?'

'I do, and less of the Miss, please; I am not a child any more.'

'I think that this is a man who is struggling. He had started his own business and was doing alright until this awful depression came along and knocked him, and thousands of others all over the world, off their perches. He soon won't have anywhere to live and his landlord isn't willing to negotiate on the rent. *We*, on the other hand, live in *your* very large house. We don't use the upstairs at all. Your bedroom was redecorated after the theatre fire, remember?'

'I do.'

'And you wouldn't let it be touched again when the rest of the place was done later on. Let's face it, most of the house hasn't seen more than a dab of paint in years.' Isobel reached out to touch the wall with floury fingers. 'I remember coming here for my interview before you moved from Bruntsfield. The walls were just bare plaster and it all had to dry out before it could be wallpapered. And your mother was ill, so everything was done in a rush. It wasn't looked at properly again until after the war.'

Ann was briefly transported back to a time when not knowing was worse than certainty. 'Even then it just got a lick and a promise. We were all still wondering what had happened to Finlay, and none of us were in the slightest interested in wallpaper.'

Isobel left Ann with her thoughts and gathered together the mixing bowl, the knife and the rolling pin, and carried them through to the sink in the scullery. She came back, rubbing her hands on her apron, and dragged the conversation back to the present. 'Perhaps it's time to give the place a new life? I mean, in spite of the fact that we have electricity now, the soot from the fires has dulled all the colours. No amount of me brushing the walls down will change that.'

'I suppose you're right.'

Isobel took a saucepan down from a shelf. She pushed a bit further. 'You'll think I'm being cheeky but if you wanted to invest in a proper gas cooker instead of just that single burner, it would be an improvement.' She checked inside the pan to make sure it was clean. 'If you offered Keith a room, he could pay the rent with his time and his skill. You would end up with a nicely decorated house to sell or keep or whatever you want, and he would have a roof over his head.' It was rare for Isobel to offer such a complete case for anything.

'You have thought about all this in considerable detail,' said Ann.

'It's true, I have.'

'If we were to do it, where would he sleep? Which room would he have?'

'I have some ideas about that.'

'Why am I not surprised?'

'He can sleep upstairs, it doesn't matter which room. He could have any one of them.'

'Not Finlay's room.'

'Alright. Not Finlay's room.'

Ann seized the opportunity. 'He could have *your* room above the scullery that you refuse to move out of, and you could have a nice room upstairs . . .'

'I suppose I could. But then you and he would be sharing a bathroom and you might not want that.' Isobel picked up the open jar of plum juice and poured the deep crimson liquid into the saucepan. Tiny splatters of red landed on the tabletop and seeped into the wood.

'My head hurts. There are so many problems with this.'

'List them, then.'

'Meat. Would he want to eat meat?'

'He can eat meat away from here if he wants, just not in the house. Not cooked in our pans.'

'What about rent? Although I can see your point about getting the walls painted and everything tidied up, it's all a bit tired now.'

'You don't have to decide about that just yet. After the place is painted, you could charge some rent.'

'How much?'

'I don't know, do I?' Irritation crept into Isobel's voice momentarily. 'How much do you *want* to charge?'

'I have no idea. And I'm not sure that he would be able to do the work on his own. The ceilings are high and I don't think the staircase could possibly be a one-man job.'

Isobel began to patiently tick off the objections on her fingers, one by one. 'See if he has a friend; he surely must know someone who would give their best shirt for some work at the moment.'

Ann's eyes widened at Isobel's suggestion. 'Wait a minute, are you saying that we ask not one, but *two* strange men to live in the house?'

'I don't know, but you are making obstacles where there are none. What I do know is that he seems decent and quietly spoken and needs a place to live. You have that place.' She paused before pulling out her trump card. 'And I think Ursula would approve. She would have done anything to have Finlay back. Think of it as Finlay's legacy, helping other people when he isn't here to do it himself.'

Wisely, Isobel left the idea to percolate, while she added sugar to the plum juice in the pan and put it on the hotplate.

Ann watched her as she worked. 'If we offered Keith a room, how long would he stay? I don't want him to move in and live here for a few weeks while he does some painting and then move out again. I mean, it might be awful and I might *want* him to leave,' she paused, 'but if we did this and it worked then maybe . . .'

'Maybe what?'

'There might be other folk who need a room. There's far more space than we need, even with Keith staying.'

Isobel concentrated on stirring the plum sauce. 'I don't think either of us would want it to be like a tram ride with people only stopping for a week or two.'

'Definitely not.'

'You could tell people you expect them to stay for a year. Or perhaps two years would be better. Time to get settled and be part of the family, if you know what I mean.' Isobel couldn't help smiling. 'But of course, you might want a different rule for Keith?'

Ann ignored the loaded question. 'What about the rent?'

'Oh, for heaven's sake, will you stop worrying about the rent!'

'But people will want to know what the arrangements are.'

Isobel could see that her suggestion had subtly moved from if to when. 'A quarter.'

'I don't understand.'

'A quarter of whatever they earn. If they earn a pound in a week, they pay five shillings, and if they earn a hundred guineas then they pay twenty-five.'

Ann put her head in her hands. 'But that feels wrong. I don't need the money. I have all the investments from when Father's company was sold last year. I don't even touch the capital; I can live off the interest with quite a bit left over.'

'Give it back, then. Tell whatever lodgers you have that you expect them to stay for two years and give all the money back at the end.' Isobel moved the saucepan to a cooler spot on the hotplate to stop the sugary mixture sticking and continued to stir. 'Don't tell them what you're planning, just do it when they leave.'

'I could.' Ann's mind whirred. 'A quarter is twenty-five per cent, and this is 25 Library Terrace. It fits together quite nicely.'

'Miss Ann, I pay no rent here. I earn a little from working in the greengrocer in Morningside but they can't give me more hours, and you still don't charge me anything. I don't think worrying about the rent is really what all this is about. If it makes you feel better, I'll pay a quarter too.'

'Absolutely not.' Ann put her hands on her hips and smiled. 'But would you really move out of that little room? It would be worth doing this just to get you out of there!'

'I could move upstairs, into your old bedroom if you like,' Isobel conceded. 'If that's what will persuade you. I don't mind sharing a bathroom.'

Ann reached for her diary. 'I need to think, and I need a pencil and paper to help me do it.'

Chapter 39

Mid-May 1931

The next time Keith appeared at the scullery door, Ann was ready for him. 'I'm so pleased to see you again,' she began. 'There's something I've been meaning to ask you.'

He put down the toolbag he was carrying. 'I know. I do owe you an apology. I said I'd get that front door fixed weeks ago and it's still not done.'

'It doesn't matter.'

'It matters to me. I don't want you to think I'm a man who doesn't keep his word.' He bent down and opened the bag. On the rough canvas the name G. ANDERSON was painted in worn letters.

Ann shook her head. Why did he have to be so obtuse?

He pulled a carpenter's metal plane from the bag and inspected the blade. The handle on the top of the frame was painted purple and there was a turquoise stripe along one side. 'This should deal with the problem. It won't take more than five or ten minutes, and I'll come back and give the edge a touch of paint tomorrow. I'd have done it before but I had to move out of my flat last week and hand back the keys. It all took longer than I expected and the landlord isn't the most patient of men.'

This wasn't what Ann was expecting at all.

He saw her looking at the lettering. 'My brother's tools. Gregor Anderson. He was a joiner before he got called up. The oldest of the three of us.'

Ann immediately remembered what Isobel had said about his brothers and was again lost for words.

Keith didn't notice and pressed on. 'On a building site, see, there's a lot of men with the same planes and chisels and he told me that he'd picked up another man's tools by accident more than once. He happened upon some leftover paint from the end of a job he was doing and we spent an evening marking up all his tools.' He put the plane down on the kitchen table. 'A few of his friends did the same thing. It's not that anyone would try to steal someone else's kit – you'd be off a site and not asked back if that was the case – but every joiner sharpens in a way that suits him, and let's just say some tradesmen are better at looking after their tools than others.' He tried to find a better explanation, mistaking her silence for a lack of understanding. 'It would be like using someone else's fountain pen after you've got the nib to write the way you want.'

'I see.' She clutched at the most important thing he had said. 'So you've found somewhere else to live?'

He shrugged. 'Well, I have and I haven't. My friend Rab has asked his mother if I can stay at their flat. There's just the two of them, and they're struggling as well. Three can live as cheaply as two and I'm grateful. It'll do until the trade picks up a bit.'

'But if they're having a hard time too, will there be room for you?' Her mind raced. 'I mean, will you have a proper bed to sleep in? Because—'

'I'll manage. We all will.'

'It's just that I was going to put a proposal to you.'

'You are proposing to me?' He grinned. 'That's not a thing I ever thought would happen.'

Ann could feel herself getting tied in knots. 'Not that sort of proposal.'

'What a pity.' He was laughing now.

'Oh, for goodness' sake!' Frustration flooded out of her. 'I was going to offer you a room here. A free room. Without any rent.'

His laughter evaporated as soon as it had surfaced. 'Absolutely not!'

'But I have plenty of space and you need somewhere to live.'

He frowned at her, a heavy expression she had never seen on his face before. 'I do *not* need charity. Not yours and not anyone else's either. I've known Rab's mother since I was a wee lad in primary school. She has made me a kind offer and I will take it because I can help them out while I'm staying there. I am *not* a charity case.' He picked up the plane. 'Now if you'll excuse me, I have a door to sort out.'

Chapter 40

Mid-May 1931

'Keith didn't stay long,' said Isobel as she came back into the scullery from upstairs.

Ann didn't reply. She picked up a potato and dunked it in a basin of water in the sink to get the last of the earth off.

'That's the bedroom fireplaces all cleaned properly at last,' continued Isobel. 'I needed to check no soot had fallen down, with them not being used for so long.'

'Thank you.'

'I don't expect we'll be needing any more fires until October.' Isobel watched as Ann removed the potato skin with the peeler.

'You're probably right.'

'And it might be a good idea to get a sweep booked; it's cheaper in the summer.'

Ann finished removing the outer skin, and kept peeling, taking away more and more of the creamy flesh in a single long, paper-thin strip. 'Good idea.'

Isobel couldn't remember the last time she'd had such a one-sided conversation with anyone, let alone with Ann, who was normally so chatty. She tried again. 'All the rooms are going to need a proper scrub if we're going to have people sleeping up there. And there's the drawing room. I haven't started in there yet.'

'It won't be necessary.' Ann lifted the almost transparent curl of potato up high in the air and dropped it into the bucket beside the sink. She rinsed what was left of the potato, chopped it into quarters and added it to the saucepan beside her before drying her hands. She turned to look at Isobel. 'Let's just say my conversation with Keith didn't go according to plan.'

Confusion was written all over Isobel's face. 'I don't understand.'

Ann examined her fingers one by one; they had become prune-like in the water. 'I didn't get the chance to explain it to him properly,' she replied eventually. 'I said I had a proposal for him and he laughed at me. I'm telling you now, I never want to hear that word ever again. I feel like a complete fool.'

Isobel tried again. 'You are upset because he laughed at the words you used?'

'No.' Ann could still feel the embarrassment. 'I mean, yes, a bit. I said I could offer him a free room. And I stupidly thought he would be pleased about it, but he wasn't. He was furious. He said he didn't need charity and he'd manage without my help. And that was it, more or less.'

'But what about doing the decorating as payment?'

'I told you. He cut me off before I was able to tell him that part.'

Isobel sighed.

'I did my best. There's no point in standing there with that look on your face. He went and fixed the front door and then he said he might be back to paint it tomorrow if he has time, but I'm not sure that's going to happen now. He didn't even say goodbye when he left.' Ann's voice had a catch in it. 'So you see, I've messed everything up. I'm not sure when he'll be back. It might be never.'

Isobel wasn't given to displays of physical affection, but there were times when only a hug would do, and this was one of them. She put her arms around Ann and didn't let go until Ann herself started to pull away.

'I think you care about him having somewhere decent to stay more than you are letting on,' Isobel said softly. 'I expect if you both leave things for a few days it will sort itself out.'

'I'm not sure how.' Ann sat down on one of the kitchen chairs, suddenly feeling as though her legs wouldn't support her. 'I have no idea where he's going to be staying.'

Isobel reached into the deep pocket on her apron.

'I don't need a hanky.' Ann sniffed. 'I'm fine.' She straightened herself. 'I doubt he'll come back. I mean, why would he, after I've offended him so badly?'

Isobel smiled. 'Oh, I think he'll be back, and sooner than you expect.' She laid the contents of her pocket on the kitchen table; the chisel had a smooth wooden handle around which had been painted two stripes, one in purple and one in turquoise. 'I was in the parlour upstairs and I saw him go up the front path when he left. He wasn't hanging about.' She paused. 'He didn't look quite right, though, and that's why I kept watching.'

Ann picked up the chisel, feeling the weight of it in her hand. She rested it on her middle finger, feeling for the balance point before putting it back down. 'This belonged to his brother. He must have left it by mistake.'

'Oh, there definitely wasn't any mistake. He did walk off pretty quickly, it's true, but then he came back after a couple of minutes. I saw him put his bag down beside the gate and he bent down and took something out.' She pointed to the chisel. 'And then he walked back up the path with that thing in his hand and he tucked it in beside the geraniums

217

next to the doorstep.' Isobel tapped the side of her nose. 'I went out to investigate when I came downstairs and there it was, with the purple stripe matching the flowers, as though it had fallen there by accident.'

Ann sat down at the table and ran her finger along the painted handle. She sensed a link to a young man she would never meet. 'You think he'll be back?' She was hard pressed to keep the hope from her voice.

'Sure as eggs is eggs. It's just a matter of when.' Isobel picked up the chisel. 'I'll put this back where I found it, and perhaps by the time he's ready to talk the two of you will have learned to stop dancing around one another and kidding yourselves there's nothing going on.'

Chapter 41

June 1931

'Do you think,' said Ann to Isobel in the garden, as they hung the sheets on the washing line, 'that the house will ever *not* smell of paint?' She finished pegging out the last pillowcase. 'I mean ever-ever? And will we be able to get rid of the dust from all the old wallpaper and plaster?'

'But don't you think it's starting to look better?' Isobel fitted the split end of the long wooden pole they used to hoist the washing line into position and pushed it upwards.

'I suppose so. I would really have preferred more pattern in the rooms but wallpaper is so expensive, and Keith says plain walls are the thing now. Art Deco has arrived in Edinburgh, apparently.'

'He is very meticulous.'

'And so knowledgeable. I mean, I know it's his trade, but I'm sure he's saved me a lot in the cost of the materials. He said the other day that Ursula had made a good choice in selecting the Lincrusta paper for below the dado rails. He says it's very hardwearing.' Ann looked up at the sheets and pillowcases moving gently in the breeze. 'Let's sit here for a bit, away from the smell of that paint.'

'You seem to have become a bit of an expert in wallpapers. I wonder how that could have come about?'

Ann blushed. 'I'm not at all! But I do like the pine-needle colour he suggested below the rail in the hall, and the pale sage above. I wasn't sure about the green, because of all the worrying stories about arsenic, but he says that's not used any more, and anyway it was a lot of nonsense. You would have had to eat a whole roll of wallpaper before it had any effect.'

Isobel smiled to herself and lifted her face to the sunshine. 'It's a good job you like all the embossing, I expect it would be a beast to scrape that stuff off. At least the plain paper isn't so difficult to remove.'

Ann wrinkled her nose, and sniffed. 'Do you remember the Lincrusta being hung? The whole house stank of linseed.'

'How could I forget? The decorator took over *my* kitchen and boiled the paste up on range in a great big pot. He told me it took at least three pounds of flour to a gallon of water, and it had to boil thoroughly so the flour would open up. He didn't trust me to watch the pot for even a minute. And then he beat the mixture over and over until it was soft, as though he was making a cake. I remember thinking I could make an awful lot of cheese scones with three pounds of flour.'

'The work is going so much more quickly now Rab is helping him. It's wonderful how bright the rooms look without all those dark colours, but it does feel quite strange.'

'How do you mean?'

'It's just all a bit sad, as though I'm erasing my family. Ursula took me to choose the wallpaper for my bedroom after the fire. And Father objected and said the colours were too modern, and that he liked things the way they were.' She shook her head. 'And now we are making a bonfire in the garden every week and burning the papers she chose for the rest of the house.' She paused. 'I wondered, you know, when I was older, whether she was getting rid of my mother. Papering over all the surfaces she would have seen.'

'Like a dog marking its territory, you mean?'

'Ugh, what a horrible thought.' Ann shuddered. 'But yes, I think you may be right. Obliterating her and all her nasty ways. I remember going to the decorator's shop to choose the paper for my room from big sample books. I knew it was perfect as soon as I saw it. Cream background with forget-me-nots and pale green leaves. It was our secret, Ursula's and mine, a suffragette bedroom under their very noses. The decorator kept putting books of deep red florals in front of us and we kept saying no!'

'It's such a pretty pattern.'

'It's going to be your room, as soon as you get on and move your things. I don't know why you won't take one of the bigger rooms, though?'

'I like small. I've spent all my life at the back of houses. But I will move, I promise, and I'm very much looking forward to seeing the cherry blossom on your tree next spring. It will be strange to open the curtains in the morning and see the street.'

'I just wish you would get on and do it. I'm sure Keith would help with moving your things. You know, if you want to change the paper or paint it a new colour, that's fine with me.'

'I'll think about it. But the rest of the house should be done first. And anyway, it means I have the advantage of seeing all the colours when they are on a wall instead of just in a tin and that will help me choose. What are you going to do with all the furniture?'

'I'm not sure yet. Most of it is very old. Some even belonged to my grandparents. It's not valuable, but it doesn't suit the place any more, it's all dark and brooding.'

'Maybe Keith could paint it?'

'Possibly. It depends what we're going to do with the house.'

'We?'

'I was thinking of offering you a proper job.'

'A job? Doing what?'

'Just part time. Instead of you looking for extra hours at the greengrocer. Of course, you don't have to say yes. You might prefer parsnips to parkin.'

Isobel smiled, and then became serious. 'I spoke with Rab the other day. He told me that his mother is moving to Glasgow to be with her sister in a few months' time, and that means he'll be in the same position that Keith was in before he moved here. It'll not be long before he needs somewhere to live too.'

'I'm sorry to hear that.' Ann leaned forward, looking up the garden at the herb patch. 'You know, I've been thinking. I know we talked about having other lodgers before, and having Keith here has worked out alright . . .'

Isobel laughed. 'Well, there's a surprise. I can't imagine why you would think so.'

Ann poked her friend in the ribs. 'You're never going to let me forget that, are you?'

'No, I'm not. Watching the two of you pretend not to be interested in each other was highly entertaining.'

'Keith and I have resigned ourselves to a lifetime of teasing.'

'And I will enjoy every minute of it. My work here is done.'

'Not quite, my friend, not quite. If you take my old room upstairs, that leaves three rooms including the parlour. So I've been thinking that two people could share that because it's the biggest.'

222

'Go on . . .'

'Well, you said that Rab might need somewhere to stay soon, so if he took one of the other rooms and if you include Keith, that's four lodgers.'

'We would offer Rab a room too?'

'Why not?' Ann saw that Isobel hadn't even considered this as a possibility. She left the suggestion to settle. 'It was your idea to set the rent as a quarter of earnings, and you were right, Keith is starting to agitate about how much he will pay once the decorating is done.'

'Even though the two of you are . . .?'

'He is happy to not pay anything at the moment while the work is still going on, but he is determined to pay after it's finished.' Ann frowned. 'I will find a way around it, trust me.'

'I hate to say it, but I told you this would happen . . .'

'You did.' Ann pointed a finger at Isobel. 'So, I've been thinking that we could use your plan.'

'Mine?'

'You thought of it, not me. A quarter of earnings for the rent and the food. And at the end of two years, I give it all back to them. And it would be our secret, yours and mine. The lodgers wouldn't find out until the day they leave.'

'Food as well? Are you sure? Groceries aren't given away in the shops for free.'

'I think we can manage. As you said, it's Finlay's legacy. The house would have been part of his inheritance, if he had ever come home.' Ann looked back down the garden towards the kitchen, past the washing blowing gently on the line. 'I don't know that I'll ever be able to lock the back door, but he's gone. However much I want the impossible to happen, it isn't going to. I know that, deep down. Maybe it's time to find a different way of remembering him.'

Chapter 42

October 1931

The letter was delivered on Monday morning. Black ink, scribed on a small envelope, the paper stiff with prosperity. Isobel picked it up off the doormat and studied the handwriting.

Not elderly, but they are uncertain about the address, she reasoned. And there was something about the E for Edinburgh that was familiar. She placed the envelope carefully on the hall table with the other post, and stepped over the canvas rucksacks and abandoned walking boots which had been deposited in the hall the evening before by Keith and Ann, so urgent was their need for sleep.

In times past it would all have been left for her to tidy away: boots polished and put in the hall cupboard in a neat row, bags emptied of wet and muddy clothes and taken through to the kitchen to dry in front of the range while the contents were sorted and scrubbed clean. Not any longer. Times had definitely changed and Ann would have her guts for garters if she so much as moved a bootlace.

Isobel returned to the kitchen and ran her hand along the back of the chair and across Rab's shoulders. He was sitting at the table in his working trousers and braces, a collarless shirt, and socks that needed attention from a darning needle. He had moved into the house at the end of September, and over the last week, ever since Ann and Keith had waved goodbye and headed off to the bus station, things had started to change.

They had enjoyed having the place to themselves; laughing and chatting with no one to hear. He had told her about the accident which had happened more than twenty years before in a house on Library Terrace, although he couldn't be sure which one. He had been thirteen and not big enough to be labouring on many of the building sites even though he'd been out of school for a whole year. His uncle had known that money was tight and found him a few hours' work but afterwards he had never forgiven himself for what happened. Rab explained how a dod of lime plaster had fallen from the plasterer's hawk and landed square on his face as he looked upwards from below. The hawk had been full and heavy and it had taken a minute for the tradesman to get down the ladder safely and scoop him up. All the while he had been screaming his head off, and then he had been held under a tap, dunked into a bucket of water and got soaking wet and half frozen in the cold. He told her how the man whose house it was going to be had handed over his good coat to stop him from freezing half to death; a coat which had been stored safely in the wardrobe with mothballs stowed in the pockets until he had been old enough to wear it. He had used it for years until it had eventually become threadbare.

Isobel had stroked his face and kissed the burn scars and the blind eye and said how pleased she was that he had come back to this street and not been frightened away. Neither of them cared about the age gap; six years was such a small thing to bother about when so many had lost everyone who mattered. For three nights now,

225

they had slept side by side in her narrow bed in the room above the scullery, and she wanted him never to leave.

'Porridge?' said Isobel. 'Or toast and mar-mal-adeee?'

He smiled at the deliberate mispronunciation. 'Toast, please.'

She opened the bread bin and took out the wholemeal loaf, made the day before with Dr Allinson's best flour.

'I suppose I may get used to this . . .' he paused, not wanting to offend, ' . . . this wholesome bread.'

'Since you live here now, you've got no choice,' she replied, setting about the loaf with the bread knife. 'You'll not get that white stuff in this house, so if you're wanting it you'll need to be buying it yourself and eating it on the street corner.' She put the slices between the mesh of the wire toaster and set it down on the hotplate.

'I wonder what time they'll rouse themselves,' he said.

'About now, actually,' said Ann from the doorway, taking in the scene, the comfortable space between her friend and this man who had been chief ladder-steadier for the last couple of months.

Rab jumped up from the chair and Ann could have sworn that he blushed.

'I'll just get my shoes,' he said and disappeared up the scullery stairs, stopping halfway up as he realised he had just revealed everything that needed to be known about the sleeping arrangements over the last few days.

Ann raised an eyebrow and smiled at Isobel.

Isobel ignored her. 'Do you want some toast as well? There's another loaf; I made two.'

'Toast and mar-mal-adeee,' said Keith as he entered the kitchen. 'The second-best breakfast after porridge. Yes, please!'

'Was the youth hostel good, then?' Isobel didn't under-stand why anyone would want to stay in such a place. 'Worth going all that way in this October weather to stay in a draughty hut in the country, far away from your creature comforts and your own bed?'

'It was.' Ann sat down at the table. 'Youth hostels are the future of holidays. So much more fun than guest houses, even though there are chores to do.'

'We met some interesting young people, but I think we were the oldest folk there,' added Keith. 'It was marvellous to be away from the city for a little while, in spite of the draughty dormitories.'

Rab returned, and the four of them sat around the table, eating the toast, spread with a little butter and a scraping of marmalade to make the jar last.

Ann listened as the room filled with stories and ideas, and thought that perhaps she was creating a family of a different kind.

*

After the men had left, putting their plates in the scullery sink and donning coats and caps to go to the next street to give an estimate for the painting of an entrance hall and staircase, Ann and Isobel stayed at the table and refilled the teapot halfway, eking a fifth and a sixth cup from the tea leaves.

'So, am I right in thinking you might be a little bit smitten with our Robert?'

Isobel reddened. 'Just a touch.'

'You still haven't moved upstairs, so I was going to suggest you choose some paint for your old room.' Ann pointed to the room above the scullery. 'The one you have been so determined not to give up. But I'm now wondering if that will be necessary.'

Isobel sighed and got to her feet. 'Miss Ann, sometimes you are so sharp you'll cut yourself.'

'I'm right, though, aren't I?' Ann took a last mouthful of tea. 'It's about time you had a little happiness, and if Keith and I can find it so unexpectedly, then why not the two of you?'

'Maybe.'

'Now, have there been any letters? Post that came when I was away?'

'On the hall table. It's all next to the heap of hats and gloves that you left there last night.'

Ann went to investigate, returning with the five envelopes.

'A bill. Another bill. An official letter about . . .' she tore open the envelope, '. . . repairs to the pavement. Yet another bill. And,' she paused, 'a hand-addressed letter from person or persons unknown. How intriguing. I hope this is a nice surprise and not something unpleasant.' She turned the envelope over and examined the back. 'Thick paper. No seal. No return address. Curiouser and curiouser, as Alice would say. Pass me the bread knife before you go upstairs, there's a dear.'

But Isobel had already left. Ann leaned forward and grabbed the knife herself, shaking the crumbs from the serrated edge.

Chapter 43

October 1931

When Isobel came back downstairs, she found the scullery door wide open. A brisk breeze was coursing through the kitchen, causing the fire in the grate of the range to burn more brightly than it had before. The opened envelope lay on the table. She assumed the door had been blown open by the wind and went to close it, but was surprised to see Ann standing at the bottom of the garden, leaning against Finlay's plum tree. She seemed to be slumped against the trunk, using it for support.

Isobel pulled her cardigan more closely around her. 'Is everything alright?' she shouted. There was no response. She hurried up the path which led to the far end of the garden. 'Is everything alright?' she called again.

Ann didn't seem to hear the words, and it wasn't until Isobel was standing right in front of her that she looked up. She held out the letter and shook her head, as though she had run out of words.

Isobel took the sheet of paper and steered Ann back towards the house. It really was too cold to be standing about outside without any stockings on.

'Read it,' demanded Ann. 'The absolute cheek of it.' She had changed from being silent to positively sparking with anger.

'What?'

'Just read it. I can't . . . just *read*.'

Isobel sat down at the table. 'You make another pot of tea; it looks as though we'll be needing it.' She settled in the chair and unfolded the paper. 'I must make an appointment to have my eyes tested,' she said under her breath as she peered at the unfamiliar handwriting.

9th October 1931

Dear Miss Black,

I am writing to you today to very belatedly express my condolences on the loss of your father and Mrs Black, and of your brother Finlay.

I need to give you what may or may not be welcome information. I am aware that what I am about to say may cause either acute distress or joy, and if it is the former, please allow me to apologise in advance.

My name is Beatrice Sidcup. I am writing to introduce you to Olivia, my daughter. She is seventeen years of age now, and a hardworking, bright young woman.

She is also your late brother's daughter.

Isobel gasped.

'It is nonsense, of course,' said Ann. 'Finlay had no children, no girlfriend, no fiancée, nothing at all like that.'

'Well, not that we know of . . .' Isobel's voice drifted off under a glare from the other side of the kitchen and the clatter of the kettle being slammed down on the hotplate. She went back to the letter.

I am sure that you will have many questions, and I look forward to having the opportunity to explain further. I would like you to meet Olivia, but would prefer to see you privately first to discuss the rather sensitive circumstances of this revelation.

'She wants to meet you.'

'I know she does. It is quite ridiculous.'

'But will you do it?'

There was no answer. Isobel went back to the letter.

Please be assured that I would not be contacting you after seventeen years if it were not absolutely essential.

If I might be so bold, this is a matter of some urgency, for reasons I will explain in person. I will call on Friday at three o'clock.

Yours sincerely,

Beatrice Sidcup (Mrs)

Isobel tried again to remember where she had seen the handwriting before; it was just at the edge of her memory and she couldn't bring it back. 'That is *quite* a letter.'

'Isn't it just?'

'What do you make of it?'

'She clearly wants money.'

'She doesn't say that.'

'Something must have happened and now she needs to blackmail me about this girl's parentage. What other possible reason could there be to keep such a secret, if in fact it is true, which I very much doubt.' Ann's voice was brisk, as if she was talking to a disobedient child. 'Well, she's on a hiding to nothing. I'm not paying her a penny.'

Isobel read the letter again. 'It says that she is married.'

'The girl? Unlikely.'

'No, this Beatrice Sidcup.'

'It doesn't.'

'It does. It has "Mrs" in brackets, see?' She held out the letter but Ann was shaking her head.

'The barefaced cheek of it. Anyone could write that. I could do it myself and no one would know if it was the truth or a lie.'

'She's coming on Friday. And this is Monday. It's hardly any time at all.'

'That's what she thinks! I'll write and say she is not welcome.'

'I don't think . . .' Isobel turned back to the first page. 'There's no return address. I'm not sure you can stop her.'

'No address? There must be.' Ann seized the letter. 'You are correct.'

'It's bold,' ventured Isobel.

'Bold? It's rude, that's what it is.' Ann paused. 'And that's what I will say plainly to her face when she turns up on my doorstep.'

Chapter 44

October 1931

'I don't know what you're worried about.' Keith sat on the edge of the bed, dressed for work apart from his socks and shoes. 'You don't know this woman and you certainly don't need to impress her.'

Ann leaned forward and examined her reflection. 'I look like her.'

'You look like her?' He shook his head. 'You haven't even met her yet.'

Ann closed her eyes, pushed the fingers of both hands into her hair like giant combs and ruffled it, gently at first and then vigorously, turning it into a nest a rook would have been proud of.

'What on earth are you doing?'

'I look like her. No matter what I do, I still look like her.' She kept poking and twisting, creating more and more knots.

He got to his feet and took the three steps required to stand behind her. He rested his hands on her shoulders. 'What are you talking about?' he said softly.

She pushed the tangle of hair back from her face and studied her reflection. 'Marginally better, I suppose.' Tears formed in the corners of her eyes and began to spill over onto her cheeks, making little channels in her just-applied face powder.

He waited.

'It's no use. As soon as I brush it again, she will be back.'

He leaned forward so that their reflections were side by side. 'Who will be back?' He kept his voice low and quiet.

'My mother. I look like my mother.' She flopped the tangle of hair forward and flipped it back again. 'See?'

He didn't immediately respond. It seemed important not to dismiss the outburst with anything flippant.

Eventually, after perhaps a minute of consideration, he spoke. 'I mean, I never met her, but I've seen the photographs of your family, and she's very different. Your face is rounder, and she had a high forehead and you don't have that. I'm trying, but I can't see anything of her in you.'

'I'm not talking about Ursula. My mother was called something else, and there are no photographs of her in this house. I burned them all after Father died. I couldn't do it before then because he would have objected, but I did it afterwards. I burned them or I cut her out of the pictures with my needlework scissors. You wouldn't have known about her because I don't speak about her at all. I haven't said her name in more than twenty years. She was a despicable, wicked, unkind woman who abused Isobel and I will never forgive her for it.' She rubbed her hair again, tangling it even more. 'And I look like her and every time I catch my reflection in a mirror she is in this house again and I cannot *bear* it.'

Keith straightened up. He didn't know what to say.

'And now look at me. I've made it worse, if that were even possible.' She lifted up a wedge of hair. 'How am I going to sort this out before Friday? Beatrice Sidcup will have a field day with her opinions about how I look.'

Keith ran his forefinger gently across the back of her neck. 'Perhaps we need Isobel's advice?'

'She has gone to help Agnes at number 38 this morning and won't be back until lunchtime.' Ann glared at her own reflection. 'My mother has been dead for more than two decades, but she is still having a malicious effect on me, on this house, on everything. I should have sold the place as soon as I inherited it.'

He shook his head slowly. 'I'm sure it feels like that at the moment, but I'm afraid I don't agree. If you had sold it, then when I knocked at the door looking for work it would have been someone else who answered and we would never have met.'

'I suppose . . .'

'And,' he continued, warming to his theme, 'you would have bought a little flat to live in by yourself and there would have been no room for Isobel when she needed a home. That plum tree down the garden might have been cut down to make way for a summer house, instead of giving us spiced fruit for our pies. And most importantly, Mrs Beatrice Stuckup wouldn't have been able to find you and you wouldn't have that letter about your brother.'

Gradually, Ann began to feel calmer. Everything he said was true and she wasn't thinking logically at all, which, for someone who loved nothing better than a proper plan and a good list to go with it, was most out of character. 'You know, you really should stop calling her that. I am quite likely to say it in front of her and then where would we be?'

'I'll try to remember.'

'Just see you do. It's your fault we called her that in the first place!'

'I think,' he said carefully, 'that you look like Finlay. And like your father. You have curly hair, and I can see in their photographs that they did too, despite their best efforts to control it.'

'My mother had straight hair. Fine and straight. She hated my curls and always insisted that my hair was brushed flat and put into plaits. Sometimes she pulled it so tight it gave me a headache. It was as though I had grown curls on purpose to spite her.'

He changed the subject. 'Tell me about Finlay.'

She sighed. 'Finlay was kind. He was everything she was not. He could be annoying sometimes, but after he rescued me from the fire things seemed to change between us. It was as though we were sort of stuck together, in a good way. He was untidy, and he was impulsive, and loved adventures, and he wanted to learn to fly, but never had the chance. You're right about his hair, it was always escaping somehow, and he tried using all sorts of oils and potions on it because curly hair wasn't the fashion, but he hated the smell of them so in the end he just gave up trying. In the photo he had taken before he went away, the last one, where he was dressed up in his uniform, you can see a little twist of hair under his officer's cap. That was what he was like; trying to do the right thing and be responsible but somehow a little bit of fun always escaped.' She looked at the photograph of her brother on the dressing table. 'And even now, I don't know where he is. He vanished and never came home. There are days when I wonder if it's a game he is playing with me. I know you understand, because your brothers are still missing too.'

'They are, yes. In my head Harris is still sharing his marbles with me and Gregor is pulling me out of all sorts of scrapes.' Keith folded his arms and hugged himself tightly in an effort to keep his feelings under control. 'This is the real reason you never sold the house, isn't it?'

She nodded. 'Just in case, because Finlay told me, he absolutely *promised* that he would be back, and I believed him.'

'I think I would have liked your brother.' He touched Ann's comprehensively messy hair and hauled them both back to the present. 'So what would he have done with all this?'

She thought about the question for a moment before replying. 'Scissors, definitely. And he would have been the one holding them.'

'And is that what you want to do? You always wear it braided, which is a little surprising, given what you've just told me.'

'It's habit. Ursula braided it too, but not tightly. And then I put it up of course, as I got older. But mostly I simply can't be bothered with it. I have more important things to be thinking about than hairpins. And the fashion is for sleek hair, and little pin curls, and mine will never behave like that. I'm a lost cause.'

'Will you let me brush it?'

'You?'

'To get rid of the tangles. I've never brushed anyone's hair but my own, but we are going to have to do something before Friday.'

'Perhaps I should go out now and find a hairdresser who can chop it all off. I'm sure people think I should be able to forget about that horrible woman. That I should just put it all aside and go on with my life.'

He laughed. 'I wouldn't dare.'

Ann spun round and pointed an accusatory finger at him. 'Don't you understand? She is *here*. Here in this house, every day. It's not something to laugh about. There's not a single day that she isn't in my head. All her nasty comments and snide remarks. And as I get older it's getting worse because with every day that passes I look more and more like her.' She smashed her hairbrush down on the dressing table. 'I cannot escape her.'

Keith knew he needed to say something, and quickly. 'Does Isobel know you feel like this?'

'I haven't said anything to her. It's not anyone else's problem but mine.' She waved her hand towards the front of the house. 'I talk to myself about it all sometimes, when I'm up on Blackford Hill and no one can hear me. I practise what I would say to my mother now, if she were here. But she isn't, so it's pointless. It doesn't change anything.' Ann looked out of the window, trying to focus on the bird table, where a house sparrow with a twisted foot was pecking at an apple core that had been put out that morning. 'I look at the birds outside, and that helps. They are all slightly different so I try to work out exactly which one of them I'm seeing and it gives me something else to think about.' She paused. 'I wasn't joking about moving house, you know? For a while, after Ursula died, I really did think that if I moved, it would be better. I even got as far as looking at other places. I went on trips to Linlithgow, and Glasgow, and Perth. And I was shown new properties, just built. Houses without any ghosts.'

'And did it help?'

'It did not.' She sighed. 'So I am *stuck* with her.'

'I'm sure—'

Ann didn't allow him to finish. 'At least when Ursula was here, I could talk to her about it.' She stopped, and her voice softened. 'And I spoke to Finlay, of course. He was the only one who really understood, especially after fighting at Ypres. He knew what it was like not to be able to forget things he had seen and heard, even when that was all he wanted in the world.' Ann stood up quickly and walked to the door. 'I am going out. I cannot bear to be in this place for another minute.'

Before Keith knew what was happening, she was gone. Her shoes clattered along the tiled floor in the hall, and he heard the front door slam. He rushed through to the drawing room just in time to see her march out of the gate, leaving it to swing in the wind. She had grabbed the Fair Isle hat she had knitted for him off the hall table on her way past, and her hair was shoved haphazardly underneath it with just a few straggly locks trailing. If she had been going any faster, she would have been sprinting.

Chapter 45

October 1931

Keith was sitting at the kitchen table when Isobel returned from helping Agnes. She dumped her basket of groceries on the table beside him.

'I thought I'd go to the shops since I was out already. Is Ann in? I need to ask her about the baking for tomorrow.'

'She is not.'

Isobel began to unpack the brown paper bags. 'I was thinking I might make sly cakes. It seems like the right thing, under the circumstances.' She reached up to the high mantelshelf and took down the well-used copy of *Allinson's Cookery Book*. 'I was looking through this last night for inspiration and found the recipe. I used to make them for Ann and Finlay when they were younger. They called them fly cakes. I thought I might put some in the oven this afternoon so you and Rab can test them out and give your approval.' She turned around to find Keith with his head in his hands.

'Or I might not, of course.' She put the book down on the table. 'Keith?'

There was no reply.

'Keith?' She was alarmed now. 'Has something happened? Is Rab alright? Is it Ann?'

He looked up at her with red-rimmed eyes. 'I don't know. I was trying to help and it all went wrong and she stormed off and I don't know where she's gone. She was not right.'

'Not right?'

'I'm frightened for her. And I should have gone after her and I didn't and now I don't know what to do.'

'Tell me. Tell me everything.'

Keith took a deep breath. 'Have you seen her looking in a mirror lately?'

'A mirror? I can't say I have, although she's not really one for primping and fussing, that's for sure. But now you come to mention it,' she looked down into the scullery, 'the little mirror beside the door there, the one I use to check myself before I go out, that's gone. She moved it a few weeks ago, told me the glass was cracked, which it was, in one corner. The crack wasn't bothering me in the slightest; it was still perfectly serviceable. But she hasn't replaced it.'

'Any others?'

'There's the one in the drawing room above the fire, but we never go in there anyway, and the same goes for the parlour upstairs and there's the one on her wardrobe, of course, but that's usually draped with scarves and wraps. So that only leaves the one on her dressing table and the one in the downstairs bathroom, and it was still there this morning. Why are you asking about mirrors?'

'She says she looks like her mother.'

'Like Louise?'

'Was that her name? She wouldn't even say it.'

'But she doesn't look like her. Well, maybe a little, but she's much more like her father, and Finlay, of course.'

'She said that when she looks in a mirror, she can see her mother looking back at her. And she messed her hair up, rubbed it into knots and made it all tangled. I think she was trying to get rid of the person she could see in front of her.'

Isobel sat down suddenly as though all the strength had gone from her legs. 'So Louise is back, is she? I thought that nasty piece of work was gone for ever. She made everyone's life a misery, apart from her husband. She had to hide her evil ways from him or I'm sure he would have had something to say about it.'

'I'm not sure I should ask any more.'

'She never wanted Ann; she wanted another boy. Louise hated her. I mean *really* hated her. The thing with her hair comes from that. It was all about control. Louise used to brush Ann's hair so hard the curls were stretched out until they were quite invisible. And she put oil on it so it would stay flat, plaited it very tightly so that no stray bits would escape. Ann wasn't allowed ribbons or clasps like the other girls.'

'That's a disgusting way to treat a child!' Keith could barely contain his anger.

'She used to get a lot of headaches, but after Louise died, I used to do her hair for her here in the kitchen, before she went to school, and there were no more headaches. And when Mr Black remarried, Ursula would plait it into very loose braids, and loop them around her head like a halo.'

'Well, I'm sorry to say it Isobel, but this Louise woman has never gone away, in Ann's head at least.'

'That bitch!' Isobel put both hands flat on the table and pressed down, as though to squash something. 'I'm sorry but there isn't another description I can think of. When she was unwell, Louise used Ann like her personal servant. She would send her to get things from me in the kitchen instead of ringing the bell like any normal person. As soon as Ann was settled to read a book or draw a picture, she would be interrupted and sent on an errand. The poor girl got no peace at all. Ann would sometimes sit here in the kitchen where you are sitting right now and ask me questions. "Isobel, am I an impossible child? Am I an awful girl?" And I would say no, of course. And then one day I asked her who was saying these things to her, I think she was about eleven years old then. She said it was Louise. I'm ashamed to say that I didn't believe her, because what mother speaks to her daughter like that? I just thought she was lying because she was in trouble over something. I mean, all children tell tales, you know?'

He nodded.

'I didn't understand until one day when I was carrying the tea things through to the drawing room. I must have been particularly soft-footed that day, so I heard it with my own ears. It was to do with Ann's name. Louise told her that she was *an* awful child, and that she was just *an* inconvenience. She was using her name as a weapon against her.' Isobel stood up and began to put the dry goods away in their labelled jars. 'I don't think she would want me to have told you about it, though. It's been a secret all these years.'

'I won't say anything, I promise. I do sometimes think there have been too many secrets in this house. Perhaps it's time to bring them out into the daylight where they can be seen for what they are.' He got to his feet. 'I'll put the kettle on. I think tea is in order.'

As he spoke, the back door opened and Ann walked in, chilled from the wind.

'Oh, you're here at last,' said Isobel, trying to bring some normality to the situation. 'I was wondering about making a sly cake for our visitor tomorrow, or do you think just parkin will be enough?' She looked at Keith's Fair Isle hat, still pulled down haphazardly on Ann's head.

'I have been to the hairdresser,' said Ann, ignoring Isobel's question, 'but there were no appointments available.' She pulled off the hat. 'I think I need to take you up on your offer of brushing the tangles out, Keith. I can't see the back at all, and it may take some time. It's either that, or you'll need to just cut it all off.'

Chapter 46

October 1931

The drawing room at the front of the house hadn't been used for almost a year. Ann and Isobel stood in the doorway and took in the vastness of the task ahead of them.

'I'll find you one of my working headscarves to tie over your hair,' said Isobel.

Ann made a snipping motion with her hand. 'I was serious about the scissors!'

Isobel surveyed the room. 'I don't think we should add haircutting to the list of jobs to be done before tomorrow. There's more than enough to be getting on with as it is.' She put her hands on her hips and took a deep breath. 'Come on. Let's get started. If we work steadily, it won't be so bad.'

Ann hoped that Isobel's confidence was well placed. The room hadn't been touched since the previous December. Even then Ann had wondered why she had bothered when there had only been herself in the house, but as she had walked back from the shops in Morningside, she had caught glimpses of Christmas trees in her neighbour's front windows. She had reluctantly tried to join in with the festivities, opened the shutters just a peep, and had even hung some paper chains on a large plant she had placed in the bay window. It had almost ended her, trying to carry the heavy earthenware pot through from her room at the back of the house. Eventually, she had edged it onto a wooden trolley with wobbly wheels and managed to get it through that way. The trolley had then died and so had the plant, left alone through the spring months in a dark, unheated room.

Isobel shivered. 'We'll need to light a fire.'

'The chimney hasn't been swept for two years. I didn't bother last winter.'

'Do you think we could risk it?'

'Definitely not,' said Ann hastily. 'I should have had them done in the summer when you suggested it. Mind you, the chill may speed her visit up somewhat. Maybe the four of us should just go out for the day and avoid seeing her altogether.'

Isobel shook her head. 'If she has something to say, and if it's about Finlay, you *are* going to let her visit, and you *will* be polite and make her welcome, at least until you know what it's about.' Isobel walked over to the big bay window. 'We need to draw these curtains and air the room at the very least. That should help a bit.'

'I know, but it's such a mess in here. We can't use the parlour upstairs. Keith and Rab stripped the wallpaper off last week, remember? And the two of them work fast, but with the best will in the world they aren't going to paper and paint a room that size overnight.'

'Well, she can't go into the old dining room. That's your bedroom now and it would be too much effort to start moving furniture for what might be a ten-minute visit. So really, we don't have much choice.' Isobel bent down and ran her finger along the edge of the skirting board. 'This place needs more than a quick clean. It's the one room I haven't been into properly.'

Ann sighed. 'I know it's my house and I should feel proud of it and want everything to be perfect, but it wasn't me who asked her to visit with just a few days' notice. I suppose we could plug in an electric fire to warm the place up a bit. Thank goodness Keith and Rab have finished the hall and the stairs, at least it looks respectable when you walk through the front door. But honestly, Isobel, why am I worried what a stranger will think about the decoration of my home?'

'Everyone does. It's human nature.' Isobel walked around the room slowly, her fingers stroking the canvas dustcovers on the furniture. 'You know, if you like how the room looks when we've got it clean and tidy then maybe we could all be sitting here with a roaring fire and some chestnuts on Christmas Day? Wouldn't that be nice?'

Despite the cold wind, they opened all four of the sash windows, and began to get the room aired. They carried Keith's tall A-frame ladders down the newly painted stairs very, very carefully, and started attacking the ornate cornice with feather dusters, before moving on to the lights. Ann steadied the ladder and Isobel climbed up to remove the glass globes, one at a time.

'When were these last cleaned?' said Isobel, horrified.

'Not since you left, I don't think.'

'It's a wonder anyone can see a hand in front of their face with the state of them. They need a proper wash and polish. I'll go and put some hot soapy water in the sink. I'm sure we'll soon have them looking much better.'

On her return from the kitchen Isobel brought the wireless with her and plugged it in. The Home Service was broadcasting music, which seemed to speed up their work.

They removed several years' worth of spiders' webs from the corners, and when Keith and Rab came home at lunchtime, they helped to take down the heavy crimson velvet curtains and hung them over the washing line in the back garden for a good beating.

Fortunately, the dustcovers had kept the worst of the grime off the furniture, and when Ann had hard-brushed the carpet, and Isobel had washed the black painted edges of the floor with a mop and bucket, and polished the mantelpiece and the tiled grate, the room looked quite presentable. Clean, but cold. It was still not somewhere anyone would want to linger, but that suited Ann very well.

'Tomorrow morning, I'll get up sharp and get the windows washed so we can get the curtains back up,' said Isobel. 'Mrs Stuckup isn't coming until the afternoon, so we've got plenty of time.'

*

Isobel was as good as her word, and in the morning the sash windows were washed inside and out. And that was when it happened.

The storm door had been left ajar while the tiled vestibule and the front step were drying. A gust of wind blew through and caught one of the unhooked windows. It swung back suddenly, clattering against the frame. A large crack appeared in the glass, and then a second one, and then a third, and finally a section of the windowpane crashed to the ground, leaving a snaggle-toothed gap in the glazing.

Isobel gasped and lifted her hand to her mouth. 'Oh my! Oh my goodness.' She turned to look at Ann, who had heard the crash and run through from the kitchen. 'I am so sorry. So, so sorry. I should have been more careful, Miss Ann,' she said, reverting to the past.

Ann took Isobel by the shoulders and studied her closely. 'Are you hurt?'

'I'm so sorry,' Isobel repeated.

'Stop that. Are you hurt?'

Isobel shook her head. 'No, I just got a terrible fright and I'm so—'

Ann left Isobel and walked over to the window to examine the damage. And then she started to laugh.

Isobel looked at her in astonishment. 'This isn't funny.'

'Yes,' squeaked Ann. 'Oh yes, it is.'

'I will pay for the window, I promise.'

Ann could barely speak.

Isobel waited, not seeing the amusing side of it at all.

Eventually, Ann managed to draw breath. 'You will do no such thing.' She sat down on a newly uncovered chair. 'Look at us. We have turned ourselves inside out and back to front trying to get this room ready for a complete stranger and for what reason? So that we can look as though we are something we are not.'

'We have?'

'I think Mrs Beatrice Stuckup is going to have to sit in the kitchen like any normal person. I mean, this is a great improvement already, even though there's a howling gale coming through that window, but I don't think it's fair to make her sit in such a draught, no matter how unpleasant she is likely to be.'

'I said I—'

'And I said no. Absolutely not. I'm sure Keith will be able to fix it with a new pane of glass and some putty.' She paused. 'The smell of it always reminds me of Finlay. It's the linseed oil. He used to rub it into his cricket bat.' Ann pulled herself together. She walked over to the fireplace and looked around at everything they had achieved. 'This room looks a lot better now, and all our hard work has given me the nudge to get those chimneys swept as soon as possible and think about lighting a fire. Maybe if Keith and Rab have any energy left on their Sundays, they might be able to help us get it wallpapered before Christmas. We might even put a Christmas tree in the window. That will scare the rest of the street.'

'We could do that.'

'Since Ursula died, I've barely been in here.' Ann ran her fingers along the mantelpiece. 'This was her favourite room.'

Isobel allowed a respectful period of silence before pushing on. 'Unfortunately, if we're going to be entertaining in the kitchen then it will need a proper clean, and it's already noon. I haven't made the sly cake yet, and she will be here at three.'

Ann folded her arms. 'Nonsense. We have parkin; you made it on Monday, as you do every week, and it will be lovely and chewy. If the sly cake is ready, that's fine, and if it isn't then we can just have it for supper instead. The kitchen *is* clean, you scrubbed it down yesterday. There might be some soot on the range but nothing a damp cloth won't sort out. We have the perfect excuse to be there, should we even need one, because she won't be able to miss the broken glass in the window as she walks up the front path. And with the price of coal I expect we aren't the only household who are lighting fewer fires. I'm sure even the most well-heeled citizens of the city are thinking about how much fuel they use and whether they really need to have a fire lit in every single room on every single day.'

'You might be right. I spoke to Agnes up the road just last week and she said they've cut right back on the coal order. Between you and me, she is rather worried about her position.'

Ann frowned. 'She won't be the first, nor the last, sadly. What age is she?'

'I'm not sure. Older than me; she might be fifty. The family sort of inherited her from their parents.'

'Times are definitely changing, and a lot of people are going to be caught up in that.' Ann walked over to the window, tiptoeing around the shards of glass. 'But for now I'm just going to clear up this mess and wedge some thick card over the hole. That will have to do until the menfolk get back. I need to tidy my hair, and there's the cake to make. It might still be warm when Mrs Stuckup gets here but that's alright. It's not the Jenners Tea Rooms she's visiting.'

Chapter 47

October 1931

At three o'clock on the dot there was a knock on the front door. The wireless was back in its usual place on the kitchen dresser and Isobel turned it off as she walked past on her way to the hall.

'What do you think you're doing?'

Isobel looked down at her dress. 'I've taken my apron off. Do I not look respectable enough?'

'You look perfectly respectable. Now sit there and just wait.'

'I'll go upstairs into the parlour; she might hear me if I go up there.' Isobel pointed at the stairs to the maid's room.

'You will do no such thing. I want a witness. I have no idea what this woman wants. And people always want something in circumstances like this. I need you to sit right here and be my ears. And please don't bob up and down serving tea either; this is 1931 not 1831.'

The knock came a second time and Ann hurried away down the hall. The outer storm door was open, and she could see through the stained glass that there was a tallish figure waiting on the path. Despite her previously stated opinions, she was glad that the brass door knocker and the letterbox were polished, and the tiled vestibule smelled slightly of beeswax and lavender. She was not Finlay's poor relation; she was the owner of this house and that suddenly mattered. It mattered a lot.

She glanced in the mirror. Keith was making her practise. Quick looks, not five-minute examinations. They had given up trying to get the rest of the knots out of her hair and Isobel, after much persuasion, had chopped fifteen inches off it in the kitchen the night before. She tucked a couple of escaped tendrils behind her ears and opened the door.

The woman outside was expensively and stylishly dressed, but she seemed unsure of herself. This was not what Ann was expecting at all.

'Mrs Sidcup?'

The woman nodded.

Ann didn't give her a chance to speak, but opened the door more widely and motioned her to come in. 'May I take your things?'

'I have an appointment to see Miss Black at three o'clock.' The woman unbuttoned her coat and handed it over before removing the hatpin from her cloche and setting both down on the hall table.

Ann smiled. She had the advantage. This could have been fun if she kept the visitor in the dark, but her manners got the better of her.

'That's me.'

'I thought . . .' The words were left dangling.

'Won't you come through? I'm afraid the drawing room is far too cold to sit in. As you'll no doubt have seen, we have had a slight mishap with the glazing and there's no point in lighting the fire and sending the heat straight outside.' She straightened her back. 'We are in the kitchen today, I hope you . . .' she stopped herself from saying 'don't mind', ' . . . haven't had far to travel. There was no return address on your letter so I'm afraid you have me at a disadvantage on that front.'

She opened the door to the kitchen and the warmth escaped into the hall to meet them. Isobel, unable to help herself, stood up.

'This is my friend Isobel Clark.' The name was lost in the scraping of the chair being pulled back from the table. 'Do please take a seat.'

The visitor offered her hand to Isobel, who accepted it as though it was the most normal thing in the world for a former maid to shake the hand of someone who was clearly so wealthy. Every thread and button Mrs Sidcup was wearing screamed money in capital letters and underlined twice.

They all sat down at the table, and Ann and Isobel waited.

'I must apologise for not providing a return address when I wrote to you but I was terribly worried that you would not see me at all.'

'I confess that had there been one, I doubt you would be here now,' replied Ann. There was no point in pretending otherwise.

Mrs Sidcup glanced at Isobel briefly before turning her attention to Ann. 'I had hoped we might meet in private.'

'I trust my friend completely. I am sure you won't be surprised to find that I have equipped myself with some company, under the circumstances. I mean, a letter from a complete stranger inviting herself to my house? I simply could not have risked having you in my home at all if I had been alone.'

Shock was momentarily written on Beatrice Sidcup's face, as though this possibility had never occurred to her, but after a moment she nodded, slowly. 'I understand; it must have seemed very odd. Please, if you can, I would like you to call me Beatrice.'

Ann stood up and retrieved the steaming kettle off the hotplate. She poured boiling water into the kitchen teapot and added the handknitted tea cosy, not caring how this might appear. She was not ready to be on first-name terms. 'Perhaps you should explain your letter, Mrs Sidcup. I confess I was surprised and not a little disturbed that you mentioned my brother after so many years.'

'It's a long story. I'm not very sure where to begin.' The visitor appeared to be struggling to gather her thoughts. 'My husband Daniel was in the same regiment as Finlay, and before that they were at school together here in Edinburgh.'

'I remember Daniel,' said Isobel, before she could stop herself. 'He often visited this house.'

Beatrice Sidcup continued as though she hadn't heard Isobel speak. 'I was so sorry to hear that Finlay was missing.'

Ann got straight to the point. 'So, what is it that you need from me?' She turned the brown teapot round and back and round again, in the usual way, before pouring the tea into three cups and handing them out.

'This is rather embarrassing.' Beatrice Sidcup was clearly uncomfortable.

Ann mellowed a little. Whatever this was, the woman was struggling. 'Perhaps if you start at the beginning,' she suggested, pushing the plate of warm cakes towards the visitor and taking a piece of parkin for herself.

'Daniel was two years older than Finlay, but they lived in the same tenement stair in Bruntsfield when they were children, and they played in the same cricket team at university. That's how we met. They were both studying engineering. He still talks fondly of Finlay, which can be a little,' she paused, 'well, it can be rather difficult, sometimes. Daniel and I became engaged to be married at the beginning of 1913. We were both twenty-one and our wedding was planned to happen in the early summer, after Daniel had finished his studies. All through the time they were students, I laid out the teas for the university cricket team, for the visiting side. It was a rule that the half-time cakes should be rather indigestible; the home team always made a pretence of eating them and the visitors didn't know any better and were weighed down somewhat in the second half of the match.'

Isobel smiled to herself, but didn't say anything about her part in this particular subterfuge.

Beatrice Sidcup twisted her wedding ring around on her finger. 'Finlay was such an attractive young man. So vibrant and funny and full of life.'

'He was,' agreed Ann.

'The week before Daniel and I were to be married in July, he was called away to an interview in Liverpool. I was beside myself with everything that was still to be done for the wedding and I went to see Finlay at his flat, on Daniel's instruction. I was a bag of worries and nerves. And he wanted Finlay to make sure I was alright.' Beatrice Sidcup looked at her teacup but decided against it and pushed on. 'Finlay was wonderfully kind and caring, and I wondered, not for the first time, if I had chosen the wrong man.'

The room was silent apart from the ticking of the kitchen clock.

Quite suddenly, Ann knew what was coming next.

'Daniel and I got married a week later. And almost nine months after that I had a daughter whose name is Olivia. She arrived a few weeks early, but she was healthy and that was all that mattered. She is a delight and rather clever and next year she hopes to be a student at the university here in Edinburgh. She has inherited her father's engineering brain and wishes to study mathematics.'

Ann took a good mouthful of tea, allowing it to wash the oats off her teeth before speaking. She was determined not to leap to conclusions. 'And what has this to do with my brother? I mean, I am pleased that he and Daniel were such good friends. I think men need close friends more than they realise. But—'

Beatrice Sidcup raised her hand to put a stop to the questions. 'Forgive me but this is difficult and I just need to keep going until the end before you ask me anything.' She put her hand back in her lap. 'Daniel and I have never had any other children. We do not know why. There is only Olivia. When I was at university I studied biology. I was interested in genetics; indeed it was my passion. Finlay had curly hair. Daniel and I both have straight hair. In the future someone may disprove what biologists now theorise but there was at the time a belief by some that it was impossible for two people who have straight hair to have a curly-haired child.' She looked at Ann's tightly corkscrewed hair which now reached just above her shoulders, unconstrained by combs or pins. 'Daniel does not know this. He is an engineer, not a biologist.' She took a sip of tea. 'I am as sure as I can be that Olivia is Finlay's daughter. And, when you meet her, you will see why I think this is the case.'

No one spoke.

Ann didn't know what to say. If only Finlay were here, she thought, he would be able to confirm or deny this rather preposterous story. 'If this is true, and of course I only have your word for it, did Finlay know?'

Mrs Sidcup shook her head. 'I suspected Olivia might be his daughter, or at least that it was possible, but it wasn't until she started to get older that I was sure. Olivia had no hair at all until she was almost two years old, and it was another six months after that before I was certain. I wrote to Finlay, just the one letter, but I never got a reply. Shortly after that I heard that he had been posted as missing. Daniel served in France right from the start of the war and there was nothing to be done. He loved Olivia dearly, so how could I ever tell him that the daughter for whom he was fighting a war was a child who belonged to someone else?' She stopped speaking quite abruptly.

'I see.' Ann tried to take it all in. 'And why are you coming here now, seventeen or eighteen years later, to tell me about this?'

'Finlay always spoke well of you. Because of that, I am here to ask for your help. Or rather it is Olivia who needs your help – although she doesn't know any of this, and I would prefer that it stays that way, for obvious reasons.'

Ann took charge at last. 'The only evidence you are providing is the fact that your daughter has curly hair and you and your husband do not. My brother never mentioned this to anyone.'

'I told you, Finlay didn't know. Even if he had suspected, he was Daniel's friend and he could hardly announce that we had—' She broke off in mid-sentence.

'I suppose not,' Ann conceded. 'Exactly what is it that you need help with?'

'It's complicated.' Beatrice Sidcup took a sip of tea. 'As I said, my husband is an engineer.'

'As Finlay would have been.'

There was a nod. 'He works on improving the railway systems. Three years ago, he was invited by the Canadian Pacific Railway to travel there and advise them on a particular project, and he jumped at the opportunity. He was away for six months and Olivia and I stayed here because

258

I didn't want to interrupt her education. When he came back all the talk was of how good the life in Canada was and he persuaded me that all three of us should visit for a month, over Christmas. And then a year ago he was offered a position, in Calgary. After much thought we decided that we would go, but we discovered that it would mean we had to emigrate. We did our research and discovered we had sufficient funds to support ourselves and that in turn meant we fulfilled the criteria of the Canadian government. Olivia was not keen to leave Scotland, but we got all the paperwork ready anyway.' She took another sip of tea. 'We were due to leave in April this year. Daniel sailed for Calgary and the plan was that I would follow with Olivia after she had completed her final school examinations. Unfortunately, because of the Great Depression, which is reportedly as bad there as it is here, the Canadians have changed the rules. Daniel has a job, and is needed by the railway company, so he can immigrate. And as his wife, I can go to be with him. But Olivia is now seventeen and not at school so we think she may no longer be regarded as a dependent minor. It might be that they allow her to enter the country, but it has been impossible to get a firm answer to the question. While all this has been happening, Olivia has now decided that she does not want to travel with us. She hopes to enrol at university here in Edinburgh next year. Her friends and her life are here. And when we were in Canada for that holiday I mentioned, it was winter; Olivia is not enamoured with the severe cold weather and the large amounts of snow. In short, she is now refusing to go with me. I must therefore choose between my husband and my child.' She looked down at her hands and twisted her wedding ring around her finger again. 'Daniel does not understand and is somewhat annoyed; he forgets that

Olivia is almost a grown woman. I have tried everything I can to persuade her but she is unmoved by my opinions and is becoming more determined in her position. I am turning to you, therefore, in the hope that you may be able to help.'

'How?' Ann was disinclined to be anything but direct.

'Unfortunately, neither of us have family here in Edinburgh any more. I managed to find a respectable lodging house for her. It's not like staying at home, but she insists that she would have preferred not to live at home while she is at university anyway, even if we were here in the city. I am hoping that you may agree to be a sort of guardian for her. Someone she could come to if she needed assistance with anything.'

'But she has never met me. I am not part of your social circle. I am a stranger.' Ann looked directly at the visitor. 'How do you propose to explain this arrangement to her? I assume you do not intend to reveal to her, *if* what you say is true, that I am, in fact, her aunt.'

'I would say that you are the sister of a friend.'

Isobel spoke out loud without meaning to. 'Instead of the truth, which is that Ann is the sister of her fa—' She stopped herself before the final syllable.

'My friend is correct,' said Ann. 'This is quite a deception.'

Beatrice Sidcup was almost in tears. 'I am not sure you appreciate how difficult it has been for me to come here today. I cannot think of another way forward. I have spent so many nights with it going around and around in my head. I do not want to leave Olivia, at not quite eighteen, with no older woman to look out for her in case—'

Ann finished the sentence for her. 'In case she makes the same error that you did.'

The reply was almost inaudible. 'Yes.'

No one spoke.

Eventually, Beatrice Sidcup seemed to pull herself together. She sat up straight and waited for a response.

Ann stood up. 'I need to think about this. As I'm sure you can imagine, it has all been rather a shock. I think perhaps it would be best if you leave now, Mrs Sidcup. If you are willing to provide me with your address, I will write and let you know what I have decided.'

The visitor took a card from her bag and handed it over. At the front door, before she stepped back into the chill of the late afternoon, she turned to Ann as though to add something.

Ann pre-empted her. 'I do understand that there is some urgency about this but I will not be rushed into a decision. It would not be in anyone's interests. Or rather, without wishing to be unkind, it is perhaps in your own, but not in those of the other parties in this matter.'

Chapter 48

November 1931

'Will you and Rab be going up to the High Street on Wednesday?' Ann was sitting at the kitchen table and in front of her was a cardboard box filled with brown envelopes and seed packets.

'On Wednesday?' replied Isobel. She lifted one of Rab's collarless work shirts from the pile in the ironing basket and put it on the ironing board. It might just be an old shirt, worn when he was stripping wallpaper, but she still wanted him to feel loved and cared for.

'Yes. For the Armistice parade.'

'I'm not sure.'

Ann took the envelopes out of the box and began to put them all face side up so she could read what was written on them. 'Keith and I are going.' She looked across at Isobel, who was positioning a chair below the central ceiling light. 'Stop! Don't do that until I've turned it off at the wall. Do you want me to steady it for you?'

'Please.' Isobel waited for the switch to be flicked and then climbed up and removed the lightbulb before fitting a two-way connector into the hanging socket. She refitted the bulb into one side of the Y junction. 'Pass me up that cable for the iron, would you? And then do the switch for me again once I'm finished so I can make sure it's working.'

When the iron was safely plugged into the light fitting and they could smell it starting to warm up, Isobel got down off the chair. She licked her finger and dabbed it quickly on the soleplate. 'Not hot enough yet.'

'You can walk with us if you like?'

'Mmmm?'

Isobel arranged the shirt across the ironing board and dabbed the soleplate with a wetted finger a second time. 'That's more like it.' She pressed down firmly on the slightly damp cotton, hearing a gentle hiss as the heat met moisture.

Ann knew her offer was being ignored. She went back to arranging her collection of seeds in alphabetical order. 'I thought I might try some more vegetables next year. You know, in the borders. I know that's not how anyone else around here does their garden, but I don't care.' She looked across at Isobel. 'What do you think?'

Isobel appeared to be lost in thought as she pushed the nose of the iron into every pleat and fold of the shirt with a precision which absorbed her completely.

'I was thinking giant leeks and perhaps a few zebras and a fleet of tadpoles?'

Eventually, Isobel realised she was being spoken to. 'Sorry, I was miles away.' She lifted the shirt off the board and arranged it on a coat-hanger.

'What do you think about the seeds?'

'I'm sure whatever you are planning will be splendid.'

'Isobel!'

'What?'

'You haven't been listening to a word I've said.'

Isobel propped the iron up where it wouldn't scorch the ironing board. She came over to the table and sat down. 'I *was* listening, actually. I just didn't know how to answer you.'

'About Wednesday or about the tadpoles?'

'Rab doesn't want to go.' She picked at a bit of rough skin on her thumb. 'He says it's too difficult.'

Ann nodded. 'I thought there had to be something. Keith asked him and couldn't get a straight answer.'

'It's different for Keith. He was too young to be called up, wasn't he? And all his classmates were the same, so they never went.'

'But?'

'Well, Rab's a couple of years older than Keith and most of his friends *did* go. Once Kitchener and Derby got their hooks in, it was bound to happen.'

Ann poked around at what Isobel wasn't saying. 'Rab only has the use of one eye, though, because of the lime plaster thing. He would have been exempt, surely?'

'The government still tried to call him up. They said that as long as he could fire a rifle, he could serve his country.'

'So what happened?'

'It's all very difficult for him.' Isobel shrugged. 'It wasn't straightforward. He wanted to go and do his bit, but of course he had to pass a medical. It was the same for everyone.'

Ann waited. She had a dozen questions.

'He went for the tests and they told him he had a problem with his heart, and it meant he couldn't fight or be anywhere near the front line.'

'That wasn't his fault, though.'

'I know that. And he knows it too. But almost all of his friends signed up, and quite a number didn't come back.'

'Like Finlay.'

'And Harris and Gregor.' Isobel rearranged the shirt on the ironing board. 'And a lot of those who did get home weren't the same afterwards.'

Ann leaned forward, trying to touch Isobel but she couldn't reach her. 'Like I said, it wasn't his fault.'

'You don't understand.' Isobel felt for the old penny which she still wore around her neck and rubbed it as though it might help her explain. 'He has this guilt. He thinks he should have gone, regardless. It's nonsense, but it's how he feels. And when he has gone to the Armistice parades in the past, he thinks everyone is judging him. His friends that are there have medals on their chests, and he has nothing.' Isobel pulled her handkerchief from her pocket and her eyes filled with tears. 'He wants to go so his friends will understand that he respects them, and that he believes what they did for the country, and for *him*, matters.' She sniffed and wiped her nose. 'But the guilt is terrible and he can't stop thinking about it.'

Ann ran her fingers along the grain of the wooden table, backwards and forwards, backwards and forwards. 'I don't think any of us are in a position to judge other people.'

Isobel sat up straight. 'I know that, but he won't be told. Last year he went to see a Pathé newsreel at the cinema and it was all about the Armistice parades around the country. He watched the ceremony at the Cenotaph in London, and he said the King put his wreath down, then turned his back on it and walked down the steps. And then he saw more news reels about other cities and he says everyone does it. All these important people lay their wreaths and then they turn around and walk away, back to where they came from. He says that's what the world has done to all the men who were injured. They have just walked away and left them to sort themselves out. And he says it's not enough.'

Ann nodded slowly. 'I can see why he doesn't want to be there.'

'He is so angry about it. And guilt and anger at the same time is not a good combination.' Isobel stood up again and picked up another damp shirt from the ironing basket. 'So, if it's alright with you and Keith, I think we'll just stay here. We might go for a walk instead.' She shook out the shirt. 'He said last night that he wants to talk to me about something important, so we'll enjoy just being the two of us for a few hours and we won't go anywhere near any ceremonies.'

Chapter 49

November 1931

Three weeks after her first visit, Beatrice Sidcup stood on the doorstep of 25 Library Terrace again, but on this occasion, she was not alone.

It was Isobel who answered the door and took their coats. 'You must be Olivia,' she said to the young woman. 'I am Isobel. Welcome to number 25.' Seeing Olivia at close quarters, she wondered how Ann was going to react.

In the intervening weeks there had been many discussions at number 25. Every breakfast and dinnertime had been dominated by the decision about what to do. Furniture had been moved around in the upstairs bedrooms, and the house had been thoroughly cleaned under Isobel's exacting guidance. The drawing-room window had been repaired but the chimney had not yet been swept and the room was still too cold to be welcoming, and anyway, Ann had reasoned to the others, 'We are not accustomed to entertaining in there and I refuse to pretend to be something I'm not.'

Isobel had made a lemon cake. The men were out at work but would be back in time to meet the visitors. The occasion had been carefully planned.

Ann stood at the end of the hall, beside the kitchen door. Every thought in her head evaporated as Olivia started to walk towards her. The young woman was clearly her brother's daughter. The same blonde curls, the same eyes. She even had the same slightly turned-out feet that she had herself, that her father had always teased her about, and told her it was because someone had forgotten to tighten her legs up properly.

Isobel rushed ahead of the visitors and rescued the situation. 'We are in the kitchen again, Mrs Sidcup. I'm afraid we are still waiting for the chimney sweep. They are so busy at this time of year when people are thinking about getting ready for Christmas.'

By the time they were gathered around the kitchen table, Ann had regained some composure. Isobel had seated Olivia opposite Ann and placed herself and Mrs Sidcup at the other end of the table.

'Thank you for inviting us to see you, Miss Black.' Beatrice Sidcup's voice was cool and polite. She seemed to be in a much more controlled frame of mind than she had been on her previous visit.

'It's my pleasure,' replied Ann evenly, her heart racing. She looked across at Olivia. 'I understand that you hope to study at the university. Perhaps you might begin by telling me a little about that.'

Mrs Sidcup frowned and cleared her throat and it was all Isobel could do not to kick her under the table. Any semblance of desperation and gratitude had vanished.

Olivia got there before her mother. Her voice, the tone, the consideration of each word was so much like Finlay when he was younger that Ann found it quite distracting.

'As I expect my mother has told you, I plan to study mathematics. I hope to start my first year next autumn, and my mother had arranged perfectly adequate lodgings for me. However, on Monday the landlord terminated the arrangement without warning. He thought that my name was Oliver, not Olivia, and used that as justification. I now need somewhere else to live. My mother feels that once she travels to Canada it will be necessary for me to lodge *with* someone, and that I cannot manage alone. I'm not sure why she feels this to be the case, as I am perfectly capable, but as I'm not the person paying the rent, it seems I do not have a say in the matter.'

Ann tried hard to concentrate. This young woman had spirit and was prepared to say things older ears might find difficult. She liked her already. 'I am not sure if you know this,' she replied, 'but I knew your father.'

Mrs Sidcup's eyes widened.

'I knew him when he was a young man. He spent a lot of time in this house.' She was determined not to lie. How her carefully chosen words were interpreted was up to the listener.

Olivia turned to look at her mother. 'You never mentioned this.'

Ann pressed on. 'After discussing the situation with the other members of the household over the last few days, I would like to offer you lodgings here.'

'Other members?' Mrs Sidcup was blindsided.

'There are four of us living at number 25. Myself, Isobel, her fiancé Robert Buchan and my friend Mr Anderson. Perhaps you would like to look around?'

Olivia was first on her feet. 'Yes, please,' she said, before her mother could object. 'I would be very interested to see where I might be living.'

For several days, Ann had been walking around the house, talking to herself as she practised giving a guided tour.

'This is the kitchen, as you can see, and the scullery is through there with a lavatory at the end, and then there is the garden.' She pointed to the wooden staircase. 'That leads to the maid's room, but this is 1931, and we don't have a maid, so we all join in with the cleaning and cooking. Isobel is using it temporarily while her own room is being decorated,' she said firmly. 'And after that it will become my office.' She led them into the hall, improvising rapidly. 'There is a bathroom downstairs, and that's the one the ladies use.' Ann was careful to address her explanations to Olivia, and not to her mother.

'Through here is the drawing room, which is where we entertain guests and we will have bigger events like Christmas; it's the next room on the list to be decorated, and I hope it will be finished in time for the festive season.' She pointed at the dining-room door but didn't open it. 'That's my room. And then if you follow me upstairs you can see the rest of the house. Please count these stairs as you go up, it's very important.'

The four women made their way up the stairs and paused on the landing at the top. 'Here we have a second bathroom, and four other rooms. Two are bedrooms for Mr Buchan and Mr Anderson. One is empty for the moment, and the fourth room is the parlour.' She threw open the door. 'We haven't used it as a parlour for many years and, as you can see, it's in the process of being wallpapered. This might be yours, Olivia. It's the biggest room in the house, and I've been thinking that when you start your course next year, there may be a fellow student who might like to share it with you? It would make it a little less costly for your parents, and it might help your academic work if you have someone with whom to discuss your studies.' She anticipated Mrs Sidcup's protest. 'It would also mean you have a friend of your own age here. I would not want you to feel you are stuck in this house with a collection of antiquarian residents.'

Ann could see Olivia processing all the information log-ically, just as Finlay would have, examining the arguments and possibilities.

'I am sure there will be someone suitable,' Olivia replied. 'And while I wait to begin, I can look for a job.'

Beatrice Sidcup could no longer contain herself. 'Perhaps we could leave your maid and Olivia together to look around more thoroughly. I have some questions about the unusual living arrangements in this household.' She turned and left the room.

Ann nodded at Isobel. They had both forecast this reaction.

Downstairs in the kitchen, Beatrice Sidcup was incandescent. 'I cannot believe that you have hoodwinked me.'

'I beg your pardon?'

'I know Isobel is your maid – Daniel told me about her, and her history of thieving.' Ann looked at her, saying nothing and allowing Mrs Sidcup to hang herself. 'And I was unaware that you had men staying in the house. There are no keys in any of the locks on the doors, and you aren't going to tell me that Isobel uses the downstairs bathroom in the night.'

'Oh, she does,' replied Ann, crossing her fingers quickly in her pocket, 'it's not a word of a lie. We both do.'

'I simply do not believe you. I think you are an ...' she searched for a description, '... an extraordinarily manipulative woman.'

Ann stiffened. 'That's your prerogative, Mrs Sidcup, but I invite you to examine the contents of the medicine cabinet in the downstairs bathroom and to smell the fragranced soap which sits beside the sink. It is not a place a man would use.'

They didn't hear Isobel and Olivia coming down the stairs and along the hall to the kitchen.

'And as for Isobel being my maid, she is no such thing. Isobel is my friend. She is my equal. As are the two gentlemen who live here.'

As she said this, the scullery door was pushed open from the garden and Keith and Rab appeared.

'Perhaps you would like to meet them? Keith, Robert, this is Mrs Sidcup. She is the mother of Olivia, who I hope will be joining us at number 25.'

Keith offered his hand, but it was ignored. He put it back in the pocket of his overalls. 'Keith Anderson. It's me that's wallpapering the room for your daughter . . .' he paused, 'if she wants it, that is.'

Olivia smiled at Keith. 'Oh, I do want it. I really do.'

Rab walked over to stand beside Isobel. 'And I'm Robert Buchan.'

'You're Isobel's fiancé, Miss Black told me.' Beatrice Sidcup's tone made it seem as though she doubted the truth of the matter.

He looked at her and stood a little taller. 'Yes, that's right, I am. We were talking about setting a date for the wedding just last week. We're saving for a place of our own, but for the moment we live here.'

'Is there anything else?' said Ann. 'Is that everything settled now?'

'Twenty-two stairs,' said Olivia. 'Counting from the bottom, two, fifteen and five.'

'Very good. You passed the test.'

Beatrice Sidcup knew when she was beaten. 'It seems as though everything has been arranged rather more quickly than I was expecting.' She picked up her handbag.

Ann looked at Olivia. 'Before you leave, there are just a few rules you need to agree to. As soon as you are twenty-one you must register to vote. This is compulsory. And this is a vegetarian house; we don't eat meat or fish here. Is that likely to be a difficulty?'

Olivia didn't give her mother a chance to answer. 'Not at all. It's absolutely fine. I do have one question, if I may?'

Ann nodded.

'What should I call you? Would you prefer Miss Black? Or Ann?'

Beatrice Sidcup butted in. 'You must call her Miss Black; that's only polite, of course.'

Ann shook her head, and her corkscrewed hair quivered. 'Definitely not.' She paused momentarily. 'Ann is the name I was given when I was born, but I never liked it and I recently decided to change it. My brother used to call me something else.' She looked across the room at Isobel and Rab, who were holding hands, and at Keith. 'You may call me Annie.'

Keith looked back at her, and mouthed the three words he said to her, every single day.

1951

Chapter 50

April 1951

Census weekend

Georgia sat beside Keith in the Second Class compartment of the train. Although she felt quite grown up at almost twelve years old, she had seized the opportunity to sit beside the window on the long journey from Waverley station to King's Cross, and had watched the countryside change from Arthur's Seat and the coast, to the open fields of the Ouse plain, to the industry of Darlington and the steel country before rushing on to fertile fields in Cambridgeshire. And now they were almost at their destination. If she could have done the entire journey without blinking once, she would have.

The engine pulled into the station's long platform with a blast of its steam whistle, welcoming them to the capital. Keith gathered their bags from the racks above the bench seats and opened the sliding door onto the corridor that ran the length of the carriage.

This is a different country, thought Georgia as she jumped down onto the platform. It's like being abroad. She bent down to tie her shoelace and her blonde plaits fell forward, almost touching the ground. 'Are we nearly there?' She had been saying this ever since they had passed through York, trying not to let her increasing excitement show.

'Not far now,' replied Annie. She took Georgia's hand despite her almost grown-up status and neatly shifted the responsibility for her safety onto the child. 'Just hold onto me in case I get lost.'

Keith stepped off the train last, carrying the two canvas haversacks in one hand before slinging one of them over his shoulders. 'Annie, you'll need to let go of her while you put this on.'

Georgia sighed. She had her own small bag with two dresses and clean socks and underwear and a book and a raincoat just in case. What else could anyone possibly need on a four-day trip to London?

They threaded their way through the crowds of hurrying passengers, ignoring disappointed porters looking for bags to carry, and headed out past the ticket collectors and into the street.

'Where are we staying?' Georgia squinted in the sudden brightness.

'We have lodgings in a guest house near the Old Street tube station,' replied Keith. 'It's about two miles away and quite easy to find.' He glanced across at Annie. 'We could walk there or we could take the Northern line on the Underground.'

'I think we should take the Underground,' said Annie firmly, over the head of Georgia who had bent down to tie her other shoelace. 'I'm tired after such a long journey and I need to freshen up.'

'I'm not tired at all,' proclaimed Georgia, 'so I don't mind what we do.'

Keith smiled at the young girl he thought of as his own granddaughter and turned back into the station. 'Very well. But the Northern line is the deepest line, so the escalators are very long and it may be rather warm.'

No stairs to count, thought Annie.

*

'You're a bit early for the Festival of Britain,' said the landlady as she handed them their room key.

'We know,' said Keith. 'I hear the preparations are well under way.'

'They've started building the Skylon,' she replied. 'I think it's going to be quite something when it's finished.'

'We have come to see Whitehall and the Cenotaph,' Georgia butted in. 'My parents worked there in 1941, when I was rather small.'

The woman smiled, and then froze as Georgia continued.

'They were killed in the Blitz, which was very sad, but I don't remember them at all so it's sad for other people more than it's sad for me.'

'It's what one might call a rite of passage,' explained Keith apologetically to the landlady as the two women in his life headed up the stairs to the bedrooms. 'She has wanted to see where they worked in Whitehall for years and the Festival preparations are such a good reason to come to London. We're killing two birds with one stone, so to speak.'

She winced.

'Sorry,' he shrugged, 'but you know what I mean.'

'Breakfast is at seven-thirty sharp and I stop serving at eight. It's vegetarian, of course. Would you like mushrooms with your potato cakes and tomatoes?'

Natalie Fergie

'Thank you, that would be wonderful. I expect the lass will be awake with the dawn chorus anyway, so you may find her in your kitchen.'

'It wouldn't be the first time.' The landlady tapped a folded paper on her reception desk. 'It's the census tomorrow night.'

'I know. We would have preferred to be counted in Edinburgh, but rules are rules, as they say.'

'I'll check your details in the morning, and make sure everything is correct.'

*

'I thought it would look more interesting,' said Georgia as they walked past the entrance to Downing Street before coming to a stop at the Cenotaph.

'You've seen it in photographs, though?'

'I know. It's just a bit . . . I don't know. A bit plain.'

Keith laid his hand gently on her shoulder. 'I think that is rather the point, Georgia. It represents all the ordinary people who died. Everyone is ordinary but at the same time we are all special. Usually, it's only the generals and kings who get statues that look like them. Keeping it simple like this means that I can look at it and remember my brothers who were killed in the Great War, and Mr Simpson from across the road, who was lost at sea. And Annie can remember her brother Finlay, and you can think about Mummy and Daddy. It lets us all have our own thoughts.'

'I see.' Georgia was not at all sure.

'As soon as it's made to look like a person or a symbol, like a cross, for example, it stops being for everyone and it belongs to only a few.'

Georgia shrugged his hand away. 'If you say so. I preferred seeing the grand office where they worked. I could imagine them going up the steps and through the doors. This is just a lump of stone.'

Annie took a breath, ready to interrupt, but Keith shook his head at her and took Georgia's hand.

'Georgia, why don't we walk along the road a bit and we can take a look at the Houses of Parliament?'

Annie dropped her handkerchief purposely on the ground. 'I'll be right behind you, just carry on.' She bent down to pick it up. 'I won't be a minute.'

She watched them for a moment before turning back to look up at the huge block of Portland stone; the same white stone that had been placed in cemeteries all over Europe, and beyond. She bowed her head and remembered the far-from-ordinary brother who had saved her on the night of the Empire Palace Theatre fire, and who had bought her ice cream on Sunday afternoons and teased her endlessly about this or that. In particular, she remembered the day he had left 25 Library Terrace for the last time. She could see him shaking Father's hand and finding himself pulled unexpectedly into a great embrace. And she had squeezed Finlay as tightly as she possibly could and whispered, 'Remember, your stick and your signature' in his ear, unaware that, although he didn't know it, the former had already got him into trouble. She remembered him saying, 'I love you, Annie Bee. You're the best sister, ever. I promise I'll be home as soon as I can.' And she remembered how Ursula had held back until the last minute before hugging him and had then handed him a tin box. 'Parkin,' she had said. 'It's well wrapped and should last for at least a week. Isobel and I made it for you yesterday.' Isobel had simply nodded at him from the kitchen door before disappearing back beside the warmth of the range, leaving the family to take their leave without her.

And that had been it.

*

They were at King's Cross in plenty of time, and when the train allowed passengers to get on, Keith spent some time trying and failing to find an empty six-seat compartment. He knew Georgia was tired and, with a bit of luck, she might sleep on the journey home. In the end, their fellow travellers didn't get off the train until Newcastle, finally leaving the three of them alone. As the evening light began to fall, Georgia dozed off, and he covered her with his jacket.

Annie stretched her legs out on the seat, against all the railway regulations, and leaned into Keith so they could watch the day fade across the North Sea together.

'I've been wondering about something,' he said.

'What's that, love?'

'A long time ago, you said you had a proposal for me. You were asking me if I wanted to live at number 25. I've been wondering if it's worked out the way you intended.'

'I remember it very well. I don't think any day in my life has ever gone quite so spectacularly badly as that one.'

He stroked her hair, feeling the curls under his fingers. 'You were just being kind, and I was filled with so much stupid pride I couldn't say yes.'

'It's a long time ago now. Twenty years, almost.'

He smiled. 'Gregor's tools saved us.'

Annie snuggled in closer.

He felt his heart quicken. 'I wasn't joking, you know.'

'Joking about what?'

'I said it was a pity you didn't mean a different sort of proposal.' He sat up a bit straighter. 'It's just, well, standing at the Cenotaph reminded me how short life is. We don't know how long we've got.'

Annie frowned, sat up straight and put her feet back on the ground. She turned to face him. 'Are you alright, Keith? You're not telling me you're poorly, are you?'

'There's nothing to worry about.' He could feel his heart beating even faster. 'But after all our years together, I've decided it's about time I offered you a proposal of my own.' He paused. 'I'm asking you to marry me, Annie.'

She studied his face, age-lined, bespectacled, familiar.

Keith felt as though time was standing still. 'Or do you need me to hide a screwdriver in the shrubbery before you decide?'

Annie smiled. 'I think it was a chisel, not a screwdriver.' She leaned forward and kissed his lips gently, as she had the first time, all those years ago. 'And my answer is yes, I will.'

2011

Chapter 51

February 2011

Tess looks up to the top floor of the Edinburgh tenement, four sets of sash windows above, and sees that the
curtains are partly closed, and there is pale light behind
them. It's a few minutes after eight. Politely late, her
father would have called it. Fiona will have been as good
as her word, Tess thinks, and will probably be uncorking
a bottle of something red, to go with the pizza. There will
be a pile of recycling needing to be sorted, and a fort-
night's worth of dust bunnies in the crevices of the hall.
It's all quite comfortingly predictable.

She presses the entry buzzer and waits for it to crackle
into life.

By the time she gets to the top floor she is out of breath,
but Baxter is not troubled in the slightest. The door to the
flat is open, and as she goes in, she can see that a mountain
of laundry is stacked up on the sofa in the living room.
Fiona is attempting to pair up school socks, holding them
up to the light in an attempt to work out the difference
between newish black and three-months-old-washed-a-
dozen-times black.

'I'm just about finished, I think.' Fiona abandons the task
with relief. 'Would you like wine or something soft with
your pizza?'

Natalie Fergie

'Both,' replies Tess, 'but I'll start with a can of that San Pellegrino you've always got in the fridge, and a bowl of water for Baxter.'

Fiona scoops up the bundles of paired socks. 'I'll be through as soon as I've put these away.'

In the kitchen there is another heap of clean clothes lying beside the dryer, waiting to be ironed into submission, and there's a higgledy-piggledy stack of library books on the worktop next to the fruit bowl. The bananas look well past their best.

Tess exhales slowly. She is needed.

'I hate laundry. Have I mentioned that before?' Fiona says as she comes into the kitchen. She opens the fridge and hands over a chilled can. 'Tell me whatever you want to tell me. No pressure. Take your time.'

'OK.' Tess sits down at the table and studies the pattern on the red gingham tablecloth. She counts out a nine-square grid and gets all the way to eighty-one before she replies. 'Right. Well, it's over. Patrick and me. It's finished.'

Fiona wonders how many times she has seen clients to whom this has happened. How many separation agreements and divorces and endings. Too many. But it's what she does. Family law for people who don't want to be families any more. And she's good at it. There's some satisfaction in that. She sits down opposite Tess. 'I'm so sorry.'

'He's in Chicago. He went to New York two weeks ago and then on to Chicago and he's due back on Friday, a week from now.'

'Is he seeing someone else?'

Tess tugs at the ring-pull and a hiss of gas escapes from the can. 'He's been lying to me.'

'Why don't you start from the beginning, if you're able to?'

Tess has replayed the sequence of events in her head dozens of times. 'He left for the States two weeks ago, went early in the morning in a taxi. And then he rang me from the airport, I was half asleep and a bit groggy, you know? He said he had lost his phone, and must have dropped it in the house or the street outside and would I go and look for it. I was still in my PJs so I looked downstairs and couldn't see it anywhere, and he was really odd about it. Just told me to leave it.'

'It doesn't sound *that* odd . . .'

Tess studies the squares again. 'And after that a man turned up on the doorstep and said he had a phone and he thought it might be mine. I couldn't work out how he knew to come to the house and then I saw the black cab in the street and twigged that he was the taxi driver from the airport run. He said that a small child had found the phone down the side of the seat and had made a bit of a mess of the cover and he was really sorry. I said thank you and took it into the house. And after a bit it pinged, and there was a message. It said, "I will tell her if you don't" and it was signed with a kiss.'

'That doesn't sound good. No idea who it was from?'

'Just a number. An international one. And then Patrick rang back a bit later and asked if the phone had turned up. He was upset because it was a new one and the software was telling him it was either in the house or in the garden. I made a pretty theatrical show of opening and closing squeaky doors in the house before going outside. It was pissing down with rain and my slippers got soaked in a huge puddle.'

Fiona risks a smile.

'I told him I couldn't see it. And there was a bit more chat and he rang off. And then there was another message.'

Tess can feel tears forming as she relives the moment. 'It only flashed for a minute and then the battery went dead. I couldn't be sure what it said so I plugged the phone in and waited for a bit. Of course, the fates then decided there was a software update, so I had to wait until that was downloaded. And *that* meant I couldn't get into the phone because you have to put the PIN in to restart it, and for some bloody reason, well I now *know* the reason of course, he had changed his PIN.' She wipes her eyes with her sleeve and takes a slug of fizzy grapefruit from the can. Condensation beads dribble down the side of the metal, making it slippery. 'I read online somewhere that you only get a certain number of goes and then it turns into a brick. Not sure if it's true. I got it on the third try. It was his birthday, backwards. Burned into my brain for ever, that number.' Tess finishes the can. 'I think I need some wine now, please.'

Fiona has had years of practice waiting for clients to feel able to speak and understands the need for an occasional nudge. 'And then what happened?' She wins the battle with the cork, and pours Tempranillo into the glasses, just to the widest part of the bowl as she was shown on the wine-tasting course last year, leaving plenty of room for swirling and releasing the aromatics. She stops. And then she pours again, because the occasion seems to demand a full glass and to hell with sommelier rules.

Tess studies the red liquid. 'Well, the message I saw, or didn't see, was there.' She puts her head back and looks at the ceiling, not trusting herself to look at Fiona. 'It said, "Have you told her yet?" with a kiss at the end. And then there was another one which arrived about an hour later and I knew Patrick would still be in the air so he wouldn't have seen it. That one said, "I MEAN IT" in capital letters, and I thought whoever it was really didn't need to shout, I got the idea.'

'Was that everything?'

'Isn't it enough?' Tess takes a large mouthful of wine and swallows. 'After that I took Baxter for yet another walk along the canal and fed the ducks. And then Patrick rang me from Chicago and sounded completely bloody normal, and we talked about the flight and the food on the plane and the delay at immigration and how he'd got a taxi to the hotel with the most talkative cab driver ever. He said he was quite tired and would speak to me the next day, and that was when I told him I had his phone and that there were some messages. And he went very quiet. I was standing in the kitchen looking at the garden and it was as though the world slowed down and stretched while I waited for him to speak. In the end he said that his American colleague Xander had been trying to get in touch with him, but he thought his phone was lost so he hadn't mentioned it.'

Fiona seizes this new fact. 'Wait, you mean it wasn't a kiss, it was an initial?'

'Yeah. And eventually, after I insisted on knowing what was going on, he said he was busy but that he would be sure to ring me later.'

'Oh, *fabulous*.'

'Tell me about it.' Tess has almost finished the glass of wine. 'I knew he was giving himself enough time to get his story straight. If he had met someone else, it would almost be easier. At least I would have someone to be mad at.' She takes another drink and holds out the empty glass for a refill. 'The problem is that he's changed his mind about something very important.'

Fiona pours, and waits.

'We always said that we didn't want children. Neither of us did. I was really happy being a sort of auntie when necessary, and it's not that I don't *like* children, but I've never wanted any of my own. And we agreed. We talked about it a lot when we first met; I never hid how I felt, and he said he felt the same.' Tess runs her finger along the red gingham grid, tracing the line of boxes across and back again.

'And?'

'And now he doesn't feel that way. He's spent a lot of time with Xander and his family, and all his American colleagues have children, and he's decided the clock is ticking and he wants what they have.' Tess takes a slug of wine from the refilled glass. 'It probably wasn't the best way to have that sort of conversation, you know, when we were on opposite sides of the Atlantic? But once he started speaking about it, he didn't stop. He said that I was being inflexible, and that we should talk, because I might change my mind. And I said that what he *really* meant was that he wanted *me* to make a decision because he was being a coward.'

'People say things they don't mean when they're upset,' observes Fiona.

'I'm not going to change my mind. Other people's kids are great, but I don't want any of my own. Never have. It turns out that he's been thinking about this for more than a year, maybe two. And our conversations about what he'd been doing with his friends' kids in the States, which, looking back, I now realise were all started by *him*, were attempts to bring me around to his way of thinking. He is *such* a liar.'

Fiona swirled the wine around in her glass. 'Maybe he didn't want to bring the relationship to an end without trying to persuade you?'

'That's not the bloody point! All of this is about what *he* wants. He is the one who has changed his mind and he didn't have the guts to be honest about it. And in the end he wanted me to be the one to call it a day, so he didn't have to. I am so angry, Fiona. I moved to Scotland last year and gave up my nice apartment in Lisbon, and my whole life there, for *him*. This is, or rather was, pretty fundamental stuff about our future together and he should have damn well told me.'

'And he definitely hasn't met someone else?'

'He absolutely denied it. I asked him a lot of times in all sorts of ways and he stuck to the story. But to be honest I really have no idea. For all I know he's been trawling make-me-a-daddy-dot-com for suitable baby carriers.'

The doorbell rings and Fiona gets to her feet. 'That'll be the pizza. I was back late so I just ordered from Domino's.'

'Good,' replies Tess. 'I need as much carbohydrate as I can get. No more diets and no more stupid step counting either. I am so *done* with trying to be someone I am not just to make him happy.'

Fiona comes back and slides the pizza boxes onto the table. 'Shall we bother with plates?'

Tess shrugs. 'Just tear the lids off and we can use those.'

'I ordered one meat and one veggie. Might as well try and be a *little* bit healthy. If there's any left the kids can have it when they get back tomorrow night.' She opens the boxes. 'A moment on the lips and all that, but oh, *so* worth it.' The smell of pizza fills the room. 'Is there anything else?'

'He said that if I wasn't going to change my mind then he wouldn't ask me to leave the house immediately, and he would stay in a hotel until I had found somewhere else. That was really big of him, don't you think? And he said sorry a lot.' Tess stops for a moment as though trying to make sense of it all. 'In between all the bad things, there was an apology. I asked him why he hadn't said anything before and he said he didn't want to hurt me. I told him it was a bit fucking late for that now.'

Baxter sits at their feet, ever hopeful.

Fiona picks up a small piece of chicken. 'Can Baxter have this?'

Tess nods. 'Baxter eats everything and anything apart from chocolate and dried fruit, both of which could kill him. And onions. And grapes.' She looks at the two pizzas. 'You got extra-large ones.' She takes a slice and watches as a piece of green pepper slides off onto the tablecloth. 'I'm making a mess. Story of my life.'

'Doesn't matter. It's what washing machines are for.' Fiona takes a sip of wine. 'Then what?'

'I hung up on him and blocked his number, and then the house phone started to ring so I unplugged it. And I needed time to think so I emailed all my clients and told them I was dealing with a family problem and apologised. You'll have had that email too. My brain is mush just thinking about it all.'

'And have you come to any conclusions?'

'I have.' Tess finishes the slice of pizza. 'I don't have the headspace for it all right now. You're the exception. You've made me so welcome, and I feel as though we are friends. I'm sorry if that sounds weird.'

'Not weird at all.'

'I'm glad.' Tess rearranges the pieces of mushroom on the top of a second triangle of pizza so there will be one in every mouthful. 'You don't try to add extra jobs on every week and expect them for free, unlike some people. Some folk really take advantage, you know?'

Fiona nods. 'I have clients like that too.'

'I've closed the business down for now. Perhaps for good. And because I didn't want to leave anyone in the lurch, I've found other people to do the ordering and the organising and all the other stuff and I've put them all in touch with each other.'

'Are you still living in the house?'

'I've been in a B&B in Musselburgh since last week. I'm going to make sure that wherever I end up, he won't be able to find me. There are other ways of making a statement.'

'There are?'

'After we had the "Big Conversation",' Tess brackets the words with speech marks in the air, 'I got the electric drill out of the garage, and I drilled a hole in his stupid phone and skewered it to that huge designer coffee table he is so proud of.'

Fiona's eyes widen. 'Well, that's . . . different.'

'Once I got the idea into my head it wouldn't go away, so I just did it.'

'Anything else?'

'Nothing you need to know about.'

'Oh?'

'Well, I was going to superglue the front door lock, but in the end I decided I'd done enough damage.' Tess pushes on. 'But I need somewhere to live and the landlord will have to be OK with a dog. And I've only got two days. I thought the B&B would be alright for a bit longer but they have other guests arriving on Tuesday.'

Fiona tops up Tess's glass for a third time. 'Let's finish eating, and then I have some questions.'

Chapter 52

February 2011

After the pizza boxes have been carefully positioned on top of the overflowing recycling bin, Fiona gets out a pad of paper and a pen.

'This is legal stuff, OK? I need to know how long you were together.'

'Just over eight years. I thought he was The One, you know?'

Fiona nods, but she has slipped into work mode. 'And who owns the house? Does it belong to both of you?'

'No, it's his. He bought it ages ago and then rented it out while he was away. I just assumed that when we got married . . . we were engaged too, did I mention that?'

Fiona shakes her head.

'You probably wouldn't have seen my ring. I didn't wear it when I was working in case it got damaged. What a joke.' Tess rubs the empty channel on her finger. 'We only moved back from Portugal in October. Our first Christmas in Scotland. Our first Hogmanay. I just don't understand it.' She tries to sniff away the tears which are starting to roll down her cheeks. 'I mean, we were *happy*. There was absolutely no indication that anything was wrong. Except he wasn't bloody happy, was he? And he lied over and over again, and let me believe everything was alright.'

Fiona pushes a box of tissues across the table. 'I know this is really hard, but I'm just going to keep going, OK?'

Tess nods.

'Next question. Joint property? A car? Anything in the house?'

'It's all his.' Tess looks at Fiona, suddenly alarmed. 'Unless you count Baxter?'

'I think Baxter is safe with you. Any joint debt? Loans?'

'Nothing.'

'Good. That makes it simpler, legally.'

'But I have to find somewhere to live, and I don't have much time. Your firm has a property department, doesn't it? And I've seen the photographs of flats for rent in your office windows. I thought you might know of somewhere that's dog-friendly?'

'I can ask Alasdair, he deals with that side of the business. Do you have much stuff? Books? Furniture?'

Tess laughs for the first time. 'One rucksack and a cross-breed terrier. There have been a lot of trips to the charity shops. I even wiped my laptop and my phone and sold them to that electrical place near the university. My whole life for all the time we were together was stored online, and I couldn't bear to touch them.'

Fiona stands up and retrieves the corkscrew from the dishwasher. 'I'll open another bottle. You can stay here tonight. The sofa pulls out into a bed and the kids are away until tomorrow.'

'Thanks. I'll just need to take Baxter out for a last pee.'

'Of course.' Fiona tussles with the cork.

*

297

The sitting room is big, but cosy, with squishy chairs and low lighting and real art on the walls. Tess stands in the bay window and looks across at the windows of the flats opposite through the gap in the curtains. 'This is just like that print you've got in the hall.'

'No, that's Glasgow, the tenements are a different colour. Red sandstone.'

'Yes, but it's the same sort of thing. When you look out, you can see into other people's lives. There's a family watching TV over there, and a woman doing the ironing. And I can see a kid who probably doesn't want to go to bed, having a story read to them. You can see it all from here.'

'It's one of the advantages of living high up; I always was a nosy parker.'

'Everyone looks as though they are where they ought to be.' Tess sighs. 'I was starting to be at the fringes of belonging here, but I'm not sure I feel that way any more.' She sits down and takes the glass Fiona is offering. 'Thanks.'

Baxter settles at her feet.

Fiona hands over a bowl of Lindor truffles. 'These have been in the freezer. No point in cheap chocolate at a time like this.' She really wants to reach out and give Tess a hug, but a recent client with an adulterous husband had told her that being hugged was the worst thing. All her friends thought they were being kind, but all it did was remind the woman of the person, and the future, she had lost.

Fiona hadn't forgotten it.

Tess takes a truffle and pulls the twisted cellophane wrapping slowly between her fingers. She pops the chocolate globe into her mouth, feels the cold outer shell crack and lets the whole thing dissolve slowly on her tongue. She wonders briefly if Patrick has discovered that she has removed herself from their joint photo archive.

She had done it in the company of two big tubs of Ben & Jerry's. Hundreds and hundreds of images of them smiling at the camera, standing in front of European cathedrals and monuments, sitting in restaurants or side by side on trains and planes, and opening Christmas presents. Trusting him. Everything they shared feels like a lifetime ago, and he doesn't have the right to see her face again. Not after all the lies.

They have all been permanently deleted.

Every. Single. One.

Chapter 53

February 2011

'Twenty-five.'

'Hello, Miss Williams, it's Alasdair McKay here, from M and P Legal.'

'Good morning, Alasdair, I've been expecting your call. But you really must call me Georgia; after all, we have been communicating for at least thirty years now.'

'If you insist.'

'Shall I come and see you? Or would you like to come here?'

'Thank you for the kind offer, Georgia.' He says her name carefully as though he might break it. 'Unfortunately, I'm rather pushed for time this week. I believe Ms Reid has been in touch?'

'She has.'

'In which case, you'll be aware that I may have a young woman for you.'

Georgia doesn't reply.

'I know you haven't had anyone since the difficulties with the last one, but I wouldn't be fulfilling our firm's agreement if I didn't let you know about her.'

'How young is young?'

'She is a woman in her mid-thirties, who has found herself,' he pauses, 'shall we say, unexpectedly single and in need of a fresh start. She only moved to Edinburgh a few months ago so she is quite isolated; in fact the only person she really knows is Ms Reid. There is some urgency about the situation.'

'Is she working?'

'No, not any longer. She was living as a digital nomad.'

'A digital what?'

'Someone who can take their work with them wherever they go. They often have jobs like website design or software development which can be done from anywhere.'

'Oh, I see what you mean, I think.'

'She's been living in various places over the last few years. Portugal, Greece, Germany, Sweden, and probably more. All in the European Union, of course. She travelled to find nice weather and new places to explore. It's a bit of a thing among these types of people, apparently.'

'So she was a website designer?'

'No, a personal organiser, though I'm not entirely sure what that involves. All I know is that she isn't going to be doing it any longer.'

'And would she stay for the two years, do you think? You know my usual terms for these arrangements. I don't want temporary residents, it's far too disruptive.'

'To be honest I'm not sure, but she definitely meets your usual criteria: single, willing to work – I don't think Ms Reid could manage without her, so I imagine that will provide some stability.'

'I would usually say I'd like some time to think about it, but it doesn't sound as though that's going to be possible. Is there anything else I need to know?'

He thinks about his meeting with Tess an hour ago. 'I know this usually proves to be an obstacle, Miss Williams, but she has a dog. I'm not sure what breed it is but I'd say it's probably on the small end of middle-sized. My mother would call it a Saint Mongrel.'

'It was only an obstacle when I had the cats.'

'Oh really? I thought you didn't like dogs?'

'Have I ever said that?'

'I don't suppose you have, no. I just assumed—'

'Never assume, Alasdair, it's liable to get you into trouble. In your line of work, I would have thought that was a given. Isn't it bred into law students at university?' Georgia didn't wait for an answer. 'Very well. Let me have her phone number and I'll give her a call.'

'Unfortunately, that's one of the complicating factors. She doesn't have a mobile phone.'

'No phone?' Georgia's tone is incredulous. 'How does she manage? Everyone has a phone.'

'Perhaps that's something you could ask her?'

'Yes, I will do that, you can be sure of it. Tell her to come this afternoon at two o'clock. It is fortuitous that I did my baking on Saturday. How will you get in touch with her, though, if she doesn't have a phone?'

'She's in the waiting room.'

'And is the dog with her? I would need to meet the dog.'

'I think it's a sort of terrier. I'll be sure to tell her to bring it with her.'

'I'd better go and push the vacuum cleaner around. I don't want to make a poor impression. Two o'clock sharp. Make sure she knows about the sharp part.'

Georgia ends the call and starts to make a mental list. The hall and kitchen are clean enough, but she's barely been into the bedrooms for months. She walks up the stairs, her lips moving as she climbs. There are sash windows to be lifted and fresh air to be let in before anyone can see the place.

Chapter 54

February 2011

Tess finds Library Terrace without any difficulty. Sandwiched between Morningside and Newington, just to the south of the grand houses in the Grange, it's a wide street, with café latte-coloured two-storey houses set out in pairs on both sides. Number 25 is halfway along. She stands outside the gate for a minute. The front garden has a single tree in the middle, and around it, crocuses and snowdrops poke their hopeful leaves skywards.

Baxter waits obediently beside her, his nose twitching at the new smells.

'Right, Bax. Let's see if this is going to work.' The gate squeaks as she opens it. Before she gets as far as the green front door, it is opened by a woman with surprisingly short salt-and-pepper hair who is wearing a scarlet dress and sunflower-yellow Crocs. She looks, thinks Tess, rather like Judi Dench, if Judi Dench had curls. 'I'm Tess Dutton. I have an appointment at two o'clock?'

'And I am Georgia Williams, do shut the door quickly, it's wickedly chilly today. Hang your coat up somewhere and come through.'

The coat rack is full of jackets and scarves. A purple fleece and a navy-blue waterproof hung up by its wired hood are already looped onto the brass hooks. A

303

well-worn, dark-olive waxed gilet with a piece of string sticking out of one pocket has fallen on the floor. Tess picks it up, and in the absence of any empty hooks, she drapes it over the newel post at the foot of the stairs and adds her own coat on top.

'Hello?' she calls out along the empty hall, unsure where to go next. Baxter's nose is still twitching.

'In here.' The voice comes from what seems to be several rooms away.

Tess makes her way past a hall table bearing a basket which is overflowing with gloves and mittens all jumbled together. She itches to pair them up.

At the end of the hall on the right is a doorway. The door is open and weak winter sunlight casts a shadow on the tiled floor. She keeps Baxter on his lead and walks towards the back of the house.

The kitchen is busy. It's the first word that comes to Tess's mind.

Georgia moves her shopping basket off the table and puts it on the floor, making space for a teapot and a plate of parkin, cut into squares. 'Sit,' she says.

Baxter sits.

Followed by Tess.

'Mr McKay tells me that you are looking for a room.' Georgia pours herself a mug of tea and adds milk from a bottle in the middle of the table. She turns the teapot so the handle is facing Tess. 'Help yourself; tea is a very personal matter, I think.'

'Thank you. And yes, I am.'

Georgia takes a piece of parkin and bites into it, allowing the treacly chewiness to excuse her from further conversation for more than a minute. This technique has worked many times and she sees no reason to alter it.

The residents of the house, past and present, call it the Parkin Pause.

Tess fills the gap, as Georgia intends her to. 'My fiancé and I have split up. My ex-fiancé, I suppose I should call him. And I was living in his house and I couldn't bear to be there a day longer. He is in America and I had to move out so I found a room in a B&B and he will be back on Friday and I really don't want to be around.' All this comes out in a disordered, illogical rush. 'And this is Baxter, he's a rescue from the Dog and Cat Home at Seafield. He's never any bother.'

Georgia lifts her mug and studies each of her potential new lodgers. She takes a mouthful of tea before speaking. 'I understand that you are giving up your job. Tell me about that.' It isn't a question.

'I organise things. I work remotely.' Tess looks at the parkin and realises that she hasn't had anything to eat since breakfast. 'Or rather I used to.' She glances across at Georgia, trying to gauge if more explanation is needed. 'By computer?'

'I do know what a computer is.'

'Sorry.'

'Go on.'

'I found out he didn't want to be with me any more because he left his phone in a taxi and the driver brought it back and someone had sent him a text.'

'Ah,' says Georgia, as though this half-story makes sense. She takes another bite of parkin and chews slowly.

Tess has no option but to continue.

'He wants children. We discussed it when we first got together and we were agreed on it. No children.' Her voice starts to break. 'But he's changed his mind.'

Georgia waits.

'He lied about it. I don't know how long for, but he was definitely not truthful.' Her rumbling tummy gets the better of her and she reaches across the table for the parkin. 'I am now superfluous to requirements.'

Baxter, who until this point has been sitting at Tess's feet, his eyes following every movement of hand to mouth, stands up and barks twice.

'Your dog seems to disagree.'

Tess bends down and ruffles Baxter's ears. Tears spring from nowhere and she surreptitiously wipes them away with the back of her hand. When she sits back up she finds that Georgia has placed a box of tissues in front of her and is now doodling in an open notebook. 'You can have the room, after you've seen it of course.'

'Thank you.'

'There has never been a dog in the house but I expect we'll get used to one another.'

'Mr McKay didn't tell me how much the rent would be.'

'Of course he didn't,' says Georgia, as though this answers the question.

'It's just that until I find a job, it's quite important to know. I need to see if I can afford it.'

'Twenty-five per cent.'

'Pardon?'

Georgia sighs. 'The rent is twenty-five per cent of whatever you earn. After tax, naturally.'

Tess frowns. 'So . . .'

'Including food and laundry powder and toilet paper and that sort of thing. You buy your own shampoo and soap, obviously.'

'I'm sorry, I really don't understand.'

'Every week or every month you show me your payslip, or whatever evidence you have. And then you pay me a quarter.' It's always the same with new lodgers, she thinks. What is so hard to grasp?

'But what if I don't earn very much? Or anything at all?'

'Then twenty-five per cent of not much is not much and twenty-five per cent of nothing is nothing.' Georgia rubs her hands together and grins, there is no other word for it. 'And if you earn a million pounds a month, then you pay a quarter of a million.'

'And what about electricity and insurance and . . .' Tess looks around her, ' . . . window cleaning?'

'That all comes out of the twenty-five per cent.'

Tess tries to find a hole in the arrangement. 'You mentioned food.'

'Yes. This is a vegetarian house,' says Georgia firmly, 'though you can of course eat what you want when you are away from here with your friends.'

'I don't have any of those in Edinburgh.'

Georgia ignores this statement. 'Within these four walls we are vegetarian. There are a couple of other rules but we can go over those when you move in.'

Tess doesn't notice the 'we'.

Georgia pushes her chair back from the table. 'You'll be needing to see your room. Actually, there are two possible rooms so you can choose which one you prefer.' She walks towards the hall.

Baxter stands up and tugs at his lead to try to follow, and after a glance at the remaining parkin, Tess decides that it's probably better that he comes along. While he is definitely house-trained, she isn't sure he can be trusted in the presence of cake.

'Count the stairs, please. You never know when you might need to know how many there are.'

Georgia climbs slowly and waits at the top.

'Twenty-two.'

There is a brief nod. 'I haven't rented out the rooms for a couple of years, so the décor is a little tired,' she waves her hand artistically, 'but it's nothing a tin of emulsion won't fix. You can paint a wall, I suppose?'

'I can. My dad taught me when I was a teenager. I made a fresh colour request at least once a year and he said that if I wanted it done so often then I had to learn to do it myself.' She smiles at the memory. 'My room had so many coats of paint the bumps in the wood-chip paper almost vanished.'

'There is an expectation that you will work, whether that's paid or as an unpaid volunteer. I'm not talking about sixty-hour weeks or anything foolish like that, though, just whatever you feel is right for you, even if it's just a few hours. If you don't have a job at the moment, I might ask you to help me with some things that need doing. Cutting the grass in the summer or going to the supermarket. That sort of thing. Obviously, if you are ever unwell and unable to work for any reason, that would be different. Everyone is entitled to be looked after if they are poorly.'

Tess follows Georgia into a big room at the front of the house. An elaborate plaster cornice runs around the walls at ceiling height, and the room is dominated by a huge fireplace with a correspondingly large draught coming down the chimney.

'Not the warmest room, but rather beautiful in its own way. I usually save this for women who are expecting because there's room for a cot and all that sort of paraphernalia.'

Tess doesn't know what to say. She feels her stomach lurch. And suddenly Patrick is back in her head again, unbidden and unwanted. She cannot think of an appropriate reply, or indeed any useful response at all. She is saved by Georgia, who ushers her out and walks across the landing to a second room, which is smaller and has a less impressive fireplace.

'I think you should have this one.'

Tess realises that she is now above the kitchen, and she can already feel the difference in temperature. The room is empty apart from an old-fashioned mahogany wardrobe and an outrageously fluffy purple rug. She wonders why Georgia doesn't have the big room for herself. As the thought comes into her head, Georgia answers the question.

'In the old days the big room was the parlour, but that was long before my time. When my mother was a student at the university, she shared it with a friend, and then she lived here with my father after they got married.'

Tess isn't sure if she should respond to this morsel of family history, but Georgia doesn't wait.

'My own room is downstairs, and there's a shower room next door to it so we won't need to queue in the mornings. I hardly ever come up here these days. We can share the kitchen and the drawing room, and you can have this upstairs bathroom for yourself,' she pauses, 'unless I take in another lodger, of course. It's not terribly likely, though. I always used to have a houseful, but I think I'm too old for that now.'

Before she can stop the thought, Tess is adding up the twenty-five per cents of three lodgers in her head. Three people at, say, £300 a month each. More if there were four or five. It would be a nice profit.

Georgia interrupts her thoughts.

'Stan has a big estate car. I'll ask him to take me to IKEA before he leaves on his trip north and I'll buy you a new bed. Can't have you sleeping on the floor, can we?'

It's on the tip of Tess's tongue to ask who Stan is, but Georgia is already leaving the room.

At the foot of the stairs, it becomes clear that the meeting is over.

'I'll see you tomorrow then. I assume you have somewhere for tonight?'

Tess nods. She realises she hasn't actually been properly asked if she wants the room; Georgia has simply assumed that she will take it and accept the rather unusual rent arrangement, which means she will be showing this new landlady her wage slip, if she has one. She has never done that before in her entire life. It seems that there are going to be a fair few never-befores in her future.

Before she has time to ask Georgia any questions, she finds the decision has been made and she is standing in the street outside with her coat on. She looks up at the house, and then down at Baxter. 'Come on, Bax,' she says as she bends down to ruffle his ears. 'Let's go and pack our bags.'

Chapter 55

February 2011

After Tess has left, Georgia goes back to the kitchen. She picks up her phone and sends a text.

> *Afternoon, Stan. I am getting a new lodger. Is there any chance you could take me to IKEA? I need to buy a bed.*

The phone rings and a man's face appears on the screen as the caller ID.

'You know I hate using the phone, Georgia, but I just had to ring and ask if you are quite sure about this. I thought you were done with lodgers after the last time.'

'You know me, Stan, I'm a sucker for a hard-luck story.'

'Well, just you be careful. Did you tell her about what happened before?'

'No, I did not.'

'And what about the rent? Usual rules?'

'I don't see any reason to change them.'

'And she was alright with that?'

'To be honest I'm not sure she has another option. She has a dog. There won't be many places she'll find in a hurry that will take a dog.'

He begins to laugh. 'You? A dog? You surely have gone soft in your old age, Georgia.'

'Never mind that. Can you help? I need to buy a new double bed PDQ and a mattress, and your car has a roof rack.'

'A double? Is she bringing someone with her?'

'No, Stan, she is not bringing anyone with her. But someone who has been used to sleeping in a double bed might find it hard to sleep in a single. And there is more than enough room.'

'She's going in the front?'

'No, the back, above the kitchen.'

'It'll need a paint.'

'She knows that.'

'If you're completely sure?'

'I am.' Georgia looks around the kitchen. 'It's time. Just the one, though. My days of having a houseful are finished.'

'Until someone else appears.'

'Stop it, Stanley. Will you take me to IKEA or not?'

'Half an hour. I just need to make sure Hazel is comfortable and I'll be over.'

*

By the time the bed is built and the Allen keys and instructions have been put away in the filing cabinet drawer that Georgia allocates for such things, it's dark outside. They sit in the kitchen.

Georgia leans forward. 'How is Hazel today?'

'She's alright.'

'Still determined to go?'

'Yes. She wants to spend her last days in our cottage on the west coast, where she can see the sea from her window.

It fronts onto the beach and she'll be able to hear the waves and the wind. She says it will remind her of when we were young, and who am I to deny her that?'

'And the health people?'

'It's all arranged. They aren't sure how long she has. Could be six months, or a year, or it could be just a few weeks, who knows?'

'I'll miss her. Three years as next-door neighbours may not be terribly long, but sometimes you just click with people, you know?'

'She asked me if you would go and see her. She's got something she wants to ask you.'

'Of course. I'll pop round tomorrow morning, before I get this new girl settled in.'

'Thank you.' He stands up. 'And you are sure about the allotment? I've explained my circumstances to the committee and they're happy for it to be left mostly fallow this year. There will be asparagus and rhubarb soon, and strawberries and rasps in the summer.'

'Leave it with me. I can't promise it will be as beautifully kept as you manage, but I'm sure I'll be able to keep the weeds down.'

'I really do appreciate it. I've had the same plot since 1962 and I don't want to give it up if I don't have to.' He looks at his watch. 'I'd better be getting back. Hazel will be wanting her Horlicks. It's the least I can do for her after all these years.'

Chapter 56

February 2011

The red front door of number 27 is propped open with a curling stone. Georgia knocks, but doesn't wait for an answer before stepping inside.

'Hazel?' she shouts. 'It's just me.'

A tall, slim woman appears from the kitchen. 'Georgia. I'm so glad you could come. As you can see, we are in a state of disarray.' A dozen boxes are stacked up against the staircase wall, and four suitcases are set beside them. 'Two more days left here, and then we'll be off.' Hazel holds up her hand to stop Georgia responding. 'I'll be sorry to leave and I'm going to miss you, but I want to be in the old place while I can still enjoy it. I need to be able to get out onto the beach and paddle in the waves.'

Georgia laughs. 'In February?'

'Yes, of course in February. When we were young it was the rule that you put your fingers or toes in the water every single day, no matter what the weather was like.'

'You're made of hardier stuff than me.'

'So it would seem! Now come along through to the back and I'll get us a coffee. There's something I want to give you.'

The house is a mirror image of number 25, the other half of the semi-detached pair. It will be very odd indeed for it to be unoccupied, thinks Georgia.

Unlike Georgia's own house, Hazel's home has been gutted and little remains of the original kitchen. The standard issue 1900s fitted kitchen dresser is gone, and has been replaced by an enormous fridge freezer and a wall of sleek high-gloss units. Georgia cannot imagine how Hazel and Stan can possibly need all this storage space. It's not as though they need to stock food for ten people. The previous owner was a builder who had stripped everything out and built a sunny extension with inset ceiling lights and triple sliding doors out to the back garden. Lovely, thought Georgia, if you like that sort of home-interiors-magazine look, but the noise and the dust had gone on for almost a year.

Hazel drops a coffee pod into the shiny stainless-steel contraption which is built into the row of cupboards. 'Cappuccino?' She puts a mug beneath the spout of the machine without waiting for an answer. It hums for a moment in a very smooth Italian fashion and the scent of fresh coffee starts to swirl around the room. 'It's funny how you and I always sit in the kitchen even though there's the rest of the house to play in.'

'I'm the same next door.'

'Stan tells me you're getting a lodger?'

'I am. And she has a dog.'

'I confess I'm surprised, not so much about the dog but about you doing it at all.'

'So am I, to be honest. You never met any of my young women because all that was before you moved in, and the less said about the last one the better. I really don't want to revisit that particular episode.'

'Understandable. Let's talk about something else.' Hazel places the mug of froth and coffee on the breakfast bar in front of Georgia. She takes a small box from her pocket and puts it down next to the coffee. She splays her fingers

315

out on the granite worktop. 'My fingers are useless. Look at them, all puffy from the lymphedema. I'll not be wearing my rings again.'

'Your rings?'

'I'm keeping my wedding ring and my engagement ring, of course – perhaps the undertaker will be able to fit them on my finger after I'm gone – but I thought you might like this one.' She opens the little box. 'I found it when I was clearing things out. I hope it fits.'

The box is lined with silk and embossed with the very Edinburgh name of Hamilton & Inches, the poshest jeweller on George Street. But the ring inside is certainly not the sort of thing such a grand establishment would sell. It's a circle of unpolished metal.

'It's not much, so if you don't want it, I won't be offended.' Hazel is apologetic. 'I've had it a long time, but it's just brass. There's the outer channel, and the inner ring slides around it, like a racetrack. I used to wear it all the time, before my hands got impossible. It was my thinking ring. If I had a problem, I would find myself twirling the inner ring around and around and it seemed to help.'

'A bit like a set of worry beads?' Georgia slips the ring onto the middle finger of her right hand, but it's too tight. She swaps it onto her third finger and it fits. Her hands are not swollen, as Hazel's are.

Hazel smiles. 'I'm sure it would polish up with a bit of Brasso.'

Georgia rolls the central ring around in its channel with her thumb. 'Or just by wearing it. I'm not one for fancy rings and jewellery really, they just get in the way of whatever I'm doing, but this is . . . well, it's very kind of you.'

'Good. That's settled then. My pendants and things are going to my friend in York, but I wanted you to have the ring.' She looks down at her flattened chest. 'You've been so helpful with everything. And I thought you would see the value, rather than the price tag.'

Chapter 57

February 2011

On her first morning at 25 Library Terrace, Tess stirs early, before the wintry dawn has lightened the sky. Barely awake, she reaches automatically with her right hand for her phone, realising as she does so that not only is the phone missing but the room smells different from the house in Craiglockhart. Halfway down the bed lies the warm lump that is Baxter. He had started off lying obediently in his new basket, but despite her instructions, he has ended up on the bed beside her. She has no idea what time it is. Her alarm clock, along with her banking, her Instagram feed, endless amounts of fitness data and the weather app, are all gone. She lies quietly; another day without a smartphone stretches ahead of her.

She rolls over carefully, but it's too late; Baxter's ears twitch and his head rises from the folds of the duvet and that's it, the day has begun. They play a game of chicken, each trying to pretend they are still asleep, but eventually he stretches, and nuzzles her arm. Last night she fed him with biscuits, and there's a handful left in the top pocket of her rucksack, but it has occurred to her that Baxter is not a vegetarian, and the tinned food he usually eats is not likely to be acceptable here. She gets out of bed and pulls a baggy sweater on over her pyjamas before opening the bedroom door.

Baxter sweeps past her, all four paws in the air, racing for the stairs. 'BAXTER!' she hisses in a stage whisper, grabbing the bag of biscuits from her rucksack. He stops suddenly on the top step.

'Sit!'

She holds on tightly to the bag and sees his nose twitch. He sits.

'Heel,' she says, and he waits for her to start walking down the stairs, his nose in the air, following the smell from the biscuit bag.

The door between the scullery and the kitchen is locked. Tess walks around the kitchen looking for the key and eventually spots it hanging on a nail next to a narrow wooden staircase. She unlocks the door to the scullery, fills Baxter's steel bowl with fresh water at the old sink, and opens the back door, surprised to find it unlocked.

She slips her walking boots on and tucks the laces in without tying them. There has been a frost overnight, but there's no sign of any return of the huge snowfall they had in December. The insides of her boots are cold against her bare feet.

'Stay!'

She walks slowly up the garden, dropping a trail of biscuits into the grass behind her.

Baxter waits.

'Find!'

He bounds from biscuit to biscuit, and ends up sitting at her feet, his tail swiping from side to side. She rubs his ears and they walk around the garden together for a few minutes. 'We'd better go in. You'll get cold, and I need to find you some proper food.'

Georgia is waiting for them in the kitchen.

'I've put the kettle on for CT1,' she says.

'CT1?'

'Cup of Tea One. I need at least two and preferably three before I'm any use at all.'

Tess hesitates. 'I need to speak to you about food for Baxter. I assume you'll not be wanting tins of dog food in the house.'

'Yes.' Georgia shakes her head. 'I mean no.' She sighs. 'I told you I was no good until I've drunk CT2, at the very least.'

'Sorry. It's just that he's hungry and I'll need to go and get him something to eat.'

'No tinned food, please. But there's a vet on the main road, I'm sure they'll have something suitable.' Georgia looks at Baxter. 'And after that perhaps you can order some for him online?'

'I could.' Tess struggles to explain. 'But I can't do computers at the moment.'

'Not at all?'

Tess shakes her head.

'Part of the no phone thing, I suppose?'

'Sorry. I'm a bit of a mess.'

'Well, maybe in a few weeks you'll feel better about that. I always include food in the rent but I'm not sure I want to extend that to dog food. I think you should pay for that yourself. If you can decide what you want, I'll order it online for you and you can pay me at the end of the month.'

Tess smiles. 'Thank you. Thank you very much. I need to take him out for a bit of a walk. I'll just throw some clothes on and I'll call in at the vet on the way back.' She glances up at the kitchen clock. 'They probably open at eight or maybe half past. Do you, or do we, need anything while I'm out?'

Georgia shakes her head. 'No, thanks. Fully stocked and ready for a siege here. You can leave him with me while you get your coat, if you like. No point in dragging him up and down the stairs.'

But Baxter, ever hopeful of more biscuits, is having none of it, and follows Tess up the stairs and back down again with great determination. They leave by the back door, Baxter wearing his new bright green harness.

Outside in the street Tess instinctively feels for the clip-on fitness tracker she keeps in the pocket of her fleece and pulls it out to examine it. The battery has been flat for days and there seems little point in carrying it if she isn't going to store the data and analyse it and compare it to last week, last month, last year, and look at her weight and compare that with the step count and plan the next week ahead and . . . she holds it gingerly between her finger and thumb as though it is contaminated in some way. How long has she been using it? She tries to remember. September, the birthday before last. Sixteen months? Seventeen? It was her birthday present from Patrick, bought on a trip to New York, just after it was launched. All those steps counted, notes compared as she tried to beat his daily total, and then feeling like a complete slacker when he out-stepped her. And what did any of it mean now anyway? She takes a firmer hold of Baxter's lead, and sets off for Blackford Pond and the hills behind it. As she turns the corner, she pauses briefly and discards the tracker on the waist-high wall of a random house. Baxter is already tugging on the lead, and is ready to get up to his belly in leaves and mud. He doesn't care about the number of steps he takes, and now, neither does she.

Chapter 58

Mid-March 2011

Tess and Georgia both hear the letterbox snap, and they reach the front door at the same time. Georgia is wrapped up in a tangerine bathrobe and is pink-faced from being in a hot shower for longer than usual. A white towel is wrapped around her wet hair like a turban and it makes her look even more flushed.

Tess has careered down the stairs at full pelt, chasing Baxter, who seems to anticipate the arrival of the post as though a sixth sense is sending him messages from the end of the street. The two women stand politely, each waiting for the other to bend down and retrieve the letters from the mat. They aren't yet completely at home in one another's company, and a degree of reserve is still there, despite the best efforts of Baxter, who pesters each of them for treats, without favour.

In the end it's Georgia who scoops up the mail. She studies the typing on a grey envelope and hands it to Tess. 'One for you. And this big thing is the census form.' She tucks the thick envelope under her arm and pushes the final item, a postcard, into her damp bathrobe pocket without looking at it properly. 'I think today feels like a cauliflower cheese sort of a day.'

Tess shakes her head slightly, trying to work out the connection between the census and cauliflower cheese, but quickly gives up. 'That sounds lovely. I'll give you a hand with it later.' She waits until Georgia has gone, picks up the paper knife that always sits on the hall table, and slides it under the flap of the envelope. As she pulls out the letter, she catches sight of the name of a firm of solicitors in the header.

She takes a deep breath.

He knows what she did.

This is her comeuppance for acting with sheer cold anger. There is, she thinks, hot anger, the sort that makes people thump one another, or race after a culprit without regard for the consequences, and then there is cold anger. Chilled fury, planned retribution.

Tess doesn't want to know what the letter says, but she knows she has to read it. She has tried so hard to put everything to the back of her mind but it keeps rising to the surface, particularly now that spring is well on the way. It was inevitable that he would react. Only a matter of time. She wonders how he has worked out where she is. She had used the Royal Mail forwarding service and crossed her fingers that it would catch everything that was important. Is it possible that some company or other has written and inadvertently provided him with the information? Maybe the bank requesting confirmation of her change of address? She stands very still as an alternative suggests itself. His house, in Craiglockhart, isn't that far away from Library Terrace. Maybe he has seen her? Or even followed her?

She walks through to the drawing room in a daze and stands in front of the fireplace until she can pull herself together. Tears blur her vision as she reads the letter and then rips it up as though she is a human paper shredder. She separates out a few sheets of the previous weekend's newspaper and rolls each one diagonally from one corner to the opposite one, making the rolls tight and even, and then folds each thin tube into a triangle about the size of her hand before weaving the long ends in, making a slow-burning fire starter. It's a lot easier with a broadsheet, she thinks, but these tabloid-sized sheets will have to do. She makes five, and adds them to the shreddings in the grate before putting a criss-cross of kindling on top and adding a few lumps of smokeless coal.

*

It's going dark outside when Georgia comes into the drawing room to close the shutters and draw the curtains. 'That's nice of Tess to lay the fire,' she says to Baxter, who has followed her and is taking up his now customary position on the rug, ready to absorb the warmth as soon as it's available. She studies the triangles of newspaper. 'I've never seen it done like that before.' She crouches down, and lifts a lump of coal between her fingertips to get a better look at the architecture of Tess's work. The nest of shredded paper is no longer hidden by the rolled-up firelighters and she catches sight of part of a logo on one of the strips. 'What's this?' She tugs at it and peers at the headed paper. 'Well I may have left my reading glasses in the kitchen, Baxter, but I recognise the name. Tearing up solicitor's letters is never a good thing, and I should know that if anyone does.' She rests back on her heels and strikes a match. 'One letter could be a mistake,' she reassures herself. 'But more than one would definitely be a problem. I suppose it's a case of wait and see, Baxter, isn't it? I can't tar everyone with the same brush, after all.'

*

They sit at the kitchen table, with Baxter at their feet. He is perpetually hopeful of a scrap of something tasty. The rule about feeding him in the scullery and not in the kitchen is ruthlessly enforced by Tess, but Baxter has learned that when Tess is out, Georgia is not quite as strict, and he lives in hope.

'I know mature cheddar is a thing of beauty,' says Tess as she grates the cheese, 'but this stuff seems a bit wasted on a basic cauliflower au gratin.'

'Not at all.'

'Wouldn't supermarket cheddar work just as well?'

'It might, but I don't like all the plastic. Mellis's costs more but it's wrapped in waxed paper. Aren't we supposed to be saving the planet?'

Tess thinks about the smoke that will be rising up the chimney from the coal fire in the drawing room and decides to keep her thoughts to herself.

'Save the rind,' says Georgia. 'I'll have that later.'

'You eat the rind?'

'It's just the outside of the cheese gone hard, and it's the best bit. Annie and I used to fight over it when I was a child.'

'Your sister?'

Georgia shakes her head, and the subject seems closed. 'Get the cornflour down, please.'

Tess reaches into the larder for the flour.

'Not plain flour, cornflour.'

Tess frowns, but does as she is asked.

'During rationing, which was long before you were born, we never wasted butter or margarine on making a sauce. You just heat the milk and stir in some cornflour mixed with a little cold water and it thickens perfectly well.'

Tess is not convinced. 'Anything else?'

'Yes, the Ryvita on the shelf near the bread bin.'

'Ryvita. OK.' Cauliflower cheese and crispbread? Would that be like cauliflower cheese on toast? Tess wonders, but doesn't ask the question.

'And that jar of wholegrain mustard. It's nearly empty and we can add the last dregs to the sauce.' Georgia chops the cauliflower into florets, slices the stalk thinly and puts it into a jar of water. 'We can have it in a terrine tomorrow; it lasts longer if you keep it under water in the fridge.' She gathers the cauliflower leaves into a heap and chops them up with her old Sabatier knife, forged long before they were made from stainless steel, using a rocking motion like a TV chef.

The round dish is filled with cauliflower, then the cheese sauce studded with mustard seeds is poured on top. 'See? No lumps. Absolutely fool-proof and much easier than making a roux.'

'You don't cook the cauliflower first?'

'I don't. It makes it mushy, like baby food. I like a bit of crunch in my dinner. Speaking of which, pass me the rolling pin.' Georgia takes four Ryvita from the packet, puts them onto the chopping board, and crushes them into rough gravel. 'Mix this with the chopped leaves and sprinkle it all on the top five minutes before the cauliflower is ready and then pop it back in the oven. It makes it nice and crispy. You can start it off now. That'll give me enough time to go and deal with this morning's post.'

Tess feels as though some sort of baton is being passed, as if she is being entrusted with what is clearly an old family recipe. She nods. 'Five minutes.'

'And another thing,' says Georgia. 'The census.'

'The census?' echoes Tess.

'I was going to fill it in online this year, but it'll be a bit of a performance for us to do it side by side at my computer.'

She points to the narrow wooden staircase in the corner of the kitchen. 'My office isn't set up for more than one person, so I ordered a paper form and it came in the post this morning. I'll leave it on the table for you next weekend. You can enter your details first, and then I'll do mine.'

'I'd forgotten all about it. I don't think I was even in the country when the last one happened.'

'Well, you're here for this one, and we both have to do it. And it's one of the rules of the house. You must be registered to vote and you must complete the census. Neither of us is exempt from our responsibilities.'

Tess feels like a small child who has just been given a telling-off without really understanding why.

After Georgia has left the room, wiping her hands on her apron, Tess realises she has no idea how long the cauliflower cheese is supposed to bake for, which means she also doesn't know when the all-important crispbread sprinkling will need to happen, but it's too late to ask the question. She'll just have to make a guess and hope she doesn't stuff it up completely. It feels like a milestone that matters.

Chapter 59

Early June 2011

It's the failure of a small circle of rubber that's the start of the problem.

Tess walks around the side of the house to the back door as usual, and is quite sure Baxter will be curled up in a warm spot somewhere, very possibly on the sofa beside Georgia. Her life is just starting to settle down a little and the new part-time job in the supermarket in Morningside, which Fiona had encouraged her to apply for, is going well. Much to her surprise, she's enjoying the work and the weeks have flown by. She spends her hours organising the tins and packets so they sit with the labels facing forward on the shelves, or checking the dates on exotic cheeses and bottles of freshly squeezed orange juice and making sure those which need to be sold first are at the front. It all appeals to her sense of order, and for a few hours a day it stops Patrick from running around in her head all the time, taking up space to which he is no longer entitled.

Loud noises are coming from the kitchen, accompanied by some forthright language. Tess opens the door to find Georgia standing in the kitchen in her wellingtons, mop in hand. Towels have been rammed up against the cupboards, followed by rolled-up newspapers.

Tess can see a steady trickle of water dribbling down the scullery steps. 'What on earth?'

'We have a burst pipe. Or a cracked joint. Something like that.'

'Have you turned the water off at the mains?'

Georgia points under the sink. 'I can't turn the stopcock, it's too stiff.'

Tess picks her way across the kitchen, trying to avoid getting her sandals soaked, before giving in to the inevitable. More towels are spread across the stone floor at the far end of the scullery in an attempt to deal with the damage. She kneels down, feels the water seep immediately into her jeans at the knees, and grasps the red-painted wheel. 'No wonder you can't turn it off,' she groans, 'it won't budge. Give me a tea towel or something.'

She wraps the cloth around the metal and grips it tightly. Slowly, a degree at a time, it begins to move.

'That's the best I can do. It's off, but I think we need a plumber.'

'I usually ask Stan to do this sort of job for me but he's away up the west coast.'

'Can you think of anyone else?'

Georgia shakes her head. 'There was the person who put the heating in, but that was a while ago. I suppose Stan might know of someone if I send him a message. Just depends if he has any reception.'

'Right. We need to get this cleared up anyway so why don't you go and get that sorted, and I'll deal with the mop.'

'I can manage, you know! I've lived in this house all my life. I don't need to be told what to do.'

Tess points to the bucket under the sink. 'I know. And I'm not trying to take over, but the water must have been dripping into the cupboard since before I left for work. Let

329

me do this. We need a plumber, and maybe an electrician, and we need them pretty quickly.' She isn't sure anything is safe. 'And I can't do those things, but I *can* manage a mop.'

What had seemed like a quirky kitchen with a hotch-potch of vintage appliances, a post-war enamel standalone sink under the window and an electric cooker which could easily be forty years old, suddenly looks like a death trap. Tess feels the project-management muscle inside her begin to twitch.

Georgia is gone for about twenty minutes, during which Tess has taken as much as possible out into the garden. The chairs, pots and pans and anything electrical are now arranged on the lawn with as much logic as she had time for.

When Georgia comes back, she stands in the doorway and takes in the damage. 'Sorry for snapping, I've got used to not having anyone else here.'

Tess wrings out the mop for what feels like the hundredth time. 'It's OK. But the water has gone under the lino and the floorboards are wet. And I'm not sure the sink should really be so close to those electric sockets so I've poked the switches off with that old broom handle. We're going to need to pull the table out of the way to get a decent look at the floor. It's all pretty sodden, I'm afraid.' She doesn't want to be rude, but things need to be done. 'Would you be able to give me a hand with the table? If we could move it across so it's under the mantelpiece, it would be a start, and then maybe we can get the lino up on this side of the room to begin with.'

They each take an end and manage to shunt the table across the room. It's almost in position when Georgia lets go unexpectedly, just at the moment Tess is giving it a last heave. Without Georgia to steady it, the corner of the table jabs sharply into the wall and as though in slow motion, the plaster crumbles.

There is half a minute of stunned silence.

'Oh hell! I'll cover the repair as soon as I get paid.' Tess drags the table back into the room a little to assess the damage. A chunk of plaster falls to the floor, and a vertical crack appears from lino to mantelpiece. 'I'm so sorry.'

Georgia seems unperturbed. 'Keith was a great decorator but he wasn't an expert in house building. This looks like a sheet of hardboard with a skim coat of plaster on top. I'm not sure it's going to be repairable.'

'What's behind it?'

'The beast. Otherwise known as the old kitchen range.' Georgia sits down wearily on the only chair left in the room. 'It would have been 1960, perhaps? 1961. Yes, it was 1961. We filled in the census at that very table and I remember there being a debate about whether the scullery counted as a room.'

'And did it?'

'Apparently not. Annie was quite indignant about that.'

'My dad always filled it in, not my mum.'

'Not here. Annie's stepmother was a census protester in 1911, and ever since then it's always been the women who do it in this house. The enumerators never knew anyway.' She looks at her grimy hands and shrugs before running them through her already dirty hair. 'We're going to have to sort this mess out.' She takes her phone out of her pocket and taps at the screen with the speed of a teenager. 'Right. I've left another message for Stan. Hopefully he'll reply soon, and if he doesn't, we'll just have to manage without him.'

Tess tries to take stock of the situation. 'If the pipes to that sink can be blocked off, I think things would be OK for a bit. The scullery sink has its own supply. This one in the kitchen must have been a later addition?'

'Keith put it in when he built the wall in front of the range. It was done so we could use the sink in here after the door to the scullery was locked at night. He had the wiring done at the same time, so we had a new electric cooker as well. All mod cons in the 1960s, you know.'

'What would you like me to do? I mean, I can tell you what I think needs to be done but it's your house and I'm happy to just be the labourer.'

Georgia looks around the room and sighs. 'I remember all these changes being made in the name of improvement. And it *was* improvement. No more hauling coal up from the coal cupboard at the end of the scullery. And much, much cleaner.'

Tess looks up at the clock on the wall. 'I could do with a coffee before we get started, but I'm not sure about the electrics. If we can get someone to tell us it's safe to use the sockets in the scullery, then even if we don't have power in the kitchen, we can manage with just the kettle and the toaster for a day or two. And if it's longer than that then a microwave would be helpful, but we can cross that bridge when we come to it.'

'I think,' replies Georgia thoughtfully, 'that I should perhaps see all this as an opportunity. Maybe the universe is telling me that it's time for a change.'

Chapter 60

Early July 2011

Tess had been staying at Fiona's for almost a week, helping her paint two of the high-ceilinged bedrooms. The kids had gone to stay with their grandparents and Tess had juggled the decorating project around her hours at the supermarket. The two women had walked Baxter around the Meadows in the mornings, played their favourite songs loudly on Spotify while they worked, and abandoned any semblance of healthy eating. They had sandwiches from Margiotta's for lunch, and takeaways in the evening when they were too tired to do more than wash the paintbrushes. There had been wine.

It's mid-afternoon when Tess gets back to Library Terrace and she can see there's a mini-skip sitting in the road outside. The white enamel sink has been dropped in at one end and a pile of disconnected pipes and taps lie beside it. The ancient electric cooker is upside down, its door lying open, surrounded by heaps of torn lino and wall tiles. Georgia has obviously had a clearing crew in.

If she would just tell me these things are happening, thinks Tess. She takes her new, not-smart, no-frills phone from her pocket and checks for texts.

Nothing.

As she walks around to the back garden she hears a new sound coming from the house. Is that music?

The door between the scullery and the kitchen is closed. She ties Baxter's lead to a hook beside the back door and lifts the grocery bags onto the scullery worktop. The long, narrow room is now sporting a variety of cooking appliances. A slow cooker had arrived from Fiona two weeks ago, and judging by the smell of spices in the room, it's already being put to good use. Tess opens the door to the kitchen and is faced with a scene of destruction. The only furniture left in the room is the kitchen table and the built-in dresser opposite the window. Everything else has been moved out, or disposed of. Various wires with brightly coloured insulating tape over their ends protrude from the wall. The table has been covered with dust sheets to protect it. Someone has embedded a claw hammer in the wall below the mantelpiece.

In the middle of the chaos, Georgia is dancing with a slim, white-haired man. He is holding her close and they are doing a very small on-the-spot shuffle. The radio is playing jazz so loudly that they don't hear her come in.

The man stops dancing suddenly when he sees her. 'You must be Tess,' he shouts over the music.

Georgia turns the radio down. 'Stan, this is Tess. Tess, this is Stan.' She looks around at the bare floorboards and hammer-pocked walls. 'We got a little carried away.'

Shouldn't Stan be up the west coast somewhere, with his sick wife? Tess thinks, before she can stop herself.

'Look!' Georgia points at a widening hole in the plaster. 'You can see the range properly now. I thought it might be rusted away to nothing but it's still there.'

'It must have had a good clean and some black lead before it was boarded up,' says Stan, 'and the room is dry, or it was until that pipe burst, so that will have helped too.'

Tess peers through the gap. 'It's *huge*.'

'It is indeed.' Georgia rubs her forehead, leaving a white plaster-dust trail. 'And it made the best Yorkshire puddings you've ever had.'

'What are you going to do? Cover it back up?'

'Not at all. It's been hidden away for fifty years and I want to see it again. It was Annie who was fed up with it and wanted some modern conveniences.'

'Is it usable?' Tess has a vague memory of her nana talking about making treacle toffee on the range in the house where she grew up.

'I'm not sure. Not with the coal we used to get, that's for sure. What do you think, Stan?'

He taps the wall above the mantelpiece. 'It would have to be smokeless fuel now. There are rules. It will depend on the state of your chimney, but maybe for occasional use it would be alright. I don't think you'd be wanting to cook on it all the time, even if you were allowed to.'

'Isobel used to make some amazing meals on it.'

'Isobel?'

'She was the maid, or at least she was when Annie was a child. She and Annie became good friends but they were pretty competitive in the baking department.'

Tess is still none the wiser about *exactly* how Annie and Georgia are connected.

Stan leans to right and left to stretch his back. 'There are three of us now. Maybe with some effort we could get the rest of that hardboard and plaster away and let the dog see the rabbit, so to speak. Might as well do it while you've still got that skip outside.'

'I bought some of those extra-strong rubbish sacks when I was doing the groceries,' Tess offers. 'Looks as though they're going to come in useful.'

Stan wiggles the hammer to loosen it, and as it comes away, another cloud of plaster dust escapes from the wall. He passes it to Georgia. 'Don't go at it too hard. With any luck we might be able to pull the rest of the board away.'

Georgia hesitates.

'Can I just get Baxter into the house?' says Tess. 'I don't really want him left on his own outside, he might be frightened.'

'The famous Baxter!' says Stan. 'I've heard a lot about him. Perhaps we can get to know one another later.'

Tess goes back outside and unhooks the lead. She bends down and scratches Baxter's head. 'I don't want you getting splinters in your paws,' she whispers, 'so we'll go in through the front door and you can sit in the drawing room.'

She arrives back in the kitchen in time to hear Stan giving instructions. 'Come on, lass. It's your house, your kitchen. You're the only one here who remembers it, so it seems only right that you should be the one to let us see it again.'

'I'll probably hit the wrong place and ruin it,' Georgia displays an uncharacteristic lack of confidence, 'but if you insist.' She smacks the claws of the hammer into the board, at chest height, where the space above the oven would be, and levers the board towards her. She does it again, and again, until there is a channel across the top, and she can push her fingers into the gap and give the board a tug. At first nothing happens, and she leans backwards, bracing herself, legs apart, feet planted on the floorboards. There is a cracking sound, and she starts to tumble backwards. Stan leaps to catch her as the wall gives way and a large sheet of board and plaster fall into the room. Through the cloud of grey dust, a huge black hunk of metal is visible below the mantelpiece at last.

Stan picks the hammer up from the floor and passes it back to Georgia. She starts again, pulling off smaller sections of board. Little by little, the whole range is revealed.

'You'll be able to use the frame for kindling if I chop it up for you,' says Stan. 'But first we need a brush and a shovel.' They stand aside as he sweeps the floor slowly, sprinkling water onto the mess to minimise the amount of dust that billows up. His floppy white hair has fallen forward and he pushes it back and out of his eyes.

Tess can see that he must once have been a good-looking man. He still is. She drags herself back to the present and examines the range. 'That's quite a lump of ironwork.'

Georgia nods. 'It wasn't just a cooker, it heated all the hot water when I was growing up as well. It had to be on all year, and if it was raining we used to dry the clothes on the pulley in here. It was cosy in the winter, but I can remember it being absolutely sweltering in the summer. Annie was so, so pleased to have an electric cooker instead. Nowadays we look at something like this with rose-tinted spectacles, but it wasn't easy to manage or to keep stoked up. There was definitely an art to it.'

'I expect it would polish up a treat,' says Stan. 'It's a fine example of domestic engineering.'

'I wonder,' says Georgia, thoughtfully. 'When Keith boxed it in, Annie and I were away youth hostelling on the west coast; it was at the end of my second year at university and it was a treat for doing well in my exams. We already had the electric cooker so the range hadn't been used for a while and it was just gathering dust. Soot kept falling down the chimney and Annie got so exasperated with it. So when we were away, Keith got it all framed out and plastered. Annie was so pleased.' Georgia traces a letter G in the sooty dust on the hotplate. 'But

Natalie Fergie

I remember coming into the scullery from the garden on the evening we got home and they were standing in the kitchen. They didn't know I was there, and I heard her ask if he had looked in the oven before he started the work, and he said he hadn't. He was quite upset that he'd done something wrong but she just hugged him and told him she thought she might have put something in it for safekeeping when she was having a clear-out one day. And then she said that she was probably mistaken and it wasn't important.'

Georgia bends down and grips the handle on the oven door. She turns it and the door swings open. Inside is a small box. 'What have we here then? Is a fifty-year-old mystery going to be revealed?' She reaches for it. 'Or not, I suppose. It might be empty.'

But when Georgia straightens up and opens the box, Tess can see that inside it is a small key.

338

Chapter 61

July 2011

'I need you to go in the attic for me,' says Georgia. 'I was going to ask Stan but he had to get back up north to be ready for Hazel coming out of the hospice. She's been in for a week's respite care.'

'You want me to go up there right now?' Tess is at the scullery sink, washing the courgettes Georgia had collected from Stan's allotment that morning.

'Soon,' Georgia replies, 'I'll be in my office for the afternoon,' and she disappears up the uncarpeted wooden stairs to the room above the scullery.

Tess sighs. Things have been rather strained since the little box was found.

'If only Georgia was consistently one thing or another,' she had said to Fiona just last week. 'One minute she is chatty and friendly and as soon as I think we are getting somewhere, the shutters come down again and we are back to monosyllables. I can't make it out at all.'

'She has her reasons,' Fiona had said.

'I wish she would tell me what they are. We're going to be living in the same house for the next twenty months, and this is bloody painful.'

'I expect she'll tell you in her own good time.'

That was last week, and again Georgia had gradually warmed up again. It was exhausting.

In the continuing absence of a properly functioning kitchen, Georgia has bought an Instant Pot, which does all manner of clever things without the need for a hob.

Tess chops a red pepper into chunks and adds it to the onions in the new appliance. The recipe she is using is from Sally Soodles' Spice Company. Every Thursday a box is delivered by the postman in a special flat package that fits through the letterbox. Inside is a sheet of instructions and a small flat tin containing a blend of spices. Tess unscrews the lid and sniffs, trying to work out what is in the mixture. Cumin, coriander, maybe a bit of cardamom? She gives up and looks at the label. Those three plus turmeric and sumac, whatever that is, and there's a separate little bag of chilli seeds so she can adjust the heat. It's a very clever idea.

She sprinkles the spices onto the sautéed vegetables, gives them a stir to encourage the flavours to develop and adds a tin of tomatoes, a vegetable stock cube and some sweetcorn from the freezer, for colour. She puts the lid on, sets the timer and leaves it to cook.

The big kitchen with its black iron range has become temporarily redundant as a cooking space, and to their mutual surprise, Georgia and Tess are managing perfectly well doing all the cooking and cleaning up in the scullery. They eat outside, working their way around the garden, following the sunshine from the picnic table in the morning to the garden bench at lunchtime, and later, the chairs under the plum tree, in an effort to catch whatever warmth there is. They only retreat to the drawing room with trays when the weather chooses not to behave. Tess's tentative suggestion that the scullery could be made into an efficient galley kitchen more permanently had initially been met with a dismissive 'I really don't think so', but over the last week Georgia has started to warm to the idea. She still refuses to lock the back door at night, though.

A few days earlier, to Tess's astonishment, there had been a visit from an electrician and another from a plasterer and it seems that plans are afoot. When the electrician did his estimate, she had heard Georgia say, 'I saw the light switches on Pinterest,' and had almost gasped, but managed to contain herself at the last minute.

Chapter 62

July 2011

Tess uses the door knocker at the bottom of the stairs and waits. She has never set foot in the office above the scullery. It is strictly off limits.

'Yes?'

'You asked if I could go up in the attic for you?'

Georgia comes to the office door and smiles, without a trace of the grumpiness of the last twenty-four hours. 'Yes, please. I suffer from vertigo so I've never been up there.'

'Sorry. I didn't know.'

'Why would you?' Georgia pulls her phone out of her pocket and holds it out to Tess. 'I wonder if you might be able to make a video. I can decide what to do after I've seen what's up there.'

Tess feels her heart sink to her feet. 'On your phone?'

'Yes. It's quite easy, I can show you if you aren't sure.'

'Is there a ladder?' Tess decides it's probably better to get the task over and done with. 'I could go up now, while dinner is cooking.'

'I have Keith's decorating ladders. They are quite old now, but still perfectly safe. Annie just about laid an egg every time he went up there. I don't want you to fetch

342

anything down, though. Not yet, anyway. I just want to know what there is. It shouldn't take long.'

*

Tess looks up at the hatch on the ceiling of the first-floor landing and pushes it upwards and out of the way with the end of the ladder.

'I wish I could do it myself but my legs just go to jelly if I do more than stand on a chair.' Georgia is positively chatty. 'Some of the houses around here have three storeys instead of two. You've probably noticed the pair across the road. Apparently, when they were being built you could choose what you wanted the insides to be like. Some people continued the big staircase up for another storey and had dormer windows. The maids in those houses quickly looked for fresh appointments because their workload was immense, poor things.'

'When was anyone last up in the attic?'

'I'm not sure; when I had the insulation put in about ten years ago, I suppose.'

Tess rests the ladder on the edge of the hatch. To her surprise, it feels solid.

'You'll be fine. Keith was meticulous about maintenance.'

'He sounds like a sensible man.'

'He was, most definitely. Right, you'll need this.' She hands over her phone. 'I've set the camera up to record so just press the red button and it will do it all for you.'

Tess feels the familiar shape in her hand. 'It's OK, I know how to use it. Is there a passcode on it, so I can unlock it if it turns itself off?'

'One nine one one.'

343

Tess isn't bothered by the height. She climbs confidently, steps off the ladder at the top and turns on the torch app. 'Is there a light up here?'

'There's a switch on the left, I think.'

A square of brightness appears at the hatch. 'Got it.'

'Can you see anything?'

Tess half expects the attic to be full of muddle and dust and old household implements, but it's almost empty. There are just three boxes of the sort that whisky or wine might be delivered in near the entrance hatch, and a bit further along there's an old sports bag.

'There's not much here,' she calls back down. 'I'll take that video for you.' Her hands shake as she touches the red circle on the screen and it takes her four attempts before she can make a decent recording.

She climbs back down and passes the phone to Georgia.

'Three boxes. One says "House", one has your name on it and one says "Finlay". And there's a sports bag which looks pretty old.'

'And that's it?'

'Yes.'

Georgia takes the phone and opens the photo app. 'Thank you.'

'I did a panorama and went into all the corners, see? It's definitely empty, apart from those things.'

'You need to get the boxes down.' Georgia is in instruction mode again, and then she softens. 'If you wouldn't mind?'

'I'll see how heavy they are. They went up the ladder so they'll come down it, I guess.' Tess climbs back up.

*

'Kitchen!' says Georgia, when everything has been retrieved.

Tess is taken aback by the urgency. 'I think we'll need to clear the big table first. It's covered in paint charts.'

'I suppose you're right.' Georgia looks at Tess. 'Ever had anything to do with the police?'

An image of Patrick's garden at Craiglockhart flashes across Tess's mind. She dismisses the thought. 'Never.'

'That's a pity.' Georgia picks up the smallest box. 'I think we may need some detective skills.'

Tess admires Georgia's restraint. She is quite sure that she herself would have put the attic treasure on the drawing-room floor and opened the boxes immediately. But Georgia is, she is learning, a stickler for doing things in the right order.

Chapter 63

July 2011

Over the last week the broom in the kitchen has been put to good use, as have the dustpan and brush, the vacuum cleaner and finally the trusty string mop and galvanised bucket. The table is back in the middle of the room and is acting as Planning Central with leaflets from Farrow & Ball and samples of wall tiles and flooring.

Georgia looks at the boxes. 'Let's do the sports bag first. It's probably just old kit.'

FJB is printed on the front near the clasp.

'Finlay John Black.' Georgia runs her fingers over the initials before opening the clasp. 'He lived here, a long time ago.' Inside is what's left of a cricket sweater, bound with blue around the V neck, and very much the worse for being a century old. 'Outside!' demands Georgia. 'I don't want moths in the house.'

Tess does as instructed and dumps the raggedy knitwear on the picnic bench in the garden. When she comes back Georgia is already lifting the remaining items out of the bag, one at a time.

'One pair of studded boots. These were white once upon a time, I suppose. And a pair of trousers.' She checks the pockets but finds nothing apart from some beach sand. 'Two, no, three, four cricket balls, and two bats.'

Tess catches a glint of brown glass in the corner of the bag and reaches for it. 'And a very old bottle of linseed oil.' She holds it up to the light. 'There's still some inside.'

'Put it all in the garden, please. We can deal with it properly later.'

'Are you sure you don't want to do this in private?'

Georgia lays a hand on the box marked "Finlay". 'I thought about that when I watched you carrying the boxes down that ladder. But this house is your home now, and these people lived here before either of us. You are part of the story of the place and you might even have a box of your own one day, who knows?' She traces the painted letters with her finger. 'And this is a mystery, so I need a Lewis.'

'A Lewis?'

'If I am going to be Inspector Morse, I need a Sergeant Lewis to be my bag woman. I think that's how it was described in the TV series. Someone to question what I'm thinking and make sure it's correct.'

'Alright.' Tess is still not completely sure.

'Don't worry, I'll be sure to tell you when I've had enough. Now, which box is likely to be the easiest?'

'No idea.'

'We've got to start somewhere. House. It looks as good as any of them.' She cuts the string and opens the box. 'Diaries. Lots of them.' She opens the cover of the first one that comes to hand and flips through the pages to the end. '1921. Look, there's a diary in the front half and lots of pages for notes at the back.' She turns a few pages. 'I think this is Ursula's handwriting. I've seen it on the back of old photographs.'

'What does it say?'

'It looks like the planning notes for a trip to France. There are train times and ferry costs. I wonder if she was going on holiday?'

Tess leans over the box. 'Shall I take the rest of them out so we can have a proper look?'

'Good idea.'

Tess sets the black books out on the table. 'We've got 1919, 1913 . . .' She sorts the first dozen into chronological order. 'The first one is from 1911.'

'I think these will bear closer examination in due course. Are there other years?'

'Lots.' Tess continues to check for dates. 'It looks as though there's one for every year from 1911 to 1964, right the way through without a gap. You know, I bet an archivist would love to get their hands on these. Social history on the kitchen table.'

'1964 is the year Annie died. Is there anything else in the box?'

'Two envelopes. They were underneath all the bundles. Letters, maybe?'

'Open them up, then. Tell me what they say.'

'You wouldn't rather read them yourself?'

Georgia shook her head. 'My eyes are tired. You read for me.'

The paper of the first letter is thin, creased into thirds and then thirds again. The folds are worn, as though it has been folded and unfolded many times, and the edges of the paper are uneven with age and handling.

Tess carries it over to the window to get a better light, and begins to read what was once black ink, and is now faded to brown.

Dear Ann,

I cannot tell you how sorry you have made both Father and one that you have been so naughty as to merit such a punishment. Perhaps it will make you feel it more and resolve to be more obedient when you think how very disappointed I am. Finlay was looking forward to you coming home on Saturday with such joy and now you must stay at school and it is all ruined.

You see the punishment does not fall on you only, it comes on us as well. You will have made your teacher sorry too. No one likes to punish but you make it necessary by your bad behaviour. Your grandmother is coming on Saturday and we are going to have strawberries and cream but you have spoiled all the pleasure for us.

Think, and pray that God will help you overcome your perverse spirit. I hope that next time I hear about you it will be more agreeable news.

You really are an impossible child. I am surprised we are related at all.

Mother

'"Father and one"?' queries Tess. 'It's so formal.'

'It's how people wrote in those days, I suppose.' Georgia feels for Hazel's brass ring on her finger. 'This is about Annie. She lived in this house from when she was ten years old, and never left it. It was Annie who first took in the lodgers.' Georgia looks across at the garden. 'I remember planting fruit bushes with her, but she absolutely refused to grow any strawberries. Wouldn't touch the things.' She spins the inner ring around its groove. 'What's the date on it?'

'Not sure. Oh, wait a minute, there's something on the back. "Mother's letter, June 1906."'

'Annie was born in 1898, so she was eight years old when she was sent this . . . this *tirade*.' Georgia is quietly furious. 'Eight years old! And she had been sent to boarding school at that age. Imagine getting a letter not just berating you for whatever you have done or not done, but salt being rubbed into the wound by telling you how sad your brother is. And then adding all that nonsense about the strawberry cream tea you are going to miss.'

Tess doesn't know what to say.

'It's inhuman. That's what it is.'

'Are you sure it was sent to Annie? It definitely just says Ann.'

'She changed her name. I think she was in her thirties when she did it. I don't know why. Ann and Annie are pretty close anyway. Finlay was her brother, and she told me once, near the end of her life, that his pet name for her was Annie Bee. Maybe that was the reason. We'll never know, will we?'

'Is it not an odd thing to do, though, change your name halfway through your life?'

'Is it? Women do it all the time when they marry, even though they don't have to.'

'I've never thought of it like that.'

'A name defines who you are, and if you're living your life with a name that doesn't fit, or perhaps one that has bad associations, then why not change it?' Georgia picks up the letter and peers at it. 'Annie said that Ursula's father changed his name. He came to this country as a child, and he was called Bernhard Schmidt. He became an engineer and when he set up his business, he changed his name to Bernard Smith. She said that his father, back in Germany, never spoke to him again.'

'And you've never seen this before?'

'Never.' Georgia stops spinning the ring and laces her fingers together, elbows on the table, like a child saying grace before dinner. 'When I was a child, there was a meeting here, with the neighbours. Something about the dustbins in the street not being collected regularly. They were going to write a joint letter to Edinburgh Corporation. It was after my bedtime and I was sitting about halfway up the stairs, just high enough that I wouldn't be seen. I think I was about seven or eight and I wanted to know what it was they were talking about.' She unlaces her fingers and spreads them out on the table, stretching her handspan as far as possible. 'I heard one of the women ask Annie if I wouldn't be better off at a boarding school. I have no idea who asked the question, but I heard her reply quite loudly that under no circumstances was any child of hers going to a boarding school. I remember it particularly because I knew that I wasn't *her* child. When you are young, and your parents are dead, and everyone else lives with a mummy and a daddy, or so it felt to me at the time, that was such a comforting thing to hear. It was as if she was claiming me.' Georgia paused. 'There was apparently some talk of me going to live with a relative in Canada when I was very young, but it never came to anything because the Atlantic was a dangerous place during the Second World War, so I stayed here in Edinburgh and that was that. Years later she told me that she would never have sent me to people I didn't know halfway across the world. I can hear her saying it now. She was so definite about it all. I think whoever the mysterious relative was must have died because it was never mentioned again.'

'Would you like me to read the other letter?'

'Please. We may as well finish dealing with this box today.'

The envelope is made from thick blue paper, just like the sheet of paper inside it. This one is folded in two, so it looks like the pages of a book, and then in two again. Tess peers at the spidery handwriting which has many underlinings and capital letters.

August 1911
Barry, South Wales

Ursula, My Bonnie Darling,

I returned here last night and found your letter waiting for me. I sent postcards to Ann and Finlay on Tuesday and another one to you from Ilfracombe on Wednesday, which I trust that you received all right.

I know that I am not always easy to live with, but believe me I will always return your love and caresses forty fold or more, if you will accept them, and we will not contemplate any other form which cannot be repaid by me in that way. What do you say, eh? Ma Cherie!

With regard to my staying longer as suggested in your letter I have given the matter much consideration and have decided . . . . NOT to prolong my stay, but will leave for home tomorrow (Saturday) by Fishguard Express, leaving Cardiff at 1 o'clock. I will stay in London overnight and return to Edinburgh on Sunday.

I shall be glad to see your gentle sweet face again I assure you, and the longing to have your company is all powerful with me. The time has seemed long since I last saw you and I will not willingly make it any longer, so all being well I will be home on Sunday and have no doubt you will think I have done right and be glad to see me again.

You may possibly think this rather the letter of a lover than a husband, pray consider it as coming from BOTH. I have written what I feel, there! And you must take me as I am – love and all.

On consulting my diary I see that when I was here last year, a bridegroom of just a few days was drowned in the sea in full view of his wife. How impossibly sad! How thankful we ought to feel that we have each other, so rich in love in our home.

I will forever be grateful that you said yes to my proposal ... and I will not forget what Ann had to endure for so long. You must believe me when I say that you have never been second best in my eyes.

Loving kisses and a thousand kind thoughts for my darling.

Yours always,

John

Tess passes the paper to Georgia. 'Wow. Not formal at all this time.'

Georgia looks down at the words. 'It's a love letter.' She strokes the thick paper. 'It's all so *recent*, isn't it?'

'How do you mean?'

Georgia refolds the paper carefully. 'This is the sort of letter that any man might write to a new wife who is taking the place of someone who died, and who is feeling terribly, terribly anxious that she isn't doing enough to make the family happy. Today it would be less flowery, and probably sent as an email, or a text, but the sentiment is the same. He has spent a lot of time on it and filled it with love and reassurance.'

Tess sighs. 'I read somewhere that future historians will despair at the lack of twenty-first century letters and diaries. To be honest I'm struggling to see how everyone fits together. I think I need a family tree.'

'It's all in my head, but I could write it down sometime I suppose.' Georgia slips the letter back into its envelope.

'Ursula was John's second wife. I don't know a great deal about the first one; it was a forbidden subject. Annie wouldn't even say her name. But it seems as though she was the one who wrote that horrid strawberry letter.' Georgia pushes her chair back from the table and stands up. 'I think I need to rest for a little while now, I'm quite tired all of a sudden. We can do another box tomorrow.'

Chapter 64

July 2011

When Tess and Baxter come down for breakfast in the morning, the second box is open and Georgia has already started to make an attempt at organising things.

'Tea?' offers Tess.

'It will be CT3 for me; I was up early. But yes, tea and toast. And marmalade as well, please.'

'Are you getting anywhere?'

'Sort of. This is Finlay's box. There are a lot of school exercise books, and what looks like university notes. And there are these.' Georgia has already laid some items out on the table. 'Pip, Squeak and Wilfred, the First World War medals.' The medal ribbons are bright, but the medals themselves are dull metal. 'Everyone got them, pretty much. It looks as though Finlay gave up university to go and fight because he was there from 1914 but sadly he didn't last until the end.' She picks up a letter and hands it to Tess. 'This is from his commanding officer. He was killed during an offensive in France and led his men courageously, whatever that means.' Her voice drops. 'I suppose whatever the circumstances were, being described as brave might have been some comfort to the people who loved him.'

She picks up a square of brown cardboard, folded in on itself, the diagonals looking like the start of a child's fortune teller. 'And this is a Dead Man's Penny. They were issued to the families of the fallen.' She slips the metal disc out of the cardboard sleeve and passes it to Tess. It's dark grey, almost black, and about five inches across.

'His name is on it, see? And the date that he died. Some families had special stands made so they could put the medal on a mantelpiece as a remembrance. But that happened later.' She paused. 'Annie always left the scullery door open for him, as Ursula had.'

'Why?'

'Because his body was never found. She didn't believe that he was gone, even though they went to see the place where he was supposed to have died. It's the reason they weren't here for the census in 1921.'

'Could that explain why there were all those notes about trains and ferries?'

'Possibly. She said that if for some reason he couldn't tell anyone he was on his way home, she might miss him. He might arrive on the train at Waverley and walk up from the station to surprise them, and find the door locked. Ursula was worried that if he couldn't get into the house he might go away again and they would never know, so the scullery door was never locked, just the kitchen door. And there was always a chair set aside every evening, and a piece of bread in a tin, and a bottle of ale.'

'In a tin?'

'To stop the mice.'

'But he *was* dead?'

'She never believed it. She was convinced he was still alive.'

'I suppose you can see how she might have thought that, if he was never found.' Tess turns the black disc over in her hands and reads the inscription.

'It was a compulsion. She told me that in the end everyone stopped commenting and just let her do it. And I suppose if it allowed her to sleep at night, then what was the harm?'

'You leave the door open now.'

'It's what I grew up with. I just continued with it. And occasionally a lodger has stayed out late or lost a key and I have found them asleep on the chair in the scullery in the morning.' Georgia smiles. 'But I don't leave bread and ale out for them.'

'Is there anything else in there?'

'There is a photograph of him. That's the last thing.' Georgia studies the black and white photo and automatically unpinches her fingers over it, as though to enlarge the image. 'He looks like a fine young man. Most of them were.' She draws it closer to her face. 'He has grown a moustache, see? And he's in his uniform. I think he wants to look like an officer who leads his men.' She props the photograph up against a pile of cookery books on the dresser. 'Welcome home, Finlay. I'll get you a proper frame very soon.'

'What do you want to do with his medals?' Tess says gently.

'Back in the box for now. They'll be safe there. And the Dead Man's Penny as well.' She pulls herself back to the present. 'We can do the last box after lunch. We'll eat in the garden, under Finlay's tree.'

Chapter 65

July 2011

The lettering on the last box is clear.

GEORGIA

There are school jotters marked 'History' and 'Mathematics', English essays, sports day awards, and two school ties. And there is a file containing birth and marriage and death certificates, including one for a Louise Black in 1909.

Georgia opens one of many school reports at random and reads it out loud. '"Georgia is a most interesting and talented young lady."' She laughs. 'I am quite sure that "interesting" wasn't meant as a compliment.'

'What else is there?'

'More letters, some postcards. It's all a bit of a jumble.'

'Who died first?'

'Pardon?'

'Who went first, Keith or Annie?'

'Annie, in 1964. And she couldn't have got the boxes into the attic, so Keith is the person who put all this up there. I was away for a few days and when I came home, he had already done it. A bit like when he did the kitchen upgrade without telling Annie what his plans were.'

'Was he, I don't know ... tidying up? Putting papers away that perhaps you might not feel able to look at after he was gone.'

'Maybe.'

'I mean, he didn't destroy anything. It's as though he was putting it all away safely so the boxes would be there for you when you were ready for them.'

'Possibly. Keith was like that. He had a knack for understanding what you needed before you knew it yourself.' Georgia reaches across the table for a tissue and wipes away the tears that have suddenly arrived. 'He missed Annie dreadfully. He died in his sleep a couple of months after she did.' She blows her nose and straightens herself up. 'Better get on. If we stop now, we'll never get started again.' She takes a deep breath. 'Perhaps this box is a bit of a muddle because Annie wasn't there to tell Keith what was important. There are holiday postcards from the seaside and bills for coal and old Christmas cards all mixed up together.'

'You could be right. Is there anything that stands out?'

Georgia rifles through a few papers. 'Not really.'

'May I?'

'Be my guest. Fresh eyes and all that.' Georgia sits down, lost in thought.

Tess goes through every item methodically, dividing them into official documents, more and more school papers, and general bills. By the time she is finished there are two items left. 'I think that's everything, apart from these.'

'Alright, let's see what you've discovered.'

'There's another letter. And there's a jewellery box, but it's locked and I think it's empty. It doesn't rattle or anything.'

'Let's look at the letter, then. Off you go, Lewis, do the honours.'

Tess takes a single sheet of paper from a small envelope and starts to read.

9th October 1931

Dear Miss Black,

I am writing to you today to very belatedly express my condolences on the loss of your father and Mrs Black, and of your brother Finlay.

I need to give you what may or may not be welcome information. I am aware that what I am about to say may cause either acute distress or joy, and if it is the former, please allow me to apologise in advance.

My name is Beatrice Sidcup. I am writing to introduce you to Olivia, my daughter. She is seventeen years of age now, and a hardworking, bright young woman.

She is also your late brother's daughter.

Tess keeps reading, unaware of Georgia's reaction.

I am sure that you will have many questions, and I look forward to having the opportunity to explain further. I would like you to meet Olivia, but would prefer to see you privately first to discuss the rather sensitive circumstances of this revelation.

Please be assured that I would not be contacting you after seventeen years if it were not absolutely essential.

If I might be so bold, this is a matter of some urgency, for reasons I will explain in person. I will call on Friday at three o'clock.

Yours sincerely,
Beatrice Sidcup (Mrs)

'This sounds important.' Tess looks up to find Georgia lost in thought, staring out of the window right up to the far end of the garden where the fruit on the plum tree is starting to ripen. She waits until Georgia has gathered herself back together and hands her the letter carefully, worried she might drop it.

'Olivia was my mother,' Georgia says quietly. All trace of yesterday's furious indignation about a strawberry tea has gone. She pauses as she attempts to make sense of the details. 'She was a lodger in this house, just like you. She met my father at university here in Edinburgh and they lived here too. They were mathematicians, and they worked for some important government department in London during the Second World War. I was just a toddler then, and I stayed here with Annie and Keith because it meant my parents could both contribute to the war effort.' She unfolds the letter. 'I have no memory of them at all. Of course, there are photographs. But I can't remember them ever kissing me goodnight, or reading me a story, nothing like that. They were killed in the Blitz.' Georgia sighs. 'In the Primary One school report I looked at this morning, the teacher describes me as "strong", but I don't think I was. Keith and Annie looked after me, and I was never allowed to think I wasn't loved. Not for a minute.'

Georgia reads Beatrice Sidcup's letter from start to finish for herself, then reads it again.

Tess tries to pull the threads together. 'So, Finlay is . . .'

'Finlay is my grandfather,' says Georgia softly. She walks over to the dresser and picks up the photograph of the young man in his soldier's uniform.

'Finlay Black is my grandfather, and I do belong in this house after all.'

Chapter 66

August 2011

For several weeks, Georgia has been different. Tess has found her in various rooms in the house, sitting quietly, apparently doing very little. The newly framed photograph of Finlay seems to move around with her, as though Georgia is trying to decide where to display it. Tess has asked her a number of times if she is alright, or if there is anything she needs help with, and has had little by way of a response. Normally Georgia would be irritated by this sort of question, but she is uncharacteristically placid about it all. Eventually, one evening after dinner, Tess takes the bull by the horns.

'I'm worried about you.'

'Worried?'

'I know that letter was a shock and I'm wondering if you need to talk to someone about it.'

'I don't think I want to do that.'

Tess tries again. 'Counselling might help, if there's something troubling you.'

'I'm not troubled. I feel quite peaceful, actually.' Georgia smiles. 'A lot of questions I've been asking myself for years have been answered.'

'Do you not wonder why you were never told about him? I would be pretty cross about that if it was me.'

Georgia leans forward and rests on her elbows. 'I confess that, yes, there have been a few days where I was pretty annoyed about it. But what's the point? Annie and Keith aren't here to ask. All I can do is assume they did it for my benefit. Maybe they thought those mythical Canadian relatives I was told about might turn up on the doorstep and try to steal me away from them? I'll never know.' She sat back in her chair. 'I could spend weeks, years, trying to square that particular circle, and at best, it would be an educated guess.'

Tess waits to see if there is anything else, but that seems to be it. Eventually, she breaks the silence. 'Georgia, can you tell me what you're doing with his photograph? I can help you hang it up if you like.'

'I haven't decided where to put it.'

'Right. It's just that I found it on the mantelpiece in my room today. I got quite a fright.'

'Sorry about that, I should have asked you.' Georgia stands up and collects the photograph from the dresser. 'I'm telling him about the house, and about all the people who have been here since he left.' She hugs the frame close to her chest. 'I'm taking him into each room and introducing him to everyone who has stayed here. All the people he never met.' She points at the table. 'He sat here sometimes, you know, in this room, eating the oaty biscuits that Isobel made, and the parkin. Have I told you about her? I can't remember. She used to tell me stories about Finlay and how he used to steal a cheese scone or two when he thought he could get away with it. I had no idea he was my grandfather, but I think Isobel must have known.' Georgia looks at Tess. 'I'm sorry about being in your room. I was there because it was his bedroom, and I thought he should know about you too.'

She stops for a moment, but she hasn't finished.

'I want him to know all about what Annie was like when she grew up, because she was his little sister and I think it's important that he knows who she became. He saved her life when she was thirteen and they were very close after that. And of course, he was the reason she took in lodgers in the first place. It was his legacy. And I really wanted to tell him about Keith. He would have been pleased that Annie found someone who loved her so much. I think the two of us are almost up to date now, but a hundred years is a lot to catch up on.' Georgia studies the photograph. 'I'm telling him about myself as well, because I'm his granddaughter. I think I'm nearly finished, though. Today I was explaining about some things that are going on in my life at the moment.' She pauses. 'You see, I don't need a counsellor. I have a grandfather, and he's a very good listener.'

Tess understands at last. It all makes perfect sense now.

Chapter 67

Late August 2011

Georgia is starting to feel as though the work on the house is almost complete, even though the kitchen is far from being finished. The restlessness which she has felt under the surface all her life is settling, little by little, with each day that passes.

She is getting ready to go out when the visitor arrives. For a whole week the house has been full of Radio 2 and the singing of the plasterer who seems to know all of the words to all of the songs and is actually rather good, almost operatic, but very, very loud. He has been in the kitchen all morning, doing the last bits and pieces, but has run out of something vital and has gone off in his van to collect it from the wholesaler.

The place smells of change, which is not unpleasant, but it's all a bit overwhelming. Georgia is going to grab the chance to visit the library to exchange her books and perhaps sit and read the newspapers. She has reserved a copy of Ottolenghi's *Plenty*.

When she hears the back door open, she assumes it's the plasterer and she doesn't turn around, but continues to put her things into her rucksack. 'I'm just popping out to get something for dinner. I expect I'll be home at about three. Help yourself to tea. There are some biscuits in the yellow tin next to the kettle. Just shop ones, I'm afraid. I'm very much looking forward to having an oven again.'

'Where is she?' It's a man's voice. Someone she hasn't heard before.

Georgia turns around quickly. The visitor is standing in the kitchen doorway, both feet on the first of the two scullery steps. Brown hair, tanned, looks as though he goes to the gym; all these things rush through her head.

'I think you've come to the wrong house,' she replies.

'And I think I have not.'

Well-manicured hands. A signet ring. Never mind about the ring, he could always take it off. It might leave a white mark on his finger, though. Little finger, right hand.

She can feel herself becoming extremely calm. 'Which house is it you are looking for?'

Hard to see his eyes from this distance. Mole above his left eyebrow.

'Number 25. I know she's here.' He takes a phone from his trouser pocket and stabs at the screen.

Left-handed. Needs glasses. Same height as the hinge on the door jamb.

'Electoral roll. Tess Dutton. 25 Library Terrace.'

'You're looking for Tess? She isn't here today.'

'I can wait.' He looks past her. The kitchen table and chairs are covered up with plastic sheeting.

'I'm afraid that's not convenient; we are in a state of disarray, as you can see.'

'I'm not in a rush. I've got all day,' he replies, speaking carefully.

Is he drunk? Georgia isn't sure.

'She won't be back until this evening.'

'You're lying.'

366

He is squaring up to her; she sees him lean forward a little and put his left foot on the next step.

'I'm not lying. She is never here on Wednesdays.'

He seems suddenly unsure.

'If you tell me what it is that you want, I will give her a message.'

He raises his voice. 'What I *want* is for her to answer the letters from my solicitor. What I *want* is compensation. What I *want* is for her to understand that she can't get away with this.'

'I will be sure to give Tess your messages when she comes back, but that won't be until this evening.'

He has no place to put his anger.

'May I ask why you didn't knock on the front door? That's what visitors usually do.'

He stares at her. 'They don't. Everyone comes round the back. Delivery people, tradesmen. I've been watching.'

'I suppose you're right, but I would be grateful if you would leave now, because I have to go out.'

He wags his finger at her.

Left-handed. She looks at his feet. Definitely. The shoelaces give it away.

'Just be sure you tell her, or I will be back.'

At this point Georgia is sure he is angry, not drunk.

'I'm going to Chicago tomorrow and I want this all sorted by the time I get back to Edinburgh in a month's time. I'm getting married, and I want my money.' And he turns back to the open scullery door, and leaves.

She lifts the plastic sheet off a chair and sits down. After a couple of minutes she takes out her diary and writes it all down. Left-handed, mole, fingernails, ring. Just as she is finishing, the plasterer arrives.

'I'm back!'

'So I see.'

'OK if I have a brew before I start?' He turns on the scullery tap to fill the kettle without waiting for an answer.

'Of course.' She looks at him. 'Just stand there for a moment, would you?'

He frowns. 'Sure. Is there a problem?'

'Not at all, I just want to check something. Stand on the first step there for me.'

He moves towards the kitchen and stands in the doorway, as requested. She moves back to her earlier position in the room and eyeballs his height against the top of the door hinge.

'How tall are you?'

He looks puzzled. 'Five foot ten. One metre seventy-eight and a bit, according to my GP. I was there yesterday and she said I could do with losing a few pounds.' He pats his tummy. 'So I probably shouldn't be eating your biscuits, Miss Williams.'

'Taller than that, so he must be about six feet then,' she mutters, and writes it down. 'I don't suppose one biscuit is going to hurt you, but I'll stop leaving temptation in your way.'

'Is everything alright?'

'Yes, everything is fine. I just had,' she pauses, 'I just had an unwanted visitor but I've sent him away. I don't suppose we'll see him again, but perhaps it would be an idea to close the back door while you're here.'

'You're the boss. No one will get past me, though; your worldly goods are safe as houses while I'm here.' He looks around the room. 'I should be finished in a couple of hours, there's just a bit of tidying up left to do.'

She tucks her diary into her rucksack and shoulders the bag. 'Thank you. As I say, I don't think he'll return, but that's very reassuring to hear. I'll be home at about three. If my lodger arrives before me, and I don't think she will, please don't mention the visitor; I wouldn't want her to be alarmed.'

He nods. 'My lips are sealed.'

She leaves by the scullery door and pulls it closed behind her.

Chapter 68

August 2011

The next day, exactly a month after the last grey envelope, there is another one. The mail falls onto the doormat on the same day as the spice parcel from Sally Soodles and this time it's Georgia who picks it up. She studies the envelope for a moment and then carries both items through to the freshly plastered kitchen where the new smooth finish is a sun-kissed pinky brown, and not yet completely dry. The way the old lumpy walls, pockmarked with rawl-plug damage and a hundred nail holes, have been transformed into this completely flat surface seems almost magical, and Georgia is eagerly awaiting the day when the first coat of paint can go on.

She stands in front of the window where the enamel sink had previously been and looks out along the garden to the chairs under the plum tree, and wonders if she should open the envelope. When there had been a lot of official envelopes a few years before, she had been respectful and not asked about them, seeing it as none of her business. But eventually, after her last lodger left, there had been a final letter from the Sheriff Court.

She puts Tess's envelope on the high mantelpiece above the now gleaming range, and goes down the two steps to the scullery. Instead of the old stone divided sink, once used for laundry as well as washing dishes, there is a stainless-steel model with a mixer tap, something Georgia has secretly coveted for a couple of decades. She wonders what Isobel, who was still visiting the house well into her seventies, would have thought about this new look, and about having an automatic washing machine instead of the old twin tub, and the mangle before that.

There are now two long stretches of worktop running almost the length of the scullery on each side, and a fridge freezer, and a separate hob and a waist-high oven which means she doesn't have to bend down any more. And there is a radiator. The height of luxury.

In the winter, the heat from that new radiator will rise up to the maid's room above, where her office is now. Isobel must have been terribly cold, she thinks.

*

Tess doesn't notice the envelope when she arrives back from her walk with Baxter. She smells the gorgeous spicy aroma coming from the Instant Pot and resists the urge to lift the lid and see what's for dinner.

Georgia comes down the stairs from her office and stands, arms folded, with a rather different demeanour from usual.

'Tess, I need you to sit down. I have something to ask you.'

'OK.' She sits.

And so does Baxter, which normally makes them both laugh, but Georgia is not laughing today.

'It's about this.' Georgia reaches up to the mantelpiece and retrieves the envelope.

Tess's face falls. She looks at Georgia and then at the envelope in her hand and then at the floor and then finally back at Georgia.

'I need to know what this is about. I know that you shredded one of these letters and used it to light the fire in the drawing room, I saw it with my own eyes. Is this the second letter? Or maybe the third?'

'I will sort it out.'

'Not before you tell me exactly what is going on here.'

'I said I will sort it out.'

Tess gets up to take the letter from Georgia but it is snatched out of her way.

'No!' Georgia doesn't budge. 'I want you to open that letter right now and show me what it says.'

'It's private.'

Georgia lifts her diary from the table and searches for the correct page. 'Does this ring any bells? Almost six feet tall, left-handed, mole above left eye, neat finger-nails, signet ring.' She looks up at Tess.

'Oh my God!'

'Is this the person the letters are about?'

'You've seen him? Oh shit! He's been here, hasn't he?'

'Yesterday.'

'What did he say? I am *so* sorry.'

'He said that if you do not respond to the letters he will come back, and that he wants compensation.'

'Right. This is terrible. I am so, so sorry.'

'What exactly is he wanting compensation for?'

Tess looks up at the newly plastered ceiling. 'It could be for a number of things.'

'I think it's time you opened that envelope and let me see what's inside it.'

Tess resists one last time. 'I promise I will sort it out.'

'I'm sure you will, but you see I've been on the wrong end of letters like this before because of a previous lodger, and I'm not going to be put in that position again.

So you'll forgive me for wanting to know exactly where I stand. This is my house and I cannot have it put at risk.'

Tess knows when she is beaten. 'Just open it. I don't suppose it says anything different from the last two.'

'Two?'

'Sorry.'

Georgia puts a kitchen knife under the flap and slices the paper neatly.

Dear Ms Dutton,

Please respond to our client's request for compensation for the following items:

One iPhone: £400

One spalted ash coffee table, handmade: £1,200

Payment of the enclosed invoice regarding reinstatement and repairs to the garden at 72 Craiglockhart Green, Edinburgh: £1,800

Sundry items: £300

Georgia studies the invoice.

'This is from a gardening company. Landscapers.'

'I know.'

Georgia looks at her watch. 'It's a little early, but I would like something to drink. A small whisky is in order, I think.' She opens the tall cupboard beside the range and takes out a bottle of Glenkinchie and two glasses. 'You need to tell me what's happening. Don't leave anything out.'

Tess doesn't drink whisky, but she makes an exception. Slowly, she proceeds to tell Georgia everything. She explains about living in Europe, about coming to live with Patrick in Edinburgh, and about the text messages from Xander.

'I blamed myself to start with. I told myself that if I really loved him, I should have noticed that he wasn't happy. But I was wrong. If someone wants to hide something, they will. I just hadn't realised there were questions that needed to be asked.' She swirls the last of the whisky around in her glass and drinks it. 'It's made me quite cynical about relationships, I think, because people can tell lies, even to those they care about, without saying a single word. I talked to Fiona about it once and she said it's called "lying by omission".'

Tess can feel her throat getting tight as she tries not to cry.

'I was a mess. We had been together for ages. I loved him so much. And everything just changed in a matter of minutes. My world disintegrated. For the first few days I couldn't function, I couldn't sleep or eat or anything.' She takes a deep breath. 'And then I super-glued his phone onto his very expensive handmade coffee table, and I got his electric drill, and I bored a hole right through the app where all the messages were, and into the wood.' She stops, remembering. 'And then I did something very silly.'

Georgia waits.

'He is, or he was, very proud of his garden, even though he hadn't been living in the house for years. It was written into all the tenancy agreements he drew up when the place was rented out that the garden had to be looked after, and he always arranged for a neighbour to let him know if it wasn't happening.' Tess rolls the empty glass between her palms.

'Go on . . .'

'I got the five-litre canister of weedkiller out of the shed and poured it, almost neat, into the watering can, and I wrote something on his ever-so-perfect front lawn, where all the neighbours would see it.'

'What did you write?'

'Nothing sweary or rude.'

Georgia raises an eyebrow.

'I wrote "LIAR", because he had been lying to me for months. Maybe for years.'

Georgia lifts the whisky bottle, pours two more drinks, and tops them up with water. She raises her glass. 'Magnificent.'

'Pardon?'

'Magnificent. I would have done the same if I had half your imagination.'

'It was a crazy thing to do. And it left me with all sorts of problems. I can't bear to use a smartphone. Our relationship was bracketed by loving text messages and funny things we had seen and taken a picture of and sent to each other, and calls from far-away places and apps for booking flights and finding nice places to eat. I know I eventually caved in to your suggestion and bought that really basic one, but I still don't use it unless I have to. And my business was toast because I didn't have the energy to be creative any more. I used to organise things, mostly for business people. They would message me and ask me to arrange for flowers for their mum twice a month or buy birthday presents. One family got me to buy children's party gifts on Amazon and have them sent gift-wrapped so their child could take them to what-ever event they'd been invited to. I booked travel, hotels, arranged cleaners, organised dog walkers. I was like an online housekeeper and personal assistant and substitute wife all rolled into one. And now look at me! It took me a considerable amount of effort just to film your attic. You should have seen my hands shaking.'

'But you managed it, and it was a great help to me that you did.'

'I was completely broken.' The silence stretches into the nooks and crannies of the kitchen, filling every tiny space. Eventually Tess finds her voice again. 'After I did the weed-killer thing, I thought I'd be fine. But I wasn't. It's been six months, but he's in my head almost every day, and I'm still pretty wrecked. I'm just better at hiding it now.' Tess looks down at her left hand. 'Maybe I'll always feel like this.' She takes another sip of whisky and rubs her ring finger, unable to continue.

Georgia nods. So many of her lodgers had similar experiences. Unfortunately, she was never able to provide them with a route map back to normality which might have helped them. 'I know it's hard.' She pauses, thoughtful. 'Let me help you deal with this solicitor of his. I know just the person to speak to.'

Chapter 69

August 2011

Tess looks down at the two years of accounts which have been downloaded and printed out by Georgia, and laid out on the kitchen table. 'I thought I'd be embarrassed about you seeing all this, but it turns out I'm OK with it.'

'I didn't look at what was on the screen.'

'It wouldn't have mattered if you had, I don't have anything to hide.'

Georgia puts a box of giant lime-green paperclips on the table. 'I bought you these. I thought they might be useful. You do know the library has computers if you need to use one?' She points to the Ottolenghi book on the dresser. 'I mean, even their reservations are online. I do miss my old tickets, though. There was always a thrill when I handed them over and got my books stamped by the librarian when I was a child.' She pulls herself back to the present day.

Tess shrugs. 'I've managed pretty well for the last six months without one.'

'Yes, but it's useful. Ordering food for Baxter, for example, instead of me doing it for you. It's so much easier and quicker online.'

'I know you're right.' Tess studies her fingernails. 'It's just become like a big boulder I can't seem to shift. I suppose

I *could* try using the computers at the library, but if I can manage without having one of my own, I'm fine with that.'

Georgia taps the top of one of the piles of paper. 'Maybe that's a plan for another day. All I'm saying is that although you can do your tax return on paper right now, I'm not sure how much longer that'll be the case. I don't think any of us will be able to live our lives in a purely analogue fashion in the future, and that time may arrive sooner than we think. I've even been thinking of getting rid of the house phone. If mobile calls weren't so expensive, I would do it in a heartbeat.'

Tess seizes the moment. 'I need to say something, Georgia. You mentioned that you had trouble with one of your lodgers before, and I just want to tell you again how sorry I am about all this mess. I completely understand if you want me to find somewhere else to live.'

'Why on earth would you think I want you to do that? We manage alright, the two of us. It just brought back some memories, that's all.'

Tess waits, as Georgia had waited for her.

'My last tenant was a perfectly nice young woman. Her name was Nicola. She had lived here for almost a year and I had no idea that there was a problem.' Georgia rubs the moving band in the middle of Hazel's ring. 'She was ambitious. There's nothing wrong with ambition but she was, shall we say, *very* confident. I should have realised there was something wrong but all my other tenants had managed before her and never complained. She earned a good wage and paid her rent as we agreed, the same twenty-five per cent that everyone pays. But she liked to spend. She always had nice clothes, and she would show me them, doing twirls in the hall in some new frock or a nice jacket. Told me she got them in charity shops, but of course that wasn't the case. They were new. Everything was brand new. She bought them all on credit, and took the labels off.'

'You told me you didn't like credit.'

'I don't. But I can't roll back time. I had the same rules for all my lodgers at the beginning; nothing on tick. They were Annie's rules and I never changed them. Everything must be paid with cash.' She pauses. 'But once we all had plastic instead of pound notes I had to accept that a cash economy wasn't reasonable any more. Everyone was on the electoral roll, because of the house rule about voting, and that meant they got letters offering them credit cards. And by the time Nicola was here, you could opt for e-statements, with nothing coming through the post. I've never had a credit card so I didn't realise that, and I think she knew that I didn't know. She moved out three months before her two years were up. She was the only one who has ever done that.' Georgia picked up one of the outsized green paperclips and tapped it on the table, moving it from the long side to short, to long, to short. 'And a little while afterwards, the letters started arriving. Letters from a credit card company. I saved them, thinking she would come back to collect her mail, but she never did. She just vanished. And by the time the letter arrived from the Sheriff Court, I hadn't seen her for six months, so I opened it and that's when I realised what she had done.'

'You must have been furious.'

Georgia frowned. 'Furious? No, not furious at all. I was hurt. Very hurt. I had trusted her. In the end I asked Fiona to look into things for me and, after some checking, we realised that they were Nicola's debts and nothing to do with the house or with me. Fiona wrote to the credit people on my behalf and that was it. No more letters. But I think, reading between the lines, that she must have been intercepting the postman for a while. It was such a shame; she was a lovely girl.'

'And you've never heard from her since?'

'No. She's the only one.'

'Was it a lot of money?'

'Just over a thousand pounds. Not an enormous sum, but enough. The irony is, if she hadn't just vanished, she would have been able to pay it off quite easily.'

'She would?'

Georgia stands up from the table and goes up the narrow stairs to her office. After a couple of minutes she comes back down carrying a metal cash box, and large black book, worn at the spine, and held shut with a piece of elastic tied in a knot. She puts them down on the table. 'This is the rent book, and this box is where the rent money goes. When there are too many small-value notes, I go to the bank and get them changed into larger denominations. Everyone's twenty-five per cent has always been kept here, in cash.' She rests her hand on the cash box. 'Of course, no one knows about the arrangement. Not until later.'

Tess frowns. 'You aren't declaring it to the taxman?'

'It's not my money.'

'Yes, it is.'

'No, it's like a savings account. I give it back.'

'You give—'

'I don't need the money. I have the house and an inheritance I wasn't expecting which has been invested and which gives me an income.' Georgia stops for a moment as though not sure if she should continue. 'I live quietly, Tess. I like it that way. I have enough to run the house, pay for the council tax, the window cleaner, the heating, the phone, the repairs and the food for everyone. I don't have a mortgage. That money comes from my investments.'

'Gosh.'

'I save the rent money, and on the first occasion that my young women come back to see me after they have moved out, I give them the money back.'

'What? All of it?'

'Yes, all of it. Two years of rent. Of course, each person gets a different amount because how much I have for them depends on how much they have earned over the two years.'

'Wow. I had no idea.'

'Why would you? I never talk about it, and all my former lodgers know how important it is that it remains confidential. In fact, you are the *only* resident who has ever been told about the arrangement. It has always been a secret. No one has ever suspected.'

'And because Nicola never came back, she never got her twenty-five per cent?'

'It's all here, waiting for her. When she first arrived she earned very little, but with some support and friendship she got a better job, and then an even better one. There is just over eleven thousand pounds here, sitting waiting for her. It's not mine, it's hers. And I will keep it here safely until she comes back.'

'Wait a minute. You keep eleven thousand pounds in the house in cash?'

'More, because your rent money is here too.' Georgia opens the tin. Inside, there are two envelopes. She lifts out the one marked 'Nicola'. 'I always ask for brand-new notes when I go to the bank because I think that when I hand them over it will make it feel more special.' She opens the fat envelope and takes out the red and white notes, fanning them like a hand of cards. 'There are one hundred and ten of these, and a bit of change. The Bank of Scotland note is my favourite, of all the hundreds. The Kessock Bridge on one side, and Sir Walter Scott on the other.'

'Put it away! Someone might see.'

'Who? There's only you and me here and I have my back to the window. I've always done it like this. It's what Annie intended to do with her first lodger in 1931. That was Keith. Of course, they fell in love so it didn't quite work out the way she planned, but that was certainly her intention. All the records are here in this book right back to 1931. Every penny paid to Annie, and after 1964, to me. And every penny paid back.'

'Why is it twenty-five per cent?'

'It's the number of the house, and Isobel thought of it. I saw no reason to change it. It's fair as a rent goes; no one has ever thought it unreasonable. Even if someone is on a small wage there's enough left after they've paid their rent for them to be able to save. And they all know they will be moving out after two years, so there is a target date. All of them, even the two who had babies while they were here, saved hard because they thought they were going to need the money for a place of their own when they moved out. Nicola was the only one who didn't stick to it.'

'And you don't know where she is?'

'No. But she knows where I am, and perhaps, when she is ready, she will come back. And if she does, there is eleven thousand pounds waiting for her.'

'And if she doesn't?'

'I don't know. But I think she will. She was a nice young woman who had more on her plate than she could really deal with. Perhaps if I hadn't been so strict about the two-year rule, things wouldn't have happened this way. It's partly my fault.'

'How can it possibly be your fault?'

'She wanted to stay longer. It was just after Christmas, and she asked me if she could stay for three years instead of two. I think with hindsight, she knew she was in trouble and was trying to sort it out on her own, but I said no.'

Tess shook her head. 'I don't think you should blame yourself.'

'I could have been a better listener. It was just before Hazel next door was unwell the first time, and Stan and I were trying to support her and there were a lot of hospital visits and so on. I was distracted and I wasn't really paying attention to things. Not properly, anyway.'

'I still don't think . . .'

Georgia rearranged the red and white banknotes so they were all facing the same way and put them back into their envelope. 'As I said, I was hurt at the time, but I can't walk around feeling like that for ever. And if she ever comes back, I will be pleased to see her. You don't live with someone for almost two years and share their birthdays and Christmases, and their successes and failures, without coming to care about them, do you?'

'I suppose not.'

'Anyway, now you know how it all works, perhaps you won't want me to save on your behalf. After all, you are older and probably wiser, financially speaking, than my usual collection of residents, and I'm well aware you have excellent money management skills already.'

Tess leans back in her chair and thinks for a minute before speaking. 'Honestly, I'm very happy with the arrangement. I'm a bit worried about all the cash, though.'

'I've been thinking about that ever since your man called.'

'He is definitely not *my* man. Not now.'

'Of course. Sorry.'

Natalie Fergie

'You could lock the scullery door.'

'Definitely not. But I'm thinking that maybe you could go up the ladder again, and put Nicola's envelope into the attic for me. You and I will both know it's there, so if I lose my marbles or something, you can retrieve it and give it to her when she comes back. Because I think she will. One day.'

'Deal. And perhaps something more anonymous than an old cash box for the rest of it might be a good idea too.'

'Probably,' concedes Georgia. 'I'll look in the charity shops next time I'm in Morningside.'

Chapter 70

September 2011

'Fiona is coming for dinner tonight,' announces Georgia over breakfast. 'And she's bringing a friend with her who may be able to advise you what to do about your situation.'

'I'm not sure I'm up to explaining it all again.'

'Don't worry about that.' Georgia opens the Ottolenghi book. 'I've renewed this twice but it's due back to the library tomorrow. I want to try his recipe for grains and squash and pomegranate seeds. Lebanese, I think. Look.' She pushes the open book across the table. 'Don't you think that looks really tasty?'

Tess glances at the page. 'It's pretty, certainly.'

'Jolly good. You can do the shopping for it; just take the grocery purse off the dresser over there.'

'I'm sure I can afford to buy a pomegranate and some bulgur wheat.'

'Please don't undermine how things are done, Tess. We have the bulgur wheat already, it's the fresh pomegranate that's missing. And perhaps something deliciously wicked for dessert? I shall leave it up to you to choose.'

Tess shakes her head. 'You pay for all the food and I don't think it's fair.'

'Please just *stop*.' Georgia's voice has a sudden edge. 'I am immensely privileged. I have a lovely house, albeit one in need of some care and attention in the garden department. I have chosen to share it with various young women over the years, at my own expense. None of them, not one, not the most broke, nor the most broken-hearted, would have lived here with me and shared their lives for a couple of years if they thought I was offering charity. Every single one of them was far too proud to be beholden to me or anyone else. They have given me so much, Nicola included.'

'But—'

'But nothing.' Georgia's voice gives away her exasperation. 'Perhaps you will feel differently if I remind you that Keith paid rent when he first moved in. My own mother took a job in the year between being at school and going to university; she refused to let anyone pay her rent for her. She took a job at the greengrocer on Morningside Road and apparently that caused *quite* a stir among the well-heeled at the university.' Georgia stops as a piece of the family jigsaw slots into place. 'Annie made me study the ledger when I took over, so I would understand how it all worked. I always wondered why Olivia was allowed to stay for longer than two years and we now have the answer to that question. But even though Annie knew that Olivia was her niece, the accounts show that she paid rent. It wasn't a lot, but she paid it. It is the way things are done here.'

'I'm sorry.'

Georgia glares at Tess. She is not finished. 'You are not so special, I have to tell you. Not so special that you are going to avoid the rules which have been in place here since 1931.'

'That's me told, I suppose.' Tess stands up and reaches for the little grocery purse, which always has cash inside. 'Pomegranates and pudding.'

As suddenly as Georgia's frustration had arrived, it vanishes. 'I don't think you'll be able to find a Lebanese wine, but it's called Chateau Musar if you happen to see it. Just get a bottle of something nice. In fact, get two.'

Tess tucks the purse into her pocket. 'I'll take Baxter, he likes going to the shops.'

Georgia raises her hand like someone stopping traffic. 'Actually, I've been hearing that dogs have gone missing recently when they are tied up outside shops.'

'Really?'

'Yes, it was on Facebook.' Georgia looks down at Baxter. 'And we don't want that to happen to you, do we? Oh no we don't, so I think you should stay here with me.'

'That's just so you can fuss over him when I'm away. He's spoiled rotten when he's with you.'

Georgia smiles. 'I'm expecting a parcel today and he will protect me from the delivery driver.'

'As if you need any protection . . .'

'Be off with you. I have to weed the herb patch and try to stop the mint spreading even more energetically than it usually does. He can keep me company.'

*

They cook together, side by side. The routine has fallen into place quite naturally. Tess opens jars and chops vegetables, and peels garlic. Tess is the percussionist, Georgia the conductor of the orchestra.

'Eton mess?'

Tess nods.

'That was my thought. I went to Stan's allotment for the fruit. It's easy to make and I haven't met a person who doesn't like it, so it seems like a safe option.' Georgia walks over to the larder. 'You know, I think there are some bottled redcurrants in here. I found a bush growing wild in the park two summers ago and I took advantage. Free food. It would have been terrible to let the birds get away with them all.'

Tess scoops the seeds out of a particularly large butternut squash. 'I told Fiona about the weedkiller, a while ago.'

Georgia puts the jar of redcurrants on the worktop. 'Fiona is so utterly discreet; I promise you, she never said a word.'

'Good practice for a lawyer, I guess.'

'The extra person is a friend of hers, someone she thinks might be able to advise. I expect they may have some questions for you, but you aren't in trouble.'

'I don't want to be made to feel like someone who is not in control. I can assure you I was *very much* in control of that watering can.'

'I'm sure you were. Pass that wooden spoon, please, this needs a stir.'

*

The guests come around the back of the house, as everyone does, except those delivering parcels or flyers for the local pizza place.

'Hello there.' Fiona is carrying a bottle. 'My goodness, Georgia, what a difference.' She looks up and down the new scullery-kitchen. 'Very nice indeed.' She nods to Tess and thrusts a bottle of fizzy white wine at her. 'This could do with cooling down, I think.'

Georgia is standing on the steps between the kitchen and the scullery. 'If you like that, just wait until you see what's been happening in here.'

'It's all so exciting.' Fiona follows Georgia up the steps. 'Let me see what you've been doing to the old place.' She stops. 'Wow! You said you were ripping things out and you've certainly done that. He's a good plasterer, my cousin, isn't he?' She strokes the smooth surface, now a delicate shade of very pale peach. 'I keep trying to get him to do the ceilings in my place but he never has time.'

'A case of the cobbler's child having no shoes?' says a voice from the doorway.

'Sorry, Georgia. This is Cait. I've known her since Primary Five and she's an expert in all things financial.' Fiona looks around the kitchen as though seeing it for the first time. 'Amazing. Look at that old range. I shouldn't really say this, but if you ever want to sell, that's a property photographer's dream shot.'

'It was behind the chimney wall all the time,' says Georgia. 'It was when I was at university, the summer before I went to Germany for third year. Annie and I went away for a couple of weeks and when we came back it had all been covered up and the wall was painted.'

Fiona laughed. 'When I think about all the times we used to sit here having dinner with the others and listen to you reminiscing about it, and we had no idea.'

Tess caught the scrap of information. 'Did you live here too, Fiona?'

'I did indeed. Two years.' She points at Georgia. 'I don't know how this saint put up with me.'

Tess suddenly has a hundred questions but it's already too late, and the conversation moves on.

'Does it work?' asks Cait.

'Stan says that it's sound enough, the fireplace in Tess's room upstairs uses the same chimney stack. But I think I need someone a bit more expert to look at it, and of course the chimney will need to be swept.' She points at the grate which is full of pinecones. 'I picked those up in the park and they look pretty enough for now. I think I'd need to use smokeless fuel, so I'm not sure I'll ever light a fire in it.'

Fiona smiles. 'It would be such fun, though.'

'It's a beast. Isobel was the only person who could get any sense from it. You have to coax it, and know its ways. It was always warm and cosy in the winter in here, but in the summer it was roasting and not pleasant at all. And it ran the hot water, so if you let it go out then your clothes went unwashed, and there were no hot baths either.' She raises her arm, sniffs her armpit theatrically and pulls a face. 'We started getting smelly pretty fast.' She points at the table.

'Shall we eat?'

*

There is homemade pitta bread, bulgur and butternut salad studded with pomegranate seeds, and courgette and yellow peppers dressed with lemon and oregano. And Eton mess, and what turns out to be not Prosecco, but Cava. It's a good meal. The four women chat and laugh, but Tess can't forget the reason for the visit. After the last of the meringue has been scraped from the bowl and the dishes have been cleared away, she knows that she has to get this over with. She looks at Cait. 'I think Fiona has told you about my predicament? What do you think?'

'You aren't denying it was you who did the damage?'

'Oh no, it was definitely me.'

'In theory, Fiona says you need to pay the bill, but . . .'

'But?'

'But it may be that the cost of the reinstatement is very, very small beer when compared with the cost of years of unpaid tax on rental income.'

'Pardon?'

'Fiona mentioned that when your ex was out of the country he rented his house out?'

'Yes, that's right.'

'And he didn't declare the income?'

'No. He said he didn't need to because it was a private arrangement, not done through an agency.'

'Unfortunately for him, that's not the case.' Cait takes a sip of Cava. 'And he would also need to have had a buy-to-let mortgage, not a regular one. Banks are pretty fussy about that. And insurance companies too.'

'But I couldn't possibly drop him in it.'

Cait pulls a calculator from her bag. Her fingers hover over the buttons. 'Have you got any idea how much he charged?'

'No idea, but it's a nice three-bedroom house in Craiglockhart.'

'OK. If we play with some numbers for a minute and say that hypothetically the rent was a thousand a month? That's twelve thousand a year. How long did he rent the house out?'

'I'm not sure, at least eight years.'

Cait stabbed at the screen. 'Ninety-six thousand pounds.'

Tess goes white. 'But if he had to pay tax on all that, it could be, well, quite a lot would be an understatement.'

'And you're not going to tell Her Majesty's Revenue and Customs, but he doesn't know that.'

'I'm not?'

'No one is. However, it can be suggested that not declaring rental income to HMRC is unwise. It's quite possibly all that would be needed to get him to back off.'

'Seriously?'

'If he has any sense at all, yes. It's likely he owes a not inconsiderable sum, especially when compared with the cost of some gardening and grass seed.'

'And a phone. And a designer coffee table.'

'Even with those things too.'

'But you aren't going to tell HMRC either? I don't want that.'

'No, I'm not. But I can't imagine it'll be long before he decides to voluntarily pay the tax anyway, once the situation has been explained to him by his solicitor.'

Fiona, who has been silent during the discussion, joins in. 'I'll draft a letter and you can see it before it gets sent.'

Tess frowns. 'Solicitor's letters are expensive.'

'You can pay me in ironing. I have a Munro-sized heap of it, and it's only Thursday.'

'Are you sure?'

'M and P Legal have always been,' she makes inverted commas in the air with her fingers, '"helpful" to Georgia's friends. Let's just say the sisterhood supports when necessary.' She wags her finger at Tess. 'And I will extract my fee in pressed T-shirts and pillowcases, you can be sure of that.'

'Ironing I can cope with. I just don't want to be pulled into a huge argument over all this.' Tess looks at the three women with whom she has just shared an excellent meal. 'I think I've finally got to the point where I'm thinking about what comes next in my life, and I don't want to get dragged backwards.' She stands up. 'And since we are talking about what comes next, who would like coffee and chocolate?'

Chapter 71

September 2011

'I'm going to France,' announces Georgia as they are finishing lunch. 'I assume you'll be able to look after everything while I'm gone?'

'To France?' Tess cannot keep the surprise from her voice.

'Yes. Stan asked me to remind you there are lots of blackcurrants which will need to be picked at the allotment.'

'France is a big place.'

'I'm going to visit one of the Commonwealth War Graves Commission cemeteries on the Western Front. Finlay might be there. All I really have is the letter from his commanding officer, and that might not be accurate. He's listed on the big Memorial to the Missing nearby, but according to their website he doesn't have a headstone with his name on it. I want to go and look for myself.'

'How long will you be away?'

'Two weeks; I'm leaving the day after tomorrow and going on a bit of a tour. Not sure exactly where I'll end up.'

It isn't the first time that Georgia has made sudden decisions and Tess is getting used to expecting the unexpected: getting the kitchen plastered out of the blue, going to an apparently excellent folk concert where the band sang entirely in Welsh, walking up Blackford Hill at dawn for the solstice. She half expects Georgia to come home one day with bright pink hair, just because she wants to see what it feels like.

'I'm wondering about taking his medals with me. What do you think?'

'You could.'

'I'm not sure.' Georgia spins the inner ring around its brass racetrack on her finger. 'I don't know if there is an accepted protocol for these things.'

'I expect that whatever you choose to do will be fine.'

'And there is something else.' Georgia twists around in her seat and picks a box up from the dresser. 'I need your opinion about this.'

'That's the jewellery box that was locked. We couldn't open it.'

'Yes, but remember the other box, the one with the key inside that Annie put in the range oven for safekeeping?'

'Yes.'

'I found the little key again last night when I was getting my things organised for going away. Look what I found.' Georgia puts the key into the jewellery box lock and turns it. The lid springs open. 'See? It's another letter. I'm not sure what to do with it.'

Tess picks up the envelope. 'Isn't this the same handwriting that was on the letter from Beatrice Sidcup?'

'I think so. I tried putting them side by side and they look the same to me.'

'It's still sealed.'

'I know. It's strange to think she is actually my grand-mother.'

'What are you going to do with it?'

'I'm not sure. It's addressed to Finlay, and it's postmarked as the third of July 1916. I looked in Annie's diary for that year to see if there are any clues and there's a list of the dates when he was on leave. He was here in the house at the end of June, and then he went back to France. He was posted as missing a few days after that.'

'So, if it *is* from Beatrice Sidcup, she might have hoped it would reach him before he left?'

'It's all guesswork.'

Tess turns the envelope over. 'I wonder why it's never been opened.' She hands it back.

'I know. I've been trying to work out why that might be.' Georgia runs her fingers along the sealed edge. 'It was in Annie's jewellery box, so she knew about it, but she didn't open it either. I've been trying to imagine what I might have done if I'd been in Ursula's shoes. If a letter arrived for someone who was missing. A personal letter for someone I thought of as my son. Would I open it? And what if I wasn't totally convinced the person was dead? Would that make a difference?'

Tess frowned. 'You might keep it safe for them, for when they got home?'

'You can see how that might happen.'

'What are you going to do with it?'

'I don't know.' Georgia gets up quickly, as though there are suddenly a hundred things to be done. Her phone, which is lying on the table, gets caught in her sleeve as she stands and is launched across the room. It lands with a thud on the corner of the stone hearth and they both watch in horror as the screen smashes.

Georgia is first to speak. 'Well, that changes things a bit. There won't be enough time to get it fixed before I leave. I suppose I'll just have to print off all my tickets and hotel reservations. It will be quite like the old days to be going away without being in touch with the world back home.'

Chapter 72

September 2011

The maître d' of the small hotel where she is staying has provided Georgia with a map, and circled her destinations in incongruous purple pencil.

She walks along the pavement, following the route he has suggested. At the edge of the village, past the last of the houses, she sees the tree-green sign.

Commonwealth War Graves Commission.

She opens the low gate and steps into the cemetery. It's a warm day. Above her are swifts, swooping across the blue sky. They do not scream. The grass is closely mown. This is a place that's looked after with pride, she thinks. She sits on a bench near the side wall for almost half an hour, feeling no pressing need to wander among the graves, no urge to read the names so carefully carved on the headstones. It's enough to simply be present.

Eventually, she gets to her feet and begins to walk along the rows. A lesson in regimental history, and in lives cut short, unfolds with each step. Every so often she comes upon a stone without a name. And another, and another, and another.

She makes her way along every row, finding more and more nameless white slabs.

'Is this you, Finlay?' she says to each one. 'Is this you?'

She tries to imagine Ursula and John being here in 1921, with Annie by their side. She would have been twenty-three years old. Would she have been remembering the boys she teased in the school playground, as she stood among the graves? Or the lads who surrounded her at the roller-skating rink on Saturday afternoons? Perhaps she had a boyfriend or a lover who was called up but never returned. Other than Finlay, Annie had never spoken to her about the missing. Not a word.

In her online research, Georgia has seen a photograph of the cemetery from 1921, and knows that it would then have been filled with temporary wooden crosses with scratched-on details, not the carefully placed slabs of Portland stone professionally engraved with a cross or the occasional six-pointed star which are there now. She is quite sure that Ursula and John would have looked at every grave hunting for Finlay's name; but they hadn't found him. All they had was the letter from his commanding officer, saying that he had led his men courageously.

They would never have been asked about the personal words the stonemason might have carved at the foot of his headstone at a cost of threepence ha'penny per letter, because in the chaos, the Army didn't know where Finlay was.

Did they guess? Did John choose a grave at random and decide that it was the one where his son lay?

She goes back to sit on the bench again and thinks about the scullery door, always left unlocked, just in case.

It's almost noon when she stands to leave. The sun is over-head and there are few shadows. She has done her research and knows that when farmers or builders uncover the remains of a soldier, the Commission tries to find relatives. They look at dog tags and cap badges and regimental buttons and engraved hip flasks, and anything else that might help, but there is no guarantee of a correct identity because in the thea-tre of war, when men were killed by the thousand all around the battlefield, their uniforms were sometimes reused; taken off the corpses and put on by others who needed warmth or just something less worn out than what they were standing up in. She knows that occasionally there is a definite identifi-cation and sometimes it is discovered that the person already has a named grave, with a headstone placed there in error, bearing the name of another man. When this happens the Commission does not exhume the incorrectly identified sol-dier and try to establish who he might be. The original grave remains respectfully undisturbed, and a new headstone is carved and placed there instead.

Known Unto God.

She cannot take a photograph because her camera is on her phone, and it lies smashed to bits in Edinburgh, but she doesn't feel the need anyway. She opens her daysack and removes an envelope from the inside pocket. Her grand-mother's neat handwriting is easy to read in the bright sun-light. Georgia holds the still-sealed letter close to her heart. 'This is your secret, Beatrice, not mine, so I'm not going to read what you have written. I'll put it back in the box with the other things when I get home, just as it is.' She puts it back into her bag and looks again at the long rows of white headstones. 'I don't think you are here, Grandpa,' she whis-pers. 'I think you would have spoken to me, if you were.'

*

On the way back into the village the cars swoop past, taking their owners home for lunch. They kick up little stones that sting her legs; her sandals are covered in road dust. She walks right through the centre of the village, ignoring the bistro offering two courses and a glass of wine for a dozen euros, and past the sweet, sticky temptations of the boulangerie. She looks at the map and heads for her second destination.

At the gate there is a different sign.

Cimitière Militaire Allemand

Instead of the rows of pure white stones, there are lines of simple black crosses stretching out in front of her. There is no central monument pointing up into the sky. It feels different, she thinks. There is so much space here.

She walks among the crosses, and is aware of a quite different arrangement from the straight paths she had seen an hour earlier. Each cross has two names, and two sets of dates on its horizontal limbs. And on the reverse, there are two more names. 'Four graves for one cross,' she says softly. 'And no unknown soldiers. Or not here, anyway.'

Georgia walks slowly, reading the names, and recognising their youth as she goes. Near the boundary wall ahead of her is a slab of carved stone, set into the ground.

IN EINEM GEMEINSAMEN GRABE RUHEN HIER

Below is the word SOLDATEN, and some numbers. She dredges up the German she learned at university in her twenties and nods to herself.

IN A SHARED GRAVE HERE LIE . . .

This is the explanation. The unidentified soldiers are buried together beside a low wall at the edge of the cemetery.

She looks back towards the gate, and at the trees which make dappled shade in places. 'So different, and yet the same,' she whispers. 'I know you are not here either, Grandpa. But I don't think you would mind if you were in this place, beside these men.'

Chapter 73

September 2011

The house is quiet. Tess wanders around, tidying books, dusting mantelpieces. 'I've forgotten what it's like to live alone,' she says to the silent rooms.

The first postcard had arrived from Stan the day after Georgia left, and then on the third day, another was delivered. His handwriting is precise. It does not fit with the man who was dancing about in the kitchen while his wife is in a hospice, she thinks. She has seen postcards arrive regularly ever since she moved to Library Terrace. It's impossible not to sneak a peek at the words if she is the first to collect the mail landing on the doormat. The cards are often plain, with a diagram on one side, a circle, filled in with green dots and squiggles, and fireworks of coloured arrows leading to unfamiliar Latin names in tiny lettering.

Georgia had once found Tess studying the design on one of the cards. 'He was a roundabout designer, before he retired. You wouldn't think a roundabout was something that needed to be designed, but he won prizes for his work. And an international award, I believe.' And she had snatched the postcard away and stomped up the hall in a mood. After that, Tess only looked at the cards when Georgia was out; she never intended to pry, but her curious streak always got the better of her. And anyway, if he wanted privacy he would send a letter, she reasoned.

There was always news of Hazel, and the cards were signed 'Love, Stan x'. This did not sit well with Tess at all.

*

There are no more cards after the third day, but on Monday a familiar grey envelope takes their place and lands on the tiled vestibule floor. Baxter is asleep upstairs on Tess's bed; a lost cause. She can feel her heart racing and she doesn't look at the address, but takes the letter to the kitchen and sets it on the table, face down, beside her coffee. Fiona had assured her there would be nothing more to worry about, but now this has arrived. She retrieves the largest knife from the drawer and sets about slicing the flap open, resting her hand on the envelope to stop it moving away from her.

She pushes the folded paper into her pocket and takes it up the garden to the plum tree, a habit she has adopted from seeing Georgia do it. 'What has happened now?' she says, as she unfolds the letter.

Dearest Georgia,

She reads Stan's handwriting without making the conscious decision to do it. In contrast to the precision of the postcards, his fountain-penned words sprawl in royal blue ink across the page.

I wanted to write to you and not telephone because what I have to say bears the effort of pen and ink.

My sister is gone now. She slipped from this life to whatever does or does not come next, last night.

Tess reads on, entirely missing the most important piece of information.

> She did not want a funeral of any description, there is really only me here that knew her, it was where we came on holiday every year when we were young. But this is where she wanted to die, and more importantly it is where she wanted to be scattered, in the sea, where we played in the waves as children, shouting and splashing, and learning to swim with black tyre inner tubes around our waists. I agreed to her wishes. There will be a cremation very quickly, on Tuesday.

Tess gasps; this means either tomorrow or next week.

> After that she asked that I let her drift away in the waves. Just me and her in the sea together for one final time. You were a good friend to her and I know she would want me to let you know.
>
> There is one last thing, and I am writing it here but I do not want to speak of it, unless you are of a similar mind.
>
> I was not free until now, to say these things, and I will not give voice to them with breath unless your answer is positive, so please do not tell me that you would like to discuss it.
>
> This is a yes or no.
>
> Hazel was widowed, as you know, and she was the only family I had left here. My wife has been gone for nearly twenty years, and our children are spread across the continents. David is in New Zealand and Hannah and her family are in Uruguay.

I would like to spend my last years with you, Georgia. But if you are not interested then all you need to do is stay silent. I will not mention it again.

Hannah has bought me a ticket to Montevideo and I leave in a week's time. I can delay the trip, but if your answer is no, simply do not reply, and I will go and spend the winter in the Southern Hemisphere in the sun, with my grandchildren. I would never want to embarrass you.

I am sorry I could not come to France with you, but I hope it went well and was a comfort.

Yours ever,

Stan

Tess folds the sheet of paper back up. This is not her letter to read.

And yet.

Something niggles at the edge of her mind. She unfolds it and reads it a second time. There it is, staring her in the face.

My sister is gone now

Stan was not Hazel's husband; he was her *brother*.

There is no date anywhere on the page. Cursing herself under her breath, she rushes down the garden, back into the house and puts the letter down on the table. That'll teach me not to make assumptions, she thinks. Not about people, and not about grey envelopes. She examines the postmark but it's smudged and unclear and no help at all.

Still furious with herself, she leans across the table to pick up her abandoned coffee. A vase of garden flowers is beside the mug and, in her haste, she nudges it. The vase wobbles like a child's toy, and falls onto its side and, as though in slow motion, it begins to roll across the table. Tess reaches out to catch it just as it falls off the edge, but she doesn't have a good enough grip and it slips from her hand, lands, and smashes. Shards of glass and water and bent flower stems are strewn across the floor. She had cut a fresh selection of pink cosmos from near the herb circle just an hour ago and filled the vase almost to the top with water. The same water which is now running across the floor, spreading out into a small lake as she watches. She shuts the door to the hall to stop Baxter wandering through and hurries to the scullery to get a mop and bucket, and two copies of the *Evening News* from the fire-lighting pile. It takes a good fifteen minutes to pick up all the tiny pieces of glass and then to mop up all the water, and another five to rinse the mop thoroughly and make sure the tiny glitters are gone.

She turns her attention back to the table. The water has coursed across Stan's letter. The sheet of paper upon which he had poured out his heart is a puddle of pooling ink, and getting more and more soggy by the minute. There is no paper kitchen roll in the house because Georgia sees it as a waste of trees, and right at this moment Tess curses her landlady's eco credentials. She grabs the only alternative and lays a clean tea towel gently over the paper. Both ink and water soak into the white linen and Tess can barely bring herself to peel back the fabric, but knows she has to.

Some words remain. The salutation 'Dearest Georgia' and the first paragraph have survived but after 'she did not want a funeral' only snippets are left.

Tess opens the door again so Baxter can find her and sits down on one of the kitchen chairs, all of a lump. She counts the problems off on her fingers. 'Georgia is in France. She does not have her phone. That means she also won't have email unless she happens to be staying in a hotel with internet access. She told me she doesn't want to be disturbed. She said it was an opportunity to get to know her grandfather, and that not having her phone was a sort of blessing.' She runs out of fingers. 'I can't even quote from the letter.' She looks at the narrow staircase that leads off the kitchen, up to Georgia's office, and for a moment she finds herself grumping like an obstreperous teenager. 'It's not as if it's any of my business anyway.' But she already knows the answer. For as long as she has lived in the house, there have been postcards. Every few days, another postcard came through the letterbox; sometimes they had the annotated circles drawn on one side, and other times there were views of the mountains of the north-west of Scotland, somewhere beyond Ullapool. She had judged him. Judged them. Tess is furious with herself. 'I am such an idiot! Georgia even said something about Stan having terrible phone reception when the pipe burst in the kitchen and she needed his advice.' She sighs. 'All the clues were right there in front of me and I've been so obsessed with my own nonsense I haven't been paying attention.' She sits down at the table and picks up the soggy sheet of paper by one corner. 'Fat chance of deciphering this now. If Georgia sent postcards as well, there wouldn't have been enough room to tell him where she was going. Not in any detail anyway.'

She takes a deep breath. This isn't going to be easy. Over the last few weeks she has started to use a computer at the library. It's not that she can't do it, she has discovered, she just prefers not to. In many ways Stan is the person she has become. Doesn't like the internet. Prefers paper and pen. The difference is that he has probably always been this way and she hasn't. Among the three of them, Georgia is the exception: internet banking, emails, messages to the neighbourhood WhatsApp, booking tickets for concerts and ordering books. In administration terms, her life is organised online.

Tess walks over to the staircase which leads to the office and puts her foot on the first step. The uncarpeted stairs are steep and narrow, and painted chocolate brown; it looks as though they haven't had any attention for many, many years. Her feet clatter on the bare wood. It would have been impossible, she thinks, for a bone-tired servant to nip up the stairs quietly and grab a few minutes to herself. There would have been no privacy in her daily life at all.

She gets to the top and turns the brass doorknob.

A long bench, made from what looks like sanded scaffolding planks, runs along one wall below the window. Beneath it is a pair of utilitarian two-drawer filing cabinets. The room is above the scullery with its sinks and stone floor and seems to have no heating at all apart from a small electric blow heater. She tries to imagine what it would have been like to be the maid here. The cream wallpaper is speckled with brown, and near the ceiling is a paper border that runs all around the room. Cream and mint and coffee. 'Very 1930s,' she says out loud.

At the end of the room is a wall of photographs. Each one shows a young woman, standing beside Georgia; they have all been taken in the garden with the scullery door as a backdrop. Judging by the clothes, they span from the 1960s to a few years ago. These, Tess realises, are her predecessors: Georgia's lodgers. She leans closer to look at them. I wonder where they are now, she thinks, sent off into the world with unexpected funds to make a new start. She finds Fiona, a nervous-looking girl, squinting into the sunlight of a summer day. Did they remember Georgia with fondness, she wonders, or was she just a footnote, a passing acquaintance? The last photo is of a tall girl, looking confident, smiling into the camera. 'Is this you, Nicola?' she says.

She drags herself away from the photographs, and turns to look at the workbench, and the Apple computer with its pristine white keyboard and equally white mouse set out neatly, ready to use.

'A fruitarian to your core, Georgia, of course you are. Granny Smith all the way.'

Chapter 74

September 2011

The filing cabinets are not locked, and Tess discovers that everything is neatly itemised and tabbed, albeit according to Georgia's rather idiosyncratic system.

There are files labelled 'NECESSARY' and 'THINK' and 'DELICIOUS'. On a shelf above the planks is a long row of black diaries with the date on each spine. The first one is dated 1951. Without thinking Tess takes it down from the shelf and opens it.

'We went to London on the train. The tube was hot. We missed the census at home,' she reads, and then snaps the book closed. This is none of her business. 'I'm sorry, Georgia, I shouldn't have done that,' she says and puts it back on the shelf carefully.

A small pile of papers lies beside the computer, and she rifles through them, looking for anything relating to train tickets or hotels. There is nothing useful.

'Which means the information I need is in here,' she says, tapping the top of the computer screen. 'I wonder if you are password protected?'

She sits down on the office chair, presses the power switch, and rests her fingers on the keyboard. The Mac comes to life. Enter password, it demands. She remembers trying to guess the PIN on Patrick's phone and feels a sudden chill, but pushes on. She cannot afford to waste any attempts.

She looks around her for clues. Beside her, the filing cabinet with its idiosyncratic ordering system is still open. Would Georgia have written them down and filed them? She opens the drawer and checks through the tabs. It is there, right in front of her. DROWSSAP (S).

Inside is a single sheet of paper. In Georgia's neat handwriting are all the passwords for utilities and online shopping and the library. Tess runs her finger down the list.

There is no password for the computer.

Where would she have put it? Tess's thoughts are racing and she tries to slow them down and apply logic. 'Georgia knows that one day someone might need to get into her papers, so she's sure to have written it down. But where on earth is it?'

It has to be somewhere a burglar wouldn't look, she reasons, but at the same time easy for anyone who actually knows Georgia to work out. Tess gets up from the chair and begins to pace back and forth along the small room. She looks under the keyboard, and kneels down to look behind the filing cabinets, but there is nothing. She cannot afford to make an error. She stares at the screen and the image of Finlay fades and is replaced by the screen saver. She wiggles the mouse and he reappears. She looks again at the password list, and there it is.

MOTHERSHIP.

And beside it, 'Finlay1916' has been crossed out, and a single word is written below.

She lets her hands rest on the keys and types with her eyes closed, as though being able to touch type is the most natural thing in the world. Dots appear one after another with each keystroke.

GrandFather

And there in front of her is the image of Finlay, in his officer's uniform.

She rolls the cursor down to the dock at the bottom of the screen. 'Where now? Browser history will just be the research, I need to look at her email for the bookings.'

In less than ten minutes, she has printed off all the information she needs.

She gathers the sheets of paper and closes down the screen. It hasn't been so bad after all.

*

Tess lifts the phone handset in the hall. There is no dial tone. She looks at it in confusion before remembering that Georgia had unplugged it from the socket a few weeks ago in protest at the number of sales calls she was subjected to. The curly cable twists this way and that, and Tess vows to make it coil properly just as soon as she has spoken to Georgia. She bends down and plugs it back in, and then, her heart in her mouth, she dials the number for the hotel.

'*Bonjour, je m'appelle Tess Dutton, et je voudrais parler avec Madame Georgia Williams qui est votre invitée à l'hôtel ce soir.*'

'Good evening,' comes the reply. 'You would like to speak with Madame Williams.'

'Yes please, and forgive my poor French, monsieur, it is many years since I learned it at school.'

'It is not a problem. But unfortunately, madame left this morning.'

Tess consults Georgia's itinerary. 'Are you sure? I have her staying with you for three nights.'

'Indeed,' replies the voice, 'but she decided to change her plans and to leave a day early. I believe she was going to a new destination before visiting Paris.'

'She told you about her visit?'

'*Naturellement.* It is an important time for her, I think.'

'Do you happen to know the name of the new hotel?'

'I do, but I cannot say, madame.'

'Oh?'

'It is a matter of privacy. I can leave a message with the manager there if you wish. They may ask her to telephone you?'

'Thank you so much, monsieur. I appreciate your assistance more than you can imagine.'

She ends the call, and exhales. Baxter appears beside her, wagging his tail enthusiastically. 'Good idea,' she says to him. 'After all that, I think we both need a walk in the fresh air.'

Chapter 75

September 2011

For two days, the phone in the hall is silent apart from calls about double glazing and boiler replacement. Tess becomes highly accomplished at simply walking away and leaving the caller talking to themselves.

It's on the evening of the second day that Georgia rings. There is no preamble. 'You have been in my office.'

'I am sorry about that but you—'

'This had better be good. I don't like people going through my things.'

'I'm sorry—'

'You have looked in my files too. We *will* talk about this when I come home.'

'Yes.'

'And what is it that is so important that you have invaded my privacy?'

'There has been a letter from Stan.'

'A card, you mean.'

'A letter.'

'Stan never writes letters.'

'It wasn't good news, I'm afraid. He wrote to tell you that his sister has passed away. He wanted you to know that there isn't going to be a funeral, and that this is what she wanted, and that he is going to see his daughter in, I forget where . . .'

'Montevideo.'

'That's it, Montevideo.'

There is a pause. 'That's an awful lot to get on a postcard.'

'I told you, it wasn't a postcard. It was a letter and I opened it by mistake; I'm terribly sorry.'

'We will talk about this when I come home. I am very disappointed. If that's what he wanted to tell me then why was it necessary for you to track me down? I cannot think of a single reason why you would need to do that.'

Tess is fed up with being berated. 'There is a very good reason, *actually*.'

'Oh? Enlighten me.'

'It was in the letter.'

'Read it to me, then.'

Tess sighs. 'I can't, I spilled water all over it and the ink ran. I'm sorry, but it was important that I get in touch. Very, very important.'

'Go on.'

'I feel very weird about this.'

'Not any more weird than I'm feeling right now, I can assure you.'

'I have what's left of it.'

'Read it then, my dinner is waiting for me.'

Tess begins.

'"I wanted to write and not phone you because what I have to say bears the effort of pen and ink."'

'He never phones me.'

'"My sister is gone now. She slipped from this life to whatever does or does not come next, last night. She did not want a funeral of any description, there is . . ." And then he talked about a cremation and said she wanted him to let her ashes wash out to sea, and then . . . well, then it says, "not free until now, to say these things, and I will not give voice to them with breath unless your answer is positive, so", and then some stuff about Montevideo, and then it says, "I would like to spend my last years with you, Georgia. But if you are not interested then all you need to do is stay silent. I will not mention it again, ever. I would never want to embarrass you."'

'Oh,' says Georgia.

'And the part that's missing says that if he doesn't hear from you, he will go to Montevideo in a week's time and that basically you will be just friends and he will understand.'

'MEN!!!'

The volume is so great, Tess holds the phone away from her ear. 'I'm really sorry.'

'It's not you. It's him.'

'I wish you could have read the rest of it. He seems to be saying something that's been inside for a long time. And if you aren't interested then he will go and see his daughter, that's all.'

'Hmmm.'

'Had you honestly no idea?'

Georgia sighs, all the way from France. 'I suppose I did. I even tried to talk to him about it once but he said that his sister needed him and he couldn't do anything until, well, until she wasn't here any longer. But it's a bit of a leap from "let's get together" to "if you're not interested, I'm off". I'm not sure I like being given an ultimatum.'

'What age is he? Come to that, what age are you?'

'I'm seventy-two, or I will be in a couple of months.'

'And Stan?'

'A bit younger. I've never thought about it properly.'

'And,' Tess pauses, 'without being all agony auntish about it, are you interested?'

There is a silence.

'I met him three years ago when Hazel first moved in next door. He was helping her to move furniture and get herself sorted. His wife died a long time ago but he still has the house they lived in. It's in Murrayfield, near his allotment. When Hazel was first diagnosed she had chemo, and he moved across the city to look after her. I suppose we got to know each other then. There were times when I thought there was a hint of something else happening between us, but as Hazel became more poorly, it was as though he closed that particular door. We were still friends, but it couldn't progress to anything else because he saw his job as being there to do whatever she needed. They're twins, you see. And I think that's a special sort of together. More than just being siblings. She never had a seventieth birthday, I'd have known. So he's probably in his late sixties. He promised her he would be there for her and that was it.'

'And now you think he's rushing it.'

'Yes. Why on earth can't he just give me a month or two so we can work out if we actually *like* being more than friends?'

'I suspect that he's written this letter, word for word, many times in his head.'

'Possibly.'

'And now it has all come out in a rush, and if he's been thinking about it for a long time, perhaps he doesn't see the flaws in what he's asking.'

'Have you ever thought of being a professional at this?'

'Relationship advice? Oh hell, no. I'm hardly the person to offer anything like that.'

'And he's still at the cottage?'

'I think so. He said that he's planning to meet her request about the sea just before he leaves in two weeks' time.' Tess frowns as she does mental arithmetic. 'Actually, I think it's one week now. Can you not phone him?'

'He hates the phone. That's why we do the postcards. And anyway there's no landline and the mobile reception is rubbish. If he needs to make a call, he has to go up the wee hill beside the cottage to get a signal.'

'How long would it take to send a postcard from France? Or a telegram. Do telegrams still exist?'

'You've been reading too much vintage crime fiction. No telegrams since the 1980s.'

'I could go back on your computer and sort out a next-day-delivery Amazon parcel? If I do it now, he'll have it tomorrow.'

Georgia's voice brightens. 'You would do that for me?'

'What do you want to send?'

'I have no idea.'

'How about a stop sign?'

'You mean the kind of thing you get at a road junction? Yes, that's perfect.'

Tess laughs. 'I was kidding.'

'No, a stop sign is an excellent idea.'

'Red and white, octagonal? I bet I can find you something like that. Give me a chance to plug this phone in next to the Mac, and call me back in ten minutes.'

*

In the gap between phone calls, Tess doesn't once think about her anxiety. She is completely focused on ordering a pillarbox-red stop sign from Amazon.

She loads up the website, and has all the options ready for Georgia by the time the phone rings.

'You can have metal, like the kind you get as a proper traffic sign, or you can have stickers that would go on a wall?'

'You've found one already? I wasn't sure you would manage it.'

'It was fine. It turns out that doing something for someone else isn't the same as doing it for myself. Do you want metal or a sticker?'

Georgia laughs. 'I think that I would like to make a statement, and there isn't a much bigger statement than a whacking great metal road sign being delivered, is there?'

'How big, exactly? You can have thirty centimetres, forty-five or sixty.'

Georgia doesn't hesitate. 'Sixty. He's not the only one who can make bold pronouncements.'

Tess smiles. 'Right.'

'My card details should be stored on the site so just go ahead and order it. He's on the account as a person who gets parcels because I've been sending him things while he's been up north. He hasn't been able to get out much.'

'Stanley Goodwin?'

'That's him. I'll go and have my dinner now, and leave this in your capable hands. And in the morning, I'll try and work out how to get to the north-west coast of Scotland from the middle of France.'

The phone clicks and the call ends.

Tess looks at the list of items that Georgia has sent to Stan over the last six months. Thornton's Treacle Toffee, Derwent coloured pencils, warm socks, some quite expensive binoculars, a book about the creatures of the British shoreline, and two pairs of rainbow-striped bootlaces. 'Oh, Georgia,' she says, 'I think you've been kidding yourself. This is not what you do if you aren't sure you're interested. It's how you show you care very much.'

She finishes the order and adds a message to the 'Is this a Gift?' box.

Dear Stan, Georgia asked me to send this. Please follow the instructions TO THE LETTER. Tess.

She closes the computer down. It has been quite a day.

Chapter 76

September 2011

There are no more phone calls.

Tess is desperate to know if the stop sign has done the trick, but has no way of finding out. She convinces herself that she will be given her marching orders as soon as Georgia gets home, and she starts to look at the adverts in letting agents' windows to see if there are any flats she might be able to afford. Unfortunately, Baxter is an obstacle. No dogs, no pets, no animals.

Another letter arrives in a grey envelope and she opens it without taking deep breaths or having butterflies in her stomach.

Dear Ms Dutton,
  Our client has instructed us to inform you that no further action will be taken in respect of the goods and property damaged by yourself.
  Yours sincerely.

She puts the envelope into the paper drawer in the drawing room ready for winter fire-lighting, and carries the letter upstairs where she has started a new filing system in a box under her bed. She flips to U and files it under UNPLEASANT.

She leaves the phone in the hall plugged in, in case Georgia calls. People still ring to sell conservatories and double glazing and there are numerous calls from men (it is always men) telling her that her computer has a virus.

She buys a new iPhone at the Apple shop in Glasgow and doesn't care that it uses most of her savings, because she hasn't needed to ask anyone their opinion about it. She opts for a brand-new phone number but doesn't give it to anyone. Not yet.

She sets up a new email account at 25LibraryTerrace@ gmail.com and uses it to join the library.

She doesn't download Twitter or Instagram or Facebook. She listens to podcasts about birds and knitting, and takes photographs for her own pleasure, not for sharing with anyone else.

She looks at the weather forecast, and dances around the kitchen to the Proclaimers and Deacon Blue.

She doesn't count her steps or feel guilty for not reaching a goal. Instead, she browses in the local charity shops and chooses things for her room, even though she isn't sure if Georgia will want her to stay. She buys an old vegetarian cookery book by Rose Elliot, and a little wooden chest with twelve tiny drawers for her earrings, and a blue vintage ink bottle with the wrong kind of plain glass stopper. And she looks at the Gumtree app and buys herself a second-hand yellow bicycle.

Chapter 77

October 2011

Four weeks after she had sent the enormous metal road sign, and three weeks after Georgia had been due to come home from France, Tess rounds the corner on her way back from the swimming pool on her bike, and stops.

Two people are walking towards 25 Library Terrace. One has short pepper-and-salt hair and is carrying her trademark green backpack. The other is white-haired and taller, wearing brown trousers and a red jacket, and he is pulling a small suitcase. They are holding hands. She watches them go through the gate. The man touches the cherry tree in the front garden. He puts his arms around the woman and leans in to kiss her. And then they disappear around the side of the house.

Tess is suddenly reminded of *The Railway Children*, where Father comes home, but the reader doesn't see what happens when he goes into the house because that part of the story is not for public consumption.

She wheels her yellow bicycle round a hundred and eighty degrees and decides to go to the library to see if there are any books she has missed in the vegetarian section.

Baxter is at home.

He will look after them.

2021

1808

Chapter 78

July 2021

Tess's eyes are streaming with onion tears when her phone rings. She sniffs loudly and debates whether or not to answer it. She has never quite worked out why sniffing might suck the tears back up, but it does seem to help.

'Damn.'

She taps the green icon and shouts at the phone, 'Hi Fiona can you wait a minute I'm chopping onions give me a sec to sort myself out,' all in one burst without stopping. She washes her hands in the scullery sink and comes back into the kitchen and sits down at the table. 'Right. I'm here, what can I do for you?'

'There's Mount Washington in the utility room and the Great Ironing Pile may turn into an avalanche, but I don't want you to feel guilty about it *at all*.'

Tess groans. 'I'm really sorry, but I'm just trying to limit the number of people I see. I still think of Georgia and Stan as being vulnerable, you know?'

'It's OK. I understand, I'm just winding you up. You'll be dealing with a big backlog when this pandemic is over, though, I should warn you.'

'I will have my yellow Marigolds ready.'

'How are they getting on?'

'Pretty well, I think. Georgia seems quite happy now they've moved to the new place, and Stan's relieved to be allowed back on his allotment. What about you?'

'Still working. Family law is classed as an essential service, so I'm just as busy as ever, but at least it's better than last year when I was mostly working from home in between teaching my offspring about the finer points of sourdough baking and whether Hamlet would have made a good king. Speaking of work, I know I go on a bit, but you really should make your will. I've been nagging you for years.'

'I know, I know. I'll do it, promise.' Tess sits down on the chair beside the kitchen table. The old hand-crank sewing machine she found in a cupboard upstairs is set up at one end, and her chopping board is at the other. 'But that's not why you rang me, is it?'

'No, it's not.'

'Go on . . .'

'Alasdair is off sick so he asked me to call you. We know you haven't had any lodgers for a while but this is a bit of an emergency.'

'No one since Yvette moved out just before the pandemic. Lovely girl.'

'What's she doing now?'

'She moved into her own place in Musselburgh, and she's making hand-dyed embroidery threads to sell online.'

'The secret rent stockpile will have helped with that, I suppose?'

'Yes, although I confess that this time I did tell her about it a couple of months before she moved. I don't usually, but she was talking about getting a business start-up loan from the bank, and it seemed unkind to keep her in the dark.'

'That's why I'm ringing. It's about a possible lodger. I'm wondering if you might consider it again?'

'I'm not sure I can. I mean, is it allowed?'

'It is. Of course there's guidance for viewings about masks and Covid testing. It's different for actually moving house.'

'I don't know. I'm really concerned about catching it. I have a friend who ended up in hospital on oxygen and she was double-masking and stripping off in her hall when she got back from the shops and putting her clothes in the wash immediately and then showering every single time. *And* she was bleaching all the groceries too, so if she can catch it there's no hope for any of us.'

'That was before the vaccines, though, wasn't it?'

'I suppose so.'

'I wouldn't ask but this man is quite desperate.'

'A man? I've only ever had female lodgers. It was Georgia's rule, I suppose. The only other men were Keith and his friend Rab, and that was at the very beginning. It's never occurred to me to have men.'

'I suppose Alasdair knows about Georgia's wishes and never sent any your way. It may have become a self-fulfilling prophecy.'

Tess imagines her friend doodling on the pad in front of her. Fiona is so talented she could have gone to art school instead of doing law.

'So would you consider it?'

'I might. We live in strange times.'

'His name is Benjamin Weaver. He has two children who go to South Morningside Primary Sch—'

'Wait!' Tess stands up and starts to pace around the kitchen. 'Children? I'm not sure about children.'

'Two girls. They're six and nine.'

'Why does he need somewhere to stay?'

425

Natalie Fergie

'He's a widower and has used all his savings to pay his rent until now. He has his own business and is really quite desperate.'

'And the government won't help? There are grants, aren't there?'

'He's one of those people who hasn't been self-employed for long enough to have done his first tax return so he's fallen through the cracks of official support.'

'How long would he want to stay? It's two years, you know that. I don't want people here for less time, it's too disruptive. Georgia always says that it's not an emergency bed for a month or two, it's a proper commitment.'

'I told him that.'

'And what did he say?'

'To be honest, Tess, I think he was quite relieved.'

'I suppose I should at least think about it, and I'll ring Georgia to discuss it, of course. She's coming over at the weekend with Stan. We're having lunch in the garden. It's allowed now.'

'So, you'll meet him?'

'Is he allowed to come *into* the house?'

'Government rules say it's permitted, because people have to look at properties.'

Tess thinks about the dust bunnies which will undoubtedly have gathered in the corners of the rooms upstairs. She has definitely let things slide.

'I'll speak to Georgia this evening. It's such a nice day that I'm sure she'll be at the allotment with Stan just now. If she says it's OK, then he can come on Saturday, while she's here. He can have lunch with us.'

'With the children? I don't think he has anyone to leave them with.'

'I guess he'll have to bring them with him, then. Tell him to come around the back.'

426

Chapter 79

July 2021

Tess is in the scullery, tossing olive oil and balsamic vinegar into a bowl of allotment lettuce and grated carrots with her bare hands. She turns when she hears the footsteps on the gravel.

About five feet eight, she thinks. Reddish hair and beard, going grey, the bits she can see at the side of his turquoise mask, anyway. Skinny, under his linen jacket. Glasses. He is flanked by two little girls with equally red hair, each holding on tightly to one of his hands.

'Hello, I'm Tess, and you must be Benjamin.' She looks at her hands and then back at him. 'Sorry, I'm covered in salad dressing, just let me wash my hands before it gets all over everything.'

'My friends call me Ben,' he replies. 'I've never much liked Benjamin.' He looks down at the children. 'This is Lucy, she's nine, and Joanna is six.'

Tess hesitates. 'Would you like to look at the rooms before lunch or afterwards?'

'May as well look now, if that's not inconvenient?'

She takes a couple of steps back into the room. 'OK. There's a sink in here and you can all wash your hands before you come in. I'm not usually quite so fastidious when it's just me, but I don't want to put anyone at risk.' She soaps her own hands first to get rid of the oil and vinegar, singing 'Happy Birthday' in her head and wondering if the song will ever be sung again without being associated with hand-washing and viruses.

'I'm done, it's all yours. There are facecloths to dry your hands on next to the sink, just throw them in that basket beside the washing machine when you're done.' She pulls a mask from her pocket with finger and thumb and waits for them to finish, internally questioning if the tidying she had done the previous evening is sufficient. Whatever, she thinks. It's not a show home. If it puts him off then he isn't right for the place anyway.

She beckons him through. 'We shouldn't really be spending too much time indoors so I'll just walk you around quickly and you'll be able to see what it's like. If you're interested then you can join us for lunch in the garden and we can decide if this is going to work.' He nods, and the girls follow him inside, now holding hands with each other.

'That's the scullery, all the usual things, washing machine and stuff, and the cooker and fridge and the larder at the back. This is the old kitchen.' She points at the black range. 'Sadly, we aren't really supposed to use that but we have been known to put some smokeless fuel on it on a wintry afternoon. Haven't done it for a while, though, what with the lockdown and everything; not much point when I'm here on my own.' She waves a hand around the kitchen. 'This is where we eat, whoever is staying here, I mean. Meals are always eaten together, downstairs, never in the bedrooms.' She points to the narrow wooden staircase that leads off the kitchen. 'My office is up there.'

They troop into the hall. 'That's my room, next to the kitchen, and then there's the downstairs shower room, I use that one. And this is the big drawing room; we've had some great parties in here.' She catches the older girl whispering something to her younger sister.

She leads the way upstairs. 'Up here there are three bedrooms and a bathroom and the parlour, which is the poshest room in the house. In normal times we usually keep the parlour as a guest bedroom so there's plenty of space for people to stay if the lodgers want that. I usually have two lodgers at a time but there are sometimes three. There's no one at the moment, though.' She turns to look at him. 'And that's it.'

The girls have disappeared into the parlour and she can hear their voices, but not exactly what they are saying.

'I'll leave you to have a think without me peering over your shoulder. Take your time and have a proper look. Just come up to the end of the garden when you've finished. The owner and her husband will be here shortly, I think. I'll introduce you when they arrive.'

It will be strange to share the house again after almost a year, she thinks. To begin with she had struggled with the emptiness and the echoes. But she had begun to enjoy the silence, and the fact that she didn't have to consider anyone else. She alternates between relishing the peace and careering from room to room so quickly she thinks her bones are rattling. At times she fears her voice might dry up with lack of use. But the house is not meant for one person. She remembers Georgia saying that. The silence is nice, but it isn't the purpose of the place. It's time for whatever comes next.

Chapter 80

July 2021

They all sit around the two picnic benches under the plum tree at the bottom of the garden.

'Tell me, Mr Weaver, how did you come to know Fiona?' asks Georgia.

'It was three years ago. She was my solicitor after Zoe died.' He realises that more explanation is required. 'My wife. She collapsed at work and was blue-lighted into hospital. They found she had sepsis, and she died six days later. There was no time for anything, no plans, no preparation for the girls. It was brutal. We hadn't made wills or even talked about all the what-ifs. That had always seemed like an old person's thing. It took a while to sort everything out and Fiona was the person who did it for us.'

Tess realises that this is why Fiona has been nagging her about making a will.

'And your family?' Georgia continues.

'They're up north. My sister is in Aberdeen and my parents are in Brora, which is even further away. I could have moved back, but the girls are in school here and it seems better to stay so they still have their friends. My wife's family are in France.'

Stan reaches for the bread basket and offers it to the girls. 'What is it you do, Benjamin?'

'Call me Ben, please.' He studies his hands. 'I'm a cleaner. I used to work night shifts in a warehouse, and Zoe worked in a shop. We never needed nurseries or childminders because we covered the girls between us and it all worked well until . . .' He stops. 'But after it all happened I couldn't do nights any more, and it was obvious that working days and paying for childcare wasn't going to work if I wanted to stay in Edinburgh because the rents are so high.'

Georgia is listening intently, nodding with each painful revelation.

'So I set up a business doing things for older people. Folk who need a bit more than just the vacuum cleaner being pushed around. They might need sheets changed, duvet covers put on, lightbulbs replaced, meters read, lemons sliced. Anything that is high up or tricky if your hands or your legs don't work as well as they used to. I do it in school hours and I go in at weekends as well if there's a problem, and I take the girls with me, when it's allowed.' He smiles. 'My customers love to see them and they've really missed them when we haven't been able to visit, but kids are germ magnets and it's not worth the risk.'

Tess takes a sip of elderflower cordial. 'I used to do something similar, a long time ago. That's how I met Fiona. I would be at her flat when her supermarket deliveries came, and put all the groceries away for her, renew library books, that sort of thing.'

'Exactly! You'll understand then.' He shrugs. 'Unfortunately, I set the business up the year before the pandemic, and I hadn't submitted any tax returns because they weren't due, so I wasn't eligible for government support. I ended up on benefits.'

'Nothing wrong with that, young man,' says Stan. 'We pay our taxes to look after the community, not to look after ourselves.'

Tess looks across at Georgia. 'Would you like to explain the rules?'

'No, it's fine, you go ahead. Perhaps the girls would like to have another look at where they might be living?'

He nods. 'Off you go, you two.' The girls don't need to be asked twice. 'And . . .'

'We *know*, Daddy,' says Joanna.

Tess waits until the children have gone back into the house. 'Assuming you're interested in living here . . .'

'I am. I mean yes, *we* are.'

'Right.' Tess is used to doing this now, but not usually in front of Georgia. She never knows what sort of reaction there will be.

'There have been lodgers in this house since 1931. All sorts of people. Until now they have all been women, apart from the very first two. And Keith ended up marrying the landlady so I'm not sure he counts. Fiona's firm has always suggested people to the owner,' she points at Georgia, 'and so far, no one has ever been turned down. There have been women who were escaping their past, a couple were just out of prison, at least two were pregnant, some were running away from abuse, others were just stuck, being evicted, with nowhere to go.' She leans forward, resting her elbows on the bench. 'I was one of these women, ten years ago.' She doesn't give any clues about which category she had fitted into. 'The deal, if you want to call it that, has always been the same. There are five things that you would have to agree to.'

'Go on.'

She counts them off on her fingers.

'First, you commit to staying for two years, but not *longer* than two years. This isn't somewhere to stay for a few months and then move on. There must be a feeling that it's your home.'

She taps the next finger. 'Second. It's a vegetarian house, so there is no meat or fish. I think I'm correct in saying it's been like that since 1911. If you want to eat fish and chips or McDonald's that's fine, but it mustn't come in the house. And no smoking.

'Third. If people are around, we all have lunch together on Sunday. The neighbours sometimes come, lodgers invite their friends or their families – if they have a family – and sometimes their boyfriends or girlfriends come too. We might watch the Six Nations and shout for Scotland or just drink coffee and wine and eat pizza. We obviously haven't been doing that for the last wee while, but hopefully we can go back to it.

'Fourth, there must be no credit agreements. Some of the lodgers have been terribly in debt and they've used their two years to get themselves back on an even footing. Georgia never had to make this rule explicit until the woman who was here before me bought all sort of things on credit, didn't make the payments and skipped off, leaving Georgia to sort out the mess.

'And the last thing is that you must be registered to vote. Georgia takes voting very seriously. Doesn't matter who you vote for but you must be on the electoral roll so you can do it.

'That's everything, I think.' She glances at Georgia. 'Oh yes, I almost forgot. If it's census year you have to fill that in. In England it's already been done but in Scotland we'll do it in 2022. And it must be done properly. No Jedi Knights.'

Ben listens intently. 'I've no problem with any of that, but you haven't mentioned the cost of the rent.'

Georgia takes over. 'The rent is twenty-five per cent.'

'Twenty-five per cent of what?'

'Of whatever you earn. After tax, of course. You are trusted to pay the correct amount.'

He frowns and shakes his head. 'I don't understand.'

Georgia continues. 'This is number 25 Library Terrace. In the very beginning the rent was set up that way because of the house number. It covers the room, or rooms in your case, all the gas and electricity and broadband and the TV licence and insurances and that sort of thing. Food is included and there is an honesty purse and whoever is doing the shopping takes it with them. There is always money in it and you are trusted not to buy gold-leaf-covered birthday cakes or 1934 Cabernet Sauvignon. It's done that way so we don't end up with separate shelves in the fridge or five individual jars of identical coffee.'

Tess can see him doing mental arithmetic. 'It means that if you earn, or are given in benefits, a hundred pounds, twenty-five pounds comes to the house. If you clean for a billionaire who pays you ten thousand pounds a week to clean their diamond-studded bathroom taps, then the house gets two thousand five hundred pounds in that week.'

'But—'

Georgia cuts him off. 'It has worked like this for ninety years and I don't see any reason to change it.'

'Is there a deposit? Something in case of breakages?'

'No. It's never been necessary.'

The girls are making their way up the garden path.

'We are back,' says Lucy, stating the obvious.

'And?' replies Ben.

'Twenty-two,' replies Joanna. 'Two and fifteen and five.'

'Or five and fifteen and two, if you are going down,' adds Lucy. 'Is there any ice cream?'

'Well done.' He turns to Georgia. 'They always count the stairs when they go somewhere new. It's a family thing.'

'There are some in the bottom drawer of the freezer,' says Tess, sending a mental thank you to Fiona, who had suggested it. 'Help yourselves.'

Georgia is uncharacteristically quiet.

Stan takes over. 'And why do you do that, Ben?'

'It's a bit complicated.'

'We have all afternoon,' he encourages, pouring a second glass of wine.

'Thank you. Well, it's a long story, but my father was a firefighter before he retired, and so was his father, and my great-grandfather as well. There are four generations of us now, because my sister is in the fire service in Aberdeen. Counting the stairs and planning your exit whenever you go into a new building is just something we do. I was brought up with it. When I was a kid, if we went on holiday, we had to read the fire evacuation maps on the back of the hotel door, and not just read them quickly, but count how many paces it was to the nearest exit, and then check out the alternative exit too. Our friends all thought we were odd because if we went on a school trip, or stayed in their houses, we counted. Quite quickly we learned not to tell anyone so we didn't get talked about, but we always did it, regardless.' He takes a sip of wine. 'Fortunately, I've never needed to use the information in anger, so to speak.'

Georgia leans forward. 'But you've never been a firefighter yourself?'

Ben shakes his head and digs in his pocket, pulling out a blue inhaler. 'My asthma is bad enough that they wouldn't take me.'

'I see.'

435

His tongue loosened by the wine, Ben continues. 'So it's in the blood really. My sister lectures on it now, and she did her master's degree on the two-and-a-half-minute rule and whether it's still valid today.'

'The what?' Georgia is hungry for more information.

'She could tell you about it in a lot more detail, but the short version is that my great-grandfather was a fireman here in Edinburgh, and in 1911 there was a fire in the Empire Palace Theatre – you know, where the Festival Theatre is today, on Nicolson Street? And when the fire broke out, the audience didn't realise it was an emergency because of some pyrotechnics that were part of the act. The orchestra saw there was a serious problem and they started to play "God Save the King". The audience stood up because people did, didn't they, when the national anthem was played? There was a raging inferno behind the safety curtain, and the place was evacuated. It took two and a half minutes to play the national anthem, and to get everyone out. Three thousand people, and the orchestra as well. It must have been quite a sight, that many folk pouring out onto Nicolson Street in two and a half minutes.'

Georgia doesn't take her eyes off him. 'And the rule is still around today?'

He nods. 'It's used all over the world as a sort of gold standard. If you are in a public building, you must be able to get to a place of safety in two and a half minutes. As I said, my sister is a real expert on it and would be able to tell you about the Occupation Capacity of buildings and the importance of Door Exit Widths but I won't attempt to explain them. There's a lot of debate about whether it's still valid as a standard, but I guess if you change it, you have to have evidence for what it should be changed *to*, and perhaps that's more trouble than it's worth when the rule seems to work.'

He laughs. 'You can imagine Christmas dinner at my folks' house, though. My mum and I just go out into the kitchen and sort out the roast potatoes and leave them all to it.'

'We will be getting new smoke alarms here,' said Georgia. 'Stan put the old ones in, but that was years ago and there are new regulations coming soon.'

'Tell me, did you want to be a firefighter?' Stan asks.

'When I was small, yes, of course. But once I had the asthma diagnosis, I just stopped thinking about it. There was no point. It wasn't something I could train for. It doesn't matter if you can pass all the physical tests if your asthma isn't stable. I was a bit jealous of my sister I suppose, but I could spend a lifetime cursing nature, and what would be the point? I have a good life and I have the girls, and I was loved very much by a marvellous woman. You can't regret what's not possible in the first place.'

Georgia sits back in her chair. 'When I was a child, we had to do a project in school about the fire at that theatre. I was at South Morningside Primary, actually, where your girls go. I don't suppose the place has changed much. And Annie, my aunt, told me all about it – she was there, in fact, on the night of the fire, seeing The Great Lafayette. He was a friend of Harry Houdini, and Houdini had given him a dog which died while he was in Edinburgh. He was heart-broken. He somehow persuaded the owners of one of the cemeteries to let him bury the dog there.'

'A dog? In a cemetery for humans?' Tess is incredulous.

'Indeed. I have no idea how he did it. He was a very wealthy man, a millionaire in today's money. Piershill is a private cemetery and I think they made him promise that when he eventually died he would be buried in Edinburgh beside his dog, and he agreed. They probably thought it would be a tourist attraction, and *he* probably thought it would be decades away. But because of the fire, he died four days after the dog did. His memorial stone is huge, right at the front near the gates. Annie told me that the funeral was on a Sunday and half of Edinburgh turned out. There were black horses with big plumes on their heads and it was quite a spectacle. The whole family went and stood at the roadside to watch it.' Georgia took a sip of wine. 'But she didn't tell me she was at the theatre on the night of the fire until many years later. I still have her bag, green suede with purple lining and a white pocket. Suffragette colours, you know? And inside it there are some things; some coins, and a handkerchief, and there's a programme from the show. She showed it to me when I was doing the project and there's a burn mark in the middle of it.' She laughs. 'Of course, I wanted to take it to school and show it to my friends but she wouldn't let me. I remember being rather cross about that.'

She puts her right hand on the table and walks her first two fingers across the surface. 'The thing is, she counted the stairs too. Not once, but every time she went up them here in the house, even when she was quite old. You could see her lips moving. I thought she was quite the most fascinating person I had ever known, and I wanted to be like her, so I counted too. Everyone here counts the stairs.'

2022

Chapter 81

May 2022

It's early evening and still warm in the garden. Joanna and Lucy have gone to a friend's house, and Ben sits at the picnic bench with a pencil in his hand and an open notebook in front of him. He taps away at the calculator app on his phone and writes down the results in a long column of figures. His soft two-week-holiday beard has more than a sprinkling of white, and he strokes it as he concentrates.

Tess, grass-stained after emptying armfuls of lawn clippings onto the compost heap, plonks herself down on the bench opposite him.

'Georgia and Stan are coming for lunch on Sunday. They've been vaccinated and Georgia told me that nothing but an edict from the First Minister herself would stop her from being here – and even then she would be inclined to be disobedient. It's Stan's birthday, so I want to make sure there's a good spread.'

Ben abandons his arithmetic and looks up. There is grass in her hair and a smudge of earth on her left cheek. 'The girls will want a Colin the Caterpillar cake.' He blows gently into the air. 'With candles.'

She smiles. 'Of course they will. We can get one at Marks and Sparks in Morningside.'

He doodles a pattern of intersecting 2 and 5 symbols in his notebook. 'I've been meaning to ask if you think there might be more lodgers eventually?'

Tess can see his design from across the table. 'Probably not while you're here.'

He draws more numbers, linking them together with swoops of his pencil. 'You know, it's been nearly a year since we moved in, but I've never felt able to ask you . . .'

'Ask me what?'

'Well, I'm assuming you aren't a former prisoner, although nothing is impossible. And there are no children here with you. So that leaves . . .'

She sticks to the facts. 'I was dumped.'

He is embarrassed at having asked the question. 'I'm really sorry.'

'Well, not dumped exactly. It's a bit more complicated than that.' She wonders how to explain in a way which won't alienate him. 'My ex and I always said we didn't want children, but he changed his mind. I remember telling Fiona at the time that other people's kids were fine, I just didn't want any of my own.' She decides on the spur of the moment to be totally honest. 'I think he must have been thinking about it for a couple of years before he actually said something. With hindsight there were all sorts of clues but I couldn't see them at the time. I think he wanted me to be the one to end it because then it would have been my fault, and not his.'

He doesn't know what to say.

'Pretty much overnight I went from being one half of a couple to being completely and utterly wrecked. I tried to put on a good face and pretend I was coping, but the truth is that I was suddenly unattached, or separated, or solo, or whatever you want to call it.' Her voice drops to barely a whisper. 'But not in my heart.'

Ben thinks about reaching out across the table, but decides against it. He picks up his pencil again and doodles a few more numbers instead. 'When Zoe died it happened so fast, I felt as though I couldn't breathe. One minute she was her usual self, planning trips to the beach at Portobello with the kids, and reading the paper, and drinking coffee, just doing all the normal stuff. And then she was gone in less than a week.'

Tess shakes her head. 'I'm sorry. I'm not for a minute saying what happened to me is as bad as what you went through.'

'I know you aren't. Doesn't mean I can't relate though. It's four years since she died and I loved her to bits but I was absolutely furious with her for leaving us. They say grief is not a logical thing, and it's true.' He pulls himself back to the present.

Tess rubs her dirty palms together slowly. 'It's not something we have any control over. It just smashes its way in. One minute you are loved and safe, and the next, it's all gone.' She examines the green tinge on her fingers, left by the grass. 'A distant acquaintance told me recently that he has three kids now, so I guess that means he got what he wanted. I suppose it probably wasn't exactly easy for him either. These things are difficult for everyone. I've seen enough broken hearts in this house over the last eleven years to know that.'

'So when you came here, did Georgia look after you?'

Tess shakes her head. 'Absolutely not. Nobody here is looked after. Annie started it all, Georgia took over and now it's my turn. Number 25 offers people somewhere to stay at a time in their lives when they have no idea how to wash, or eat proper food, or speak in whole sentences, let alone organise things like going to the dentist. When I took

443

over from her, Georgia told me that everyone takes a different amount of time. Some need six months, others need a year or even longer.'

'Time to do what, though?'

'To reach the point where they can think about what comes next.'

'Gotcha.' Ben closes his notebook. 'The girls kept me busy, but it wasn't until we moved here last summer that I was able to make a proper start.' He thinks about Zoe, and what she would want for them. This isn't the life they planned together, but he is sure she would approve of the line of walking boots in the hall, and the waterproofs hanging on the hooks above them, always ready for the next adventure. Number 25 is not a magazine-perfect house, despite the neatly paired socks and never-late library books. In the kitchen the girls' colourful paintings of the four of them are stuck to the freezer door, and Tess never makes any attempt to remove them until the next piece of art arrives.

After a year of sharing veggie chilli and visits to the library, and coping with forgotten homework and vomity sick nights, they bumble along pretty well, but they are not a couple and are very careful not to stand on each other's toes. Despite this, there are new acronyms in the house, the kind of secret code created by families, which no one else understands. The girls have shortened the important instruction to "Count The Stairs" to "CoTS" and they all use it whenever they are staying away in a youth hostel, because no one wants to be weird in public.

Ben thinks about how relaxed and settled the girls are now and how much everything has changed. He wonders, not for the first time, if he is brave enough to have a conversation with Tess about how much she matters to him.

They sit quietly together, enjoying the evening, and not feeling any further need to talk about the past.

The side gate creaks as it opens. Tess catches half a glimpse of movement near the house. 'Are you expecting someone?'

Ben gets to his feet. 'I'll go,' he says, 'it's probably something to do with the girls anyway. You know what they're like. They'll have left some important possession behind, it's always happening.'

He comes back a couple of minutes later with a tall woman, who looks distinctly nervous.

'This lady is looking for Georgia. She says her name is . . .' Tess finishes his sentence. 'Nicola?'

The woman looks even more anxious. 'Have we met before somewhere?'

Tess has often thought about what she would say if Nicola ever knocked on the door. 'We haven't, but Georgia is a friend of mine. I started out as a lodger here too, more than ten years ago, so you and I have something in common.' She smiles and points to an empty chair beside the bench, an invitation to sit down with them in the sunshine.

Nicola is still standing, unsure of the welcome. 'I wasn't sure if it would be alright.'

Tess keeps talking, explaining, trying to put their visitor at ease. 'Sometimes people come to see us, and others stay in touch by phone. Georgia is always delighted to hear what everyone's been doing.' She leans forward, hoping to encourage a response. 'I think I may have seen your photo in the office?'

Nicola risks a hesitant smile, and sits down on the chair. 'I remember that day. It was really sunny and I was squinting into the camera but she said it didn't matter.'

Ben takes his lead from Tess. 'You aren't disturbing us. I live here too, with my daughters. Being a lodger has been

445

an interesting experience.' He has no idea who this woman is, but Tess doesn't look as though she needs any help. He picks up his notebook. 'I think I'll go and make us all a cold drink.' He leaves them to chat, and heads for the kitchen, hoping against hope that the girls have remembered to refill the ice cube tray.

Tess knows there is nothing for Nicola to worry about. All she can do is try to make her feel comfortable. She smiles again at her fellow lodger.

'A long time ago, Georgia told me that one day you would come back to number 25. I can't wait to let her know you are here.'

Parkin

Parkin is often known as Yorkshire parkin, and is some-times eaten on Bonfire Night. If you've never tasted it, try to imagine a sticky, oaty gingerbread which simply *has* to be eaten slowly.

Isobel baked it in the kitchen of 25 Library Terrace in 1911, and both Annie and Georgia used it to great effect as the years passed, either to silence their visitors, or to create a situation where their potential lodgers felt compelled to speak to avoid an awkward silence.

There are many recipes online for parkin, and they are all slightly different. This is mine.

Preheat your oven to 130C if it's a fan oven, or 140C for conventional.

You'll need what used to be called a 2 pound loaf tin which measures about 21cm x 11cm.

If you have greaseproof paper liners for the tin, that's a help.

Ingredients

60g salted butter
50g dark soft brown sugar
40g golden syrup
85g treacle
110g medium oatmeal

50g self-raising flour
1 teaspoon ground ginger
0.5 teaspoons nutmeg
0.5 teaspoons mixed spice
1 egg
25ml milk

Method

1. Put the syrup, treacle, butter and sugar into a pan and melt them over a low heat. The mixture needs to melt, not bubble.
2. Mix all the dry ingredients together in a bowl.
3. Pour the treacle mixture over the dry ingredients and stir until blended.
4. Beat the egg and milk together and add to the bowl. Stir well.
5. Pour into the lined tin. If you don't have a paper liner, grease the tin well and sprinkle a little flour in it to create a mock non-stick surface.
6. Bake for 55 minutes. The parkin will rise a little, but really not very much. This doesn't mean it's not cooked. It should feel firm(ish) when you press the top of it. All ovens are different, and if you feel the parkin needs a little longer, go for it.
7. Remove from the oven and allow to cool in the tin for half an hour. Turn out. When completely cold, wrap in foil and store in a tin.

Notes

- Make the basic recipe first, and then play with it once you have an idea of how the mixture should feel. It will not be as stiff as normal cake mixture, and may seem quite runny.

- I prefer salted butter. If you use unsalted, you might want to add a pinch of salt to the dry ingredients.
- You need a total of 125g golden syrup and treacle. The proportions are up to you. I prefer to make it with more treacle and less syrup because I like the slightly burnt 'edge' this gives.
- You may prefer dark muscovado sugar to dark soft brown. Muscovado retains the molasses so the flavour will be more treacley. However it's also a bit more moist. Make the base recipe first before experimenting.
- Isobel would have used Allinson's flour. I have also tried it with gluten-free self-raising flour and it works pretty well.
- Most parkin recipes (and I have looked at a lot of them) ask for a miserly amount of ground ginger. I add *at least* 2 teaspoons, sometimes more, but I've only used 1 teaspoon in this foundation recipe.
- I like nutmeg in my parkin. if you don't like it just leave it out. Play with the spices to make the parkin your own.
- If you want to make a double quantity, I would use two loaf tins rather than one 20cm square tin. Parkin can be quite reluctant to rise in a square tin, I find. And making a smaller quantity means it's more fun (and less of a commitment) to play with the balance of spices.
- This is what you might call a foundation recipe. Please experiment. Add sultanas or crystallised ginger. Vary the spices and try a different syrup-to-treacle ratio. Make it your own.
- The crucial thing to remember is that parkin is *much* better after being stored for five days in an airtight tin.

It becomes gloriously sticky, and even more of a useful conversation stopper. If you can keep it for ten days, even better. It's also very, very good with a chunk of strong cheddar cheese.

- If you do make it, please let me know. You can tag me on Instagram @nataliesfergie and post a photo, or just email me at n@nataliefergie.com. I'd love to know how you get on. And if you have a family recipe to share, please tell me about it.

Happy Parkin Production,
Natalie

Acknowledgements

There is more than one Ann in this book. Woven beneath the narrative is the support and encouragement of my friend Ann Carrier. She is my sounding board and my research buddy, and this book would not exist without her.

Neil and Vanessa live in a house identical to 25 Library Terrace. They have answered endless questions, counted their stairs for me several times, and shared Hogmanay celebrations, breakfasts and soup. Sleeping in the maid's room in their home allowed me to think about Isobel's life in a way I could not otherwise have imagined. The fact that their dog is a terrier called Stan is a complete coincidence. Thank you.

My great-grandmother wrote the original letter about the strawberry tea, and my great-grandfather wrote the love letter on blue notepaper from Fishguard. I altered their words only slightly to fit with the names of my characters. My great-grandfather's punctuation is both real and astonishing.

Alan Bradshaw is the originator of CT1 (and CT2 and CT3). He is a birdwatcher and the originator of the (true) story about inedible cricket teas. There is a lot of weather in this book, from a surprisingly dry and warm January in 1911, to several record-breaking summer droughts. Alan is my go-to weather expert, always ready to dig into meteorological data on my behalf.

Andy Arthur has had a significant influence on my work although he may not realise it. His website www.threadinburgh.scot is a mine of information about things Edinburgh

Natalie Fergie

and Leith which are both obscure and interesting, including macaroni pies, plain bread and experimental council housing. He is the person I scrambled a message to when I needed to know about the council's drainage plans in 1906, the manufacturing history of the ice cream cone, tram routes to Portobello, and Sunday postal deliveries in 1911.

The military historian behind www.oldfrontline.co.uk is Paul Reed. He kindly provided information about WW1 medals, and explained about WW1 cemeteries in France and Belgium. His help was invaluable when I was writing about Georgia's trip to France. It's important to note that the cemeteries in the book are my own invention and won't be found on a map.

In addition, please note that Finlay Black, Gregor Anderson and Harris Anderson are entirely fictitious. No one with these names appears on the Commonwealth War Graves Commission website which provides a record of 1.7 million Commonwealth lives lost.

I was privileged to listen to the experiences of several members of HM Forces, and this informed my understanding of the experience and treatment of veterans, past and present.

Dorothee Venn helped me with a sensitive translation of the wording in German war cemeteries, for which I am very grateful.

For detailed information about the questions in the 1911 Census I turned to Ruth Boreham. Her knowledge of the period and about suffragettes in Edinburgh is second to none.

David Blaikie of David Blaikie Architects assisted with information about the construction of my imaginary house.

Wendy Hough told me about the need for buy-to-let mortgages when renting property.

Susan Masterton gave me invaluable legal advice.

David Blair and Dave Furries (QFSM) from the Museum of Scottish Fire and Heritage on McDonald Road in Edinburgh shared their expertise, and gave me a proper explanation of the present-day significance of the two-and-a-half-minute rule. I had read academic papers and looked at historical documents, but they told me all about Occupation Capacity and Exit Door Widths and explained the formulae that make it possible for all of us to escape a building which is on fire. Any errors in explaining these engineering and safety rules are mine. My thanks are offered to all firefighters, past and present.

Mary Whitehouse, Fiona Hulme and Ann Carrier were my beta readers. They each brought different talents and perspectives to the task I gave them. I hope they like the end result.

The floorplans of 25 Library Terrace were expertly drawn by Peter Kelly, Architectural Technician.

From the publishing world I must first thank my agent Charlotte Seymour, who has guided me through several iterations of 25 Library Terrace. Thanks also to Anna Dawson and Ed Wilson.

Thank you to Hayley Shepherd, Imogen Denny, and Tamsin Shelton for editing support and advice. From Embla, Emma Wilson and Anna Perkins.

Various friends were surprised by a gift of parkin in 2024. It was usually delivered in several boxes because I was trying out more than one version of the recipe at a time, and it was accompanied by an inquisition about which one they preferred and why. My thanks (and more parkin) are offered to Mary, Julian, Helen, Adam, Graham, Fran, Susan, Iain, Petra, Alison and Richard.

My friend Sally Atkinson test-baked the final parkin recipe in a way only a scientist can. There was mention of

Natalie Fergie

lab books, her ingredient weighing was gram-perfect, and the oven timings were precise. If you enjoy your parkin, Sally was a big part of it.

Mary Whitehouse did equally important parkin-testing involving different sugars and crystallised ginger.

Warm thanks are also due to Lesley Harcourt who brought the voices on the page to life in the audiobook, with skill and sensitivity.

Annie's handbag can be found on the Victoria and Albert Museum website. It is just identified as Handbag ca 1910, but from the description of the colours and the image itself, I think it simply has to be a suffragette bag. You can see it here https://collections.vam.ac.uk/item/O353733/handbag-unknown/

Lastly, a huge thank you to my Mum, Adam, Simon and Becky. This is for you.

About the Author

Natalie Fergie has a love for social history, and a particular interest in the domestic lives of women in the twentieth century.

She lives on the outskirts of Edinburgh, Scotland's capital city, and can be found online at www.nataliefergie.com

About Embla Books

Embla Books is a digital-first publisher of standout commercial adult fiction. Passionate about storytelling, the team at Embla believe our lives are built on stories – and publish books that will make you 'laugh, love, look over your shoulder and lose sleep'. Launched by Bonnier Books UK in 2021, the imprint is named after the first woman from the creation myth in Norse mythology. Embla was carved by the gods from a tree trunk found on the seashore; an image of the kind of creative work and crafting that writers do, and a symbol of how stories shape our lives.

Find out about some of our other books and stay in touch:

X, Facebook, Instagram: @emblabooks
Newsletter: https://bit.ly/emblanewsletter